The Secret Weapon

A Novel

by

Michael A. Campbell

1945

Sergeant Richard Cartwright stopped for the twelfth time in the past hour to catch his breath. The shuddering roar of the subway train passing in the tunnel overhead drowned out his gasps for air.

They were following him, and they were gaining. Cartwright was much too much of a realist to believe that he had managed to elude his pursuers. For the last four hours, he had fought a running gun battle with German agents, ducking in and out of the nooks and crannies of the New York docks.

After an endless chase, Cartwright had finally run into a subway station, hoping to catch an early morning train and put some miles between him and his enemies. The train never arrived, and his pursuers had caught up with him. He ducked into a labyrinth of service tunnels that ran underneath the vast New York subway system.

The train echoes receded into the distance. Cartwright risked poking his head around the concrete pillar for a look. A stuttering burst of machine gun fire kicked up shards of stone and dust that shot into his face. His enemies were close, danger close.

Cartwright thought about a place that his instructors had talked to him about in Commando School: the last ditch. The last ditch was a place where no one wanted to go, where all options for survival had been exhausted. The only thing left for you to do was to throw everything you had at the enemy and hope that it was enough to insure your survival.

He was now in the last ditch.

There was only a short distance left before he would reach the ladder that led up out of the maze he had run into. He could see the fitful light of the subway tunnel filtering down the grates onto the floor of the service tunnel. Less than a hundred feet, but it may as well have been five thousand. Unless he negotiated the distance between where he was and the service ladder, Cartwright would never live to see another sunrise.

Cartwright steadied himself and started to run. He had traveled less than fifty feet when there was another burst of automatic weapons fire. The bullets ricocheted off of the rotting brick pillars next to his head. Cartwright threw himself onto the ground, flattening himself against the earth. They were close now; in another few seconds they would have him.

Dragging himself over to a pile of filthy rags and debris, Cartwright readied himself for his final stand. The pile would give him a small amount of cover and concealment.

He reached down into his trench coat and found a small round metal object. It was a fragmentation grenade, the only one he had. It would kill anyone within ten meters of its blast. Cartwright grimly calculated that the narrow confines of the tunnel would amplify its lethal effects and probably injure him severely as well.

It was a chance he had to take; there were no other alternatives left. Cartwright was no stranger to killing people. A trained agent in the deadly game of military intelligence, Cartwright was a professional soldier who had mastered the arts of mayhem and sudden death. He was good, very good at his trade. So good that for the past two years, he had been entrusted with the most difficult and dangerous assignments: working alone, far beyond home, deep behind enemy lines, setting up resistance cells in occupied countries.

Now he was going to die in New York City, on an assignment his commanding officer had assured him was purely routine. Warren was joking when he said this. There were no routine assignments in intelligence work. Both of them knew the remark was not correct, but for his friend's sake, Richard had laughed politely and ignored the irony of the statement. Mechanically, Cartwright calculated his chances of survival in his present situation. There was little hope he'd survive the night.

He was desperate to reach the British Consulate. The information he had discovered had to be gotten to MI6 immediately. Cartwright knew that at the very least, he had to get in touch with Major Warren. The consulate staff would probably dismiss him as a complete lunatic if he told them his findings. The War, after all, was over, at least in Europe. Nazi Germany was a smoking ruin, her armies gone, and her military machine smashed beyond repair. At least, that is what everyone thought.

But it was not over, not as long as the terrible secret Richard Cartwright had found existed. Unless that threat was eliminated, the world would never be safe. Millions of lives were at stake, but his chances of reaching the consulate and completing his mission were ebbing away like the blood pouring from his wounded body.

The sounds of his pursuers came closer. Cartwright waited behind his makeshift rampart. He would get only one chance to do this. When the sounds seemed to be almost upon him, Cartwright rose up and fired the last burst from his machine pistol, emptying its magazine. The only sound of the silenced weapon was the chattering clack of the firing pin as it struck the shells, along with the clinking sounds of the shells as they fell to the rocky earth. The machine pistol stopped, the bolt slamming back as the last round fired. A symphony of screams and curses greeted his ears, signifying that his burst had caused damage.

A wave of pain came from Cartwright's stomach as the result of his exertion. Reaching down, he felt around his middle. His hand came back wet. There was no doubt: the bleeding was getting much worse. They had shot him in the abdomen less than half an hour ago. He knew that he would bleed to death unless he went to a hospital. It was time to end this contest. Cartwright steadied himself, reaching over and clutching the grenade. Pulling the pin and counting to three, he raised up as far as he could and threw the grenade into the darkness before him.

Throwing himself to the ground, Cartwright flattened his body against the earth as he anticipated the grenade explosion. Five seconds later, the world erupted in a nerve-shattering blast of noise, light and pure force. A hurricane of shrapnel howled past him as he huddled behind his makeshift rampart. Once the noise had subsided, the only sound Cartwright heard was the ringing in his ears and the thumping rhythm of his pounding heart.

Cartwright waited for a few more minutes, listening for any sound that might signify that his pursuers had survived his ambush. There was only silence in the darkness before him. He raised himself to his feet, dropping his now-useless machine pistol. Cartwright continued to totter down the old tunnel towards the ladder that led to the subway above him.

A crushing heaviness had settled in on his chest, making every breath an agonizing effort. The world seemed to swim in slow motion before his eyes. Richard Cartwright knew he was dying. There was nothing else he could do. Reaching down into the pocket of his coat, he got out a scrap of paper and a pencil stub. With his last ounce of strength, he scrawled a word onto the paper. Falling to his knees, he tucked the paper back into his coat.

"I'm sorry, Major Warren. I've failed you," Cartwright gasped as the world fled before his dying eyes.

Then he remembered nothing more...

1

"Where's that lieutenant of yours this morning, Meyers?" Howard Vinson's gravelly voice interrupted Detective Sergeant Ron Meyers' review of their current case files. Ron once described Vinson's voice as a cross between a cement mixer in full operation and someone raking their fingernails across a blackboard. Hearing it first thing in the morning was not Ron's idea of starting his day.

"I don't know, Captain," Meyers replied cautiously, hiding his chocolate glazed donut from his commander's glaring stare. "She hasn't come in yet."

"Guess she's at the gym this morning. That's where you should be, Meyers, instead of eating that fat pill," Vinson said with a grimace. "Let me know when she comes in. I have an assignment for you two."

"Right, Captain, I'll let her know when she gets in," Meyers acknowledged as Vinson moved on to another desk to dispense more dour wisdom to reluctant detectives. Meyers stared at his donut sadly for a few moments and finally decided to dispose of the rest of it.

"I'm so sorry," he whispered to the offending cruller as he tossed it into his wastebasket. The donut obediently fled from sight under a pile of crumpled papers. Ron was silently mourning the departure of his breakfast when a shadow crossed over his desk.

"Get over it, Ron. You'll get another one before the morning's out," Brenda Reynolds said in an ironic tone. She had come up to the desk as Ron was paying respects to his late donut.

"Hey, Lieutenant, you just missed Captain Vinson," Meyers hastily recovered himself, "he's got a new assignment for us." He looked up at Reynolds with a sheepish grin on his face.

Looking at Brenda Reynolds was not a hard thing for Meyers to do. In fact, Ron spent the better part of most days looking at her and daydreaming. It was an unhealthy and futile activity, given his partner's prickly, acerbic temperament.

Brenda was about five-six, with medium length light brown hair pulled back into a highly unflattering bun. She had an outwardly attractive, well-defined face with gray-blue eyes and a nicely shaped mouth. Unfortunately, Brenda seldom, if ever smiled, and her face was usually set in a perpetual frown. There was talk around the precinct that Reynolds was allergic to smiling. No one ever mentioned this to her face.

At thirty, Brenda was an expert in martial arts and an accomplished long distance runner. She'd managed to pass the detective exam on her first try, and was one of the sharpest investigators in the precinct. Vinson would have promoted her to section supervisor a year ago, except for two major problems.

The two problems were these: Brenda took herself much too seriously, and she had a violent temper. These defects were highly visible most of the time, and Reynolds made no attempt to control them. She had gone through a series of partners, both male and female, in blindingly fast fashion. Ron Meyers was the latest and to date, the longest lasting partner Brenda had had in the five years she'd been a detective.

Howard Vinson had frequently told his superiors that if it weren't for the fact that Brenda was such a good investigator, he would have fired her years ago. Brenda had heard all of this, and frankly didn't care. She didn't care how people felt about her. All she cared about was police work. That was her life, and if no one understood that, too bad.

This morning, Ron was staring a little too long for Brenda's comfort. "What's wrong, Meyers? Do I have soap in my ears?"

"No, Lieutenant, your ears look fine. In fact, you look fine. I mean, you look fine all the time, I mean," Meyers stammered, turning beet-red. "How was the gym session today?"

"Meyers, stop babbling," Brenda commanded, her steel-gray eyes sparking with a flicker of amusement. "Since you're interested, I ran about six miles around the track. Then I did a few sparing sessions with McKinsky."

Her voice took on a stern, lecturing tone. Ron was familiar with it. He called it Brenda's You-Need-to-Get-In-Shape tone. "You need to get down there, Meyers. It'll do you some good. Your annual physical's coming up in a few months, and you need to get ready."

"Come on, Lieutenant: that's not fair," Ron Meyers hauled himself to his feet. He slapped his protuberant belly. "See this? It's all muscle. I can still bench press two hundred pounds in the gym, remember?"

"That was a year ago," Brenda reminded him. "Wilkins had to pry the bar off your chest after you did it. You nearly died before he got the weights off of you. Come on, Meyers; you need to start working out now, or you'll flunk the PT test."

"Okay, Lieutenant, I'll see if I can sometime," Meyers remembered Vinson. He looked nervously towards the captain's door. "Vinson said we needed to see him right away, Lieutenant."

"All right, let's go," Reynolds started off for the captain's office without looking behind to see if Meyers was coming. Meyers caught up with her as she reached the door. He paused for a moment, not knowing if he should hold the door open for Brenda. Holding doors open for ladies was a reflex for Meyers.

Unfortunately, it was the wrong thing any man could do for Brenda Reynolds. She had told him two years ago when they became partners that she did not want to be catered to and treated with any sort of deference because she was female.

"Come in," Vinson's voice grated through the door, solving Meyer's dilemma. The voice of his captain suppressed Meyer's chivalrous impulses. The two detectives entered the room simultaneously, bumping into each other as they crossed the threshold.

"You two need to decide who's going in first," Vinson observed laconically. "It solves problems. Take a seat."

Meyers and Reynolds sat down in front of Vinson's desk. He

tossed a flimsy sheet of paper across to Reynolds, who caught it with ease. "Dispatch called in a triple homicide over in the East Dock area this morning at five. Subway Authority units found three male victims in one of the access tunnels underneath the abandoned subway station at Seventeenth Street. As you guys know, we're sweeping through all areas of the city right now getting ready for the convention in July. These tunnels haven't been inspected in years, if ever."

"Captain, we've got four major cases we're working on right now," Reynolds objected briskly. "Putting three more homicides on our plate is going to slow us way down."

That statement was a tactical error on Reynold's part. "Lieutenant, I don't recall asking you if it was convenient for you and your partner to take on another case," Vinson snapped back. "I'm transferring your cases over to Donelley and McCutchen. Brief them after you get back from the crime scene."

He paused for a moment, looking at his two detectives intently. "The reason why I'm giving you this case is that it involves some sort of foreign intelligence agency. One of the cops on the scene said that one of the bodies had some ID that looked like he was a British secret agent. I've called the consulate and they're sending over two people to help you check out that angle of the story."

Reynolds nodded. "Sounds good, Captain. Anyone we might know?"

"Their liaison's name is Donald MacKay," Vinson replied, squinting at a piece of paper in his hand. "Oh yeah, and there's a forensic scientist they're going to bring in to help with the crime scene. Woman by the name of Charlie Warren. You may have heard of her. She was involved in those homicide cases out in Long Island last year."

Brenda reacted suddenly when Charlie's name was mentioned. It was not a favorable reaction. "Yeah, I know her, Captain. That little twerp married my ex-brother in-law back in December."

"Well then, isn't that cozy? This will be a nice little family gathering for you, Lieutenant," Vinson said in an acid tone. "Maybe you can share photographs or recipes."

"Dave Stone's a really great guy," Meyers chimed in, making things much worse.

Controlling herself mightily, Brenda shot him a black look. "Yeah, he's super," she finally ground out. "Okay, Captain. Sounds good. Anything else you want to tell us right now?"

Vinson stood up and looked across his desk. "I have a personal suggestion for you, Reynolds. Put a lid on that temper of yours. I don't want to hear any stories about you blowing your cool. This is a sensitive case. I'm giving this to you because you're the sharpest investigator I've got in this precinct. Don't disappoint me. Is that understood?"

"Yes sir," Brenda replied stonily. She and Meyers left the Captain's office and returned to their desks.

"Meyers, do I ever loose my temper?" Reynolds asked as picked up her coat. Meyers was in the middle of taking a sip from a cup of coffee when she asked him this question. He nearly strangled to death trying not to spray her with coffee as he fought to come up with a diplomatic answer.

"Lieutenant, do you want me to lie, or do you want me to tell you the truth?" Meyers wheezed once his airway was clear of hot coffee.

This was not the response Brenda wanted to hear, especially from her partner. "What's that supposed to mean?" she asked in a snippy tone. "My temper's fine, except when I'm dealing with knuckleheads and idiots and people who don't give me straight answers."

She put on her coat with a series of short, angry motions. "I'm completely self-controlled at all times, Meyers, in case you haven't noticed. Let's get out of here."

The rest of the detective squad watched the exchange and their departure with barely suppressed amusement. Once the door to the section closed, one of the detectives turned to another. "How come Meyers puts up with that witch?"

"Can't you tell?" his partner replied. "Meyers has it bad for her. It's been that way for the longest time. Of course, she won't give him the time of day, but he just keeps hanging on, hoping something's going to change."

"Right," his skeptical partner shook her head. "The only way Brenda Reynolds is ever going to change is if lightning comes down and strikes her on her thick skull. That's never going to happen."

2

Erasmus Krinklefeldt loved dairy farming. It was safe and predictable. Nothing ever happened out of the ordinary, and that's the way Erasmus liked it. Boring and routine: that's the way Erasmus' life had been for the past forty years. In a few years, he was looking forward to a comfortable retirement.

It was a hot day in early June, a day like any other day at Contented Cow Farm. Heat waves were already eddying up in the pastures. Erasmus was up at five, and after having breakfast with Ernestine, his wife of thirty years, he went out to the dairy barn and hooked up his thirty cows to the milking machines.

He stopped by the pasture to check on his new calves. There had been three born the past month, and Erasmus wanted to make sure they were doing all right. His hike out to the east pasture took him about ten minutes. The summer insects were already tuning up, counter pointed by the lowing of the dairy cows.

Erasmus was slightly deaf, so it took him a few seconds to hear the new sound that morning. The cows heard it first, and they started to get skittish. A few seconds later, Erasmus picked it up. It was high-pitched, and definitely mechanical. The sound was also growing louder and deeper. Erasmus was used to the sounds of farm machinery, and this definitely didn't sound like any farm engine he'd ever heard before.

His eyes detected some movement in the distance. Something

gray and green was coming at him, over the pasture, headed directly for him. Erasmus could tell it was the source of the ever-increasing noise.

It was an airplane, coming towards him, low and fast. Its shape looked vaguely familiar, like something Erasmus had seen in old movies about World War Two. The plane was so low that it looked like its propeller was actually touching the ground. Erasmus did what anyone would do under the circumstances: he threw himself on the ground, flattening himself against the earth. Unfortunately, the part of the pasture that he landed on was covered in substances other than grass.

By the time Erasmus had wiped the steaming, smelly muck from his overalls and face, the airplane had howled over his head, missing it by only a few feet. He managed to catch a glimpse of it as it receded quickly into the distance.

Cursing and muttering to himself, Erasmus stomped off to his farmhouse. Ernestine smelled him coming, and insisted that he take a shower in their barn before entering their home. After a quick shower at the barn, the enraged farmer called the sheriff.

-0-

The desk sergeant's phone at the Compton Police Department rang thirty minutes later. Everyone was at shift change, so an irate Chief Carl Davis rushed out of his office to pick up the phone.

"Doesn't anyone answer phones around here?" he grumpily asked the desk sergeant, who was busy eating the last of her glazed donut.

"I would have gotten it, but I had sticky fingers, Chief," the desk sergeant replied, wiping her fingers quickly with a paper napkin. "You know how much you hate it when a phone has goo on it."

"Right," Carl glowered at the desk sergeant as he swept the still-ringing phone off its hook. "Compton Police Department. Chief Davis speaking."

"Carl? This is Mort Grayson at the Sheriff's department. I just got a call from an irate farmer who said that someone in a gray and green airplane buzzed his pasture this morning. He said it had some sort of weird markings on it, like it was from a World War Two movie. Does that ring a bell?"

Carl rolled his eyes heavenward. Not again. "It was a gray and green prop-type airplane, right?"

"That's right, Carl. Sounds like you know something about this. What is it?"

"It's a Spitfire, Mort. That's an old World War Two airplane. I also know whose plane it is; Charlie Warren's at it again."

Grayson started chortling over the phone. "You mean the Medical Examiner? That Charlie Warren? She's in trouble now, Carl. The guy who called in said he took a cow pie bath because it buzzed him. He was really steamed. He wants me to file a report with the FAA."

"That was a really bad choice of words, Mort," Carl told Grayson, grimacing horribly. It was a horrible joke, but it was morning and Davis couldn't help himself. "Cow pies and steam usually go together."

"Cow pies and steam? I didn't even think of that. You are one sick dude, Davis," Grayson chortled. The two policemen laughed for a while. Mort finally managed to control himself after half a minute. "Okay, Carl: I'll let it slide this time. You tell Dr. Warren to ease up on buzzing the locals. If it happens again, I'll have to call the FAA."

"All right, Mort," Carl replied. "I'll pass on the word. Call the farmer back and tell him the problem will be taken care of. Let him know we won't need to get the FAA involved in this one."

Joan Richards, the Head of the Detective Section, had entered the office during the conversation. Carl's face told her wordlessly that Charlie Warren had done something again. She waited politely until Carl was through. "Okay, Carl: you have that Charlie Warren look on your face. What's the redhead done now?"

"Buzzed a cow pasture," Carl grimaced. "Farmer wound up diving headfirst into a cow pie. He called the sheriff up and filed a complaint."

"Figures." Joan shrugged elaborately. "Fifth time this month, isn't it?"

"Yup."

-0-

The pilot of the Spitfire was completely oblivious to all of the mayhem she was causing on the ground. Charlie Warren, M.D., liked flying low and fast. The faster her old fighter went, the more she liked it. As far as she was concerned, the airplane was nothing more than her own personal roller coaster.

She felt a thrumming vibration next to her waist. Glancing down briefly, Charlie saw it was a message from David: *Need you back now!*

"Blast. All right, old girl," Charlie said regretfully to her airplane, "time to head back to the shed."

Turning the plane upward in one final inverted roll, Charlie reluctantly headed the Spitfire back towards the open field where the plane was berthed.

The airplane had arrived at Compton one day in March, transported into town on the backs of four flatbed trucks. Jane's father had the airplane shipped piecemeal over from Great Britain, where it had been languishing in a back shed on their family estate. Charlie had often told Jane that she'd wanted to restore the old plane, and Jane's father finally decided to give Charlie the plane as a wedding gift.

David Stone, Charlie's longsuffering husband who was used to having all sorts of odd things appear at his doorstep, signed for the delivery. Unusual things had become the norm for David ever since he married Charlie last Christmas. He looked at the parade of flatbed trucks with their odd assortment of plane parts and just shrugged his shoulders.

"I hope it came with model cement," was his only comment as he signed for the bizarre arrival. "Take all that stuff over by that large shed in the back. We'll sort it all out later."

"What kind of nut job would put together an old airplane?" the truck driver asked.

"That would be me," Charlie appeared at the doorstep with a delighted grin on her face as she saw the caravan of trucks. "I'll have to e-mail Jane's parents and let them know the plane finally made it."

David simply shook his head and went back into the house.

Charlie was delighted with the belated wedding present. For the next several weeks, she and her half-sister Katya were busy in the barn, putting the old plane back together. With help from Sean O'Grady, a Catholic priest who ran an auto shop at the edge of town, they managed to get the aircraft airworthy. The project kept her busy for a while, and as long as Charlie was busy with something, she generally stayed out of mischief. Generally.

The key for Charlene Warren to staying out of trouble was to keep her life as full as possible. Charlie worked as the Chief Medical Examiner for Compton and the surrounding towns. She also helped her godfather, Angus McKendrick, at Trinity Church. All of these activities filled her life with purpose, and made her very happy.

She also had other "interests" that came her way on occasion. From time to time, Charlie would receive calls from law enforcement agencies in the New England area. As a forensic scientist, she would sometimes be called in to help with difficult or troubling cases involving murders or crimes of a complex nature. She sometimes ran into trouble dealing with local law enforcement officials, as well as some of her medical colleagues, mainly because of the way she acted and looked. People had a tendency to judge her on the basis of her behavior and looks. This was an unfortunate mistake that rapidly dissipated once Charlie came onto the scene and got down to business.

Charlie was thirty-one years old, but looked about half her age. Being a little over five feet in height failed to help matters, along with her red-gold hair and splashes of freckles across her face. She looked like an intellectual lightweight, and sometimes acted a little too playfully for her own good. Her outward appearance and behavior concealed a very complex character and a highly developed intellect that rapidly became apparent once people got to know her.

There was another, darker part of Charlie's life that occasionally intruded on her daily existence. Sometimes her phone would ring at night, and David would waken to find his bed empty. When this happened, it meant that Charlie had been summoned for cases that involved work of a secret, clandestine nature. David never asked Charlie about those cases, and Charlie never volunteered any information. Sometimes she would be gone for a day or so, sometimes for weeks. David had learned to accept it. Fortunately for them, those incidents were few and far between.

"Can't you tell them 'no' some time, Charlie?" he asked one time.

Charlie fixed him with an icy stare. "David, you were in Special Forces one time. Could you ever tell your superiors, 'I'm sorry, but I really don't want to go on this mission.'?"

"No."

"I think you've answered your own question," Charlie replied, softening her response by kissing him. "Besides, you knew what I was when you married me."

"Yeah, a pest."

One of the last things her old plane needed was a functioning radio. Charlie was in no hurry to install it. She enjoyed the peace and freedom of flying around without the mundane distraction of talking to people as she flew. The lack of a radio irritated David, who pointed out that if the old airplane were to develop engine trouble, there would be no way for Charlie to radio in for help. Charlie's solution to the lack of a radio was to put a GPS tracker in the plane. The radio box, however, remained empty.

That morning, Charlie brought the Spitfire in for a perfect landing in the field behind their home. The grass was now cut short, and made a perfect landing field for the vintage aircraft. David was waiting for her.

"It's still running a bit rich, but Sean did a wonderful job tuning the engine," she called out to David as she climbed out of the cockpit once the propeller stopped turning. "What's going on?"

David came up to her. He wrapped his arms around Charlie picking her up and twirling her five-foot, two-inch frame around as he kissed her. "David, put me down! You'll break your back doing that!" she said laughingly.

"Not a chance, Pest," he replied, stroking her short hair as he held her. Pulling back, his face assumed an expression of mock seriousness. "We need to talk about you and your hobby of buzzing cow pastures. A local farmer phoned in a complaint to the Sheriff's office this morning."

A mildly penitent look flitted across Charlie's freckled face. It made her look almost regretful. Almost. "I'm sorry. I guess I got carried away. It just felt so good to let the old girl feel her oats," Charlie told him.

"Is that what it is?" David asked wryly. "Are you getting bored with Compton? Somehow I get the feeling there's not enough excitement for you in this burg. You're probably the only forensic scientist in America who will be cited by the FAA for violating airspace guidelines."

Charlie looked up at him and kissed him. "You're probably right. Anyway, as long as I have you around, there's plenty of excitement for me."

"Good," David put his arm around Charlie's shoulders as they walked away from the plane. The early morning sun glinted off of Charlie's golden-red hair, illuminating her face in a beautiful way. David's heart filled with love for her as he held her. "What's on your agenda for today, cutie?"

"Let's see: Katya and I have to be down at the high school for our first meeting today. Jackie's finally gotten all of the scripts printed out, and we're holding tryouts this afternoon."

"Uh huh," David grimaced. "Ah yes. *Ophelia*, Jackie Smythe's first great experiment in script writing, directing, producing, and Heaven knows what else. I can hardly wait. Between you and your half-sister, I can't keep track of all of these projects you're involved in. I have to carry a list with me just to keep up."

"Get over it, chum," Charlie playfully punched David's arm. "You're getting involved as well. I've got you helping Steve Morton with the set construction after we get back from England."

"Yeah, I figured as much. Now run this by me again: we're going off to get you and me knighted, then in July after the play we're going up to Edinburgh for Megan and Donald's wedding, then back to London for the Gresham wedding. All of this is happening in one summer, right?"

"That's it."

"Fine, so who's going to run the show while we're off in the UK this next week?"

"Jackie's going to be handling the directing, along with Joanne, and Steve Morton's going to be supervising the construction," Charlie explained patiently. "Katya's staying behind over at Joan's house while we're away."

"Charlie, I'd like to know something: is there anyone else in this town who hasn't been dragged into this thing? It looked like most of the town was down at your organizational meeting last night."

"It's a community project," Charlie replied with an amused glint in her emerald eyes. "Keeps everyone together."

David sighed. "All right. Whatever you say. Now look: you really have to stop flying your toy low and fast over farm country. The farmers are going to have your head on a pitchfork if you keep this up. This is America, and they're not used to eccentric English ladies taking Spitfires out for morning joy rides."

Charlie held up her hand. "You've made your point, David. From now on, I promise to keep my aircraft at the thousand foot minimum over the countryside at all times."

She playfully pushed on his shoulder. "And I am NOT eccentric. That's a term reserved for fussy old ladies in large, frowsy hats who knit doilies for their large collection of spoiled cats."

"I never said you were frowsy."

"All right," Charlie conceded, "I promise to behave. A little."

An evil flicker flashed in her eyes. "I do reserve the right to drop down over bodies of water."

David groaned. "Uh huh. Just keep our phone number handy and your cell phone on so you can call me when I have to bail you out. And the FAA's going to ground you permanently if they ever find out that you don't have an operating radio in that crate. You know that's illegal."

"Whatever."

They continued walking over to the back of their house. "Katya was showing me her set designs last night. They look very elaborate," David noted bleakly. "How fast does she expect us to build all of that stuff?"

"She thinks we can get most of the major construction done in about two weeks," Charlie replied brightly as they came up to the back door of their house. "She and Megan went through the high school stock of existing flats and platforms last week. Most of the stuff can be refitted and painted to make the new set, so there won't be that much to build."

David was skeptical. "Right. You're all nuts. Katya's starting to get just as bad as you are. And I had such high hopes that she'd turn out normal. I saw the plans, kiddo. They look more in line with a Hollywood production than a community play."

"She's my sister, David; there's no way she's ever going to be normal," Charlie explained patiently. "Besides, being normal is boring."

The smell of eggs and bacon greeted them as they went inside. Katya had already fixed breakfast for them. "Good morning, Charlie," Katya said as she kissed Charlie and hugged David. "I have breakfast ready for us."

"I can see you have, love," Charlie said, looking at her half-sister with pride. "David can help you set the table while I get changed."

"I'm going to rent you out as a cook, Katya," David winked at his sister-in-law. "It'll pay for your sister's aviation gas bills."

"I heard that, David," Charlie called out from the bedroom.

"I think you're in trouble again, David," Katya said as she poured orange juice into the glasses.

"What else is new?" David replied as he got out the silverware. He helped Katya set the table while Charlie changed out of her flying clothes. Their household had managed to settle into a well-oiled routine over the past six months. At least the house had enough room, despite its ghastly past.

The house had belonged to David's parents. After they died in a car accident a few years back, David's twin brother Bryan had moved in. Bryan and David resembled each other in physical appearance only. A pathologist by training, Bryan had been the local Medical Examiner, and David had worked as a detective in the Compton Police Department. The two brothers were poles apart in temperament, and they had barely spoken to each other except when absolutely necessary.

The previous September, a hideous murder occurred in Compton, the first ever for the sleepy New York town. Bryan became a suspect, but had died of a brain tumor before being arrested and brought to trial.

After his death, the police had found evidence in the house that other murders had taken place. Bryan had used the carriage house as a makeshift operating room, killing twenty women and burying their bodies in the field behind the house.

Charlie had been summoned from England to help with the original investigation, and had stayed on to help with the hideous aftermath. The task of identifying the bodies kept her busy for several weeks. She decided to stay on in Compton after the work was done, having fallen in love with David.

After Charlie and David married, they moved temporarily into David's home in Compton, leaving Bryan's house deserted. The property had gone to David after Bryan's death, and considering the house's history it had no resale value. They decided to have the house demolished at a later date. Charlie told David that in her opinion the house needed to be leveled and the acres around it sowed with salt.

Their plans and lives changed completely in January. Charlie's half-sister came into their lives. Katerina Chernenko's arrival had been a complete surprise. While they were over in England on their honeymoon, Charlie and David found out that Charlie's father, John Warren, had remarried some years ago while living in the Ukraine.

John Warren had been working for British Intelligence when he had been forced into hiding. Settling in the Ukraine, Warren had lived there for about eleven years and had married a local doctor. Their daughter, Katerina, or Katya as she liked to be called, was eleven when John and his wife died in an outbreak of influenza. A talented figure skater, she was sent to a Ukrainian school that specialized in training young athletes.

Katya had become a national skating star, and was on tour in London with the Ukrainian Figure Skating Team. Charlie and David met her in London, and decided to adopt her and bring her home with them to America. After a difficult court battle, they were granted custody of Katya, and she had come home with them that January.

David and Charlie had planned to move into a larger home, but Katya's arrival had made their plans more complicated. Despite her earlier threats to have the old home leveled, Charlie decided after careful consideration that having Katya in the family made their needs for more space imperative. The problem for space became even more glaringly apparent when they went down to the storage area in January and found that there was no way they could fit all of the new pieces of furniture Charlie had bought in England into the house they'd picked out.

"You miscalculated on square footage, Charlie," David told her that day. "We need a bigger place."

"That's right, David. We'll move out to your parents' old home," Charlie replied cheerfully. "There's no way we'd get all of your books into this house and have any room left. We now have an extra family member to think about."

David's eyes nearly fell out of his head. "You want to move out to Murder Mansion? What about all of that stuff you said about having the house plowed under?"

"That was before Katya showed up. Things have changed. We need the space, David."

"Doesn't it bother you that we'll be living in a house where all of those killings took place?"

"David Stone, I don't believe in ghosts and all that rot," Charlie said briskly in a no-nonsense tone. "This is an empty house that happens to belong to you, and that's all it is. We need the house, and that's final. It's a perfect solution to all our problems."

David sighed. "All right, I'll call up Carl and give him the bad news." Carl Davis, the Chief of Police and David's best friend, had already picked a home down the street from his. Sarah, Carl's wife, had been ecstatic when she discovered the home. It seemed just right for Charlie and David.

Carl took the news in stride. "It works for us, Dave. I was worried about having that place stand empty. We won't have any weirdoes buying up your parents' old house and turning into some sort of nightspot for freaks. If you guys are living there, that won't happen."

"No, instead you'll have Charlie living in it and that could be so much worse. You know what that girl's like. She'll probably stir up every ghost, goblin, or whatever you can think of," David replied. He was looking at Charlie as he said those words. She responded by making a horrible face at him and punching his shoulder.

"Beast," she sniffed. "You're maligning my character again."

"How? Tell me one thing I've said that's not true." David asked, massaging his shoulder.

Charlie thought for a moment. "Nothing really. It's just I didn't care for your tone, dear sir. Besides, there's no reason in paying property taxes on two pieces of land. We'll have room to build a skating rink if Katya decides to take up skating again."

"Charlie, she told us she never wanted to skate again."

She fixed him with a why-do-I-put-up-with-this-man expression. "David, she's thirteen. She can and probably will change her mind. Trust me on that."

"Woman's prerogative?"

"Precisely."

Charlie's words proved to be prophetic. Katya decided after two months in America to take up skating again. She reluctantly confided this one night to Charlie.

Charlie explained to Katya that she could live in Compton and skate if she wanted to. Katya was overjoyed that she could continue to live with Charlie and David. The little girl was terrified of being sent off to some place to continue a skating career.

After Katya's parents had died, she had been sent off to a special school where she lived with the Ukrainian figure skating team. Skating had become "her job," an endless source of joyless misery and pain. When she initially came to Compton, she wanted nothing to do with figure skating.

Now that she was no longer under the heavy hand of her former coach, Katya's skating was better than ever. Charlie encouraged her gently, biding her time. She knew that eventually Katya would probably want to compete again, but she refused to pressure her sister into making a decision.

"Katya, David wants us to be normal," Charlie came back into the kitchen. "I told him that was a horrid thing to say. I explained to him that normal is boring. What do you think about that?" Katya said nothing for a moment and spent the time toying with her food.

"What's wrong, darling?" Charlie asked gently, half-guessing the answer to her question.

"Charlie," Katya finally began, "I've really enjoyed skating the past few months. I have learned to love it again. The other day I met a lady down at the skating rink who said she would like to be my coach. Ms. Robeson wants to see if I could get on to the American Olympic Team. I would like to try. What do you think?"

Charlie glanced over at David, who nodded slightly. "Darling, I think it's a wonderful idea, if that's what you want to do. Is this what you want?"

Katya lowered her eyes. "Yes, Charlie. I have thought long and hard about it. I love you and David, and I want to stay here in Compton with my friends. I do not want to be sent away to a skating school. Can I skate and also stay here? Is it possible?"

Charlie reached out and put her hand in Katya's. "Of course it is, love. We'll make arrangements for you to work with a coach. We can even see about building you a skating rink here on our property, if you like. Whatever you need, we'll do it."

"Hold on, Charlie," David held up a hand. "I'm all for helping Katya out with the skating thing, but the Olympics is a whole other deal. Katya's got to be an American citizen to compete on the U.S. Olympic team. She's still a Ukrainian national."

"Yes, but we've officially adopted her," Charlie pointed out. "That means she can apply for American citizenship. The Winter Olympics are in 2006. We need to get the ball rolling in that department, David."

David looked at Charlie and Katya. "Seems reasonable. I'll see what we can do about that."

"You are so tractable, David," Charlie said with a twinkle in her eyes. She turned to Katya. "We'll work on that part of the problem, Katya. Even if you can't skate in the Olympics, you can still skate for America at the World competitions. If you're not ready for 2006, there's always 2010 to shoot for."

Katya came out of her chair and came over to Charlie and hugged her tightly. "Thank you, thank you, Charlie! I was so worried you would be angry about my decision! I told you a few months ago that I never wanted to skate again, but now I have learned to love it, and I want to skate to honor you, and God."

Charlie said nothing for a moment. She held her sister close, stroking her blonde hair. "Darling, there's nothing you could ever do that would make me angry with you," Charlie whispered through her tears. "I have been so very proud of what you've done over the past few months."

"Did I hear you say something about a skating rink?" David asked cautiously. "Where is this money going to come from? I don't think I've gotten a raise recently. Did you find a buried treasure chest when you were spading up the back yard last year?"

"We'll think of something," Charlie replied confidently. "Grandfather's estate was finally sold. We cleared around a million pounds after the taxes and fees."

"A million pounds? How much is that in real money?"

"Around one and a half million dollars, give or take a few hundred thousand, you goose," Charlie said sternly, winking at Katya. "Mind your manners, if you please."

"Yes, ma'am." David looked at his watch. "Now if you two lovely ladies will excuse me, I need to be off to the police station. Where are you all headed today?"

"I need to stop at the Medical Examiner's office and finish up some paperwork. Katya is getting together with Jackie later on this morning and they're going to go over her designs for the set. I think that takes us up to noon." Charlie enumerated everything, using her fingers to tick off points for emphasis.

"Another typical day," David said as he put on his coat. "Try not to get too involved before supper. Will I see you at lunch?"

"I suppose so," Charlie said mysteriously. "That depends on if I get out of the doctor's office on time."

David stopped at the door. "Doctor's office? What's going on? Are you sick?"

"No." Charlie replied demurely. "It's… something else."

David looked at Charlie and raised his eyebrows. She nodded back slightly. "Why am I always the last to know about these things?"

He turned to Katya. "Did you know about this?"

"Yes David. Charlie told me not to tell you. She found out a few days ago."

"Why are you asking her?" Charlie looked at him teasingly. "I thought you'd be the first one to know."

"I… well I'm a guy, and you know…" David was flummoxed.

"Know what, David?" Charlie refused to let him off the hook.

"Stop it, you little pest," David came over and picked her up and twirled around as he held her in his arms. "I don't know what to say! I love you so much. I really can't believe it. This is wonderful! It's great!" David laughed as tears filled his eyes.

He finally recovered and looked at Charlie and Katya. "Okay, any more surprises I need to know about?"

Charlie's face assumed a deadpan expression. "Nothing else at the moment. Give me time, David. It's only eight in the morning. You never know what else might happen."

"Okay," Shrugging his shoulders, David kissed her goodbye and hugged Katya. He left the house shaking his head and muttering to himself.

"All right, darling, now that we've flummoxed David, it's time for me to head to work." Charlie kissed Katya and hugged her. "What time is Jackie coming over?"

"She said around ten," Katya gathered up the dishes and took them to the sink. "We'll meet you around eleven or so."

"Sounds good, darling. Have a good day."

David reappeared at the kitchen door. "Hold it, everyone: no one's going anywhere. Where's my car, ladies?"

Charlie's face was the picture of innocence. "Why David, what ever are you talking about?"

"You know exactly what I'm talking about," David's voice took on a tone of mock outrage. "You two come with me."

He led them out to the adjoining garage where their cars were kept. In place of his venerable heap, there was a new, dark blue minivan with a large red bow on top of it. "What, may I ask, is this?"

Katya and Charlie exploded into peals of laughter at David's reaction. "It's a minivan, David." Katya managed to tell him after her laughter subsided.

"Yes, David, it's a minivan," Charlie echoed, her face contorting with laughter as she tried to control herself. "Your car, so-called, has been abducted, and this is its replacement. I had the car dealer come out at two in the morning and take it away."

David looked at her for a moment, and shook his head. "Fine.

Okay. Just wanted to check. It makes perfect sense. You're pregnant, and we need a new car for our growing family."

He smiled and wrapped Charlie in his arms. "It's wonderful, and I'm not one bit surprised." David turned and looked at Katya with a scowl on his face. "I'm mad at you, Katya. I thought there was at least one person in this household I could trust."

"Charlie told me not to say anything," Katya replied with a smile.

"Traitor. I'm surrounded by criminals." David assumed a martyred expression.

"Here are the keys, David," Charlie handed David a key ring. "Now run off before we all get into more trouble."

"Trouble? You're telling me not to get into trouble? That's your department, Pest," David kissed her one more time before climbing into the van and driving off.

"Do you think he liked the van, Charlie?" Katya asked as they watched the van driving off down the long road to the highway.

"Yes I do, darling," Charlie hugged her sister and sighed. "I think he's very pleased. Now let's go inside and tell me all about this Ms. Robeson and what she thinks."

3

Charlie left the house and drove into town in her XKE Jaguar. It was a gorgeous morning; the sun had already burned off the early morning fog, and it promised to be a beautiful day. Charlie drove the few miles into town with the top of her sports car down, negotiating the turns in a quick, professional manner. It was a fast drive, but one that relaxed Charlie and allowed her to focus on the tasks of the day ahead.

Lucy Kelson, the lab director, was waiting for her in her office with a stack of messages. "Good morning, Lucy," Charlie sang as she took the stack from her with a smile. "Has Jason relented yet and decided to get involved with Jackie's play?"

"I don't know," Lucy replied with a mock frown on her face. "It's going to be a struggle. Jackie's an expert in wearing him down, but Jason's stubborn, so it might take time. How did your surprise with the van go?"

"David loved it, though I think I didn't surprise him much. He was still in shock about my other news."

"You hit him with everything all at once? You're a fiend," Lucy shook her head. "I'm surprised the man's still standing."

"I think he'll survive."

"Good," Lucy paused for a moment. Her face became quiet and serious. "John asked the prison chaplain the other day if you could speak at the prison prayer breakfast sometime. He's going to have the warden call you."

Charlie put her hand in Lucy's. "I'll look forward to it. How is John doing?"

A troubled look came over Lucy's face. "I don't know, Charlie. He's losing a lot of weight. John says it's the prison food, but I think something else is going on. I'm worried about him."

John Griggs, Lucy's ex-husband, had been an accomplice with Bryan Stone in the series of horrific murders that occurred in Compton the previous fall. He confessed to his crimes, and had been sentenced to life in prison. Charlie had interceded on his behalf, and the judge had sent him to a prison close by Compton so that Lucy and Jason could see him on a regular basis.

Charlie could see the concern in Lucy's face. "I'll try to get out to see John soon, Lucy. I promise."

"Thank you, Charlie," Lucy's tone improved at Charlie's assurance. "By the way, someone from the British Consulate called this morning. I think it was Donald MacKay."

"Really?" Charlie's face immediately broke out into a delighted grin. "What on earth could our intrepid Sergeant Major want or need from me?"

"I don't know. He sounded embarrassed."

"Donald's been that way around me most of the time I've known him. I wish he'd just relax."

"It's probably a Megan problem."

"Probably."

Megan O'Grady, the younger sister of Sean O'Grady, had become engaged to Donald back in December. Charlie had managed to bring the two together while Megan was directing a play at the local high school. They had fallen helplessly in love, and were planning on marrying this summer.

Charlie walked over to her desk and sat down, an amused smile playing over her face. She dialed Donald's number at the British Consulate and was quickly connected to him. "Good morning, Donald. What can I do for you on this fine June morning? Are you having a case of prenuptial jitters?"

"Colonel Warren, we need you down at the consulate this morning. There's been an incident that requires your assistance. Can you make it?" Sergeant Major Donald MacKay was normally very lighthearted when he talked to Charlie. He almost never used Charlie's military title in speaking to her privately, except in discussing very serious subjects. His complete lack of levity meant that something grave had happened.

The light tone in Charlie's voice vanished. "Of course. I'll be right down." Charlie put down the phone and buzzed Lucy's number. "Lucy, I'm going to have to go down to the consulate this morning. Could you call Katya at home and tell her I won't be meeting her this noon for lunch. Oh yes, please call Dr. Edwards and let her know I'm going to have to reschedule my appointment with her."

"Sure, Charlie. What's going on?"

"I'm not sure. Something serious has happened in New York City. Donald was obviously not calling me about some sort of premarital problem. He sounded very concerned, and he didn't elaborate."

"All right, I'll take care of all of those calls for you. Is there anything else?"

Charlie thought for a moment. "Yes, please tell the state medical examiner that I won't be able to call him today. I don't know what's going on right now."

She hung up the phone and then called David. "I'm going to have to go to the consulate this morning, so I won't be able to meet with you and Katya for lunch."

"Someone start a war somewhere? I don't see any mushroom clouds in the direction of New York City. What's up?"

"I don't know, David," Charlie replied rather sharply. "This is serious. I'll call you later."

"Okay, just keep me posted."

-0-

Forty minutes later, Charlie pulled up to the British Consulate. MacKay was waiting for her at the entrance. "What's going on, Donald?" she asked as they went inside.

"A British subject was found shot in a tunnel underneath a subway station this morning," MacKay replied tersely, "that's all I know right now."

Donald MacKay was a Sergeant Major in the elite British Special Air Service. He was on special duty, attached to the British Consulate to assist in criminal investigations. That was his official posting. What MacKay actually did fell into two main areas: first, he was in charge of counter-terrorism and intelligence operations for the New York area. His second and more difficult unofficial duty was to ride herd on Charlie Warren. It was this second part of his job that gave him the most trouble.

They walked into the Consul-General's office. Lady Margaret Wilson was there, along with James Rosson, the Director of Intelligence and Criminal Investigations.

"Good morning, darling," James said as he kissed Charlie's cheek. "Sorry for the abrupt summons, but we really couldn't elaborate over the phone."

Charlie gave him an understanding smile. "I understand," she turned to Lady Margaret. "It's good to see you again, ma'am. I haven't seen you since March."

"Since Jane's parents dropped off their wedding present, you mean," Lady Margaret said with an amused tone in her voice. "James tells me you've got that ancient machine racketing about the countryside, terrifying farmers."

Blushing, Charlie nodded her head. "Guilty on all counts, ma'am." Being around Lady Margaret always managed to make Charlie feel as though she was in the presence of her mother. Charlie's own mother had died when she was five. Lady Margaret had stepped into the role of Charlie's mother quite naturally.

"All right then," Lady Margaret ushered everyone over to her desk where a ring of chairs waited. "James, please give us a full update on what has gone on this morning."

"At about eight this morning I received a call from the New York City Police Department telling me that a British national had been found shot in a subway station," James began grimly as soon as everyone was seated. "They were rather close-mouthed about the whole affair, refused to elaborate on when or where, or anything else about the situation."

"The reason you've been called in on this, Lady Warren," Lady Margaret smiled at Charlie, "is that your talents as a forensic scientist may be useful in trying to figure out how this man came to be shot in a subway, and why. The New York Police Department asked for our help, and naturally your name came up. We have reason to believe that there may be more than some sort of robbery involved. The man had identification on him that was most curious, and the police think he might be some sort of intelligence agent."

"I'll be happy to help in any way I can, ma'am," Charlie said with enthusiasm. The case sounded intriguing. "My schedule at the medical examiner's office isn't very busy right now."

"I'm glad to hear you're available to help us," James said with satisfaction. "We don't want to jeopardize your employment."

He paused for a second or so. "Although nothing would make me happier than to have you on our staff full time. There's enough work in this office to keep all of us quite busy."

An amused light flickered in Charlie's eyes. "Now James, you and I have had this talk several times before. I can't go racketing about the countryside on all sorts of adventures anymore like I used to. There's David and Katya to think about now, as well as the rest of my family. Besides, you know full well that I've been involved in plenty of other things that you've asked me to do."

"That's enough arm twisting, James. Dr. Warren has been extraordinarily helpful to us on several occasions. Her life is quite full right now. Congratulations on your news, by the way," Lady Margaret said in her most maternal tone. "We'll expect regular updates on your progress."

She rose from her chair. "Donald, I need you and Dr. Warren to head to the crime scene to find out about this man. James and I will stay here and contact Sir Leslie Gresham. Since the man might be an intelligence officer I took the liberty of informing him of the situation this morning. He promised me he'd look into it."

"Very good, ma'am," Charlie said as she and MacKay stood up. She glanced over at Donald. "Looks like the Sergeant Major and I are off to a crime scene."

"That we are, Colonel," MacKay replied, "and yes, I insist on navigating our car through New York traffic."

"Chauvinist."

-0-

Charlie had tried over the years to convince Donald MacKay that women were capable of driving just as well as men, but it was a lost cause. MacKay in turn refused to yield on that point, which was unusual since Charlie had pretty much mastered the art of wheedling MacKay into doing anything she wanted.

"We don't need you getting that guided missile of yours mixed up in one of New York's famous traffic accidents," he said firmly. "I've been in this city for six months now. I'm far more qualified in getting us where we want to go in the least amount of time. Blast this traffic!"

"Of course, Donald; you're far more capable than I am in getting us there on time," Charlie remarked with a straight face as their car's progress was promptly halted by a traffic snarl. Two cabs had merged simultaneously into the same lane ahead of them. The resulting crash caused a fusion of their bumpers and an eruption of metal, steam, and filthy language from their drivers.

"What a beautiful New York picture: a traffic accident, clouds of steam, and inspired cursing from cabbies," Charlie mused. "The steam cloud reminds me of the time I saw Mt. Etna erupt in Sicily. American cab drivers turn cursing into an art form, don't they?"

MacKay laughed. "It's a great, bonnie cloud, but the language is pure American. Speaking of eruptions, I heard from Megan that you managed to get rid of David's car. How did he take his loss?"

"Rather well, actually. He was in shock from the pregnancy news, though," Charlie replied mirthfully. "I think he's starting to get a bit used to me, Donald. I don't seem to be able to surprise him much anymore."

"That I doubt, lass," MacKay replied laughingly. He sighed and leaned his head on the wheel. "What I wouldn't give for a few guided missiles right now! This traffic is abominable."

"Courage, Sergeant Major," Charlie said in a mock serious tone. "It will get better in a while. You always reminded me of that when we were soaked to the skin in the Cotswolds."

"And I was right, wasn't I, lass?" MacKay replied smugly.

They waited in silence a few moments more while the traffic problem undid itself.

"I was certain that your call this morning was about Megan," Charlie finally said.

Donald blushed and looked straight ahead. "It was, originally. I am really having misgivings about staying in the Army, Charlie. Colonel Rosson's teasing aside, I really have enjoyed my tour at the Consulate. The problem is, if I continue in SAS, I'm almost certain to be posted away from America eventually, and I can't bear the thought of separating Megan from you and the rest of her friends and family. She really loves Compton."

"Have you talked to her about these things, Donald?"

MacKay was silent as he turned onto the street where the subway station was located. "We've talked about it a bit. Megan tells me that she's willing to go anywhere, but I look into her eyes, and I know how much it would hurt her to leave all of you. I can't be selfish anymore, Charlie. I've got to think about her."

Charlie looked at him with admiration. "Bravo, Sergeant Major. You've exceeded my expectations in every single way. If I didn't know you before now, I'd know now that you're absolutely the right man for Megan."

"I'm glad you think so, Charlie." MacKay replied with gratitude. "Your opinion has always meant a lot to me. Megan loves teaching school in Compton, and I'm not going to take her away from that. I'm planning on talking to Colonel Rosson later on today about all of this. I can always get a job with Sean at his automotive shop. He told me I could help him any time."

"I'm sure you'll find something, Donald. You are one of the most resourceful people I've ever met," Charlie laughed as they pulled over to the curb next to a row of squad cars and a van marked "NYPD Forensic Unit."

"This station looks a bit on the seedy side," MacKay observed as the came to the entrance.

The Seventeenth Street Station had been abandoned a number of years back, and the entrance had been sealed until a few days ago. Subway security had opened it up for a routine inspection. A uniformed officer standing at the door allowed Charlie and MacKay to enter after seeing their identification cards.

They walked down the crumbling concrete stairs to the subway station. Brenda Reynolds and Ron Meyers were waiting for them. Since they were a few minutes late, Brenda was pacing back and forth like a caged animal, and looked elaborately at her watch to indicate her displeasure with their tardiness.

"This must be our friends from the police department," Donald said, coming up to Brenda and Ron.

"Good morning, Mr. MacKay," Detective Reynolds said brusquely. She shook Donald's hand and studiously ignored Charlie for the moment. "I'm Lieutenant Brenda Reynolds, and this is Sergeant Ron Meyers. We're investigating this case."

"Donald MacKay. I'm pleased to meet you, Lieutenant," MacKay replied formally, noting the deliberate and egregious lapse in Brenda's manners. "By the way, this is my colleague, Dr. Charlene Warren, a forensic scientist who has been called in as a consultant by the British Consulate in this matter."

"I know all about Dr. Warren," Detective Reynolds said in an annoyed dismissive tone as she stared at Charlie. She finally shook Charlie's hand briskly. "We don't need help in forensics. Our CSI guys can handle this case without your help," she said coldly.

Brenda Reynolds had been at war with herself ever since she'd heard about Charlie being assigned to the case. She had never met Charlie before, but the prospect of meeting and working with David's new wife was not a pleasant one for her. There was no humor in her cold gray eyes as she looked at Charlie, who immediately decided that Brenda needed to be shaken up a bit. Brenda for her part decided to hate Charlie from the moment she laid eyes on her.

"Why, I'm sure they can, Detective," Charlie replied brightly in her cheeriest voice, determined not to let Ms. Reynolds' snide attitude get to her. "Don't worry about me. I'm just tagging along right now at the request of the British Consulate." She flashed a six-megawatt smile at the surly detective and her partner.

MacKay picked up on her tone and rolled his eyes heavenward. *Lord help us; Charlie's going to toy with this irate detective.* It was never a good day when Charlie decided to play with someone.

Ron Meyers sensed his partner's hostility and decided to play peacemaker. "I'm glad to finally meet you, Dr. Warren," he said warmly as he clasped Charlie's hand. "I read about that Shakespeare play you did a couple of months ago. It sounded great. I wanted to get out to Compton to see it, but it was sold out every night."

"Meyers, spare us the theatrical reviews and focus on the case," Detective Reynolds broke in rudely. Meyers looked crushed, and Charlie eyed him with sympathy. *That was truly uncalled-for*, she thought to herself. *This woman needs to be taken down a notch.* Charlie controlled her features, but her eyes flickered up to Sergeant Major MacKay, who shook his head slightly.

Reynolds resumed her terse, colorless briefing. "As I was saying, here's what we know. At about four this morning, Subway security was busy checking the access tunnels below the subway line when they ran across three bodies. It was obvious that they had all been shot. The bodies were completely decomposed, and there were signs that they had been involved in some sort of gunfight. This station has been closed since the 1950's, so there's no telling how long the bodies have actually been down there.

"One of the men had some really strange ID which identified him as a British citizen. That's why we called the consulate, to see if you people might know who he is." Brenda's tone indicated that she doubted that MacKay and Charlie would be any use to her at all.

"This is one of those cases that turns up every once in a while. Someone knocks down a building or comes into an underground room that hasn't been opened in years and discovers some dead bodies no one knew about. We get a couple of cases like this every few months or so. It happens in New York all the time."

"That's New York," Meyers added cheerfully. "It's summer and bodies are just popping up all over."

Charlie giggled at his remark. Reynolds rolled her eyes heavenward at Meyers' lame remark. *Could this English twit possibly be more of an airhead?*

She crushed Meyers with a glance and looked directly at MacKay. "What I want to know, Mr. MacKay, is do you or the British government know anything about those bodies? Is there anything you want to tell me, Mr. MacKay? Were any of your intelligence agents snooping around New York tunnels sometime in the past?"

MacKay looked at her impassively. "Detective Reynolds, I don't know what you're talking about. When your police department contacted us this morning, it was the first time any of us heard anything about them. I don't know why you'd think I would know anything more about them personally. I just work at the consulate assisting with criminal matters."

"Right," Reynolds was unconvinced. "I have friends who work in Intel, MacKay. I know what your post is at the consulate, and I know who you work for. Listen: I don't know who this guy was, or what he was doing down in that subway. All I know is that we want to get this cleared up as soon as possible."

"That's why you're here. We found multiple shell casings fired from automatic weapons, along with evidence of a grenade explosion. It looks as though this British guy was involved in some sort of firefight underneath the city.

"Additionally, we have two unknown male subjects. The bodies have been dead for a long time. Our CSI says that they got blown up by a grenade or something."

Donald MacKay raised his eyebrows. "Really? That is unusual. When can we see this crime scene?"

"In just a minute. You have to understand, Mr. MacKay, we generally don't have people blowing each other up with grenades here in New York, but the times are changing," Meyers quipped, winking at Charlie, who giggled in return.

"Can the humor, Meyers," Brenda said grimly. "So what do you think, Mr. MacKay?"

Donald looked at Charlie for a moment. Charlie was his superior officer, and Reynolds was deferring to him. It was obvious to everyone that she was deliberately ignoring Charlie. MacKay decided it was time to set things right. He coughed and looked directly at Charlie. "It sounds reasonable to me. What do you think, Colonel Warren?"

The use by MacKay of Charlie's military rank startled Brenda. "You're a colonel, Dr. Warren? A colonel of what? Fried chicken?"

Ron let out a strangled laugh. Brenda Reynolds had just made a joke, one that was almost funny. It was a milestone of sorts, since Brenda was one of the most humor-impaired people on the planet. Charlie and Donald smiled tolerantly at Brenda.

"No, Lieutenant. I'm commissioned as a Lieutenant Colonel in the Royal Army Medical Corps, actually," Charlie said indulgently. "Sergeant Major MacKay was just trying to be polite."

"Okay, fine. Whatever. Now that we've got all that straightened out, let's head to our crime scene," Brenda started to turn and walk down the stairs to the main subway platform. "It's down in an access tunnel underneath the main subway corridor."

"Excuse me, Lieutenant Reynolds," Charlie looked at MacKay for a second. It was time for her to make her move. "I hate to be a bother and all, but I could use a bite to eat before we begin. I saw a donut place down the street. I'd like to go over there for just a moment and get a donut and a cup of coffee. We could bring back some for everyone."

Brenda stopped dead in her tracks and turned around. "Excuse me? You want to do what?" She couldn't believe Charlie had actually said something that ridiculous.

"It will just take a moment, really," Charlie replied cheerfully with an indulgent smile. She tugged at Donald's coat sleeve. "We'll be right back."

"Charlie... I don't think this is a good idea," MacKay said reluctantly, looking at Charlie as though she'd just sprouted another head.

"Come along, Donald, come along. We won't be a moment," Charlie urged him up the stairs, leaving the two New York detectives staring in their wake.

"Well, I could use a donut now," Meyers said haltingly. Actually, he thought it was a wonderful idea. His stomach had been growling ever since he pitched his donut that morning.

Brenda for her part was speechless. "Donut?" she finally said in a strangled tone. "This is unbelievable! That... that woman acts like this is some sort of picnic! That's the stupidest thing I've ever heard anyone say!"

"I don't know, Lieutenant. I think they were just trying to be nice to us." Meyers stared sadly at Brenda for a moment. Brenda's bad temper and abrasive personality were not going to make this easy for either of them. Ron Meyers had been assigned to her because he was easygoing and could handle her moods and temper. Vinson had hoped that Meyers might eventually rub off on Brenda.

So far, the treatment hadn't worked. It was common knowledge around the precinct that Brenda's mouth was eventually going to get her into a situation she couldn't get out of.

Ron Meyers was extremely intelligent, a fact that he studiously hid behind his happy facade. Meyers habitually adopted an optimistic attitude, mainly because it was his essential nature. He also did it because it drove his straight-laced partner insane. "Come on, Lieutenant; the Doctor Warren's offering to buy us breakfast. What's wrong with that?"

"Meyers, stop thinking with your stomach for a moment," Detective Reynolds snapped. Just then, her cell phone rang. "Hello? Yes, we're almost there. Yes, we've got them. Sir, I just don't understand why we need them on this case. It's a complete… What? Yes sir, we'll be there in a minute."

"Let's get going, Meyers," Detective Reynolds turned and stalked off with Meyers in tow. "We can't let the FBI wait."

"What about MacKay and Warren?"

"I don't care. They can catch up with us. That agent will take their heads off. I can't wait to see when that happens," Brenda replied, a little too gleefully. She stopped long enough to let a policeman assigned to the subway know that two more officers were on the way.

"There will be two more people coming down to the crime scene. One of them is a tall Scottish dude and the other is a short stupid little English girl who'll be carrying some donuts and coffee. Send those morons down when they show up."

"Yes, ma'am," the officer said, maintaining a completely straight face as Brenda talked to him. When she turned away, he shot a sideways look at Meyers and winked. Meyers winked back.

"You know, Warren and MacKay seemed okay to me," Meyers observed in a neutral tone as they walked down the subway platform to the access tunnel. "They want to help us, Lieutenant."

"We don't need their help!" Reynolds snapped back. "She's completely unprofessional. Warren's not a police officer, and this isn't her case. Having those two idiots around is a complete waste of time. I knew it was a dumb idea to get them involved in the first place."

Meyers realized this conversation was going nowhere and

decided to change the subject. "What did the FBI say?"

"They told me that because there was a foreign national involved, and because he may be an intelligence agent, they had jurisdiction in the case. We'll be kept on to handle the local details," Reynolds explained in a disgusted tone. "We'll also have babysit that MacKay guy and his English twit doctor friend."

Brenda was on a tear, and refused to let go of her issues with Charlie. "Did you know that Stone moron married that little idiot only six months after Karen died? Can you believe it? It figures, though: Stone and Warren are both idiots. They deserve each other." Brenda stormed as they climbed down the ladder to the access tunnel.

"You really don't like Charlie Warren, do you, Lieutenant?" Meyers said, barely hiding a smirk. "I always thought Dave Stone was okay. We went through the NYPD Academy together."

"I'm so happy you get along with Stone, Meyers. Stones' a clod, and that wife of his is a total twit! She's...she's too happy! She smiles too much!"

"Idiot or not, we're going to have to put up with her this morning," Meyers observed as he saw the lights of the crime scene up ahead. A tall middle-aged man with close-cropped dark hair came up to meet them.

"Detective Reynolds and Meyers, I presume, I'm Ken Rawlings, Special Agent in charge. It's nice to meet you," the man held out his hand to Brenda, who shook it perfunctorily. "Where are our two friends from the British Consulate?"

"They stopped to get donuts and coffee, sir," Meyers answered reluctantly, expecting an explosion from the FBI agent.

Instead, Ken Rawlings nodded his approval. "Good. I could use some breakfast. Let's get over to the crime scene and I'll show you around." He sneezed violently. "I hope you don't have allergies to dust. This place hasn't been open in a long time."

"Looks like we'll have to wait on seeing their heads taken off," Meyers said quietly to Reynolds as they went to the scene.

"Shut up, Meyers," Brenda grated back.

4

"What a sweet and charming lass Lieutenant Reynolds is," Donald proclaimed ironically to Charlie as they walked down to the donut shop. "So warm, so caring," he shuddered in revulsion. "I feel a great wave of pity for that poor sergeant of hers."

"My thoughts exactly, Sergeant Major. Reynolds is a real beauty," Charlie agreed. A mischievous light started to glow in her deep green eyes.

Donald spied the look and blanched. "What's going on in that devious mind of yours, Colonel Warren? Would you care to explain to me why we are toddling off to the bakery for crullers in the middle of an investigation? Other than pure malevolence, I can't see any reason why we are doing this."

Charlie assumed a beatific expression. "You're accusing me of malevolent intentions? Why Sergeant Major: I'm cut to the quick. How ever could you think such terrible things about me?" Charlie batted her eyes for emphasis.

"Because I know you, lass, and stop that. I know that look, and I know it bodes ill for everyone. I had you pegged from the first day you arrived at SAS school. You know I can't stand it when you do that." MacKay chuckled, attempting to control himself.

"Do what, Donald?" Charlie asked, turning her face towards him with a dewy look. MacKay hated that look. It always broke him up.

"Stop it, you little imp!" MacKay roared with laughter. "We

need to focus on the case, Colonel. You are completely incorrigible. Now please behave yourself."

"Why?"

"Och, Charlie! Why in Heaven's name are you wanting to do this? You know this is not going to be pretty. Please, if not for you, for my sake: just try to not badger the woman too much," Donald pleaded as he opened the shop door for her.

"I'm not badgering anybody. That nice sergeant of hers deserves to be treated well, and she needs to be shaken up a bit. She was very unkind to him, and I can't stand it when people mistreat each other," Charlie replied with a beatific smile. "He only puts up with it because he's rather sweet on her."

"Oh please, Charlie," MacKay groaned. "Let's not go down that road this morning."

They walked into the store, and Charlie swiftly chose a dozen chocolate glazed donuts. "That beastly female detective is going to be furious." Donald observed dourly as Charlie paid for the donuts and four cups of coffee.

"That is precisely why I'm doing it, Donald," Charlie replied sprightly, gathering up her merchandise. "That sergeant has to put up with that martinet all day long. We might as well make life at least a little more bearable for the poor man."

"Of course, Charlie, that's exactly why we're doing this." Donald said as they returned to the subway platform. They came up to the uniformed police officer standing over by a corner of the subway next to the tracks.

"Good morning, officer," Donald greeted the policeman politely. "My slightly insane colleague and I are from the British Consulate. We're assisting the police in an investigation. Could you show us where we need to go?"

They showed their ID's to the police officer who looked at them and nodded. "The lady detective said I should be looking for a Scottish dude and a short stupid little English girl carrying donuts," the officer said, looking at them and their ID's. "That must be you two. Tunnel's down that way." He pointed to the corridor to their right. Those are her words, not mine, by the way."

"Thank you, Sergeant," Charlie replied calmly, not batting an eye. "I could tell you were quoting Lieutenant Reynolds when you were saying those things."

Her lack of response to the insults confused the officer. "Hey, don't you care what she thinks about you?" he asked incredulously.

"No, what she says doesn't bother me in the slightest," Charlie shrugged. "Actually, it's exactly what I expected she'd say."

Charlie and MacKay looked at each other and then at the donut box. "Would you care for a donut, Sergeant?" Charlie offered.

The officer didn't have to be asked twice. He'd been eyeing the donut box ever since they came up to him. He reached into the box and took out a still-warm donut. Biting into it, he rolled his eyes with pleasure. "Man! They're still warm! You got these at that little bakery a block west from here, right? I love their stuff!"

"Yes we did, and I'm glad you appreciate them," Charlie replied. "Thank you again, officer."

"I'm not short, am I, Donald?" Charlie asked as they walked away from the officer.

MacKay thought for a moment. "I've never thought of you as short. Petite, perhaps, but never short. You are, however, a nuisance at all times," Donald MacKay observed affectionately, "try to behave."

"I will," Charlie rewarded him with a vacant smile and crossed her eyes slightly.

MacKay shook his head mirthfully. "Charlie, if you'd been around during the Second World War, we would have wound up fighting the Americans instead of the Germans and Japanese. You are seriously deficient in your diplomatic skills, my dear colonel."

"Touché, Donald. Touché. I never said I was a diplomat," Charlie said as they arrived at the ladder leading down into the access tunnel.

The area beneath the subway had been brilliantly illuminated with portable lights, and the area cordoned off with barrier tape. Detective Reynolds was predictably fuming by the time they arrived. "It's about time you two showed up," she barked as they strolled up to the crime scene.

"Come now, Lieutenant: selecting the right donuts and coffee takes some time. Any police officer knows that. Since you've been so kind and gracious to us, we wanted to treat you properly,"

Charlie said breezily as she handed Ron Meyers a cup of coffee. She offered the box of donuts to Ron Meyers.

"What kind did you get?" Meyers asked eagerly, peering into the box.

"Chocolate glazed: the international favorite of law enforcement officers," Charlie pointed out. "You look like a glazed chocolate man to me, Sergeant." With a warm smile, she handed him a still-warm donut. "The kind officer at the subway platform already had one. He was nice enough to direct us down to the crime scene."

"They're still warm. You have no idea how much I appreciate this," Meyers took the donut with a delighted smile on his face. Charlie knew at once that she'd made a friend for life.

"You're most welcome. Would you care for some coffee and a donut, Lieutenant? We have plenty." With an ingratiating smile, Charlie offered a cup of coffee and the donut box to the incredulous Lieutenant Reynolds.

Brenda looked as though she were about to explode. She ignored the donut box and snatched the cup of hot coffee from the smiling Charlie, spilling it onto her clothes. "Dr. Warren, this is not a picnic. Your behavior is highly unprofessional. This is a crime scene, and I plan on filing a personal complaint against you with the British Consulate, as well as the New York State Medical Examiner's office!"

"I'm really terribly sorry you feel that way, Detective," Charlie's voice dripped false contrition. "I was only trying to help. You are most welcome to file any sort of complaint you like with whomever you like. In the mean time, may I talk to your crime scene investigator, please?"

A man in a NYPD jumpsuit labeled "CSI" came up to them. "You most certainly can, Dr. Warren." He held out his hand after taking off his plastic gloves. " Detective Joe Thomas, CSI. I've been an admirer of your work for some time. I've read some of your papers on forensics. You really know what you're doing."

Charlie shifted her box of donuts over to her left hand and shook Thomas' hand. "It's a pleasure to meet you, Detective." She caught Joe eyeing the box. "Would you like some donuts, Joe? I bought a dozen. We've run out of coffee, unfortunately."

Thomas didn't have to be asked twice. He peered into the box. "Sure. I'm glad you have chocolate glazed. They're my favorite. Give me a chocolate glazed, and I'm set for the day."

As Joe happily munched his chocolate glazed donut, Charlie decided it was time to get down to business. "What do you have down here?"

Thomas finished his donut before replying. "That sure hit the spot. Thanks, Doc. Okay, let me introduce you to the crime scene. This is unusual, even for New York City. It's more like a battlefield really than anything else. It looks like a firefight from Iraq in a New York subway tunnel. This station's been closed since the 1950's so no one's been down here since then, except for homeless people. We occasionally stumble into dead bodies from time to time in these tunnels, but nothing like this."

He led Charlie, Donald, and the two NYPD detectives over to a scorched area of concrete wall. "This is a blast area. Looks like a fragmentation grenade went off here."

Charlie stooped down at the fragments that had been tagged where they lay. "I agree. What do you think, Donald?"

Donald said nothing for a moment. As a military professional, he was taking the whole scene in. Finally, he nodded in agreement. "I agree with you, Detective Thomas. This most certainly is a battle site. I've seen my share. Looks like he got whoever was chasing him."

He looked down at the two shattered bodies. "At this range, in this confined area, a grenade blast like that goes off and you have bits and pieces left. Messy, very messy."

MaKay moved closer to the old concrete walls. "There are lots of bullet strikes in this surface. Looks like automatic weapons fire."

"Then we have our man from England over here. We found old shell casings over by a mound of dirt and wood," Thomas walked over to a body stretched out towards the tunnel exit. The man was clothed in what looked like an overcoat. He was prone, his right arm was stretched out over his head, the left arm tucked underneath him, cradling his abdomen as though it had spasmed just before his death. "He shot it out with the bad guys over there, then tried to crawl away. He was trying to get to the ladder, but he never made it."

Charlie stooped down to the body. "Remains are partially

mummified, owing to the dry atmosphere. He's probably been down here for years, judging from the extent of decomposition."

She pointed to an area beneath the body. "Look here: he bled out. See the dark stain underneath his body? The man was bleeding all the time, even as he fought back. Abdominal wounds cause terrible pain. It's obvious that his last moments were agonizing."

The implicit tragedy of the scene was evident to everyone. "That's the way we train them," MacKay observed with a slight catch in his voice. "The lad was determined to sell his life dearly."

"This coat's in pretty good shape," Charlie said, lifting up part of the jacket. "You found identification on his body. Anything else?"

"Just a scrap of paper in one of his pockets," Thomas held up a plastic bag with a scrap of paper in it. "Looks like he wrote something on it. Our lab will enhance it and let us know what it is."

"May I see that please?" Thomas handed the bag to Charlie, who studied the paper inside intently for a moment. "The handwriting is uneven and hurried. This is probably the last thing he wrote before he died."

"I agree with you, Dr. Warren," Detective Thomas nodded.

"Charlie," Charlie corrected him with a smile, handing the bag back to him.

"'Rache' is the German word for 'revenge.' Could the word possibly be 'Rachel'?" Charlie asked, frowning. "Perhaps it was the name of someone he was supposed to contact."

"It could be. Right now, anything's possible," Thomas agreed. He picked up a badly corroded weapon. "Let me show you my next item. Ever seen one of these before, Sergeant Major?"

"I most certainly have, Detective," MacKay took the weapon from Thomas, "This is an American M3 Grease Gun. It's a type of machine pistol the Americans used during World War Two. Looks like it's been modified with a silencer. This is a commando's weapon. You found this down here this morning?"

"Yes, we did," Thomas smiled. "I was actually able to lift off a set of prints from the barrel. We might be able to find out who this guy was."

"That's why were down here," Charlie touched Donald's shoulder. "If nothing else, we're here to take him home, whoever he is."

She walked over to the other two bodies. "It's obvious the man was an expert in handling firearms. These bodies show evidence of multiple gunshot wounds as well as fragmentation damage from the grenade blast."

"I saw that the moment I first examined these bodies," Thomas crouched down next to her. "All of his shots seem to have hit center of mass, as near as I could tell. These guys were also carrying some sort of machine guns." He pointed to two lumps of rusted, corroded metal next to the bodies. "Their weapons are so badly rusted, I can't really tell what they were."

"My guess is they are probably Schmeisser machine pistols," MacKay said as he came over and glanced at the weapons. "The Germans used them during World War Two. Any idea on who our two friends might be?"

Thomas shook his head. "Not a clue. No IDs on either of them. We know how they died, and that's it."

"We need to find out answers about who they are, and about who this man is, or was." Rawlings joined them. "Good morning; I'm Ken Rawlings, Special Agent in Charge. I work with the Counter-terrorism Task Force."

He turned to Charlie and MacKay. "Dr. Warren, Sergeant Major MacKay: it's an honor to meet you finally. Sorry I wasn't here to greet you. I had to go up topside for a minute to talk to my office. Phone reception down here is lousy. We've heard a lot about you, and believe me, we want to make up for the rotten experience you had last fall with Jacobsen. Thanks for bringing the donuts, by the way." He helped himself to one of the last donuts in the box.

"You're most welcome, Agent Rawlings," Charlie replied with a smile. "We wanted to start things off on the right foot."

Brenda had had enough. "Sir, this… this doctor and her British friend show up at the subway and act like this is some sort of field trip instead of a criminal investigation. She's been highly unprofessional from the very start, and I resent her attitude towards me, and towards this whole investigation!"

There was a long, awkward silence after Reynolds spoke. Rawlings looked at her and his face started to turn dangerously red. "That's an interesting way to look at things. Your comments have been noted, Lieutenant. May I have a word with you in private?"

He steered Brenda away from the others without waiting for her to reply. Rawlings pitched his voice low so that no one else could hear him.

"Lieutenant Reynolds, I'm a tolerant man, but I don't appreciate your attitude. I've worked with NYPD for twenty years, and I've got a lot of respect for cops in this city. Now tone your attitude down. There's no reason to behave like this. MacKay and Warren were sent by the British government to help us. Please control yourself."

His tone took on a cold edge. "This is not a routine homicide, regardless of how trivial you may think it might be. We're here because this case may have issues concerning national security. That's why I'm here, Lieutenant. Dr. Warren and Sergeant Major MacKay are here because we wanted them to help with this investigation.

"You will cooperate fully with us on this investigation, and you will give Dr. Warren and Sergeant Major MacKay your respect. Is that clear? These people have done nothing to you to merit the kind of treatment you've been displaying this morning. Now get a handle on your temper, Lieutenant, if you wish to continue with this investigation."

Reynolds nodded mutely, her face a mask of stifled fury. "Good," Rawlings exclaimed with satisfaction. "I'm so glad we got all of that straightened out. Now let's get back to the investigation."

They walked back to the crime scene. Charlie was busy talking to Detective Thomas, who was delighted that Charlie was there to help. "Detective Thomas, do you need any assistance in processing the crime scene?" Charlie asked. "I noticed you seem to be the only investigator down here at the moment, and I'd be happy to help."

"We're shorthanded down at the lab this morning, and I'd be honored if you gave me a hand," Detective Thomas replied enthusiastically. Brenda Reynolds shot a black look at Thomas, and then at Charlie. Realizing there was nothing she could do about it, she sighed in resignation.

She paused for a moment, and a malevolent grin came over her face. It was time to take a different tack. "By the way, Dr. Warren, I don't think you realize it, but we have a family connection. I'm Karen Reynolds' sister. Karen was David's first wife."

Brenda had wanted to spring this news on Charlie with the hope that it would somehow crush and disconcert her. Her statement produced the reverse effect. A delighted grin broke out on Charlie's face. Charlie crushed her in a sisterly embrace.

"Why of course you are! I should have noticed the family resemblance when I first met you! How wonderful!" Charlie gushed. "I'm so very happy to meet some of Karen's family! We sent all of you invitations to our wedding, and I'm so sorry you missed it! David will be so pleased to know that we've finally met!"

Okay, that didn't work, did it, Brenda? Meyers thought to himself, struggling to keep his face straight as Brenda speedily freed herself from Charlie's embrace. *She's about ready to have a stroke.* Somehow, he managed to control the wave of hysterical laughter that was rising up inside of him. He masked his reaction by a fit of coughing.

"Well, isn't this nice," Rawlings commented with a deadpan expression. "Now that the family reunion is over, I'll brief MacKay and you two on what's going on with the other aspects of this case. We need to let these two scientists get to work." He steered MacKay and the two detectives away from the crime scene.

"Let's take a closer look at this crime scene, Dr. Warren." Joe Thomas walked over to the site where the grenade went off. "As you can see, I have two bodies here, or what's left of them. The grenade was thrown from a position about fifteen feet away from here."

"This area?" Charlie asked as she went over to a small pile of debris about five yards away from the British agent's body.

"Yeah, that's it. That's where he made his last stand," Thomas replied, walking to that area. "We've got shell casings all around the place, and you can see an imprint of a flattened body lying next to all of this rubble, along with a patch of blood. Next to it is where we found that old machine gun, along with some shell casings. That British guy was shot in the abdomen, so that accounts for the blood.

"The way I see this going down is that he hunkers down behind this pile of debris, and waits till they're almost on top of him. Then he sprays them with machine gun fire and tosses the grenade at them for good measure. An overhand toss from a lying position is tricky at best, so I figure he heard them coming and threw in the direction of the noise. The bad guys got hit with his machine gun slugs, and then his grenade finished the job."

"They were only fifteen feet away from him when he threw the grenade. That's much too close, especially in a confined area. I guess he knew there was nothing else he could do," Charlie commented in a professional tone. "Hit back with everything you've got at the last moment."

Thomas paused for a moment. "He had nothing to lose at that point. The man knew he was dying and it was just a matter of time."

"He took a big risk throwing a grenade down here," Charlie said, testing the walls. "A concussive force like that could have brought the entire tunnel down. Is this a service tunnel of some sort?"

Joe Thomas made a face. "Yeah, the whole city is honeycombed with them. They go on for miles underneath the city. No one has any idea where they go in most cases."

"You said you got some prints off the one weapon, is that correct, Joe?"

"Sure did," Thomas replied. "We got some good ones. I scanned them and sent them up to the lab for ID. There are no matches in any of our existing data files. That includes INTERPOL and your Scotland Yard. I even ran him on our classified black files to see if he was a spook of some sort. No luck. Since he's been down here for a while, I'm not surprised, but it was worth trying anyway."

He peered down into the blackness of the tunnel. "We need to find out where this guy was originally shot. Maybe then we'll find out why he was down here."

Charlie stooped down to look at the darkened area on the ground. "His gunshot wound had to be fairly recent, otherwise he never would have made it this far. It occurred maybe fifteen minutes to half an hour before he got to this part of the tunnel. That gives us about half a mile at most. The blood trail should be easy to follow."

"You're right about that," Thomas agreed, shining his flashlight on the ground. He could see a trail of dark stains leading into the tunnel. "He came up from the south through this tunnel. There's a whole maze of these tunnels in this part of town going down to the docks. Most of them lead to brick walls and dead ends now."

"Well then," Charlie looked at the agents, "let's go down and take a look."

"I think there's enough blood to show us the way back," Thomas pointed out. "Let's go."

Charlie and Joe started away from the crime scene, carefully moving along the blood trail by hugging the sides of the tunnel walls. "No one's been down here for a very long time, Joe," Charlie choked and sneezed as she ran into an exceptionally heavy bank of cobwebs. The banks of cobwebs stretched over and across the walls of the tunnel, blanketing them heavily. At times they had to stop just to clear away the dusty curtains that spanned from each side of the tunnel walls.

"I'm sorry, I should have gone back to my truck and gotten you a spare jumpsuit, Dr. Warren," Joe said regretfully. "Your suit's going to be a mess by the time we're through down here."

"Don't worry about it, Joe," Charlie replied cheerfully. "I've never been interested in being a fashion plate, and I don't mind getting dirty if the work's interesting."

"Spoken like a true CSI," Joe grinned. He stooped down to look at the floor. "There's a fair accumulation of dirt and junk on the tunnel floor. In addition to the blood trail, I can see three distinct sets of footprints. The rest of the floor looks undisturbed."

"All headed in the same direction," Charlie noted, pointing to the middle set of tracks. "This is our man. His gait's shortened and irregular. Look how the blood trail weaves over it. The man's staggering from blood loss; he was in shock at this point."

"Yeah, and the guys trailing him knew it," Joe said grimly as he pointed to the track. "They aren't even running here. They kept behind him just far enough to keep out of range, but close enough so they wouldn't lose track of him."

"Tracking him like a wounded animal," Charlie shook her head. "They were waiting until he collapsed from the blood loss, and then they were going to move in for the kill."

Thomas and Charlie worked carefully back into the tunnel for at least a hundred yards. From time to time they would encounter a branching tunnel going off into some nameless direction, but the trail of footsteps never varied.

At last they came to a major intersection. Two tunnels branched off to the left and right of them. Directly in front of their path was an iron door. Thomas clutched Charlie's arm and pointed downward. "Charlie, I think we've arrived at where our man was shot."

Charlie followed the beam of Joe's flashlight down to the floor of the tunnel. "I see lots of old shell casings. Nine-millimeter by the looks of them. Our blood trail petered out about fifty feet from here. That makes sense for someone wounded in the abdomen. It takes a bit of time for the heavy bleeding to start."

Thomas nodded. "Yeah, but the trail doesn't deviate to the right or left, so I imagine this iron door was installed sometime after our man got shot. The trail goes through there."

"Yes, Joe, it does, but someone else has been down here, going through these other tunnels," Charlie said quietly. "There are no cobwebs on them, and I see numerous sets of fresh footprints. These are newer. Look at the sole markings. Those are contemporary shoe prints."

They took photographs of the footprints and left markers tagging the location of the shell casings. Thomas wrote down their observation of the scene. Charlie glanced nervously around, scanning both of the tunnels branching off either side of them.

"Someone's living down here," Thomas swept his light to the right and left one more time. "I wonder..."

Charlie stopped him by squeezing his arm and motioned him for silence. She stared into the blackness of the tunnel to the left of them. Something was down there, something malignant and alive. Charlie could sense the watchfulness, the intent concentration of purposeful intelligence, waiting for them to make the fatal mistake of going down into that inky blackness.

For a frozen minute they listened intently. "It's nothing. I thought I heard something down the left tunnel. It must have been a dripping pipe," Charlie forced herself to say in a conversational tone. Joe caught the tension in her voice and nodded mutely.

"Let's get out of this place, Charlie," he said, turning around and heading back up the tunnel. Once they were a hundred feet from the branching tunnels, Thomas leaned over to Charlie and asked quietly. "You heard something, didn't you?"

"Not something, Joe. Someone."

5

"A gent Rawlings, what's really going on with this whole tunnel business?" Brenda Reynolds demanded. "I can't believe you were called out to this scene just to look at a bunch of moldy dead bodies. There's got to be something else that the FBI's interested in."

An amused light flickered in Ken Rawlings' eyes. "You're very perceptive, Detective Reynolds. It's not just about the bodies. We'll know more in a few minutes after our two scientists finish following that trail into the tunnel. I've got my suspicions they're going to find out some things down there that will help me with a case in the here and now."

"I hope so," Brenda's face registered disgust as she glanced over to Ron Meyers and Sergeant Major MacKay, who had stepped away and were getting to know each other. "It can't come soon enough."

The two men had discovered that they had been in the Gulf at around the same time. They were busy swapping war stories. "I was a tank gunner in the First Cav. Firing up Iraqi T-72s with the Abrams was a total trip," Meyers told MacKay proudly. "What unit were you in?"

"Forty-Second SAS," MacKay replied. "Actually, I'm still with them. My current post at the consulate is a temporary duty assignment. I was attached to the consulate back in November in order to keep watch on that young officer who's mucking about in that tunnel right now."

"Dr. Warren?" Meyers chuckled. "That sounds like a full time job. She's a really cute chick, and I love her sense of humor."

"That she is, lad, and so much more," MacKay nodded sagely. "You have no idea. My wee colonel is most definitely a handful. The main burden's been passed on to her husband, David Stone. He's been a busy lad ever since they married in December."

"I know Dave Stone," Meyers said, glancing over at his violently disgusted partner who was pretending not to listen to their conversation. "Dave's a good cop. Very smart."

"I happen to agree, lad. You won't be finding me disagreeing with that statement," MacKay nodded approvingly.

The mention of David's name finally set Reynolds off. "Would you two can the war stories for a minute, please?" She looked at her watch. "Those two lab rats have been down in that hole for a good half hour now. When are they going to come up for air?"

"Right now, I think," Rawlings said with a smile. Charlie and Thomas emerged from the tunnel. Both of them were covered in cobwebs.

"Good Lord, Charlie! You look like something out of those American Halloween movies!" MacKay came over to her. Charlie was busy dusting herself off of the masses of dust and cobwebs clinging to her. Donald helped her remove some of the cobwebs from her back.

"Yeah Warren, you're a mess," Brenda observed in disgust. "You're also covered in dust. What did you do, roll in the stuff?"

"Not really, Lieutenant," Charlie sneezed vigorously a few times. "I can understand why you'd feel that way. I do look rather ghastly. We've had an interesting experience in the tunnels. Wouldn't you agree, Detective Thomas?"

"Right," Joe Thomas turned to Rawlings. "You were right, sir. In addition to the footprints made by our friends over here, we found fresh tracks in two tunnels that branched off of the main one."

Rawlings nodded and produced a notebook. He carefully wrote the information down. "That's what I thought," he replied, putting the notebook away. "Did you find out anything more about our friends here?"

"The agent was shot about half a mile down the main tunnel." Thomas replied. "Both he and his two pursuers were running down this tunnel for a good distance before the man collapsed from loss of blood. They knew they'd shot him and were biding their time. They didn't count on him having a machine pistol and a grenade. Does that summary match up with what you saw, Dr. Warren?"

"Yes it does," Charlie nodded her head. "I think we've gotten all of the basic information we need from the crime scene here. The City Medical Examiner and a forensic anthropologist could tell us a bit more once they see the bodies."

"All right then, thank you for assisting us, Dr. Warren," Ken Rawlings said with satisfaction. He paused for a moment, glancing at the tunnel entrance. "I'm going to let all of you in on something: we've been running into signs for the past few weeks that people are down in these tunnels. Not the usual homeless types. The patterns are much different. Someone's looking for something in a systematic pattern.

"We've also found bodies, or parts of them, horribly butchered. Someone wants the homeless people to stay away from this part of town, so they've killed anyone who goes down into places like that, and leaves their bodies in plain view so other people will stay away."

"We took photographs of those footprints, sir," Thomas said. "Dr. Warren thought she heard something, and we decided it wasn't healthy for us to be down there too long."

"I'm glad you came back when you did," Rawlings agreed. "I'll brief all of you tomorrow on our case. That, Lieutenant Reynolds, is one of the reasons you're here right now."

"Is there anything else you need us for, Agent Rawlings? If not, then I would like to take my grimy young officer here back to the consulate for a proper scrubbing," Donald said, smiling at Charlie.

"Yeah, get her out of here. The dust is starting to get to me too," Brenda Reynolds said after a fit of sneezing.

"I'll see all of you over at the Federal Building tomorrow morning for a briefing," Rawlings said, looking at his watch. "I'll expect a preliminary report from you two at that time. Does that sound reasonable, Lieutenant Reynolds? Check with District Seven Homicide. They're the ones running with the cases on the other bodies found down here."

"Yes sir," Brenda looked at Charlie bleakly. "Nice to finally meet you, Warren. Give my love to Stone, okay?"

"I certainly will, Brenda," Charlie replied in her most charming voice, ignoring the woman's snide tone.

Realizing that she'd failed utterly to get a rise out of her, Brenda looked at Charlie and then stomped off. "Come on, Meyers! Let's get out of here!"

"See you later, Dr. Warren," Meyers said over his shoulder with a wink as he followed his disgusted partner to the ladder leading out of the tunnel. Charlie winked back.

"It's going to be an interesting few weeks," Ken Rawlings observed to no one in particular, shaking his head. He turned to Charlie and MacKay. "I'm glad for your help on this case. Let me know what your people find out about this man."

"I just got off the phone with the ME," Thomas said, putting away his cell phone. "They'll be here in a few minutes to pick up our bodies."

"That sounds good," Charlie agreed. Glancing at Donald, who was looking at the solitary body of the fallen agent. "Are we ready to go, Sergeant Major?"

MacKay was stooped down next to the body, obviously in deep thought. He didn't hear Charlie come over to him. "Something wrong, Donald?"

Sergeant Major MacKay stood up. "No, not really, Colonel. It's just… Well, I'd like to stay here with the lad until they come to pick him up. It just doesn't seem right to leave him here after we've found him."

"You don't need to explain yourself to me, Donald," Charlie said softly, touching Donald's shoulder. "We can wait." She glanced back at the tunnel opening. "Besides, I don't think it's a good idea to leave Detective Thomas and Agent Rawlings down here by themselves, considering what we found down here."

-0-

"Did you fall into a dustbin, Dr. Warren?" James Rosson asked laughing as Charlie and Donald came into his office.

"More like a rabbit hole, James, if you take my meaning."

Charlie had managed to remove most of the offending dust from her light gray jacket. A few tattered strands of cobweb clung furtively to her dark slacks. Most of the strands were out of her hair, which fortunately was cut short enough so that it was barely noticeable. "What have you found out about our friend?"

"Not much, I'm afraid," Rosson replied with a disappointed air. "We ran his prints through the usual data bases and came up with nothing. War records were of little use. You know they're trying to put all of those War Office files onto the computer now, and the task is monumental. Sir Leslie's on the case, so we may have something later on today. What are your impressions?"

Sergeant Major MacKay and Charlie glanced at each other. "The lad was running for his life, sir." MacKay replied in his most professional military tone. "They shot him in the abdomen, and then trailed him until he dropped. He finished them off with a burst with his machine pistol and then tossed a grenade at them for good measure. The man got up and then collapsed and died before he made it out."

"Thank you, Sergeant Major," Rosson looked over to Charlie. "Do you have anything to add to Sergeant Major MacKay's assessment, Dr. Warren?"

"Not really, sir," Charlie replied. "Apparently he was shot about half a mile down the tunnel where we found him. The tracks where he and his pursuers came from ended in a steel door. We stumbled across more footprints going across our trail down a set of branching tunnels, but nothing else."

"Yes, I heard about that," James sat back in his chair. "Agent Rawlings called me just after you left the crime scene. He was most impressed with you two, by the way. He's looking forward to working with you over the next few weeks."

Charlie was puzzled. "Next few weeks? I don't understand, sir. We've pretty much done what we set out to do with our work this morning. There wasn't much left for us to do, other than stop by the NYPD crime lab and check on the man's identity documents."

Rosson looked at Charlie and pressed his fingertips together. "Actually, Agent Rawlings wants you to assist with his current investigation. That's the one he's really interested in having you help him with. He told you a bit about it down in the tunnel. I can tell you that he needs help in figuring out what's going on in those tunnels.

"They've been trying to seal up some of those old tunnel systems under New York City, and they've come across some disturbing things that indicate someone is down there looking for something."

"Rawlings mentioned that, sir. What could possibly be down there?" MacKay asked.

"That's what he's hoping you'd be helping him with: trying to find out what they're looking for. Oh yes, this arrived from Britain this morning in the diplomatic pouch, Charlie," Rosson handed Charlie a large bulky envelope.

Charlie looked at the envelope as though James had just given her a large venomous snake. "The last time you handed something to me from a diplomatic pouch, it was back in September. As I recall, it caused no end of trouble, James. What is in this package?"

Rosson looked benignly across his desk. "I have no idea, my dear. It's sealed diplomatic correspondence addressed to you. Why don't you open it?"

"Open it. Of course, what was I thinking? Another magic key into a world of unending trouble. I know I'm going to regret this," Charlie muttered as she tore open the envelope. Inside it was another envelope along with a cover letter. She read the cover letter quickly. "It's from my grandfather's solicitors in London. Apparently my grandfather owned a warehouse in the dock area along the East river, and it's now mine. How grand!"

"Wonderful," MacKay exclaimed, "you are now the proud owner of a warehouse. What on earth are you going to do with something like that, Charlie?"

"Sell it, most likely," Charlie glanced through the other documents in the envelope. She pulled out a photograph. "Ah, here's a picture of the building. Jolly old place, isn't it? Makes the Bloody Tower look like a fairy tale castle."

"Indeed it does. It's most definitely a keeper," Rosson said as he looked at the picture. "One thousand feet long by sixty feet wide. It's a splendid place to store a full-sized battle cruiser. Now see? Not everything that comes to you in a diplomatic pouch is trouble.

You really are far too pessimistic at times, Charlie."

"Right, James: I intend to bring your comments up at a later date. There's more to this wretched pile than meets the eye, I'm certain. Nothing my family's ever involved in is exactly what it seems. We'll all live to regret your remarks," Charlie predicted firmly.

The phone on Rosson's desk rang. James picked it up. "Hello? Yes ma'am, they just returned. Of course ma'am, we'll be there in a moment. Goodbye."

"That was Lady Margaret," James replaced the phone. "She wants to see us in her office now. Apparently there is some news on our mystery man from Sir Leslie. You like mysteries, don't you, Charlie?"

Charlie fixed him with a steely glance. "I live for them. James, persist in this mood, and I'll have to have a talk with Jane. You are being entirely too lighthearted about this whole matter. I'm sure that this case going to be full of delightful surprises for all of us."

They got up from their chairs and went over to the Consul General's office. "Do come in and sit down, please," Lady Margaret beckoned to three chairs arranged in front of her massive oaken desk.

"I could send for some coffee, if you like," she said in a motherly tone as her guests seated themselves. "I understand, Lady Warren, that you had a bit of an adventure this morning."

She peered at Charlie for a moment over her wire-rimmed spectacles. "Forgive me, but you look a bit dusty, my dear. Have you been poking about in old places again?"

"Yes ma'am," Charlie became acutely aware of her appearance. "I've been mucking about in an old tunnel this morning."

"So I've heard. It's quite all right," Lady Margaret replied indulgently in her best maternal tone, "you used to get into all sorts of odd places at your grandfather's estate when you were growing up. I'm quite used to seeing you a bit untidy."

She looked at Rosson. "James, I just got off the phone with Sir Leslie Gresham. "Apparently our mystery man was a member of the branch of British Intelligence known as the Special Operations Executive. Are you familiar with that organization?"

"SOE? Wasn't that the branch of British Intelligence who

spent long periods of time behind enemy lines during the War?" Rosson asked.

"Indeed it was," Lady Margaret nodded her head. "SOE's sole purpose in life was to 'set Europe ablaze,' as Churchill put it. The man's name was Richard Cartwright, and he happened to be a close associate of your grandfather's, Charlie."

"I never heard Grandfather mention anything about a Richard Cartwright," Charlie said, pausing for a moment. "That's not unusual, however. He never talked much about what he did in the War."

"That's because much of what he did in the War was classified secret, and still is," Lady Margaret said solemnly. "When you got that packet from your solicitors back last September, it was the first time that anyone in British Intelligence had heard anything about your grandfather's activities about Josef Mengele. It was a surprise to all of us, including Sir Leslie."

"I still find that whole business quite extraordinary, Lady Margaret," James observed. "I thought certainly that Sir Leslie would have had some idea about that secret mission that Charlie's grandfather had been on, especially since it concerned the possible capture of Josef Mengele."

Lady Margaret smiled. "There are levels of secrecy in British Intelligence above MI6, James. Suffice it to say that the information was not known, because at the time, it was not necessary for anyone to know about it, other than Michael Warren and his heir who was directly involved in the fulfillment of the Secret Commission."

"That's why it was called a Secret Commission, James," Charlie explained in an indulgent tone.

"Speaking of all that, Charlie's gotten another family surprise this morning," James said with a smile. "It arrived in the diplomatic pouch."

Charlie shot him a black look. "James has been bubbling with excitement ever since I opened the ghastly thing, ma'am." She handed the packet with the documents and photograph over to Lady Margaret, who glanced at them with an amused smile on her face.

"How very intriguing," she said, looking at Charlie keenly. "I have known Michael Warren all of my life, and he never once mentioned owning property in America. Most unusual. I daresay it might have something to do with his government service."

"Jolly," Charlie muttered glumly.

"That's enough out of you, my dear colonel," James laughed, looking at his watch. "I believe we've taken up enough of your time for one day. We'll see you back here tomorrow morning around eight or so?"

"Of course," Charlie rose and then sneezed. "Excuse me. I seem to still have part of that dusty tunnel in my nasal passages."

"We understand," Lady Margaret said with a smile. "Please give my best to the rest of your family, especially that delightful sister of yours."

"You'll be interested to know that she's decided to resume her skating career, Lady Margaret." Charlie said. "We've found a coach who wants to train her."

"Wonderful news," a delighted smile spread across the older woman's face. "I will make a point of letting Mary Gresham know about it. She adores Katya."

"Well then, I'm off," Charlie turned to MacKay. "I expect to see you later on tonight, Sergeant Major. Megan is counting on you. We have need of skilled carpenters on our set."

"I am as always, Colonel, your humble servant," Donald MacKay said with a twinkle in his eye. "I'll see you later on tonight at your first rehearsal. Megan has already drafted me into the set construction department."

"I'm afraid no one is going to escape set construction," Charlie laughed. "That's the way Megan and I run our shows. Everyone helps, otherwise nothing gets finished on time."

"Thank you again for coming in this morning, Charlie," James rose and took her hand. "If there's anything else we need you for, we'll ring you up."

"All right then, I'll see you later," Charlie turned and left Lady Margaret's office.

Lady Margaret waited until Charlie had left to address the two men. "Gentlemen, I want to communicate something to you about our young friend when she was not around. Now seems to be as good a time as any. Special Agent Rawlings communicated to me that there is a disturbing connection between this current case and Charlie Warren's family."

"What kind of disturbing connection?" Sergeant Major MacKay asked.

"One of the central suspects in this case is an individual who was involved in the disappearance of John Warren. He is a man who is currently believed to be in New York and actively planning some sort of operation. This business in the tunnels appears to have something to do with him. His name is Ivan Kolov, and if half the things rumored about him are true, then Charlie Warren and her family are in terrible danger."

Lady Wilson looked at MacKay with a grim expression. "There's something else even more disturbing. Detective Thomas returned to the crime scene after you and Dr. Warren left. Someone had deposited fresh tracks over the area."

6

As she drove back to Compton, Charlie talked to David on her cell phone about the case. "Who's the cop in charge of the investigation?" David wanted to know. "You've told me everything except his name. I went to the NYPD Police Academy, and I know a lot of the guys on the force."

"It's not a him, David, it's a her. Her name is Brenda Reynolds," Charlie said offhandedly. Suddenly there was a crash on the line as David dropped his phone. "David, are you all right?" Charlie asked with concern in her voice.

A moment later, David answered weakly. "Yes, Charlie; I'm fine. Brenda Reynolds? Are you sure?"

"Yes David, it's Brenda Reynolds. She's already told me she's Karen's sister."

"Great," David moaned. "Brenda's trouble, Charlie. Is Ron Meyers still assigned to her?"

"Yes he is, poor thing."

"I know Ron from the Academy. He's a great cop. About two years ago, he got assigned to Brenda. She already had a bad rep back then. No one else in the precinct wanted to be her partner, and so far he's lasted longer than anyone else. Ron will make lieutenant soon, and then he'll be transferred. After that, I don't know what will happen to Brenda. Ron's the only reason Brenda's still on the force. Her mouth and attitude have gotten her into plenty of hot water."

"What's her problem, David?" Charlie asked. "She's angry all the time."

David sighed. "I don't know, Charlie. No one knows. We can talk about it more when you get here. Speaking of here, how long is that going to be? It's after noon now, and I was headed out the door to link up with Katya, Megan and Jackie down at Sophie's. Any chance you'll make it in time?"

"I'll do more than that. I'll drive you over there. I'm pulling into your parking lot even as we speak." Charlie parked her Jaguar in a convenient parking spot just next to David's minivan.

"Okay, I'll meet you outside."

David came out of the station, along with a visibly upset Joan Richards. The Chief of Detectives was none too pleased when David told her about Brenda Reynolds.

Joan was an extremely longsuffering woman. Married to a patrolman and the mother of three teenaged girls, Joan could put up with a lot of things in life, but Brenda Reynolds was not one of them.

"Dave told me the news, Charlie," she began, her face set into a grim mask. "Let me tell you right now: if that witch gives you any grief, I will personally clean her clock. That's not a threat; it's a promise."

"Don't worry about me, Joan," Charlie squeezed her arm gently. "I can take care of myself."

Richards was unconvinced. "Uh huh. Look, Sport, I have no doubt you can. I saw what you did to Derek Jacobsen, but Reynolds is a whole different ball game. She's nasty, and she also had her eyes on David, even after Karen married him..."

David frowned and shook his head. "Don't give me that look, Dave. You know it's true. I saw it myself. Karen did, too. Karen was a sweetheart, but the rest of that family was a total loss."

"All right, Joan. We don't need to bring that up right now, okay?" David attempted to steer the conversation into less troubled waters. "Do you want to come with us to Sophie's for lunch?"

"No, I've got work to do right now," Joan fixed Charlie with a look that told her that they would be talking privately soon. "You run off and have lunch. I'll see you later, little girl. Remember what I said." She went back into the station.

David sighed and rubbed his neck. "I'm sorry about that, Charlie. Joan hit the ceiling when I told her about Brenda. She loved Karen, but had no use for the rest of Karen's family. I had to practically pull her off of Brenda during Karen's funeral."

He decided to change the subject. "This minivan's really great. I have lots of room to put my stuff."

"Stuff? Hold on, young man. This vehicle is here to transport our family," Charlie reminded him. "It's not a repository for more of your odds and ends. The rear compartment is mine, and don't you forget it. In fact, I've already claimed it."

"Really? What did you put in there?"

"A few odds and ends. Things you don't need to concern yourself with." Charlie said pointedly.

"Right, a few odds and ends," David said bleakly, looking at the van. "Knowing you, 'odds and ends' is code for enough explosives and hardware to overthrow a dozen Middle Eastern emirates."

A smile flitted across Charlie's face. "Excellent guess, David. Spot on, as a matter of fact. Now get into my car, please."

"Yes love," David got into the Jaguar. They drove over to Sophie's. Jackie and Katya had arrived, along with Megan O'Grady. Even though school had let out for the summer, Megan was busy, getting things ready for the summer play. The high school was going to be the site of the production, and Megan was in charge of coordinating everything.

They were deep into discussing plans about the play when a special pager Charlie was carrying went off. It was one given to her by the consulate for emergencies. Charlie's face turned white as the little device vibrated in her pocket.

Somehow, she managed to keep her voice level. "David, excuse me, but I've just been paged about some business at the consulate. I need to go with you over to the police station, if you don't mind."

David looked at her curiously for a moment, then he understood what she meant. "Of course, Charlie; we can do that right now." He got up along with Charlie. "You ladies have a good afternoon getting things ready for that play. We'll see you all later on tonight."

Megan looked at Charlie, who nodded wordlessly. Charlie had just been summoned to the British Consulate for an emergency.

David and Charlie left the restaurant quickly, trying not to appear in a hurry. "Does this have something to do with the business you were involved in this morning?" David asked quietly as they arrived at their cars. "You don't have to answer if it's classified, Charlie."

"I don't know, David, but I think your little wish may have been granted," Charlie's voice took on a grim tone as she stared at the little pager's readout screen. "I'll find out more when I contact the consulate over that secure line at Police Headquarters, but it doesn't bode well, whatever it is."

-0-

"Carl, Charlie got a special page from the consulate," David said as he and Charlie walked into the Chief's office, "any chance we could use your phone for a minute?"

Carl glanced up from some paperwork on his desk with a puzzled look on his face. "Sure, I could use a break from reading this report of yours about the break-in at the mall. You're a boring writer, Stone." He got up out of his chair and left the office without saying another word.

"You need me to leave too, Charlie?" David asked as Charlie dialed the secure number.

"Please, if you don't mind, David. I'll let you know what I can as soon as possible," Charlie said as the phone made the connection. David left the office and joined Carl outside.

"Trouble?" Carl asked as David closed the door.

"I don't know," David replied, frowning slightly. "We haven't had to use that line since back in November last year."

Joan came up to them, sizing up the situation swiftly. "Charlie's over here taking calls on the hot line in Carl's office and Brenda Reynolds just reentered our lives. Care to share, Dave?"

"Look guys, I'm outside the office just like you," David held up his hands. "I don't know anything more about all this than you do."

Charlie emerged from the office a moment later. Her face was set and grim. "I need to go back to New York this afternoon."

"Will you be back in time for play practice tonight?" David asked quietly.

"I don't know." Charlie replied in a carefully neutral tone. "It depends on how things go."

"Okay," David kissed her and hugged her briefly. "We'll see you later. Let us know when you're coming back."

"I will, David," Charlie said as she left the station.

"Did I hear you say Brenda Reynolds is involved in all of this?" Carl asked, deep concern registering on his face. "That's not good, Dave."

"Look guys, let's try not to jump to conclusions," David held up a cautioning hand. "Charlie ran into her today on some sort of case, that's all."

Carl shook his head. "I don't like it when people start messing with my girl, Dave. Things will get mighty ugly around here if that happens."

"You'll have to take a number, Chief, because that woman's mine. If that witch lays a hand on that girl, I'll rearrange her anatomy," Joan muttered.

"Let's back off the threats, okay?" David pleaded. "Charlie will let us know what's going on later on today."

"Okay, Dave. Just keep us posted," Carl looked at David. "Get your cases in order in case I have to cut you loose for a little extra duty in New York City."

"Aren't you jumping the gun on that, Carl?" David asked.

"No."

7

Charlie arrived at the British Consulate an hour later. She had been told very little over the phone. The terseness of the communication had perplexed her. When she arrived at the consulate, Rosson was there, along with Lady Margaret, MacKay, and Special Agent Rawlings.

"Somehow, I'm not surprised to see you here, Agent Rawlings," Charlie said as she glanced around the room. "I take it this meeting has to do with our recent discoveries in the tunnels this morning."

"Indeed it does, Lady Warren. Special Agent Rawlings is here on behalf of the FBI, and he's been cleared to hear everything I'm about to tell you." Lady Margaret explained. "It's taken some extraordinary work for us to put all of this together. Sir Leslie has been piecing things together over in the UK, and it is taking a great deal of time. We now know considerably more about Mr. Cartwright than we did earlier today. It is quite extraordinary."

She paused for a moment, looking at Charlie with sympathy. "I do apologize for having to drag you back into the city, my dear. However, the have information we have received could not wait."

"That's all right, ma'am," Charlie replied. "David has become rather used to odd things happening around me."

"David is a very fast learner," James Rosson noted with a smile. He turned to Lady Margaret. "Ma'am, now that Dr. Warren has arrived, perhaps you can fill us in on what Sir Leslie has found out about Mr. Cartwright."

Lady Margaret nodded. "Before I begin, I'd like Special Agent

Rawlings to bring us up to date on where his part of the investigation is at this time."

Agent Rawlings rose and went to a map on an easel he'd brought with him. It was an enlarged map of the New York City harbor district. "Thank you, Lady Wilson. First off, let me explain that the Federal government has assumed full responsibility for the American half of the investigation."

Rawlings paused for a moment before continuing. "The fragments of bodies recovered at the scene are from two unknown European males who died forty years ago from a grenade blast. That's all we know about them. The bodies were too badly decomposed to get decent prints off of them. However, the bullets that struck those men came from the British guy's machine gun. The ID on the body was that of a British national named Richard Cartwright."

Lady Margaret broke in. "Sir Leslie has confirmed his identity, Agent Rawlings. Richard Cartwright was an intelligence officer who worked with the Special Operations Executive back during the Second World War. He was officially listed as missing in action back in 1945. Originally, he was posted to New York City with the BSC, the British Security Coordination. He vanished without a trace while on a mission down in the New York harbor district."

"Why was Richard Cartwright sent to New York back in 1945, Lady Margaret?" Charlie asked.

"That we don't know at this time. Sir Leslie has had his research people at MI6 combing the archives, searching for some sort of reason. So far, nothing has turned up." She paused and looked at Rawlings. "I'm sorry to interrupt, Agent Rawlings. Please continue."

"That's all right, ma'am," Rawlings replied. "I need to let you all know why this investigation is now classified top secret, and why we've taken over from the NYPD. We have information which points to a major terrorist attack in New York coming in the next few weeks.

"The chatter points to some sort of operation involving the tunnel system underneath New York. This incident with Cartwright is the first solid lead we've had that indicates there's something behind the chatter. So far, we can't figure out what's down there, other than miles of unused tunnels and thousands of rats."

"I think I can speak for Her Majesty's government when I say that we will give you any kind of assistance you need in your investigation," Lady Margaret replied.

"Thank you, ma'am. I knew I could count on you," Rawlings replied with a smile.

"There is, however, a small matter that we need to let you know about," Lady Margaret said, looking directly at Charlie. "Lady Warren has an engagement over in the UK early next week."

Charlie's face immediately fell. "Ma'am, I was hoping that this situation might have postponed all that."

"Oh no, my dear," Lady Margaret said with a sparkle in her eye. "We mustn't disappoint Her Majesty. She is looking forward to investing you as a Lady of the Garter and knighting your husband. I would love to be there as well. Unfortunately, I have a conference to attend in Washington over the weekend. I will be back in New York sometime on Monday."

She turned to James Rosson. "That means you will be in charge during my absence, James. I hope you don't mind."

"Of course not, ma'am," Rosson said. "We'll manage without you and Dr. Warren in the mean time."

"I'm sure you will, James," Lady Margaret said. "Special Agent Rawlings, aside from that small event I just mentioned, we are at your service. How can we help you?"

"I think you already know my answer to that question. Give me Charlie Warren and your Sergeant Major MacKay, and I think we'll call it an even trade," Rawlings replied with gratitude. "Your cooperation in this matter has already exceeded my expectations."

A sudden roadblock loomed in Charlie's mind. "Sir, I'll be happy to help in any way, but this means I'll have to take a leave of absence from my duties as Medical Examiner."

"We've already contacted the New York State Medical Department. They'll be sending someone to take over while you're attached to us," Rawlings replied. "You should have seen the number of people vying for the chance to work with you, Charlie. I think a number of fistfights broke out. All I know is that I'm glad I've been given the chance to work with you."

"I'm not sure how to take that, Agent Rawlings. No one has

ever fought over me before," Charlie laughed.

"Take it as a compliment," Rawlings replied, looking at his watch. "Now if you'll excuse me, I have to head back to my head-quarters and brief my superiors on this meeting."

Rawlings said goodbye to everyone and left Lady Margaret's office. "Well, it's been a tiring day for us all," Lady Margaret sighed. She turned to Charlie. "I understand you have a play to direct tonight, Charlie. One of your more promising students wrote it, and I'm looking forward to seeing it soon."

"Jackie wrote a brilliant play, ma'am. I only hope it's as good on stage as it is on paper," Charlie told her. "We have a lot of work to do between now and the end of July."

"I'm sure you will do well," Lady Margaret smiled. She looked at Donald MacKay with deep sadness. "Donald, I am so sorry about your wedding. Everyone here was so looking forward to going over to Scotland to see you and Megan married. I remember meeting your parents several years ago. They are delightful people."

"Thank you, ma'am, for your expressions," MacKay said with affection. "But you don't need to trouble yourself. Megan's already figured out a backup plan in case things didn't work out. We'll be bringing my folks over from Scotland in a few days and have the wedding in Sean's church, and the reception can be done at any time."

"Might I suggest Christmastime?" Lady Margaret smiled.

"Aye, that's the very time we had planned," MacKay grinned. "Sort of a wedding and first anniversary celebration for us all." He winked at Charlie.

-0-

Charlie found it difficult to concentrate about the case on her way from New York City. Despite her cheery assurances to David, the entrance of Brenda Reynolds into her life was deeply upsetting to her. Brenda Reynolds kept flitting about her consciousness like a late night mosquito in a darkened room.

Charlie, give this to God and stop worrying about it, you twit, she thought to herself. As she drove towards Compton, she started to pray about her feelings, about David, and about the case she was now embarked upon. Her feelings lightened considerably, and she had regained her optimistic mood by the time she reached the medical examiner's office in Compton.

Lucy Kelson was waiting for her in Charlie's office. She did not look happy. "Charlie, I just got a call from the State Medical Examiner's office. They told me you were being placed on a leave of absence so you could work on something with the FBI. Want to talk about it?"

Charlie smiled at Lucy Kelson. She was more than the chief of the lab; Lucy Kelson was one of her dearest friends. They had been close since last fall, when the town of Compton had been rocked by the series of murders at Bryan Stone's house.

"Lucy, I'm sorry you had to hear the news second hand. I had no idea they'd call up this afternoon. I'm going to be working with the British Consulate and the FBI on a very sensitive case. I can't do both jobs at once, and I promise you it's only temporary. I'll be back in the saddle in a few weeks."

A look of relief washed over Lucy's face. "Good, I was very worried, Charlie. We all love you down here. I think you know that. Things are just now finally getting back to normal. I couldn't stand the idea of having you leave; that's why I was so upset."

"Trust me, Lucy: I love you, and I love working here. If anything ever came up to change that, I'd let you know," Charlie assured her. "Do you have anything else for me right now? If you don't, I have to run home and get ready for the rehearsal tonight."

"Oh yes, there's a message from David. The rest of this junk can wait until tomorrow," Lucy rifled through the stack of mail. "Here it is: David wants you to meet him down at Angelo's for supper before the rehearsal. Katya is having supper with Megan and Jackie, so that's the plans for this evening. Call him now, okay?"

"Okay," Charlie reached for her phone and dialed it. "David? It's me. Yes, Lucy just told me. It sounds lovely. No, I'll be right over. Actually, I packed a bag just in case the thing in New York went a bit long, so I'll change at the high school. All right, I'll see you then. Love you! Bye."

"By the way, Lucy," Charlie asked as she put away the phone.

"Has Jason caved yet?"

"Totally," Lucy rolled her eyes. "Jason's decided to go to City College in New York City. Oddly enough, the campus is just a hop, skip, and a jump away from Julliard. Go figure. Anyway, he's in on the play. Jackie's got him wrapped around her little finger."

Charlie laughed as she started towards the entrance. "Fancy that. What a surprise." Both the women burst out laughing.

"Have a nice time at Angelo's," Lucy called out as Charlie waved and drove off in her Jaguar.

David was waiting outside Angelo's when she arrived at the restaurant. "It seems like I haven't seen you for a thousand years," David said as he came up to Charlie and kissed her. "I've missed you so much today."

"That goes double for me," Charlie replied, kissing him back and holding him close. "It's been a crazy day."

"Tell me about it. I can't ever remember you going to and from New York City twice in a single day," David observed. "Let's go inside and have some supper. Angelo's waiting for us."

Angelo's had been a favorite spot of theirs since last September when they had first met. The owner of the restaurant, Angelo Roncelli, had reserved a special spot for them by the window. It was a beautiful view, looking over the town of Compton towards the western hills that masked Compton from the sloping land that led towards New York City.

As they sat and ate, David filled her in on the events of his day. His time had been spent with a very routine breaking-and-entering incident at the local mall. David didn't mind mundane investigations. Having Charlie around was enough excitement for him.

"Charlie," he said after they had finished dinner and were lingering over coffee. "I want to tell you about Brenda Reynolds."

Putting down her coffee, Charlie looked at David steadily for a moment. "David, is this something you want to tell me, or is this something you think I expect you to tell me?"

David shook his head. "This is something I want to tell you. I met Karen on 9/11, the day the Towers fell. I was on business in New York down at the Trade Center. I'd just gotten out of one of the buildings when the first plane hit. Karen was walking into the building, and I saw a huge chunk of debris headed straight for her.

"I grabbed her and pushed her out of the way. We must have run about half a mile before we even stopped to introduce ourselves. That's how we met, Charlie."

Charlie nodded, deeply interested. "I take it Brenda and Karen were living together."

"How did you know that?"

"Just a guess," Charlie shrugged. "I really don't know why, but it just seems reasonable. Apartments in the city are expensive. It makes sense for two women to share expenses. Go on, David."

"Anyway, we got to know each other after that. Everything was chaos, as you can imagine. Brenda was dating a cop who worked for the Port Authority at the Trade Center. He hadn't called her since the planes hit, and she was trying to reach Karen to find out about him.

"Karen talked to Brenda on her cell phone, and Brenda wanted her to go back to their apartment. I agreed to walk back with her. There was nothing else to do. There was no way I was going to get out of New York that day anyway."

David looked at his coffee. "We got to her place at about six that night. Brenda met us there and she was frantic about Pete. She thanked me for bringing Karen home, and that was the end of it as far as I was concerned."

"Obviously not," Charlie said with an amused note in her voice. She reached across the table and clasped David's hands. "You don't have to tell me any more if you don't want to, David."

"It helps me to sort things out," David shrugged. "Besides, you need to know. About a month later, Karen called me up and asked if I'd come down to the City for Pete's funeral. A lot of cops from all over Long Island were going to funerals then. There were hundreds of them. Carl said it was okay, so I went back into the City and was there for the funeral. Karen really appreciated me being there. That's when we started dating."

Charlie raised her eyebrows. "I take it Brenda didn't approve?"

"No, and neither did the rest of the family. I was a dumb cop from Long Island, and they were upper-class types from New York. Brenda had just made Detective, and she thought I was not good enough for Karen. The whole family treated me like a stranger."

David stopped for a minute, and Charlie's hands tightened on his. "David, you don't need to tell me about what happened at Karen's funeral. I can probably guess. It was probably pretty terrible."

"You have no idea. It was a total nightmare," David shook his head and plunged on. "They... they told me I was responsible for Karen's death, and that if I hadn't married her, she'd still be alive. I was so broken up, that I didn't know what to say to them. Karen's parents insisted that they take Karen's body back to New York City for burial. I let them do it, and I haven't seen them since the funeral."

"Now I know why our wedding invitation to them was returned," Charlie nodded in understanding.

"After Karen died, I was very lonely. Half the time, I didn't remember from one minute to the next what was going on. One night, Brenda came over to my house. She just showed up at the doorstep. Brenda said she wanted to talk to me about Karen. I let her in, and we had dinner together. I talked to her for a long time about Karen. We had some wine together, and... and things got out of hand..." David's voice trailed off into an embarrassed silence.

Charlie nodded slowly. She didn't know what to say. Even though she had lost her brother and grandfather in one horrific day, she had no idea how horrible it must be to lose a beloved spouse. David was trying to let her know what had happened, to give her a possible reason why Brenda Reynolds behaved the way she did.

"I'm not offering any excuses, Charlie," David continued quietly. "There are none. You have a right and a need to know. That's why I'm telling you now."

Charlie put her hand in his. "David, months ago, before we were married, you told me about your past. I told you then, and I'm telling you now, that your past is behind you.

"I appreciate your honesty. Above all else, David, I know that you love me. Brenda's issues are hers. I'm sorry for what happened, but she has no right to hold those events over your head. You were not married to me then, and to be perfectly honest, she came to you at a time when you were intensely vulnerable. She had no right to do that, and I think she took advantage of you."

David's face brightened as Charlie talked. He leaned across the table and kissed her. "Thanks for understanding, Charlie. You just needed to know the full story before you have to deal with her further."

Charlie looked at her watch. "Come on, David. We have to get to the high school. There are several dozen high school students waiting for us to get started on building a set."

8

The following morning, Charlie drove straight into New York City to the British Consulate. She arrived at around eight, only to find that James and Donald were already there. "I was so hoping to beat you into work this morning, James," Charlie said as she walked into James' office.

"You forget that in the Army, we've already been at work for four hours by the time eight rolls around, Colonel Warren," Donald MacKay reminded her. "Colonel Rosson and I have just been going over your latest property acquisition. It's actually quite an interesting building."

"Is it now?" Charlie raised her eyebrows. "What have you come up with?"

"We think that you need to look this place over before you agree to sell it," Rosson said firmly. "There must be a reason why your grandfather had a warehouse here in New York City. It may have something to do with the work that he did in the War. It bears further scrutiny, if you know what I mean."

"I'm not following you, James. What if it did? The War has been over for almost fifty years now. Any sort of military value that place might have has long since faded away. David and I were talking about it last night. We were thinking of donating it to the City so the fire brigades could set it alight and practice putting it out. I think that's a splendid idea. It would make a jolly fire."

The two men laughed. "Charlie, you should contain your enthusiasm for mischief," James finally replied. "We think it might have a little more value than providing you with an amusing bonfire."

"Really, James? Go on: I'm dying to hear what you want me to do with that wretched pile," Charlie said with a grimace.

James put his fingertips together. "The Sergeant Major and I believe there might be a connection between this Cartwright and that warehouse. We need to look at the place more closely."

"Look at this map, Charlie," MacKay spread a map of New York City out on James' desk. "You can see that the place where that body was discovered isn't more than a mile or so away from where that warehouse is located."

"Donald, half of lower Manhattan is within a mile of where that body was located. It's not that big an area," Charlie said in a practical tone.

"I understand that, Colonel," MacKay refused to be brushed off. "Remember what Rawlings said about those tunnels? We've been thinking about that this morning. Now I know for a fact that during the War, lots of coastal cities had underground tunnel networks connecting buildings with docks and other areas of strategic value. If your grandfather had a dock like that, and it was operational during World War Two, then it would stand to reason that there may be underground passageways connecting it with other parts of the city."

"I see your point, Sergeant Major," Charlie said with a sigh. "I'm supposed to meet with the legal representatives of my grandfather's law firm this morning, and then you and I have a briefing with the FBI to attend at two this afternoon. The lovely Ms. Reynolds and her longsuffering sergeant are going to be there as well."

"Yes, pity that," Rosson said sincerely. "Donald was telling me about your new found sister-in-law. What an absolute treasure."

"She most certainly is," Charlie replied, shaking her head. "David's filled me in about her."

Charlie's cell phone rang. "Hello? We were just talking about you! No, you may not know about what. If I told you, I'd have to kill you. No, they didn't like the idea about the bonfire. Yes, I'm disappointed too. Well, if you must know, I'm going over to that lawyer's place and find out about this warehouse Grandfather left me. What? David Stone, you're a complete idiot! Yes you are! Don't be silly!"

Charlie giggled. "All right, now listen: give my love to Katya. Bye."

She hung up her phone and looked at James and Donald. "This is an example of great minds working in concert. My husband's convinced that if we can't burn the place down, then that moldy old warehouse has some sort of secret treasure buried underneath it. He says that all pirates have buried treasure, and since I come from a family of pirates, it stands to reason that something of great value is hidden in that building."

"Sounds plausible to me," MacKay said soberly. "What do you think, Colonel Rosson?"

"I think, Sergeant Major, that any opinion I might have on the subject is irrelevant," Rosson replied tactfully. "You and I are treading on most dangerous ground. Given the Warren family's proclivity for piracy and unconventional activities, it sounds most plausible."

"A most excellent answer, James. Spot-on brilliant," Charlie said with a smile, rising from her seat. "Now if you two fine gentlemen will excuse me, I am off to locate this law firm and see about that warehouse of mine."

"Shouldn't I be headed off with her, sir?" MacKay asked, slightly concerned. The thought of Charlie loose in New York City was somehow unsettling to him.

"Nonsense, Donald. I'm going off to meet a lawyer in some dusty old office, not assaulting a fortified pillbox. I'm perfectly capable of handling things on my own," Charlie said nonchalantly. "What could possibly happen?"

MacKay and Rosson looked at each other. Her question required no comment. "With you, my dear girl, the possibilities are endless," Rosson said darkly.

His tone changed and he looked at Charlie soberly. "Charlie, Thomas went back to your crime scene in that tunnel. Someone was there after you left."

-0-

The law offices of Briggs and Smith, Q.C., were located in the seedy outskirts of the New York City financial district. It took Charlie the better part of an hour to get into downtown New York, and almost the same length of time to find a parking spot for her car. The frustrations of dealing with New York traffic put Charlie's nerves on edge. Again and again she thanked God that she didn't have to face commuting to New York on a regular basis.

She walked into to the building where the law offices were housed and identified herself to the uniformed security guard in the foyer. Charlie was directed to the bank of elevators, where she took an elevator to the fourteenth floor.

For a group of high-powered lawyers, the offices of Briggs and Smith were undistinguished at best. She was ushered into a tired-looking waiting room by a colorless office assistant who promptly dismissed Charlie from existence as soon as she left.

"Mr. Quimby will see you shortly," the squat, mouse-haired woman said in a monotone to Charlie. That statement could be roughly translated as, "make yourself comfortable, because you're in for a long wait."

Charlie sat down on a gruesomely overstuffed couch and started to thumb through the pile of elderly magazines on a coffee table. She managed to get through the entire pile once when the door to the inner office and Mr. Hubert Quimby's rat-like face appeared. "Come in," Mr. Quimby flashed a toothy grin.

While she was waiting, Charlie had amused herself with a mental game. She had tried to picture what Mr. Quimby's office would look like. Her imagination had proved to be spot-on. There was the usual complement of law tomes arranged in a series of bookshelves. They were brand new, Charlie guessed, as she could still smell the ink coming from the paper, and the spines of the books were in mint condition. Mr Quimby's desk was in the center of the office facing the door. Behind him, the panel of windows looked out over a wall of anonymous-looking office buildings.

"Now, then, Dr. Warren," the rodent graciously gestured Charlie to sit down in a tired-looking leather chair. "Have you had a chance to peruse the papers our London office sent you?"

"I have," Charlie replied in a carefully neutral voice. "I'm not sure at this time what to think. I would like to see the properties before I make any sort of decision. It was my understanding from my solicitors that my grandfather's estate had been settled."

"True, true," Mr. Quimby nodded his head up and down like a spring-loaded dashboard ornament. "However, a series of documents bearing your grandfather's name were found when a local company was planning to buy up properties down in the Harbor district. The company expressed its interest in buying your grandfather's property, hence we contacted you."

"I'm delighted that you did," Charlie replied courteously to the strange little man. "Now then, I think I'll take a little trip over to the properties to see them myself."

"There's really no need to do that, Dr. Warren. It's nothing more than a dock-front nineteenth century warehouse. Very unattractive. Eyesore actually."

"Somewhat like the ones down near the Thames on the North End?" Charlie asked innocently.

"Precisely; the very image I was trying to convey to you," Mr. Quimby replied.

"Intriguing," Charlie's smile froze. "There is no such place in London, Mr. Quimby. The docks are located in the east end section of London. Anyone who's lived in Great Britain for any length of time could have told you that. Your accent, sir, is all wrong as well. You sound more like a transplanted South African to me. Would you care to tell me who you really are and what's going on?"

Mr. Quimby's face went scarlet. Before he could reply to Charlie two things happened. Charlie suddenly noticed the red glint of a pencil-thin beam coming through the window behind Quimby's back. Instinct took over before thought, and she hurled herself away from the lawyer's desk. The picture window behind the desk shattered and the lower part of Quimby's face disintegrated in a cloud of blood and tissue.

Reflexively, Charlie whirled out of the chair and onto the floor, keeping the chair in front of her as a shield. She drew her gun instinctively, and nearly fired at the dough-faced secretary, who stared at the scene for a second or so before screeching and running out the door.

Charlie flattened herself against the floor, even though it was covered with shards of glass and blood. For what seemed an eternity, she waited for another burst of gunfire. No other shots came. It finally dawned on Charlie that Quimby, not she, was the object of the single assassin's bullet.

Knowing that the secretary had left the office, never to return, Charlie got out her cell phone and dialed 911. She calmly reported the details to the dispatcher. The operator assured her that help would be on the way. Did Charlie need any medical assistance? No, she was fine, Charlie told the woman in a matter-of-fact tone.

It was at this point that Charlie called David and requested the change of clothes. The sound of sirens approaching meant that soon she would have another round of explaining to do to the New York Police.

David's going to love me for this, Charlie thought to herself. Some of the glass fragments had gotten into her hair. She stood up and brushed some of the debris off of her jacket. "My best wool business suit in ruins: that's just my luck."

Charlie picked herself up off of the floor. She did not move around, since she was in the middle of a crime scene. Mr. Quimby was clearly beyond medical attention, Charlie decided clinically as she looked at his body, now slumped over his desk like a piece of sodden baggage. The pool of blood coming from his shattered corpse was now busy dripping over the edge of the desk onto the champagne colored carpet. "Looks like I'm part of a crime scene," she said to no one in particular.

The pounding of heavy, booted footsteps a few moments later announced the arrival of the ESU, the Emergency Services Unit. As the helmeted, flak vested officers burst into the room, Charlie put on her best smile. "Good morning, gentlemen. Welcome to my crime scene."

-0-

Earlier that morning, David Stone watched as Katya Warren glided around the skating rink, her pink-clad body jumping and pirouetting in effortless grace. He had brought her down to the skating rink at ten that morning to meet with Terry Robeson, the figure skating coach who had volunteered to work privately with Katya.

Katerina Warren skated with a beautiful smile on her face. As she skated, David had the impression that Katya was not doing some sort of mechanical routine. Katya was somehow worshipping God with every move and gesture she made on the ice. She had told David and Charlie in London the night they first met that she praised God as she skated. David knew that she was not speaking idly. In the months since he had come to know his sister-in-law, David knew that she was speaking the truth. Katya's skating was flawless, almost otherworldly in its grace and beauty.

Terry was busy glancing down at a piece of paper, writing notes as fast as she could. She had spent an equal amount of time looking at Katya and her paper. At the end of about ten minutes of skating, she raised a whistle to her lips and blew a short blast. Katya skated across the ice over to her.

"Good," Terry said, nodding her approval. "How old are you, Katya?"

"I turned thirteen in March," Katya told her with a smile.

Terry nodded again and looked at her notes. She looked over at David, "Where do you want her to go?"

David held up his hand. "This is her show, not ours. Charlie and I want what's best for her. Katya's the one who's driving this skating thing."

A smile broke out on Terry's face. "Even better. You wouldn't believe the number of pushy parents who browbeat their children into skating competitively. I'm so glad to hear someone with your viewpoint, Mr. Stone."

For the next hour or so, Terry sat down and reviewed her technical notes with Katya. She did all the talking, and Katya nodded frequently as Terry talked over her notes.

Katya had grown up enormously since she arrived in America back in January. She had changed her last name to Warren, telling Charlie that she wanted to take on her father's true name. Katya had plunged into American life with an absolute passion that surprised even Charlie, who was like her in so many ways. She devoured learning, and had raced through several college level courses in mathematics and science.

Charlie had insisted, for her own social development, to keep her in the eighth grade at the Compton grade school. Katya would enter high school in the fall. Although she would be officially enrolled in the ninth grade, she would be taking several tenth-grade classes, a full load heavy with advanced-level math and science courses. Katya would already have around twenty college-level credits in her record at that time.

Despite the heavy academic load, Katya was a relentlessly normal child. Charlie refused to treat her any differently despite her gifts. Katya had plenty of friends over at the house for sleepovers, pizza parties, and so on. She was involved at Trinity Church, helping out with the children's Sunday School program.

"Thank you, Katya, for showing me your moves," Terry Robeson finally said. "You can go get dressed into street clothes now."

"Thank you, Ms. Robeson," Katya rewarded her with a beautiful smile. She pushed away from the rink wall and glided across to the entrance to the locker rooms.

"She's a beautiful kid," Terry said softly, watching her go towards the locker room. "Very sweet. I'm amazed that she survived it all and is still willing to skate. The Soviet-style programs are like concentration camps. They produce technically perfect skaters, but they grind the individuality out of the kids."

"You can thank Charlie for the way Katya turned out. She's had to more or less be her mother and her sister since she got to America," David told her.

He paused. "Do you think she could go to the Olympics?"

"Maybe. We need to get her through Regionals first, and then the Nationals," Terry told him in a practical tone. "I know she's a student, so school comes first, last and foremost. What would you say to four hours a day right now in the summer, five days a week? There's a competition coming up in August in New York City. She's already a known quantity, but the Figure Skating Association needs to get her plugged into the American system. It's a good goal to shoot for."

"Sounds good," David replied. "That's up to Katya and Charlie, but it sounds reasonable to me. They do a lot of running together in the morning, and Katya goes down to the 'Y' two times a week for weight lifting and ballet lessons."

Terry nodded her approval. "That sounds good. I'd like to train her. There may be some workshops coming up during the year that I'd like her to attend, and I'll let you know when those occur. She's got talent, and the drive, Mr. Stone. It's up to her where she wants to go with it."

"All right then," David concluded with a smile as Katya came up to him and hugged him. "Thank you for your time, Ms. Robeson. We'll be in touch."

"Thank you, Mr. Stone," Terry replied. "Katya, I want to work with you. Would you like that?"

"Oh yes, Ms. Robeson. I would like that very much!" Katya said enthusiastically.

"I will be talking to your sister later today, Katya." Terry handed her notes to Katya. "Review these tonight, and I'll see you again on Wednesday, okay?"

"Okay," Katya nodded, taking the notes. "Can we go get some lunch now, David?"

David laughed. "Of course, Katya." He looked over to Terry Robeson, who smiled. "What can I say? Typical teenager."

"I have two at home, Mr. Stone. I know the breed," Terry replied, winking at Katya as they walked out of the rink to their cars.

After lunch, David drove Katya back to the house before he went to the Compton Police Station. Joan Richards was waiting for him. "How did the skating tryout go?" she asked as he came through the door of her office.

"Great," David said as he sat down in the chair opposite her desk. "You wanted to see me about something?"

"How would you feel about helping Charlie out with her assignment in New York?" Joan asked. "I've talked it over with Carl, and he thinks it's a good idea."

David frowned. He'd been thinking about the idea himself, but there were plenty of problems with it. "Joan, you know Charlie won't go for it. There's no reason for me to be assigned to her. She's been in America for almost a year now, and she doesn't need a babysitter. Charlie never needed one in the first place."

"I'm not thinking about her so much as I am about her having to deal with Brenda Reynolds, Dave," Joan replied. "Brenda's a barracuda, and you know it. I'm afraid she's going to make things difficult for Charlie."

"Joan, Brenda's got a lot more reasons to mess with me than with Charlie. As far as that goes, you know what sort of things happen when people try to get in Charlie's way. Charlie's perfectly capable of taking care of herself."

Joan looked at David and decided to try a different approach. "Look, Dave: I saw what happened to you when Karen died. What worried us most was that Brenda would come in and somehow mess things up for you. It really bothers me that she's involved in this case. She may try to stir up trouble and that wouldn't be good for any of us, especially you and Charlie. I just don't want anything to happen to you and your family, that's all."

David reached across the desk, took Joan's hand and squeezed it. "Joan, I appreciate what you're saying, and I'll do whatever you want me to do. I won't deny that I've wanted to tag along with Charlie on this thing, but I can't really see any reason for me to do so. If you and Carl come up with a reason for me to be there, then I'll go. But you're going to have to sell this to Charlie, not me. If I show up there on my own, Charlie and Brenda will both treat me like a third wheel."

A smile broke out on Joan's face. "Carl and I will work on that, Dave."

David's cell phone rang. "Hello?"

"David, it's me. I'm down at the lawyer's office. There's been a shooting, and I'm in a bit of a mess. Could you be a lamb and stop by the house and pick me up a change of clothing, please?"

"A change of clothing?" David repeated in shock. "Charlie, are you hurt? What's going on?"

"I'll explain everything later, David. Do please hurry," Charlie hung up.

David mechanically turned off the cell phone, putting it away. He got up from the chair and started for the door.

"Dave, what's wrong with Charlie? What happened?" Joan asked sharply.

"What?" David was in shock. He recovered and looked at Joan.

"That was Charlie. She went over to that family lawyer's office. Someone fired a rifle at her and the lawyer. He's dead, and she's okay, but she's stuck down there."

"There's your answer, Dave," Joan said in a business-like tone. "Get out of here. Go take care of that little girl. Don't worry about Katya. I'll call Megan and we'll take care of her."

David rushed out of the office. Joan watched him go. Carl Davis, came up to her. "Trouble, Joan?"

"Yeah. Something's happened to Charlie in New York. Dave's going into the city to find out," Joan answered.

"Well, that didn't last long," Carl observed grimly.

"What are you talking about?"

"Our little lull in action around here. Remember how busy things were around here when Charlie first came to town?"

"How could I forget," Joan said ironically. "I thought things would never slow down. Are you saying it's going to be like that again?"

"I wouldn't doubt it," Carl said. "In fact, it's probably going to get worse. I want everyone in the force to keep an eye out for suspicious people hanging around here. Keep an eye out for people asking questions about Charlie and David, and I want units to patrol out towards Dave's place. I don't want any maniacs to come into this town and start causing trouble."

"Sounds like a good plan," Joan nodded her approval. "We got lucky last time, but I don't want to count on that again."

Carl sighed. "It's going to be a long summer."

9

"What a mess! You need to clean up after yourself, Doc," Ron Meyers said genially as he and Brenda Reynolds came through the door half an hour later. Charlie was busy talking to the homicide detectives about what she saw when they arrived. Charlie immediately brightened up when she saw Meyers and Reynolds.

"I wasn't carrying my broom and shovel, Sergeant. Hello, Lieutenant Reynolds, Sergeant Meyers," she said lightly as though they were lifelong friends. "As you can see, there's a bit of a mess about the place."

"Warren, I should have known you were mixed up in this. Just what are you doing here?" Detective Reynolds asked in her surliest tone.

Charlie's patience with Brenda Reynolds was just about exhausted. The woman was being deliberately rude and abrasive. Charlie's nerves had been frayed by the events of the morning, but she somehow managed to keep her temper. "Lieutenant, would it be too much to ask you if you'd perhaps be a little more civil when asking me questions?" Charlie asked in her politest, most correct tone.

Brenda knew very little about Charlie Warren. That was unfortunate, because anyone who had any dealings with Charlie could have told her that when Charlie's tone became very polite, it meant that her patience was gone. Brenda was too wound up at this point to really pay attention to anything except her own agenda.

"Warren, I've had it with you and your meddling. Stay away from this investigation unless you are specifically ordered to be somewhere. Now why are you down here this afternoon?"

"Let me enlighten you, Lieutenant, as to my schedule for this day, since you seem to take an unwarranted interest in me and my affairs," Charlie replied steadily after half a minute's silence. She had had enough, and it was time to put this obnoxious detective in her place. "I was summoned to the British Consulate for a meeting with my immediate supervisor, Colonel James Rosson. That meeting, and the subjects that were discussed, do not concern you at this time. When my superiors authorize me to discuss it with you, I will do so."

Brenda was about to make an angry protest, but Charlie abruptly raised her hand. "Please allow me to continue, Lieutenant. You want a full accounting of my activities; I am complying with your request, down to the last detail.

"I then came down here this morning, again at the directive of my supervisor, to inquire about some property in New York that my family owns. I found out that this man, who called himself Quimby, was a fraud. It was at that point, Lieutenant, when I noticed a laser-targeting beam on his back. I ducked down just as someone fired a rifle at Mr. Quimby's head. You can see what happened as a result.

"Mr. Quimby is now dead, and the lower half of his face and most of his brainstem is spattered all over my clothes. I am now an integral part of this crime scene, and I can assure you that once the scene is processed, I will exit this place and not come back. I think that summarizes my current situation quite nicely."

Charlie came up close to Brenda, her voice assuming an icy cold tone. "Do not, Lieutenant, try my patience. I am involved in your investigation at the request of the Federal government. You may think that I am a thimble-witted amateur, but I am most assuredly not."

Brenda's face went white with fury. She was about to answer when Ron Meyers decided it was time to act. His cell phone had gone off while Charlie and Brenda had been talking. He had just finished his conversation when he noticed his partner was about to blow her stack again.

He came over and placed himself between the two women. "Lieutenant, I just finished talking to Captain Vinson."

"We're not finished here interviewing Warren," Reynolds said, never taking her eyes off of Charlie. Meyers shook his head. He knew that the two women were almost ready to come to blows. He needed to intervene, and quickly.

"Yes we are, Lieutenant. Captain Vinson wants us down at the station right now. He told me that Sims and Kubeck will handle the rest of this."

Meyers' tone finally brought Brenda back to reality, but she kept staring at Charlie. She knew that an implicit challenge had been issued, and she was toying with the idea of picking it up. Finally, she found her voice. "All right, we're going. Look Doctor, stay out of my way on this case, and we'll get along fine."

She turned around and started to walk through the door, almost knocking down David. "I was wondering when you were going to show up, Stone. Brought your little wife a change of clothes, did you?" Brenda asked in her nastiest tone.

David flattened himself against the wall to let her pass. He winced as though she had struck him. "Ow, Brenda! That hurts!"

Reynolds whirled around and was about to say something else when Meyers tugged at her arm. "Dave, nice to see you again. Come on, Lieutenant: the Captain's waiting."

David winked at Ron and glanced at Charlie. She had finished talking to the Homicide detectives and the CSI's processing the scene. "Hey. I brought you the clothes you asked for. Nice fashion statement, by the way. Brains and blood are so now."

"Wise guy," Charlie rewarded him with a mock scowl. "Your score, David, keeps climbing ever upward."

"I live to serve," David said with a mock bow. His face softened into concern. "You mentioned that your hair got spattered, so I brought some shampoo. How are you doing, kiddo?"

"I'll manage, really. Thank you for coming down and helping me get out of this mess." Charlie took the clothes and shampoo from him gratefully. "I need to find a bathroom to change before we leave."

She turned to the lead CSI processing the scene. "Do you need my garments for evidence, Lieutenant?"

"Yeah, that would be great, Dr. Warren," the Detective Sims replied, handing Charlie a bag and a pair of gloves. "You know the drill. Thanks for being so cooperative for us. I know this was a horrible experience for you."

"All right, then; I'll be back in a moment," Charlie disappeared out of the office and down the hall to a restroom.

David looked around the room at the incredible mess. Quimby's body was still where it was: pitched forward on the desk, the lower half of his head blown off. The pool of blood had stained the edges of the documents Charlie had brought. "Can I move these now, Lieutenant?" he asked the CSI processing the scene.

"Go ahead, Detective," the CSI replied. "You can take them with you, as a matter of fact. Let me get you a bag." She handed him a plastic bag to put the documents in.

"You're cleared to go, Dr. Warren," Rachel Sims said to Charlie when she reappeared a few moments later.

"Thank you, Lieutenant." Charlie replied gratefully. She turned her attention to David. "Now then, I think I could use a hug from you." David could feel her body trembling slightly as he held her.

"It's okay, Charlie," David said, kissing her. "MacKay's going to pick up your car later. You're coming home with me now. No more investigations today."

Charlie shook her head. "No, David, there's a meeting I have to go to this afternoon over at the Federal Building. Then we can go home. Fair enough?"

David paused for a moment before answering. "Charlie, let's go to the consulate first and see what Rosson thinks. MacKay's perfectly capable of handling any meeting. Let's play this by ear, okay?"

Charlie nodded, overcome by a wave of weariness. "Okay."

-0-

Howard Vinson was in the beginning throes of a migraine headache. His vision had clouded and he was seeing spots before his eyes. Sometimes, the headaches came out of the blue, with no warning or cause. Other times, stress, especially severe stress, would bring them on. This was one of those times.

He looked up at Brenda Reynolds. At this moment, she was the current and recurring cause of his physical and mental misery. Vinson made a visible effort to control himself. "Lieutenant Reynolds, I've just received two complaints about you in the past half hour. One was from the British Consulate, and the other was from the FBI. That's a department record, so congratulations," Captain Howard Vinson snarled. "I'll give you thirty seconds to explain your actions. The clock is running."

"Sir," Brenda Reynolds began. She was trembling with rage and humiliation, Meyers mentally noted. *Too bad, Bren: your mouth got you into this mess. You'd better get yourself out now.* "This Dr. Warren from the Consulate is an incompetent fool who has been nothing but trouble ever since she showed up! Somehow she got involved in the murder of some lawyer up in the financial district."

"That's enough, Reynolds," Vinson held up his hand. "Now I'm going to give it to you straight. I've had enough of you and your tempers and nasty attitude. You've been trouble ever since you showed up at this precinct. I don't care who your rabbi is down at Headquarters; you had a bad rep when you got here, and nothing's changed. You were assigned to my precinct because this was your last chance. That's straight from the Chief's office, Lieutenant. You came to me because no one else would have you, and that's the truth.

"Here's what you're going to do: you're going to fully cooperate with all Federal agencies involved in this case. You will obey without question any orders given to you by superior officers, whether they are foreign or domestic. That includes Dr. Warren, by the way. She's a Lieutenant Colonel in the British Army and a combat veteran. In my book, she's got more field experience under her belt than people twice her age. She outranks you, and if she won't tell you, I will.

"I pulled you off the Quimby crime scene because one of the other homicide detectives told me you were giving Warren a hard time. Sims told me you nearly had it out with Warren in the middle of a crime scene. That's embarrassing and unprofessional, and I won't put up with that kind of nonsense. I've had it with your vendetta against that woman."

Brenda started to protest, but Vinson was not through. "Warren may look like a high school student, and she may be a little too sweet for your liking, but she's a decorated officer from British Intelligence. You will respect her, Lieutenant Reynolds. Is that clear?"

"Crystal, sir," Detective Reynolds ground out.

Vinson slowly nodded his head. "Get out of here, and call Meyers in. I want to talk to someone with brains."

Brenda left Captain Vinson's office and told Meyers the message. Meyers went in and softly closed the door behind him. Brenda slowly sat down on the bench outside the office and stonily waited until Meyers came out.

"All right, Meyers: give me the straight story on Reynolds. Sims and Kubek phoned in and told me Reynolds nearly had a fight with Warren at a crime scene. What's her problem with Warren?" Vinson asked as the door closed.

Ron thought for a moment. "Her sister was married to Dave Stone, and I think Brenda's got issues with Warren because of that."

"Okay, so it's a family thing," Vinson said, massaging his head. "Look, I don't care if Reynolds' mother is Warren's grandmother. I want this to stop. I'm getting a lot of heat from the Chief about this case. This is major league, Meyers. Do you think Reynolds can handle this?"

"I think so, sir," Meyers replied with some hesitation.

"You've got problems with her, don't you, Meyers?" Vinson asked. "I can tell it in your voice. Come on now: it's me and you. What's your issue with Reynolds?"

"Trust, sir. I don't know if I can trust her when the chips are down," Meyers looked at his hands. "I'm afraid she's going to wig out on me, Captain."

Vinson settled back in his chair. "You want to be reassigned, is that the issue? I can make that happen, or I can fire Reynolds. I've got more than enough grounds. You can do the investigation solo without her. You're ready to make Lieutenant, and I'll sign off on your promotion this afternoon if you want me to."

"No sir, that won't be necessary," Meyers shook his head. "I want her to become someone I can trust. She's a great cop, Captain. Reynolds is smart; her instincts are good. It's just that she's a little too high-maintenance at times."

"You want to stay with her? Even after all you've said this afternoon?" Vinson was somewhat startled by Meyers' reply. His eyes narrowed with suspicion. "You're not falling for her, are you, Ron?"

Meyers' face turned scarlet. "No sir, it's nothing like that. I just think Reynolds is special. I just don't want to give up on her."

Vinson wasn't convinced. "Look, Meyers: I've seen this sort of thing before. It's bad news when detectives start to get emotionally involved with each other. I'm afraid you two will get into a situation and get both of yourselves killed, or someone else."

"Sir, it's not like that at all," Meyers shook his head adamantly. "Reynolds has no feelings for me. It's my problem, and believe me, I can handle it."

Howard Vinson looked down and twiddled with a pencil on his desk. Finally he looked up, his face set and grim. "Okay, Meyers: I trust your judgment. Reynolds stays, and you remain her partner. That's going to be a tough job, and I'm still not convinced she's going to survive this case.

"You need to keep her in line, Meyers. I'm counting on you to do that. One more incident like this afternoon, and she's out the door. She needs to watch her mouth and her attitude. Understood?"

"Yes sir," Meyers nodded, "Do you have any suggestions on how I can do that?"

Vinson grimaced. "Nothing legal, I'm afraid. Taping her mouth shut would be a good start. You'll think of something. Now get out of here so I can do some work."

"All right, sir," Meyers replied, opening the door to Vinson's office.

-0-

Ron Meyers came out of the office and sat down next to Reynolds. Brenda looked at him sullenly and promptly got up. "I'm going home. I'll see you tomorrow," she called over her shoulder as she walked down the hall. Meyers got up and followed her.

"Lieutenant, I want to talk to you," he called out. Reynolds increased her speed down the hall. Meyers rushed up and walked in step with her. "Look, can we find some place and sit down for a moment and talk?"

He touched her arm gently. "Please, Brenda."

Brenda Reynolds turned around and looked at him. She hated losing control of her emotions. She hated the fact that her eyes were full of tears, but there was nothing she could do to stop them. "Meyers, the Police Department is my life. Nothing else matters. I've worked my way up the ranks from Patrol Division on my own. No one's ever done me any favors, ever. I didn't have a rabbi or anyone else to help me. That's a lie."

Her shoulders started shaking as the tears started down her face. Meyers tried to put his arm around her. Brenda angrily pulled away from him. "Don't touch me! I don't like that sort of thing! I don't need your pity, or anything else from you!"

Meyers decided to try a different approach. "Look, Lieutenant: you're my partner. You've been my partner for two years now. Don't you think it's time you relaxed, just a little? Have I ever let you down, or not backed you up at any time?"

Reynolds thought for a moment. "No, Meyers; you've backed me up. I can't fault you for that. You've lasted longer than anyone else ever has. Why have you done that?"

Ron smiled slightly. "Let's say I like a challenge, Detective."

"Challenge? Is that what I am?" Reynolds had been softening for a moment, but the word "challenge" instantly put her back on the defensive. "I'm not some sort of prize for you to win, Meyers. You can get any thoughts about that out of your mind right now. I trust no one."

The smile vanished from Meyer's face. "That's funny, Reynolds, because that's exactly what the Captain and I were talking about a few minutes ago. You trust no one, and no one trusts you. Your life is in my hands because you're my partner, and vice versa. If you can't factor that into your life, then you have no business being a cop."

He moved in closer to her and lowered his voice so no one else could hear. "You know what Warren has that you don't? She's got people she can trust. MacKay and I were talking the other day. He was Warren's training NCO back when she went through SAS school. Warren earned that man's trust, even when he was trying his hardest to make her quit. She saved his life a few months ago, along with a bunch of other people. You don't earn the trust of a Sergeant

Major of the Special Air Service by being a fool. MacKay will put his life in her hands any day of the week, because he trusts her.

"And that's what you don't have, Reynolds: trust. You're a smart cop, but you'll never be a great cop, because no one can trust you," Meyers concluded with his voice heavy with defeat and disgust. "I can't trust you either, and I've had it. You won't be there for me when things go down, and I'm not going to take the chance that you'll flake out on me. It's over. I'm asking to be reassigned in the morning. Have a nice day, Lieutenant." He turned on his heel and walked away from her.

Brenda Reynolds stood in the hallway and stared after him. She had finally succeeded in driving Ron Meyers away, the only man in her life who had ever stood by her and taken everything she could dish out. "Ron, please," she finally managed to croak out. "Please come back."

Meyers turned around and looked at her. He just stopped in the hallway and waited. Brenda came up to him.

"What do you want?" Meyers asked sullenly, expecting another blast of invective.

Brenda looked at the ground. "Meyers, I'm sorry. You're right: I don't trust anyone. I want to, but every time I do, I get burned. It's happened all my life. I guess I got so used to having people slam the door in my face that now I slam it in my face before they have a chance to do it."

"Look Reynolds, I'm not your priest, rabbi, shrink, or whatever," Meyers looked her in the eye. He was fed up" with Brenda, and decided he had nothing to lose. "You've got problems with trust. We all do. My problem with you is this: you've got a gun and a badge, and you've got my life in your hands. All I want to know is that when the time comes, and I need you, are you going to be there or not?"

"I'll be there for you, Meyers. I promise." Brenda said with conviction.

Ron Meyers looked at her for a full minute. "You're on probation with me, Lieutenant," he said slowly. "You mess up one time, and I'll make that call. This case is big, and we can't afford any slipups. I have a feeling before it's over you and I are going to learn a lot about trust, and a lot about each other.

"I may be a sergeant, and you're a lieutenant and my superior. I'll never forget that. Just remember to watch my back, and I'll watch yours."

For a fleeting moment, Brenda Reynolds face softened and became intensely vulnerable. Meyers knew that she was about to kiss him. He wasn't ready for that, so he changed his tone back to his old joking mode. "Don't get all gooey on me, Reynolds," he cautioned her with a smile.

"Yeah, I hate that kind of stuff," she said, lightening the mood.

They said nothing more to each other until they were safely out of the precinct building safely away from prying eyes and ears. "I know a restaurant a couple of blocks away from here that serves the best pizza in the world. Are you interested?" He threw out the invitation carelessly, half expecting to receive some sort of nasty reply.

A slow smile spread over Brenda Reynolds' face. "Sure."

Ron quickly covered his surprise, hoping that his pleasure in her response wouldn't be detectable. "Let's get one thing straight, Lieutenant. This isn't a date. It's two cops hanging out after work grabbing a bite to eat, okay?"

"Okay."

-0-

David had half expected Charlie to put up some sort of protest when he insisted that he drive her back to the British Consulate and then home. Surprisingly, Charlie offered no resistance. Instead, she fell deeply asleep once she got into the minivan. She woke up when they arrived at the consulate twenty minutes later.

"Good grief, did I fall asleep?" she asked sleepily, stretching herself for good measure. "I must have been more exhausted than I thought."

"Looks like it," David said in a noncommittal tone. "James is waiting for us inside."

They got out of the car and went up to James' office. He was there, along with Donald MacKay. "We've got some more information on Cartwright," Rosson told them as they came into his office. "I think we've veered into a very complicated, dangerous case. That building of yours seems to be extremely important."

"Given what's happened this afternoon, James, I think you're right," Charlie replied ironically.

10

—————

"In May of 1945, Richard Cartwright was dispatched by Major Michael Warren to oversee the dismantling of certain aspects of British Security Coordination here in New York City," James Rosson told everyone in his office after they were seated.

"BSC was the brainchild of two remarkable leaders: Winston Churchill and Franklin Roosevelt. When Roosevelt died in 1945, Churchill knew that it was only a matter of time before his successor would order the dismantling of BSC. His removal from office in the elections of 1945 underscored the urgency to preserve certain critical aspects of the operation which might prove valuable in the years to come."

"In other words, some of those facilities were left behind, without knowledge of the British or American Governments?" Sergeant Major MacKay asked. "That's not very sporting of them."

"Major Warren was in charge of the operation. Cartwright was his second in command. SOE prided itself on being rather unconventional, and Warren was more unconventional than most," Rosson replied dryly, a half-smile on his face. "Cartwright's mission was to make sure that the bulk of the records, equipment, and other nonessential items were shipped over to Canada in compliance with President Truman's directive. The rest was, shall we say, inadvertently directed to other locations."

"In other words, BSC lied to the Americans about shipping all of that equipment over to Canada," Charlie summarized brightly. "How dreadfully unsporting of them. Sounds like my kind of organization."

"Yeah, you'd fit right in, Pest. It's something that you would have come up with if you'd been around back then." David told Charlie, who winked prodigiously in return.

"Now you're catching on," Rosson said, warming up with enthusiasm. "I happen to agree with their philosophy. Sometimes the security of the country is too dear to be left in the hands of bureaucrats and politicians. Michael Warren was ideally suited for such a role. He was the polar opposite of the 'spit and polish' types who invariably resurface after every major conflict."

"In other words, he was a pirate. Just like his granddaughter. I married into a family of pirates," David summarized, looking directly at Charlie as he did so. Charlie wrinkled her nose and stuck out her tongue at him.

Rosson laughed. "Exactly so. 'Pirate' sums up Michael Warren to a 't'."

"This brings us to Cartwright's adventure in the tunnels, Colonel Rosson," Donald MacKay chimed in. "Why was he down there in the first place?

"We still don't know the details of his mission, or what happened that night. We are still trying to piece together that part of the puzzle." James said grimly. "There are many unanswered questions about the whole affair."

He leaned back in his chair. "Now then, Colonel Warren: you managed to wind up in the middle of a real murder this morning. Care to elaborate?"

"Sir, it's obvious that someone wants to acquire that building as soon as possible," Charlie replied. "Quimby wanted me to sign the papers immediately without any sort of inspection. That's highly irregular, and legally questionable. It shows how desperate these people are to acquire that building. His enthusiasm tipped his hand, and that's why I think he was eliminated."

James nodded his head. "Clearly he was a weak link. Killing him removed any chance of him informing on his superiors. The timing of your recent property acquisition and the appearance of Mr. Cartwright's body in that tunnel seem to be linked in some way."

"Just as I suspected: that empty warehouse has more intrinsic value than just simply the ground it's standing on," Charlie said quickly. "Something is in there that's worth a lot of money. Otherwise this corporation wouldn't be so hasty in acquiring it."

"I've done a little digging myself, and I came up with the name of the corporation who's interested in that property. It's one of those international conglomerates called LuxVeritas Systems," James told her. "Tomorrow, I want you and David to go down there and find out why they want to purchase that building. Sergeant Major MacKay and I are going to track down where this building is located. We need to inform Special Agent Rawlings about our plan.

"I think I'd like to go down to the warehouse district and personally inspect that building. We need to know why it's worth having a man's head blown off."

MacKay looked uncomfortable. Rosson spied it. "You have reservations, Sergeant Major? Please speak your mind."

"Well sir, I don't know exactly how to phrase this," MacKay began slowly. "Lady Margaret was rather specific that she wanted you to watch over things. Skulking about looking for old warehouses isn't exactly what she had in mind."

"You're wrong on that, Donald" James said proudly. "Reconnoitering that warehouse is exactly the sort of thing she'd want me to do."

He looked over at David. "I could use you to help us out, David, if you're available. You know your way around the City, and your assistance would be most appreciated."

David raised his hand. "I'll be happy to help skulk."

Charlie shot him a blistering glance. "You have play duty tonight in case you've forgotten."

David immediately assumed his little-boy expression. "I never get to do anything fun."

"Actually, Colonel Warren, we could probably use his expertise, being an American and all that," MacKay suggested hopefully. David's face immediately brightened.

"Oh, all right: you can go play with the other boys tonight." Charlie allowed a maternal tone to color her response. "I can't stand it when you sulk, David. Just get home sometime before two, and don't wreck our new van."

"Yes, ma'am," David replied contritely. "All right then," James said in a business-like tone. "I just need to coordinate with my family about all of this. Jane's got a softball game tonight."

"How is she doing, by the way?" Charlie asked.

"Splendidly," James replied. "She's a born natural at pitching. Apparently she has the deadliest fastball in her church league."

"I'll bet she does," David noted wryly. "I was really impressed the way she took out those two characters in that pub a few months ago."

"What about that briefing by the FBI this afternoon?" Charlie asked.

"Rawlings told me that it's been moved to tomorrow. Quimby's murder has thrown another angle into the picture," James told her. "Additionally you have been excused from that briefing. Detective Lieutenant Reynolds and Sergeant Meyers will be attending in your place."

He looked at Charlie with concern. "I also might at that you've had quite enough excitement for one day, my dear. You need a bit of a rest, in my opinion."

"I hate it when you try to take care of me, James," Charlie grumped, "it makes me feel like I'm six years old again."

"Well, regardless as to how it makes you feel, you're not expected back here until tomorrow morning," Rosson said with a smile. "Besides, you have a play to assist with, as you're so fond of pointing out. By the way, one of our staff members arrived with your car about ten minutes ago. It's in the lot."

"Well, I'm off to my rehearsal," Charlie rose from her seat. "I left word with Megan to get started without us if we run late here."

"Off you go, then," James said with a smile.

"Darling, try not to get yourself shot or arrested tonight," Charlie kissed David goodbye.

"That's your department, Pest," David kissed her back.

"Enjoy skulking, gentlemen."

-0-

James Rosson decided to wait after dark to start their search for the old warehouse. David pointed out to him that the traffic in the dock areas would be less, and the newness of the buildings would not distract them from their search. The East River docks were a conglomerated mishmash of old warehouses precariously perched on older docks. It was not a wholesome place to be in past dark, and most New Yorkers gave the place a wide berth. The dimly lit streets with their sodium vapor lamps made the whole area look like an old yellowed photograph.

"This picture is truly terrible," Rosson stared at the grainy old photograph. "I imagine half of the buildings in this part of the city no longer exist. The place looks like some of the East End dock areas in London."

"Perfect spot for the Warrens to have a bit of family property," David pointed out. "You know: East End and the Ripper murders."

"That's quite true sir," Donald agreed. "Fortunately for us the New York City streets don't change, at least not in this part of town."

"This part of town's pretty rough, guys, so we need to be careful," David cautioned as they drove slowly through the streets. "I did some patrols down here when I was in the Academy."

Traffic was scarce, and there were few streetlights. The streets were filled with old abandoned cars and heaps of trash next to old brick buildings. The eerie light from the streetlamps made everything look strange and otherworldly.

Rosson sat up in his seat as he recognized something. "Slow down, Donald. I think I just saw the street." He pointed to an undistinguished intersection they were approaching.

MacKay slowed the car down and made a left hand turn. They were coming up on a bank of long, two story buildings. "Do you see something that looks like the building in that photograph, Colonel?"

Rosson looked up at a row of buildings before them. "Indeed I do, Sergeant Major. That building up ahead looks promising. I believe we have arrived, gentlemen."

MacKay pulled the car over to the curb. They were now in a desolate, run-down part of town close to the docks. Overhead, the hulking shadows of the skyscrapers loomed like the teeth of some great prehistoric beast. The sun had long since set, and the busy day traffic had deserted the area. They walked slowly up towards the building. Made out of crumbling nineteenth century brick, the building reeked of decay and neglect.

"Remarkable," James mused, "It's a miracle that we've managed to find the building at all, given the poor quality photograph."

"Did Sir Leslie give you any idea what might be in this building, James?" David said as they walked up to the front of the building.

"It was simply a warehouse, at least that's what the records said." James looked at the map and then up at the faded address over the door. "2417 Seventeenth Avenue. This is it. No question about it."

"There must be a side entrance," MacKay said eagerly. "We need to go around and take a look."

They edged around the front of the old building. Halfway down the side of the building, they found a rusted old door with an ancient padlock. "No one bothered to bring a key, right?" David asked with a smirk.

"There weren't any keys in the packet Charlie had," James replied, shaking his head.

"I brought a key," MacKay produced a pair of bolt cutters.

"Scottish resourcefulness: I knew we could count on you, Donald," Rosson grinned.

MacKay snapped off the lock with little trouble. "It's rather a puny lock, sir. Not much of a struggle. Let's go in and take a peek."

"Hold on, guys," David cautioned. "You have to understand that we have authorization from the owner to do this. Get your stories straight now, because I guarantee that when the cops come, that's one of the first things they'll ask."

"What about the lock?" Rosson asked. "Sergeant Major MacKay's bolt cutters are highly suspicious."

David shrugged. "We didn't have a key."

"Right."

The ancient steel door screeched open. The noise sounded loud enough to wake the entire city.

"If anyone's inside, they most certainly heard that awful racket," MacKay pointed out. "Here: turn on your torches. Let's take a look."

David, Rosson and MacKay entered the building. It was a vast emptiness. The beams of the flashlight stabbed through the darkness, illuminating the farthest walls with a ghostly glow. "Nothing," Rosson said with bitterness. "There's nothing here."

"That's weird," David mused. "Why would anyone hold onto an empty warehouse for decades? You could at least rent out the space for storage. Space like that is always at a premium here in New York, especially along these docks."

"Excellent point, David," MacKay swung his light around to the far corners of the building. The dark silence of the warehouse hung around both of them like a wet cloak, causing the men to lower their voices. Before they could investigate any further, they heard the sounds of several cars screeching to a halt outside the building.

"All right, guys: the cops have arrived," David said wearily. "Let's go outside and get ourselves arrested."

"You don't think they'll shoot us, do you, David?" Rosson asked as they walked towards the door.

"They might. Just move slowly and keep your hands where they can see them."

-0-

Charlie's phone went off in the middle of the rehearsal. "Hello?"

"Hey, Charlie. It's me."

"Hello, me. What's the problem?"

"We, uh…" David paused for a moment. "We got arrested."

"Really? This is supposed to surprise me, right?" She clamped a hand over her mouth to stifle a scream of laughter. After half a minute of muffled giggles, she controlled herself. "No, no, no, I'll be down, David. No, no, I'm not angry. Serves you right, though, running off without me. Well, now we're even." She turned off the phone.

"Charlie, what's wrong?" Megan asked in a concerned voice. Charlie was giggling hysterically next to her, trying desperately not to cause a disruption in the rehearsal.

Finally, she caught her breath. "It's… it's… well… Megan, it's hard to explain," she gasped for air for a moment, tears streaming down her face. "It seems that our men were out and about snooping around the docks, and the police caught them. I have to go down to the consulate, pick up our van and spring them from jail!"

Megan rolled her eyes upward, seeking strength. "Right. Donald's mixed up in this. I can tell. James too, right?"

Charlie wiped her eyes. "Oh yes, they're all involved, every one of them. You know Jane will never let James live it down." She gathered her purse. "Just let Katya know we'll be back in a while."

"We'll take her over to Joan's if it gets late. Give my love to the jailbirds when you see them." Megan grimaced and then winked at Charlie.

-0-

"I'm getting really tired of running after you and your band of merry men, Warren," Brenda Reynolds snarled as Charlie came through the precinct door an hour later. Reynolds had been summoned from her home by the Watch Commander, since she was the officer in charge of the NYPD part of the investigation. She was not happy.

"We caught your little pals down by the dock areas breaking and entering an abandoned warehouse. This time, they're going to jail for sure," she sneered in gleeful anticipation.

"Not so fast, Lieutenant," Charlie held up the deed to her grandfather's property. "That warehouse happens to be my property. They were down there with my permission."

Reynolds stared at her and the papers for a moment. "You mean to tell me that you had those cretins down there in the middle of the night trying to find out what was in that building?"

She shoved the papers back at Charlie. "All right, Warren: take your deed and these morons and get out of my precinct. They're lucky they didn't get shot down there. Next time they might not be so lucky."

"Thank you, Lieutenant," Charlie replied in her sweetest voice, batting her eyes for emphasis. David, Donald and James came through the door from the holding cells, escorted by two policemen. "Come along home, boys: it's way past your bedtime."

"Don't rub it in, Charlie," David looked drawn and pale. It was obvious that he was in no mood to be teased. Rosson and MacKay were also looking haggard as well.

Brenda looked at Charlie, who was still dressed in her leotard and skirt. "Were you at some sort of costume party? You look ridiculous."

"Play, actually," Charlie replied with a huge grin. "I'll make sure I send you tickets when we have a performance."

"We were about to do a bit of exploring when we were interrupted," Rosson told Charlie enigmatically, nodding slightly. He kept his tone carefully neutral, not wanting to arouse Brenda's curiosity. Charlie picked up on this and nodded slightly in return.

"At least we know where the building is," Rosson continued. He lowered his tone so only Charlie could hear. "Do not part with that property until we investigate it thoroughly."

"Right." Charlie nodded. She turned to David. "Well then; let's head back home."

"I'm with you. Nice to see you again, Bren. Thanks for everything." David grinned at Brenda Reynolds.

"Get out of this station before I arrest you for loitering!" Reynolds roared. She turned her wrath on James and Donald. "I'm going to inform the consulate about this. With any luck, they'll have you two pixies on the next plane back to England."

"You needn't worry about that, Lieutenant. You already have. I happen to be the Assistant Consul General, and I'm acting in Lady Margaret's stead while she's out of country," James informed her smoothly.

Brenda's face went scarlet. "Leave this place, Mr. Rosson. Leave now before there's an international incident. Take you and your little friends before I do something I know I'll regret!"

"Yes, let's all leave now," Charlie said indulgently, "Come on, gentlemen: we've bothered the nice detective long enough. We'll be in touch."

The sight of Charlie in her leotard triggered an evil thought in Brenda's head. She called out to Charlie just as they were leaving. "Hey Warren! Someone told me you taught hand-to-hand at the FBI Academy. Any time you want to go a few rounds, just let me know."

Charlie stopped and turned around. A strange light started to glimmer in her deep green eyes. "You want to spar with me, Lieutenant Reynolds? What an intriguing idea!"

Her face fell for an instant. "However, I'm afraid it really can't happen. I would be terrified of injuring you, Lieutenant. That would be most unfortunate."

That pushed Brenda's button. "Don't worry about me, sister. Worry about yourself. Why not tomorrow? It's been a while since I've taken on anyone who's been a challenge."

She paused for a moment. "Unless, of course, you're afraid."

"Oh no, Lieutenant, I'm not afraid at all," Charlie replied warmly. "We will be here tomorrow. I'm looking forward to it."

"Charlie, I don't think that's a good idea..." David began. Charlie stopped him by putting a hand on his arm.

"Nonsense, David; I think it's positively splendid," Charlie said brightly, never taking her eyes off of Brenda's. "I'll see you tomorrow at seven. Where shall we meet?"

"We have a gym in the basement of the precinct," Brenda said. "I'll be looking forward to seeing you."

"As will I," Charlie replied. "Have a good night, Lieutenant."

"Charlie, that was a really bad move," David said as they left the station. "Reynolds is tough and she's vicious. She could really hurt you."

"David's right, Charlie," MacKay agreed. "I think she'd like nothing better than to injure you badly."

"Nonsense," Charlie said briskly as she opened the van. "I think it will be fun. Besides, she's much too angry to be a threat."

"I suppose it wouldn't do any good for me to pull rank on you and forbid you to do this," Rosson said bleakly. The look Charlie gave him in response told him it was a lost cause.

"You are correct in your assumption, James. Reynolds has got to get this out of her system," Charlie said in a practical tone. "Once she does, we'll be fast friends. Besides, I've done nothing at all to provoke her."

"Of course you haven't. The Sergeant Major briefed me on the donut incident," Rosson replied skeptically. "Young lady, please try to control yourself for once. We really do need to have the local police force on our side."

"Yeah, we're already fighting enough wars across the pond. We don't need to start something with the Brits over here," David pointed out.

Charlie refused to be put off. "The real problem is that Lieutenant Reynolds is just lonely. We need to fix her up with some nice young man. That will change everything. I think that Sergeant Meyers might just be the ticket."

"Charlie, don't do it." David said in a pleading tone. "Ron Meyers doesn't deserve that."

"Deserve what?"

"What you're… what you're scheming."

"David, I am shocked that you think I'd do such a thing!" Charlie smirked as she opened the door of their minivan. "Where's your car, Donald?"

"I think it's still down next to your building," MacKay told her. "The police insisted we leave it there when they bundled us into their patrol cars."

"Fine: we'll drive you down there. We need to drop James off at the consulate on the way." David and Charlie climbed into the front seat, while MacKay and Rosson got into the back.

"What a lovely van," James observed. "Did you just get it?"

"Charlie kidnapped my car and disposed of it," David explained. "I'm still in mourning. I don't want to talk about my loss right now."

"I understand, David. You have my condolences," James replied soberly with a deadpan expression on his face.

"I had it buried in an unmarked grave," Charlie informed them gleefully.

"Stop it, you little sadist."

They drove to the consulate first, letting James off. "I'm sure I'm going to catch it from Jane when I get home." James remarked bleakly.

"I think you can count on that, James. She's already been fully informed on your adventures this evening," Charlie seconded.

"Thanks ever so much, love," James grimaced. "By the way, Rawlings called after you left, Charlie. You have an appointment at nine down at the City Medical Examiner's office to assist in

Quimby's autopsy. Reynolds and Meyers will meet you there after their briefing."

"Thank you, James. Have a good night and give our love to Jane," Charlie said as they drove off back to the docks. In a few short minutes, they arrived back at the old warehouse. The consulate car was exactly where Donald had left it.

"Now that ranks as a major miracle," MacKay remarked as he got out of the minivan.

"What do you mean, Donald?" Charlie asked.

"The car's not stripped or burned or up on blocks," Donald said, giving the car a cursory external exam.

"The consulate's choice of fleet cars is not the most popular model, Donald," David pointed out. "If anyone wanted this thing, it would be long gone by now."

"I see your point," Donald climbed in and started the motor. "We'll see you both tomorrow."

David and Charlie sat in the van for a moment or two after MacKay's car drove off. The long gray expanse of the warehouse gleamed dully in the yellow sodium lights. "What's inside this building Charlie? Why is it so valuable?" David finally asked.

"I don't know, David," Charlie sighed, putting her head on David's shoulder. "All I know is that we need to find out quickly. I have a terrible feeling we're running out of time.

"I think you're right, Charlie," David agreed. "Well now, are you ready to go back home and go to bed?"

"We still need to go by the consulate once more and pick up my car. I want to drive it home. With all that's going on right now, we need two cars."

"I wish you'd said something sooner. You could have picked it up when we dropped James off. I'm starting to get dizzy with all of this backtracking." David said as he turned the van around and headed back to the consulate.

Once they arrived, he let Charlie out where her car was parked. "Okay, Charlie. Just don't let that lead foot of yours get the best of you. I've had my fill of police stations for one day."

Charlie put her hand in the air. "I promise to obey the speed limit."
"Sure."

"Are you calling me a liar, dear sir?"

"No, I just know you won't keep that promise."

"You're probably right."

-0-

Ron Meyers' phone rang at eleven-fifteen. "Hello?"

"Meyers! Are you awake? I've got great news!" Brenda's excited voice jolted him into semi-consciousness.

Meyers was in bed, half an hour into a deep sleep when Brenda called. He couldn't remember the last time anyone had called him at this hour. "What's going on, Lieutenant? This is the first time you've ever called me at home. I didn't think you had my home phone number."

"I know, but I just had to tell you," Brenda gushed into the phone. "I challenged Warren to a sparring match tomorrow, and she accepted. This is so great! I'm going to pulverize that little twit!"

"Uh huh. Pulverize," Meyers repeated, hoping Brenda wouldn't hear the skepticism in his voice. "Okay, so that's why you called me up, to tell me that you're going to beat up Warren tomorrow?"

"Yeah, isn't it great?"

"It sure is," Ron leaned back in his pillow. He was getting sleepier by the minute. "Is there anything else you want to talk to me about?"

There was a pause at the other line. "No, not really. I guess you were the only one I could call and tell this to. I just wanted you to know."

"Well, I appreciate it, Lieutenant," Meyers glanced at the clock. It was now half past eleven. "I'll see you tomorrow at the gym around six."

"Okay. I'll see you then. No, wait: I'll meet you over at Mickleson's diner for breakfast at four. See you then," Brenda said, hanging up.

Meyers stared at the phone. "Okay, good night, Brenda," he said to the now-disconnected receiver. He hung up the phone and turned off the light.

11

Charlie and David woke up at five the following morning and had breakfast with Katya. They had made arrangements with Megan O'Grady to pick up Katya later that morning and take her to her skating session.

"Just let me know if there's a change in plans, Charlie," Megan said on the phone the night before. "I've got to get down to the theatre and help Steve Morton set and angle lights this morning."

"I really appreciate this, Megan," Charlie replied. "What's the situation on your wedding plans?"

"We're planning on getting married after the play's over in July. Donald's already talked to our family over in Scotland, and we've set a date."

Megan paused for a moment. "Funny, I said 'our family.' I already feel so connected with them. It's like the way I feel about you and David and the Rossons."

"I understand how you feel, Megan. Thank you so much for helping us," Charlie replied softly.

Charlie was so grateful for Megan's help. It made life so much easier. Megan adored Katya, and the two had become very close as they worked on the summer play production.

Katya was happy and excited about her upcoming skating practice. "I love Ms. Robeson, Charlie. She's so kind and patient."

"I'm glad you do, darling," Charlie kissed her cheek. "It's wonderful that you're enjoying skating now. We'll see you this afternoon in time for supper."

"Why are you going into New York today, Charlie? Katya asked as they finished washing the breakfast dishes.

"Katya, your sister is going in early so she can beat up a lady cop who's giving her trouble," David answered for her.

"I am not," Charlie said, setting down her dishtowel and glowering at David. "I'm going in early to do some training with an associate of ours."

"In other words, she's going to beat her up," David amplified with a grin.

Charlie said nothing further in reply. She left the kitchen and in a few moments reappeared in her powder blue jogging outfit. David stifled a laugh when she appeared at the kitchen doorway.

"You're not seriously going to go down there in that, are you?" he asked.

"Why not?" Charlie replied, her face the picture of innocence. "I think it's perfectly appropriate."

"It's appropriate for a morning jog, Charlie, not a sparring match. Come on, now: you look like you're going to a track meet or something," David observed. "Put on your gray sweats."

"I have my reasons, David," Charlie explained patiently. "This outfit will put her off balance. Besides, I look good in this suit. You've said it yourself."

"Right, you look adorable as a matter of fact, but that's not the point," David was not convinced. "This is not a fashion show, Charlie. You're going to be mixing it up with this woman in a hand-to-hand combat match. Brenda means business."

Charlie turned slowly and looked at her husband. All levity had vanished from her face. "So do I, David. Let's get on the road."

-0-

Captain Vinson was gleeful about the match. "It might help Reynolds' attitude to get taken down a notch or two," he told Ron Meyers that morning. "Rawlings told me Warren taught hand-to-hand at the Academy, and she's really tough."

"I'll bet a steak dinner Warren takes her down in thirty seconds," Meyers replied, looking at Brenda, who was dressed in a black sweat suit. She had called Ron at four, and they had met at an all-night diner for breakfast before coming down to the gym. All of the other cops in the gym had suspended their usual morning activities to gather around the mat to see what would happen next.

"You're on," Vinson said, shaking Ron's hand. "Well, speak of the devil; here's our little champ from the UK."

Charlie appeared in the doorway, dressed in her jogging suit, carrying her bag. "I see we have an audience this morning. How exciting," she said quietly to David. They were greeted with a wave of yells and cheers as they walked into the gymnasium.

"I knew it, Charlie. This is like high school, only way worse," David observed as they came over to the mat.

"Yes, it is. Only these people have guns," Charlie pointed out, setting down her bag at one corner of the mat.

Brenda was not impressed with Charlie's choice of outfits. "Look at that dopey blue sweat suit she's wearing," she sneered to Ron Meyers. "She looks like a complete idiot."

"Yeah, an idiot. I knew a female instructor girl in my Police Academy class who wore something like that. She cleaned every single cadet's clock in sparring matches."

Ron shook his head and went over to David. Charlie was now in the middle of the mat, doing some stretching exercises. "Hey, Dave! Nice to see you this morning."

He leaned in close and asked in a voice only David could hear. "This isn't going to be pretty, is it?"

"You've got that right, buddy," David said, shaking his head. "Charlie's got that look in her eyes, and when she gets that way, it's time to head for the tall grass."

"Hey Meyers: I've got my camera phone," one of the detectives came up to Ron. "You want me to get some pictures?"

Meyers nodded slightly, never taking his eyes off of Brenda, who was doing some serious stretching of her own. "Go for it, McKinley. Just make sure Brenda doesn't see the camera, or you'll be sipping your lunch through a straw for the next six weeks."

"I brought my pads, Lieutenant, in case you wanted to use them," Charlie said in a helpful tone, setting her bag over in one corner of the mat. "I'm sure we can make them fit you quite nicely."

A wave of snickering and laughter swept through the gymnasium. Brenda looked around with a scowl. "I don't need pads, Warren. Just get over here and let's get started." She started dancing around in a menacing, weaving manner.

"If you insist," Charlie said brightly, settling down into an on-guard stance. "Full contact, or are there any rules you want to go by?"

"Just shut up about rules, Warren. The match is over when you can't get up any more," Brenda snapped. "Let's get it on."

"Okay," Charlie replied. Brenda struck first, delivering a volley of kicks and strikes. Charlie deflected them easily, refusing to deliver any blows of her own. "I see you've studied *Krav Maga*. Your style is excellent," Charlie said admiringly as she fended off Brenda's frenzied attack with apparent ease, "my compliments."

"Come on, Warren! Is that all you've got?" Brenda snarled, frustrated at not being able to penetrate Charlie's defense. Charlie had decided to bide her time and wait Brenda out. It was only a matter of time before she would make a serious mistake that Charlie could use to her advantage.

"Really, Lieutenant, you must learn to control your anger," Charlie said as she calmly continued to deflect Reynolds' attack. "Your rage will be your undoing." To emphasize her point, Charlie quickly moved in and with one lightning-quick motion swept out Brenda's leg just as she was attempting to kick Charlie with the other. Brenda fell flat on her back with a resounding crash. A wave of shouts and yells echoed off the walls of the gymnasium.

"Ouch! That's gotta hurt," Ron remarked to David.

"Yeah, right on her pride," David said with a smirk.

"That's not the correct term for that part of her anatomy, Stone," Vinson said, looking at his watch. "Meyers, you're out of a steak dinner. First takedown happened in fifteen seconds. Want to even things up?"

Meyers thought for a moment. "Okay Captain. Warren's going to wrap this thing up in two more minutes."

Vinson nodded slightly. "You're on."

Brenda was dazed at the swiftness of Charlie's response. It took her a moment to get her wits together. Charlie waited politely until she recovered. "Do you need some assistance in getting up,

Lieutenant?" Charlie asked politely, offering her opponent a hand. Another wave of snickers and laughter swept across the gym. Brenda knocked it away and struggled unsteadily to her feet. The laughter made her lose her temper completely.

"No I don't," Brenda said viciously, resuming her attack. She moved in and tried to land a flurry of punches on Charlie. Her blows continued to land on air, as Charlie stepped back nimbly to avoid them.

"Come on, Brenda; this is getting us nowhere," Charlie said after two more minutes of deflecting more kicks and jabs.

"What's the matter, Warren? Are you getting tired? I'm just getting warmed up," Brenda puffed as she aimed a kick right for Charlie's head. Charlie deflected it and turned Brenda's leg with one hand. Brenda's body flipped over and she landed flat on her back with an earth-shattering crash. Charlie moved in, wrapping her arm around Brenda's neck in a chokehold.

"That's it! It's steak time!" Meyers shouted in jubilation. "Two minutes on the nose, Captain! You're out one steak dinner!"

Meanwhile, back on the mat, Brenda was having oxygen troubles. Lights were swimming before her eyes, and there was an ever-increasing roar inside her head as Charlie's arm inexorably cut off the flow of blood to her brain.

"Now then, Lieutenant: we are going to end this little contest," Charlie said into Brenda's ear. "I can apply enough pressure on your neck and stop the blood flow to your brain until you pass out, or I can let go and let you up in a civilized fashion. Since you can't talk right now, you can nod your head to agree."

Brenda made a series of gargled sounds through her airway and continued to struggle uselessly against Charlie's grip. Howard Vinson came over to them. "I'll answer for her, since she's too pigheaded to call a halt to this. Let her up, Dr. Warren."

Charlie released Brenda, who got up after a few seconds. "Thank you for the exercise," Charlie said brightly, receiving a towel from David. "I think it's time we went to the consulate. I think I can find a shower there." They turned and started to walk towards the gym door.

"This isn't over, Warren!" Brenda croaked after her, rubbing her neck gingerly.

"Yes it is, Lieutenant," Vinson said. "Get to the showers and get dressed. We have work to do today." He turned around to all of the other officers who had gathered to watch the match. "That includes all of you pixies as well! Get to work!"

He turned to Meyers. "You got your steak dinner, Sergeant. We'll talk later."

Meyers came over to Brenda and handed her a towel. Vinson watched with barely concealed amusement. "You're lucky, Lieutenant," Vinson said, shaking his head. "Warren could have badly injured you at any time if she wanted to. My sources over at the Bureau tell me she's vicious in a real fight."

"That girl's got a grip like an anaconda. She was just playing with me," Brenda said sullenly. "I don't think she broke a sweat."

"Be happy she didn't break anything else in this place this morning, Lieutenant."

-0-

"I'm really hating this investigation, Meyers," Brenda Reynolds snapped at Ron as they headed towards the FBI Building in downtown New York. "We have three dead bodies in a subway, and now another homicide in the past twenty four hours. And worst of all, we have to deal with the Brits and that stupid little English doctor."

"You're still sore about this morning?" Meyers asked. The morning had not gone well. Brenda had been in an especially bad mood ever since the incident at the gym.

"Of course not: I'm perfectly fine and in complete control," Brenda said, climbing out of the driver's seat gingerly. She slammed the door violently for emphasis. The alarm started to sound, but was cut short when Reynolds delivered a vicious kick to the door.

"It's all right. We're having a very bad day," Meyers said softly to the car, stroking the side of his door as he got out.

They arrived at the entrance of the FBI Building. Meyers opened the door reflexively and Brenda passed through without comment. "Isn't that interesting?" he muttered under his breath. Usually such a display of gallantry earned him a blistering comment from Reynolds.

Ken Rawlings was waiting for them in a briefing room, along with several other agents. He was at the podium, ready to start the morning briefing with his task force. "We can get started now that our friends from NYPD have arrived." Rawlings smiled slightly as they took their seats. "It's an honor to have Detectives Reynolds and Meyers from NYPD joining us today.

"Your CSI's have just given us some preliminary reports from the shooting incident over at Briggs and Smith. Quimby was shot with a 7.62 millimeter round fired from the office building across the street. They traced the bullet track to a suite of abandoned rooms on the thirteenth floor."

"We don't have any eyewitnesses on the ground or the building, other than... Dr. Warren," Brenda added. "She managed to duck out of the way when she saw the laser targeting beam on Quimby's head."

"Single shot kill: very efficient," Rawlings noted grimly. "The body count in this investigation keeps mounting. The reason why all of you are here this morning is that we need to fill you in on some other aspects of our operation."

"I'm going to turn this part of the briefing over to Rob Dubek, our intelligence expert." Rawlings sat down and a tall young man took the podium.

"We've had rumblings inside the Russian crime community that something big is about to go down, something involving this man." Dubek pushed a button on his remote. A picture of a bearded, bald middle-aged man appeared on a screen behind him.

"Ivan Kolov: former Soviet Colonel. Head of *Spetnatz;* that's the Soviet Special forces. He was in charge of infiltrating teams into forward NATO areas to capture and disable nuclear missile sites and other high value targets. Kolov has a background in nuclear physics, with an emphasis in nuclear weapons technology. He escaped to the West in 1992 after a brief, aborted attempt to steal launch codes for Russian ballistic missiles."

Dubek paused for a moment and looked at Rawlings. "Are these people cleared for what I'm about to talk about?" He indicated Reynolds and Meyers.

"If they weren't, they wouldn't be here," Rawlings nodded, turning over his shoulder to look at Brenda. "You do have a working knowledge of what classified information means, don't you, Lieutenant Reynolds?"

Brenda answered with a blistering scowl and a nod. Rawlings nodded back and turned around. "Go ahead."

Dubek resumed. "The launch codes were retrieved by a joint Russian-American-British special forces operation. Most of the people involved were captured, except Kolov. He managed to escape. There was some question that he might have help within the forces involved in the op, but that was never proved.

"Russian intelligence lost track of him for a number of years, then he resurfaced about two years ago here in America. Kolov is now deeply involved with supplying weapons systems for terrorist organizations all across the globe. He is completely apolitical, having no adherence to political ideas or ideology. The only thing he cares about is money, lots of it."

A picture of a crashed Blackhawk helicopter flashed up on the screen. "This is the most recent operation we believe he was involved in. Kolov supplied Stinger missiles to an IRA splinter cell here in New York. That group used the missiles to bring down this helicopter back in November 2003."

Meyers and Reynolds exchanged glances. Dubek looked down at his notes. "We think Kolov has the inside track on obtaining nuclear weapons systems, and deploying them in the United States. He's considered the 'Go to' guy when it comes to nuclear weapons. Kolov is smart, he knows the weapons, and he has the resources to obtain them. That's where we stand on our prime mover in this operation. That concludes my part of this briefing."

A picture of New York City flashed up on the screen as Dubek left the podium. Rawlings came up and pointed to the map. "All of this ties into what we've been seeing over the past few weeks. We've had the bodies of homeless people being dragged out of abandoned tunnels over by the East River. The terrorist chatter keeps mentioning Kolov's name along with New York, along with some sort of major op he's involved in. The incidental finding by the team investigating the triple homicide yesterday gives us another big piece in this puzzle.

"Let me emphasize, ladies and gentlemen: this case is developing hot and fast. New York City is our prime target area. Something big is going to happen here in the next few weeks. Intel thinks that Kolov and his people are somehow involved in it, and it's our job to find out what and why. If Kolov is involved, and we think he is, then it's going to involve some sort of weapon of mass destruction.

"We need to move quickly on this, people. The clock is running. You have your assignments. Our next briefing is tomorrow at 0700." Rawlings looked over at Brenda and Ron. "I need to see you two in my office for a moment."

As the meeting broke up, Reynolds and Meyers followed Rawlings down a long corridor to a medium-sized office. It was furnished with anonymous-looking imitation walnut furniture lit by a small desk lamp. On the wall was the usual assortment of school plaques, service photographs, and awards.

Rawlings motioned for the two detectives to sit down in a pair of leather chairs flanking the front of his desk. "I wanted to ask you two how things are going with your British counterparts? Rumor has it that three of them were arrested down over by the East River dock areas last night."

Brenda's face darkened. She managed to control herself as she replied. "Sir, Warren's gnomes were out last night snooping around some abandoned buildings. They actually broke into one. Patrol picked them up and took them to our precinct. I was about to book them for breaking and entering when that redheaded twit shows up with papers showing that she owns the building. These people have been nothing but trouble since we started this investigation! Warren's a menace and a pest!"

Nodding his head slowly, Rawlings turned his attention to Meyers, who was grimacing horribly as his partner was giving her opinions. "Meyers, I take it by your expressions that you have a somewhat different view on the Brits. Care to share?"

Meyers looked down at his feet for a minute in an effort to control himself. "Sir, Lieutenant Reynolds has had some unpleasant experiences in dealing with Dr. Warren," he began slowly. "So far, Dr. Warren's contributions to this investigation have been very helpful. She's, well, lighthearted, and her approach to the investigation has been somewhat... unorthodox. I can see why she rubs Lieutenant Reynolds the wrong way."

"But you don't have any problem with her, Sergeant Meyers?"

"No sir."

Rawlings leaned back in his chair and folded his hands. "Okay, let me acquaint you two with some facts of life about Dr. Warren. I've known Charlie for a number of years. She taught weapons and forensics at the Academy two years ago on an exchange program. I know how she operates, and I know her style. I'll grant you that Warren comes across as a lightweight, but when it comes to doing the job, she's a pro, through and through. Don't be fooled by her attitude."

A slight smile appeared on Rawlings' face. "I believe you've found out personally that Dr. Warren was also an instructor in hand-to-hand at the Academy, Detective Reynolds. Believe me when I tell you that you got off easy."

Brenda said nothing in reply, and Rawlings paused for a moment to let his statements sink in. "There's another facet to Warren's personality that I want to share with you. One that may help you understand what kind of person you're prejudging.

"What I'm about to tell you is classified. Remember that helicopter crash mentioned in the briefing? That was a helicopter on a black-ops mission. It took a hit from a shoulder-fired surface-to-air missile. Warren was on that bird when it went down. She took charge of defending the site after she treated all of the wounded, and then went on to disable an ambush. The Brits gave her the Victoria Cross for her actions."

Ron Meyers emitted a low whistle. "That's the British equivalent to the Medal of Honor, isn't it?"

A slight smile flitted across Rawlings' face. "Yeah, it is. She's the first woman who's ever been awarded that medal. In February, the President awarded her the Distinguished Service Cross."

Brenda was unimpressed. "And this has to do with... what?"

Rawlings leaned forward, and his voice turned icy cold. "Don't confuse style with competence. She's not some half-baked lab rat, Lieutenant. Warren is a decorated combat officer, and you WILL respect her. Do I make myself clear?"

Reynolds looked at him for a second or two. "Yes sir. I understand."

"Good. We're going to the Medical Examiner's office over by Bellevue," Rawlings said, looking at his watch. "We have a date with Quimby. Warren and her husband are going to meet us there."

Brenda's face went pale as he said this. Meyers looked over at her. Brenda Reynolds hated autopsies. "Great," she mumbled in reply.

12

David drove through the busy New York traffic to the Medical Examiner's office. While he drove, Charlie briefed him on the day's events. It promised to be a busy day for both of them.

"Megan's got Katya for the balance of the day," Charlie told David as they headed to the morgue. "She has skating in the morning, and then in the afternoon she'll be down at the high school working on construction after she helps Angus in his garden. Hopefully we'll link up with her in time tonight to be at the rehearsal."

"Hopefully," David sighed. "When do we have to be down at the airport to get on the flight for London?"

"Tomorrow at eight," the mention of the flight instantly put Charlie into a black mood. "I hate the idea of going back there, David. Getting dressed up in all of that nonsense, parading outside Windsor Castle dressed up like a Christmas turkey: I detest it all with a passion."What I hate most of all is what Katya's going through right now," Charlie sighed. "We're having to farm her out to everyone. My greatest hope was that she would have a life with a stable family situation. I've only seen her a few hours this week."

David put his hand in hers and squeezed it. "I know that, love. Everybody does. This is not the life we planned back in January. Things have changed, we've had to adapt to that change." After parking their car, they walked into the cool darkness of the morgue.

"Splendid old building," Charlie commented cryptically as they walked through the long, nineteenth century corridors. "It reminds me of the old London Hospital where I took my medical training."

"I think it looks like an old haunted house: weird and creepy. I always liked the fact that you got your medical training in the hospital where Jack the Ripper used to hang out," David said as they turned a corner. "It's like a homey family tradition."

"Mr. Stone, you are macabre and twisted at times. Sir Charles Warren tried to bring the Ripper to justice, not 'hang out' with him as you so improperly suggest," Charlie replied as they passed a man wheeling a gurney with a long black vinyl bag draping an anonymous form. "You are unjustly maligning my family again."

"Guilty as charged," David smirked. "Thank you for calling me macabre and twisted, Charlie. That's the nicest thing you've said to me in a long time. This is the place I went to last September when I was investigating the Jenny Thatcher murder. The Chief Medical Examiner's a really neat lady. You'll like her, Charlie," David said as they came into the office.

They were directed by the secretary to go to Autopsy Suite 12. Dr Evelyn Woodward was waiting for them. Evelyn was a tall, middle-aged African-American lady whose face was permanently fixed with a wry smile. She never took herself seriously. This trait allowed her to stay reasonably sane in the midst of all the gore and mayhem she was exposed to on a daily basis.

"I see business is booming, Evelyn. They're lining up in the hallways just waiting to see you," David said in a light tone as they walked into her office.

"It certainly is. Standing room only, as a matter of fact. Everyone's just dying to get into this place," Evelyn shot back in a breezy tone. "Hello, Detective Stone, nice to see you again."

"That's pretty good, Ev," David replied, grasping Dr. Woodward's hand warmly.

Dr. Woodward smiled. "I see you've brought your famous wife along with you. I'm glad to finally meet you, Dr. Warren! It's not every day that medical examiners get mixed up in all sorts of interesting adventures. Welcome to my haunted mansion."

"More like unmitigated disasters," Charlie replied, blushing. "It's good to meet you, Dr Woodward. I go by Charlie. I can see you and my husband share the same sense of sick, twisted humor."

"Evelyn," Dr. Woodward responded. "Yes we do. Dave and I became good friends last September. By the way, my teenaged daughter has finally gotten interested in a medical career, thanks to you. Andrea thinks my job is gross, but she says you're really cool. She wants to be just like you some day."

"Sounds like a great career choice," David chimed in. Charlie nudged him in the ribs. "Are our colleagues from NYPD and the FBI here?"

Woodward's face assumed a pained expression. "Yes, they are. There's a nice FBI agent and a sour-faced female detective whose sergeant just polished off all of the donuts in our break room."

"Reynolds and Meyers strike again," David said wryly. "I should have warned you about Ron Meyers and donuts."

"I know all about Ron," Evelyn countered. "He's a good friend. I had the guys buy extra this morning because I knew he was coming by."

They walked into the autopsy suite. "Excuse me, Evelyn, but I'm not dressed for this party," Charlie told Dr. Woodward. "Is there some place I can change into some scrubs?"

Evelyn was embarrassed. "Of course. What was I thinking? The tacky-looking scrub suits are down the hallway."

Charlie took out her weapon and handed it to David. "Gun-bearer: hold this."

"Yes, mem-sahib," David smirked as Charlie left the room.

"You two fit well together," Evelyn noted. Reynolds and Meyers came into the room, along with Special Agent Rawlings.

"Why are you here, Stone? Your obnoxious wife was invited, but you weren't," Reynolds said in a nasty tone.

"Hello yourself, Bren. Nice to see you again," David replied in a tone that matched hers exactly. Brenda Reynolds detested having her name shortened. "I was ordered to accompany Charlie by my superior officer. Someone had to protect you from her."

"I don't need protection from anyone, especially from that twerp doctor you married," Brenda snapped. "Just shut up and stay out of the way."

"Still sore about this morning, I see," David observed, turning to Ron Meyers. "Nice to see you again, Ron." He leaned closer to

Meyers. "Did they get the pictures?"

Meyers nodded, pitching his voice low so Brenda couldn't hear. "Yeah, they did. McKinley got some great ones with his cell phone."

"Great," David nodded. "Burn me a copy when you get one."

"Glad to have you on board, Detective Stone. You come highly recommended." Agent Rawlings came over and shook David's hand.

"I'm glad to be here," David replied, looking at Brenda. "I was told to run interference for Charlie by Carl Davis."

"Good luck on that one. I've already had to sit on Reynolds once," Rawlings said, glancing at Brenda, who was looking about the autopsy suite nervously.

Charlie reappeared a few moments later dressed in a scrub suit that was grotesquely too large for her. She looked like a little girl in pajamas. David stifled a guffaw as he looked at her.

"What's so funny, David?" Charlie asked.

"You look you just got out of bed," David snickered.

"Stop it!" Charlie said, frowning at him. She turned to Evelyn. "You'll have to forgive my husband egregious lack of manners, Evelyn. He forgets to mind his manners in public sometimes."

"Guilty as charged," David replied with a smirk.

"Let's can the comedy and get on with this, okay?" Brenda Reynolds didn't appreciate the levity. Meyers and Rawlings looked at Brenda and exchanged exasperated looks with each other.

Evelyn Woodward was deeply amused by the exchange. Walking over to the sheeted body on the table, she drew the sheet back to expose their shooting victim. It was not an appetizing sight. "Come along, children, and let me have you meet Mr. Hubert Quimby, attorney at law."

"He doesn't look too good," David observed.

"Most people don't when half of their lower faces are missing," Charlie nudged him. "Attempt to be professional, please."

"All right," David said in a falsely contrite tone. He cleared his throat and assumed a more serious voice. "Was the slug retrieved from the crime scene?"

"Yes it was," Reynolds and Meyers replied simultaneously. Brenda shot David an irritated glance. "Stone, there are plenty of real detectives here. You're just an observer, so just shut up for a while."

"He's here because I want him here, Lieutenant, and I think his question is perfectly relevant." Rawlings replied quickly with some heat. "Feel free to comment at any time when you see something, Detective Stone."

"Let's continue with our exam, people," Evelyn said in an indulgent tone. "He was shot with a high powered rifle from approximately fifty yards away. From what we got at the crime scene, the shooter was about level with Mr. Quimby when he was shot."

Charlie came up to the body. "Single shot severing the brainstem. It's obviously a professional job."

"The work of a sniper," Dr. Woodward agreed. "The round was a 7.62. That's an unusual size for a sniper bullet."

"Not for a Soviet-style round," Rawlings chimed in. "The Soviets use larger caliber rounds for their sniper rifles."

"The lab confirmed it was a Soviet round. We also recovered traces of gunshot residue on a windowsill in a building just across the street from Quimby's office. Trace ran the round through the FBI data banks, and we got a match. The round was fired from a weapon implicated in a number of unsolved shootings involving the Russian mob here in New York." Brenda said. "The sniper didn't leave any cartridges lying about."

"There are no other signs of injury to the body," Evelyn continued. "He fell face forward onto the desk. Death was instantaneous."

"And messy," David added. Charlie glowered at him. "Well, it was, wasn't it?"

"Stone, if you can't say anything intelligent, just shut up," Brenda snapped.

"Okay, children: another outburst and I'm sending you all to the time-out corner," Rawlings raised his hand. "We've established a reasonable cause of death, Dr. Woodward; is there anything else you can tell us about this man?"

"Nothing strikes me as unusual," Woodward replied. "The drug tox screen on his blood was negative. I'll know a little bit more about him when I do the autopsy. By the way, Dr. Warren, would you care to assist?"

"I'll be happy to help," Charlie replied cheerfully, moving in closer to the table and picking up a scalpel.

"Do you really need us here for this?" Brenda asked in an irritated tone.

"Yes we do, Detective," Rawlings replied quickly. "This is part of your investigation, so let's get on with it. Go ahead, Doctors; proceed with the autopsy."

Ron Meyers looked at his partner. Brenda did not like autopsies, which was strange, considering her profession as a homicide detective. Her face was turning greener by the minute.

"Are you going to need a chair, Detective?" Meyers asked solicitously. "I can get you one if you like."

"No," Brenda shot back through clinched teeth, shaking her head. Charlie noted the exchange, but wisely said nothing.

"Do you ladies need any help?" David asked the two doctors hopefully. Meyers and Rawlings looked at each other and moved away from David cautiously.

"David helped me in England on an autopsy," Charlie explained to Dr. Woodward in an understanding tone. "He really warmed up to the whole thing."

"Oh, I see," a slow smile spread over Evelyn's face. "Once you get bit by the bug, it's all over. No, Detective, this is my show today. Charlie's plenty of help."

"You are so sick, Stone," Brenda Reynolds sniffed. Her face was growing dangerously green. She swayed slightly, and Ron took up a strategic position close to her in case she started to fall.

"Go ahead, Charlie," Evelyn Woodward nodded. Charlie was about to make the first incision on Quimby's chest when there was a rustle of clothing and a thud behind them.

"Oops! Watch her head!" Meyers called out to Rawlings as they caught Brenda Reynolds' body as she slumped to the floor in a dead faint.

"Chairs are over in the corner, guys," Evelyn called offhandedly over her shoulder as she and Charlie settled down to work. "Emesis basins are in the cabinet by the sink. The mop and bucket are down the hallway. Help yourself. Meyers, you know the drill."

"Thanks Ev," With David's assistance, Ron Meyers draped his stricken leader in a chair. "Shootings, stabbings, multiple murders, she's okay. But get her next to an autopsy table, and it's light's out for Brenda."

"She's wearing her hair differently, Ron," David observed as Brenda remained unconscious. "It looks good. Are you two finally starting to date?"

"Nah. I finally got her to go out for dinner the other day," Meyers told him. "I told her it was a cop thing, so she agreed."

"And you didn't get shot?"

"Nope."

"That's progress." David said approvingly. "She looks a good deal like Karen right now."

"Yeah," Meyers said wistfully. "I just wish she'd relax a little bit."

David slapped a hand on Ron's shoulder. "There's always hope, buddy."

-0-

Brenda came to just as Charlie and Evelyn were finishing up the autopsy. "So as you can see, gentlemen, there's no other indication of foul play on the body, other than the gunshot wound." Dr. Woodward was talking to Rawlings and David. Meyers had strategically placed himself close by his fallen Lieutenant.

"Hey, Lieutenant, glad to see you finally waking up." Meyers said in a carefully neutral voice. "The autopsy's about over."

Brenda shook her head and attempted to jump to her feet. That was a mistake. She lost her balance and nearly bowled into Meyers. "Whoa! Whoa, Lieutenant! Easy does it!" Meyers said as he finally righted her.

Charlie came over to them after taking off her gloves. "Are you all right, Lieutenant?" she asked in a solicitous tone.

"Of course I am!" Brenda snarled, massaging her head. "I'm perfectly fine! I just have difficulty with autopsies, that's all. Save your fake pity for someone else, Warren."

Rawlings turned to Charlie. "Rosson told me you might be headed over to LuxVeritas. See if you can rattle a few cages, Dr. Warren."

"Cage-rattling is my specialty," Charlie replied with a wink. She looked down at her scrubs. "You'll have to excuse me, but I need to change into street clothes again."

"Why change? You look so cute in your scrubs," David said, earning another dirty look from his bride.

"David, your score is climbing ever upward," Charlie reminded him in a threatening tone.

David shrugged elaborately. "This is news?"

Meyers came up to David after Charlie left the room. "She's really great, Dave. How did you manage to land her?"

"I have no idea, buddy," David replied. "I'll tell you about it sometime when your exalted leader isn't around."

Meyers glanced over at Reynolds, who was engaged in some sort of earnest argument with Rawlings. "I wish she'd just turn it off for a minute every once in a while."

"Yeah, it would be nice," David turned to Evelyn Woodward, who had just returned from carting the body off to the storage area. "Thanks for the help, Ev. Always a pleasure to see you."

"Likewise," Evelyn Woodward smiled. "Charlie and I were talking in the hallway about a mutual friend you ran into in England. Jessica Gray was one of my pathology pupils."

David's eyebrows shot up. "Really? You know Jessica Gray? We had her and her family out to our place over a month ago. Jessica's a riot, and her family is really great."

"Yeah, they are," Evelyn agreed. She paused for a moment. "Look Dave, you need to be careful. The guys who did this to Quimby are really nasty. They'll stop at nothing. Keep your eye on Charlie. If this case has the Russians involved, it's going to be very ugly. I've had to do a number of autopsies on some of their victims. They don't play around."

"We'll be careful, Ev. I know all about the Russians," David told her as Charlie came up. He handed Charlie's gun back to her with a slight bow. "Your blunderbuss, madam. You know that cannon you carry around is about as big as you are, kiddo."

"Dispense with the personal remarks, if you please," Charlie rewarded him with a kiss as she took her pistol back from her husband. "You owe me lunch for all of the abuse I've suffered at your hands this morning."

"Abuse? What abuse? If you say that I've abused you, then it's okay," David conceded, turning to everyone else in the room. "Why don't we make it a company affair? Ev, are you up for lunch? Apparently I'm buying for everybody, at least that's what Charlie's telling me."

"Meyers and I have work to do," Brenda said, flatly. Meyers looked crushed.

"Gotta take a rain check, Dave. I have more clients waiting," Evelyn said with a disappointed look on her face.

"Okay, it's a date. Some other time. We'll see you again soon, Evelyn," David said with a smile. "I want some more Jessica stories to tease her with. She's almost as crazy as Charlie."

Evelyn laughed. She turned and shook Charlie's hand. "It was a pleasure working with you, Charlie. We'll be in touch."

A thought occurred to her. "Charlie, could I see you in my office for a moment?"

"Sure," Charlie glanced at David for a second, who nodded and shrugged his shoulders. Leaving David with the two detectives and Rawlings, she followed Evelyn down the corridor to a medium-sized but sumptuously appointed office.

"Charlie, I just thought about something. I want to make you an offer, something I'd like you to think about," Evelyn said as she closed the old oak door. "We have a position on our staff that's coming open in the next month or so, and I'd love to have you come on board."

Dr. Woodward's offer took Charlie by surprise. "Really? I'm flattered that you'd consider me for it. Right now I'm quite happy with my position at Compton."

Evelyn refused to be put off. "I understand that, Charlie, but you'd have a position that pays about twice as much, and the cases would be far more interesting. You'd also have the chance to teach, and I know you love to do that. There are at least half a dozen medical schools that would love to have you join their faculties. We're only a forty-minute commute from your home, so you wouldn't have to move."

"Thank you for thinking about me, Evelyn. Your offer is incredibly generous and very tempting," Charlie replied graciously. "I appreciate the offer, but right now my life is very full."

"So I've heard," Evelyn laughed. "Jessica and I talk on a regular basis. She told me you're up to your neck in projects in the community as well as working with your church. I wish I had half your energy. Well, I can see you're not going to take the bait, but the offer still stands."

Charlie reached over and squeezed Evelyn's hand. "Thank you for considering me. It means a lot to me to know that you'd make such a generous offer."

"All right then," Evelyn laughed, opening up her office door. "I wanted to make the offer, even though I already knew it was a long shot you'd accept. Thanks for stopping by and helping. We'll keep in touch."

"Where are you going next, Lieutenant?" Charlie politely asked Reynolds as she rejoined the two detectives, Rawlings and David.

"We're going to go over to Quimby's apartment," Detective Reynolds replied briskly. "We'll get back to you later." She turned and left the autopsy suite with Meyers in tow.

Rawlings watched the two detectives with disapproval as they walked down the hall. "Has Reynolds allowed you to help at all with this case?"

"No," Charlie replied quietly. "We've been on the outside looking in."

"That's what I figured. I contacted her captain yesterday," Rawlings explained. "Meyers is not the problem; it's Reynolds that needs the attitude adjustment. She's been put on notice to get a grip on her attitude. I'm not impressed that she freaked out at the autopsy. The whole objective of having officers attend the autopsy is to have them hear what the ME has to say. Reynolds is supposed to be pretty sharp. So far, I'm not impressed."

"I think that's because I'm around. For some reason, the woman detests me. Even if she'd been conscious, I doubt if she'd listen to anything I would have had to say to her anyway."

"She still needs to get a grip," Rawlings shrugged. "Let me give you some information about this outfit you're going to visit. LuxVeritas is a legitimate company. It's one of those multinational enterprises. Tons of overseas investments and all that. Most of its dealings are completely legitimate, though we've been seeing some shady stuff cropping up in the last few months. They've been buying up a lot of property over on the East River side of town. That's the official reason why they're interested in your warehouse.

"You two need to keep an eye on what's happening down at that warehouse, Dr. Warren. Reynolds and Meyers can do the footwork on the murders, but I'm counting on you two to keep things tied together. My agents are working the Russian angles and the intelligence parts of this operation. By the way, nice work on the autopsy today, Doctor. And yes, I will take you up on your lunch offer some other time."

Charlie held up a hand. "Wonderful; we'll be glad to have you along, and thank you for the compliment. I'm not sure how much I contributed. Evelyn could have handled everything herself."

"I still appreciate your observations," Rawlings paused for a moment. "Do you think the body of that British Intellligence agent is linked to your warehouse and this terrorist threat?"

"I don't know," Charlie shook her head. "If the time line is as short as you say it is, then we don't have a lot of time to find out."

-0-

"Did Evelyn Woodward offer you a job?" David asked once they were clear of the building.

"Yes, she did. She made a very generous offer," Charlie said as she opened the drivers-side door of their van. "One I'd almost be tempted to consider."

"Almost? Charlie, come on: you're wasting your time with the ME's job in Compton," David pointed out after he climbed in and closed his door. "Everyone in town knows you're there because it's close to home."

"I have people who depend on me at the ME's office, David. They work incredibly hard, and they deserve support. I can't just go off and abandon them simply because someone tickles my ego. Besides, I have my family to think about."

David was unconvinced. "You're thinking about this one. I can tell. No one's going to hate you if you decide to take it."

Charlie nodded as they merged into the stream of traffic. "I'll remember that, David."

13

LuxVeritas Corporation was located in a soulless glass tower on the lower side of Manhattan. As with most major buildings in New York City, Charlie and David had to pass through a security checkpoint flanked by metal detectors to get into the building.

"I'm sorry, Detective," one of the security guards told David. "We're going to have to insist that you leave your pistol with us."

"No problem," David said, handing over his pistol. "What about her?" He pointed to Charlie.

"I'm not carrying a weapon, silly. Why would I want to carry a gun?" she rewarded him with a bright, vacant smile. They had already decided before they got to the building that Charlie would play the part of an airhead. "I'm perfectly harmless." She placed her handbag on the conveyer belt.

"Right," David replied dubiously.

"She's clear," the other guard said after Charlie passed through the scanner. The guard handed Charlie her handbag and they proceeded to the elevator.

"Maybe we should have mentioned your skills in unarmed combat," David murmured as they came to the elevator, joining a group of waiting people.

"Shut up, David," Charlie muttered softly, jabbing his side for emphasis.

"Or your unhealthy interest in edged weapons."

"Stop it."

"Why?"

"Because if you don't, I may have to hurt you publicly."

"Okay."

They rode the elevator up to the fourteenth floor and proceeded to the teak-lined offices of LuxVeritas Corporation. An elegantly dressed receptionist rose to greet them as they passed through the door.

"May I help you?" she purred.

"Why yes, you can," Charlie replied in a syrupy-sweet voice, "My name is Dr. Charlene Warren, and this is my husband, David Stone. Your company expressed an interest in acquiring some property I own down on the East River."

Charlie decided it was time to turn on the drama. "Something terrible happened yesterday, something awful! I... I don't know what to do, so I came here for help. Can you help me, miss?" She turned to cry into David's shoulder.

Oh brother, this is going to be bad, David thought to himself as he held his weeping wife. *I hope she doesn't lay it on too thick.* "It's all right, Charlie," he finally said. "I'm sure this lovely lady will help us." Charlie continued to sob bitterly into David's jacket.

It's too late: she's going to lay it on. David started to shake with silent laughter, and Charlie attempted to stop him with some not-so-soft blows to his back.

Charlie's hysterical, over-the-top performance worked. The woman's eyes went soft with pity. "Of course I can," she swiftly dialed a number. "Mr. Decker? Yes, I have a Dr. Warren and her husband out here. They've come to ask some questions about some property we're acquiring along the East River. Oh you do? All right, I'll tell them you'll be out in a minute."

She hung up the phone. "Mr. Decker will be with you in just a moment. Would you like some tissues, Dr. Warren?" Charlie disengaged herself from her husband's embrace, nodded mutely and pulled out an oversized wad of facial tissues from the box the secretary offered. Blowing her nose loudly, Charlie stuffed the tissues into her purse.

Mr. Decker arrived on the scene just in time to save the day. "Dr. Warren, please come in," he puffed. Robert Decker was a rather stout gentleman with close-cropped sandy hair. He moved his bulk out of the doorway to let David and Charlie pass into his office.

"Please sit down," Decker motioned to two chairs in front of his massive oak desk. "Ms. Lipscomb told me you were here about some property?"

"Oh, Mr. Decker," Charlie began tearfully. "It was so awful! That nice man's head was blown off right in front of my eyes. I didn't know what to do! I had awful nightmares last night because of it. That's why we're here today, to see if you could help me." She started to weep violently into her wad of tissues.

Decker fell for it immediately. "That's all right, Dr. Warren," he said sympathetically. "We'll try to make things as easy as possible." LuxVeritas had been expecting a visit from the police ever since Quimby's murder. Instead of police officers asking tough questions, Charlie and David had arrived and had made their job of damage control apparently easier.

Charlie's weeping subsided and she honked loudly into her wad of tissues. "Thank you," she dabbed at her eyes with exaggerated delicacy. She glanced at David. "My husband and I were wondering if you could tell us why LuxVeritas wanted my property in the first place. It would help us ever so much in making a decision."

I'm going to lose it if she keeps this up, David thought to himself. He grimaced in pain as Charlie squeezed his shoulder tightly. "Yes, Mr. Decker. We appreciate any help you could give us," he managed to say.

"Of course," Mr. Decker sat back, relieved the conversation had gone in this direction. "I'd be delighted to show you our plans for the area. They're really quite spectacular." He heaved himself out of his chair. "Let me take you to our development department."

Charlie and David rose and followed Mr. Decker out of his office and down several corridors to a large open office area filled with cubicles. People were bustling about, and the air was filled with the sound of murmuring voices, ringing phones, and humming machines. "As you can see, we're very busy right now," Decker said over his shoulder as he whisked them along.

"Here we are," he said as they arrived at a door marked DEVELOPMENT. Decker opened the door and they passed into a room filled with people and drafting tables.

"Rick, can we see the model for the East River project?" Decker asked one of the architects.

"Sure," the man replied. "It's over by Bill's table."

They went over to the place where the man indicated. "And here we are," Decker said proudly as they stood before a model of a skyscraper. "Veritas Tower: eighty stories high. Impressive, isn't it?"

Charlie's eyes went wide with wonder. "It most certainly is," she exclaimed in an awed tone. Actually, she thought it looked like a purple soup can attempting to mate with an orange cereal box, but she kept these thoughts to herself. Instead, she turned to David with a gooey expression on her face. "Oh David; it's awfully beautiful! We really must get those papers back from the police as soon as possible so we can sign them."

Decker's happy smile froze on his face. "You... you don't have the papers the lawyer gave you?"

Charlie's face blanched. "Why no, Mr. Decker. The... the police took them from us. They said they were evidence."

"I ... I see," Decker stammered, ushering them quickly away from the model and shooing them out the department door. He moved them swiftly through the office area and back to his office with amazing speed. It was obvious that their lack of the documents had upset his plans. "I'm sorry, Dr. Warren, but we really need to have those papers as soon as possible. You understand, of course."

"Yes we do, don't we, dear?" David looked down at Charlie.

"Of course, darling," Charlie replied with utter devotion. "It's just that... that poor man's brains and blood were smeared all over the papers! It was just awful!" She broke down and started to weep violently again.

Decker came to the rescue. "You've already said that, Dr. Warren. Our legal department will draft up another set of papers as soon as we can. We're glad you're interested in selling the property. We'll contact you as soon as they're ready."

"Oh thank you, thank you so much for understanding!" Charlie replied with gratitude dripping from her voice.

"Yes, thank you," David chimed in. "You have made this awful experience so much better for us."

Decker held up a hand. "Not at all; it's been my pleasure." He walked them to the door of his office and opened it. "We'll be seeing you soon then."

"Of course, thank you again, Mr. Decker," Charlie sneezed violently and blew her nose into the tissues. She rubbed her face, wiped her hands and then offered one of her hands to Decker for him to shake. He did so reluctantly, smiled bleakly and then closed his door.

David and Charlie turned and headed for the elevator. "He was so nice, wasn't he, David?" Charlie said, leaning into David for support.

"Yes, he was awfully wonderful," David replied in a carefully neutral tone. He squeezed her shoulder, and she nodded silently back. *We're being watched*, his gesture told her.

They said nothing to each other as the elevator took them to ground level. Charlie continued to sniff and alternately dab at eyes and nose with her tissues. The door opened and they approached the security checkpoint.

"Hope everything went well, Detective," the guard said as he handed David's pistol back to him.

"You might say that," David replied enigmatically. He looked at Charlie, who was busy applying some makeup. "Are you ready to go now, dear?"

"Of course, darling," Charlie finished applying her war paint. "I'm so glad they were so understanding. Let's go."

They left arm in arm, traveling quickly to their parked minivan. Charlie took out a small key fob and prepared to open her door with her key. The fob actually was a small scanning device that swept the car for listening devices. The tiny light stayed green, indicating there were no devices in the car. Opening the door, she climbed into the minivan. David got into the driver's side, started the van, and they drove off.

Two blocks away from the building, David's composure broke. "You little pest! You nearly beat me to death while erupting into my jacket. I'm going to make sure you pay for the dry cleaning bill, and then to top everything off, you nearly squeezed my arm in two!" He said laughingly, massaging his arm.

Charlie couldn't answer him at the moment; she had completely lost it. Charlie was in the front seat of the van in the middle of a fit of giggles. "I… I couldn't help myself, David," she finally gasped, tears streaming down her face. "Every time I blew my nose, you got the most awful expression on your face. I had to do something or I was going to become completely unglued." She looked over at him and then burst out into peals of laughter.

David started laughing as well. "You already are unglued, Pest. Now stop being hysterical in the front seat, or I'll wreck this van. People are starting to look at us." He calmed down after a minute. "Do you think they bought it?"

"I don't know, David," Charlie finally calmed down and wiped her eyes. "We'll find out soon enough."

-0-

"What do you think, Ivan?" a man asked his partner, a tall, thickly built man who stared at a monitor screen. On it were the images of Charlie and David in Decker's office.

"So this is the daughter of John Warren," Ivan Kolov's voice dripped contempt. "She is a weak little fool, and her husband is a stupid man."

"Appearances may be deceiving," his friend countered. "Our contacts in the Police Department tell us she is a formidable opponent."

"Nonsense, Stefan," Kolov replied with a sneer. "She is nothing. Our plans will proceed accordingly. Make sure everything is ready."

"Yes sir," Stefan replied, carefully keeping the skepticism out of his voice. Ivan Kolov was not a man to be crossed. Once he issued an order, the time for discussion was over.

-0-

While David and Charlie were over at LuxVeritas, James Rosson drove with MacKay down to the warehouse they had visited last night. "Sir Leslie told me that Major Warren probably wanted to make sure that the dismantling of BSC operations was carried out, but not to the extent that BSC key operations would be jeopardized."

"Which means that key components of the operation may still be in place after all these years," MacKay amplified.

They had arrived at the warehouse, an anonymous block of dirty brown brick that gleamed dully in the morning sunlight. "The place certainly looks different in the daylight." Rosson observed.

"Indeed it does," MacKay agreed. "This is the last place I'd look for some sort of intelligence operation to be going on."

The old building had a stark, weathered look, as though it had seen too many harsh winters and bleaching hot summers. MacKay kicked away an old can in front of him. "Where do you want to start, sir?" he finally asked.

"Where we left off last night, Sergeant Major."

They went around to the side entrance that they had discovered last night. The door was easily opened, and once again, they were inside the empty warehouse.

"Do you notice something strange about this place?" James asked MacKay.

"There's no dust on the floor. I missed it last night because it was dark. The place is completely clean. It's empty, but it's been kept up, maintained, if you follow me."

MacKay nodded. "You're right, sir. I can feel a constant current of air in this place. There's no musty smell in here. It's as though the air in this place is being filtered and recirculated."

He turned around and looked at the entire empty space of the building. "I remember seeing this sort of thing done where there are pieces of high-tech hardware being used."

"I wonder if this place has a basement," Rosson mused. "Perhaps there is a passageway that ties into those subterranean tunnels where Cartwright was found."

"I don't know," Donald MacKay replied. "I think I'm following you, sir. There might be a connection underneath this building."

"There might indeed."

They left the empty warehouse floor and went searching for an entrance to a staircase. They found a series of side rooms off of the main floor, but nothing that indicated a staircase to a lower level.

"Looks like we've hit a dead end, sir," MacKay admitted ruefully to Rosson at the conclusion of their search. "I don't see anything that indicates this place has an access to a basement."

"Let's not give up so easily, Sergeant Major. There's got to be a way into that area. We're hearing machinery, and that means it's running on electrical power," Rosson pointed out. "Let's go outside the building and search for power lines. That might indicate where there's an access point."

MacKay looked down at the floor next to a corner and became quite still. He had finally found something. "That won't be necessary, sir. I think I've found the entry point." MacKay pushed against a section of wooden-faced interior wall in the room. The wall swung back silently, revealing a narrow spiral staircase.

Both men drew their weapons. "Well, well," James muttered softly. "Into the looking glass we go. Excellent work, Sergeant Major."

"Careful, sir," MacKay cautioned, edging down the stairs. "That panel opened a little too easily for my liking."

The two men climbed slowly down the spiral stairs, alert for any signs of danger. The air of the stairwell was surprisingly fresh; there was no odor of mold and decay that normally permeated old buildings . The staircase ended in a small landing which led to a narrow corridor. Rosson was in the lead, and he suddenly stopped, clutching the arm of MacKay in a silent order to halt.

James crept closer to an open door on the right hand side of the corridor. Carefully, he edged the door open, moving quickly into the room, sweeping it with his flashlight and gun. MacKay was right behind him.

The room stretched away from them for about fifty feet in either direction. It was filled with bank after bank of humming machines.

"Have you ever seen the like, sir?" MacKay asked in awed tones. "It looks like some sort of computer room."

"It is a computer, Sergeant Major," Rosson replied. "A very, very old computer. I've seen one like this before over in Britain."

"What is it, sir?"

"It looks like something I saw over at a place called Bletchley Park." Rosson said slowly. "I've never heard of anything like that being constructed anywhere else in the world."

Rosson was suddenly aware of the danger he and MacKay were in. "Sergeant Major, we need to leave this place. This machine has been turned on recently. The people who did that will return soon. We don't need to be here."

"Right, sir," MacKay nodded sharply, glancing about. "We've seen enough this trip."

They closed the door quietly and returned to the staircase. Rosson led the way up the staircase into the small room where the door was located. "I think we've managed to remain undetected, Sergeant Major." He said in hushed tones.

MacKay pulled the hidden panel shut. "Yes sir. We got lucky this time." He glanced about the room. "I don't think there's anything else we need to see in here today."

"I want to check the exterior of the building," James said, holstering his pistol. "I have a feeling this old building has a few more surprises in store for us."

"Right, sir," MacKay led the way out to the exterior of the building. They searched around the entire perimeter of the warehouse, but they could find no wires leading into any of the outside walls.

"Buildings of this type were simply constructed," Rosson pointed out at the end of their search. "Back when this place was built, no one wasted their time with buried cables and the like. Warehouses are built with practicality in mind, not aesthetics."

He paused for a moment. "Except this building. It's quite unusual. There are no wires or attachment points for electrical transformers."

Rosson frowned. "Perhaps it's been modified in some way to make it self-contained."

"Sir, we can call Rawlings and they can come down with sophisticated equipment that can help in our search." MacKay told him. "I'm sure they can locate power sources with some of their infrared scanners."

"Excellent point, Sergeant Major," Rosson nodded. "I forgot for a moment that we had devices like that available to us. Let's get into the car and drive back to the consulate."

"What did Michael Warren do after the War, sir?" MacKay asked as they drove through the busy streets. "Sir Leslie seemed to be a bit vague on that point of our investigation."

"That's because there isn't much to tell," Rosson replied. "I know that he taught history at Oxford. Sir Leslie said that Warren was involved in government business, but the exact nature of that business is something he knew nothing about.

"Intelligence operations following the War were thrown into chaos. All of the efforts had been bent towards defeating the Nazis and the Japanese. Once that job was done, everyone eagerly tore down intelligence agencies and bundled them away."

James sighed. "All right, Sergeant Major, I think we've done as much as we can at this building. We can come down here later on today with the FBI and see if their gadgets can yield anything."

"Sir, did you notice that we were only able to get into a rather small section of the building?" MacKay pointed out. "I mean, the building stretches on and on for several hundred feet, and we could only get into less than a fourth of it."

"I see your point, Sergeant Major," Rosson agreed. "It's as though the rest of the building was a self-contained unit. There are doors along the side for cargo to go in, but they are all sealed shut."

His face furrowed in thought. "I seem to remember seeing buildings like this along the European coast. I just can't seem to remember where, or why they were constructed this way." Rosson shook his head and looked at the picture of the warehouse in his hand.

He got out his cell phone and called the consulate. "Hello? Have Warren and Stone checked in yet? Oh, they have. All right, please let them know we'll meet them at the consulate in a few minutes. Thank you."

Rosson hung up and put the phone away. "It's been a most interesting morning, Sergeant Major."

MacKay nodded. "It has indeed, sir."

-0-

I hate pounding the pavement in scummy neighborhoods and endless interviews, Meyers thought to himself as he pulled their car up to the pavement flanking a rundown apartment building on the east side. The neighborhood reminded him of the area he used to patrol as a beat cop. The apartment building was a five-story dump with heaps of trash flanking the entrance. The odor was especially flavorful in the late afternoon sun.

Meyers wiped his head with a handkerchief. It was a boiling hot day in June, and they were stuck in a really crumby neighborhood. It was a cinch that the place they were going to had no air conditioning. This was not going to be pretty.

Brenda hated the heat, and her nerves were still raw from her dressing down by the captain last night, along with her defeat by Charlie at the gym. Dealing with the FBI and Charlie Warren that morning had left her in an even fouler mood than before.

"I love the smell of New York in June," he said to no one in particular. Brenda Reynolds shot him a venomous glance as she climbed out of her side of the car.

"Shut up, Meyers. Let's get this nonsense done now. This place stinks." She slammed her door for emphasis. The ever-sensitive car alarm went off.

"Now, now, Lieutenant: let's look on the bright side," Meyers said as he unlocked and carefully closed her door gently. "At least there won't be any dead body smelling up the place."

A particularly pungent wave of odor wafted across from the phalanx of overflowing garbage cans in front of the building. "Bets?" Brenda asked, trying to hold her breath as they ran the gauntlet to the door.

"This investigation's going nowhere," she grumbled, pressing the filthy off-white button underneath a bent brass plate labeled LANDLORD. The door opened, revealing a battered fat woman whose face looked like an old road map.

"Whadda ya want?" she rasped, looking at the two detectives as though they'd just stepped off a Martian spaceship. Her breath smelled like she feasted regularly on the garbage can outside the door.

Meyers positioned himself upwind of the old woman's breath and presented his badge and a warrant. "NYPD. We're here to search Hubert Quimby's apartment."

"Huh?" the hag choked. "I just let two of you clowns up there two hours ago. They was better lookin' than you." She hawked and spit for emphasis.

"Look, ma'am, we have a warrant, so just spare us the wise remarks and get us the keys," Brenda snarled at the woman, who looked at her and promptly went back into her hole.

"Good aim," Meyers pointed to the glob of mucus slithering down the door on the opposite wall. The hag appeared a moment later with the keys. Reynolds snatched the keys without another word, bounding up the stairs two at a time.

Meyers turned to the old woman. "Thanks," he nodded. The woman shook her head and retreated back into her lair.

Ron had negotiated the final step when Brenda called out to him from Quimby's apartment. "They've tossed the place already, Meyers." Her tone was filled with bitter disgust.

Meyers arrived at the door and peered in. "How can you tell?"

It was obvious from the layered disarray of the apartment that Mr. Quimby had not been a fastidious housekeeper. The place was ankle deep in old pizza boxes, half-eaten sandwiches, and at least two months of newspapers. All of the ancient lamps were overturned, and the few pieces of furniture had been reduced to fragments of broken wood and plastic.

"It's always a pleasure to deal with professionals," Meyers smirked as he gazed upon the destruction. His chieftain was sitting on what was left of an old chair in complete disgust. "Come on, Lieutenant. We can call CSI and they can see if they can get something out of all of this."

Brenda moodily swatted an industrial strength cockroach that was crawling across her shoe. "Right, like that's going to help. I have an idea: let's burn the place down and save ourselves the trouble."

"You know, in some countries, you could be arrested and charged with homicide for icing that roach, Lieutenant," Meyers pointed out. "It could be somebody's auntie or uncle."

"What are you babbling about, Meyers?" Brenda snarled. "Is this your attempt at humor?"

"Yeah," Meyers shrugged. "Cheer up, Lieutenant. We still might get lucky."

A stray piece of paper resting under a badly decomposed pizza caught Reynold's eye. "Hold on: the goons may have overlooked something." She picked it up. "I think we have a note on LuxVeritas stationary addressed to Quimby."

Ron came over and looked at the sauce-stained note. "'Make

sure Warren signs the papers and suspects nothing.' It looks like we've got a motive in our murder investigation, Lieutenant."

Reynolds reached for her phone. "That's a start. The morons who tossed this place may have overlooked other stuff. Let's get CSI over here and process this place."

She waved her hand in front of her face. "Let's get out of here before I hurl, Meyers."

"Okay," Meyers sauntered to the door. "You know, I think my feelings got hurt. That old hag said the clowns who did this were better dressed than us. I spent a lot of money on this coat. I think I look pretty good in it."

"Get over it, Meyers. They make more money than we do," Reynolds commented bleakly, rubbing her head. "We now have three crime scenes and four dead bodies to investigate. You and I are the only real cops assigned to this case. We're going to need help going through all of this mess."

"We could ask Stone and Warren to give us a hand," Meyers suggested hopefully.

"Did you hear what I just said, Meyers? I said you and I were the only real cops assigned to this case. I'd rather kiss a goat than ask those two for help," Brenda shot back instantly. "Those goofballs couldn't think their way out of a paper bag, let alone give us a hand."

"That's not fair, Lieutenant, and you know that," Meyers replied with some heat. Brenda's negative attitude, coupled with the oppressive heat and stench of the apartment, had finally gotten to him. "Warren and Stone are trained investigators. They were assigned with us to this case for a reason. Stone's pretty squared away. Warren taught at the FBI, and you know they don't let just anybody do that.

"So far, you've shut them out almost completely. That's nuts. Let's use their talents, Lieutenant. Don't let your personal prejudices get in the way of this investigation. You're smarter than that, Brenda."

Reynolds stared at Meyers for a few seconds. She nodded slowly. "Okay, Meyers: you may be right about this. I'll admit I can't stand either of those people, but we're getting killed on this investigation. I can't work twenty hours a day, seven days a week, and neither can you. I'll call up the embassy, or consulate, or whatever they call that bunch downtown and send them what we have."

"That's the spirit, Lieutenant," Ron replied cheerfully, thanking heaven that Brenda had finally seen the light. He dialed up CSI and gave them the address. "Let's call some patrol units and get this place secured. CSI says they're backed up, but they'll get to us in about an hour."

Brenda nodded wearily. "More good news. Let's at least wait in the hallway until they arrive. I need to get out of this stink trap before I pass out."

-0-

"We'll get some of our thermographic scanning devices down to that building this afternoon and find out what's going on," Agent Rawlings assured everyone an hour later at the Consulate. "I managed to access some of the old Corps of Engineer records. The building was built back in the 1900's by a company known as British Export Limited. That company was a front for British Intelligence. They ran a big operation out of the British Consulate until 1945."

"That was the British Security Coordination," James Rosson said dryly. "They used New York as a base of operations against the Germans back then."

"It's called strategic planning," Ken Rawlings nodded in agreement. "The Germans had an intelligence network up and running in America way before Pearl Harbor. So did your people, apparently."

"Quite correct, Agent Rawlings," Rosson agreed. "Germany and Britain had been squaring off ever since the last part of the nineteenth century. War between the two nations was inevitable. It stands to reason England would prepare bases of operation over here in America for use, especially if Britain fell to the Germans."

Rawlings continued. "The warehouse was officially listed as a place for shipping and receiving. We've gone back and checked the property listings, and Dr. Warren's grandfather acquired the building back in May of 1945. He paid three million dollars cash for it."

"Interesting," Charlie noted. "That date roughly coincides with Cartwright's arrival in the United States. It also coincides with the official demise of the BSC in America."

"Yes it does," Rosson sat back in his chair for a moment, pondering some ideas that were floating around in his head. "Is there anything else notable about the building, Mr. Rawlings?"

"Not really," Rawlings replied. "As far as the records show, it hasn't been used at all since 1945. It's never been rented or leased to anyone, despite its excellent location on the docks."

"Yet the building itself is in excellent condition on the inside, self-contained, with some sort of environmental system that keeps it dust-free," James mused. "Are there any architectural drawings on record?"

"Nothing I could find. They seem to have been lost, or misplaced."

Charlie smiled enigmatically. "More like destroyed or hidden, I think." She looked at Rawlings. "Is it possible that there are hidden tunnels connected to that building?"

Rawlings rubbed his head. "Yeah, it's possible, more than possible. I've worked in New York for the Bureau for twenty years. There are all sorts of abandoned tunnels and subways and who knows what underneath this city. Back during World War Two they had some service tunnels that connected with the docks to allow underground access in case those areas were bombed. I think I can pull a few strings over at the Corps of Engineers and see if they have some of those old plans lying about."

"That's an excellent idea, Agent Rawlings," James said enthusiastically. "Constructions like that are exactly what we're looking for. That old warehouse would be a perfect candidate for such a tunnel system to exist."

"That subway station isn't too far away from the dock areas and that building," Charlie pointed out. "It could be one of the entrance points into the tunnel system."

"I thought you said the trail you followed in that tunnel wound up at a dead end," Rawlings frowned.

"Back in 1945, it may have led somewhere." Charlie replied with a smile.

"What about your trip to LuxVeritas, Charlie?" James asked. "Any luck in ferreting out why they're so interested in purchasing that building?"

"We were shown the architectural plans of a building LuxVeritas is planning to put up on that area of the East river. Apparently our warehouse is one of the pieces of property they want to acquire." Charlie replied.

"We mentioned Quimby's death, and that seemed to make him uncomfortable," David pointed out.

"Yes, it did," Charlie smiled. "He squirmed like a worm when we mentioned that to him."

"I've got Reynolds and Meyers working on Quimby's death, trying to follow up on the leads from that end. Meyers phoned me about half an hour ago and said that they located some papers with LuxVeritas' name on them in Quimby's apartment," Ken Rawlings stood up from his chair. "I'll have a unit come down to your warehouse this afternoon with some thermographic equipment and see if we can't find some more information on your building."

"Oh yes, speaking of Reynolds and Meyers, I also got a call from Sergeant Meyers this afternoon," James told everyone with a note of triumph in his voice. "It seems that they finally want your assistance and David's in the investigation, Charlie. They are going to fax all of the reports over to the Consulate later on this afternoon. We'll send them on with you to Great Britain."

"Hallelujah, light dawns in the NYPD," Agent Rawlings observed sardonically, winking at Charlie for emphasis. "Reynolds is bright, but she has a stubborn streak a mile long. Her captain told me that he has plenty of assets available to help out, but he wants Brenda to learn to be a team player with what she's got. I'll hold a briefing on the case when you two get back from England, okay?"

"Good," Rosson smiled. He turned his attention to David and Charlie. "Now then: you two are off to London tomorrow morning, right?"

"Don't remind me, sir," Charlie's face went instantly glum at the mention of their upcoming trip.

"You're going to England to be rewarded, Colonel, not executed," Donald MacKay pointed out. "We'll manage to keep things together while you're gone."

"Charlie, I just found out that the Queen has places in Kentucky where she breeds horses. Maybe we can hit her up for a horse while we're over there." David said eagerly.

Charlie elbowed him. "David, you mention anything about a horse to the Queen and you'll be rowing back to America."

"You got a plane to play with. I want a horse."

"Drop it."

-0-

"I'll see you tomorrow, Meyers," Brenda said as she gathered her coat after getting out of her chair. It had been a very long day for both of them, and she was anxious to go home. She had just finished faxing their reports over to the British Consulate.

"Okay, Lieutenant. I'll see you tomorrow," Meyers replied, staring at his computer screen. Ron was a hopeless typist. It always took him ten times longer than Brenda to type out reports.

She came over to his side of the desk. "How much more do you have to type?"

"About three more pages," he replied stoutly. "I'll have it done in another hour or so."

"Look, Meyers: let me do that. The night shift's already here, and you know they'll be wanting to take over this spot." Brenda shoved him out of the chair and adjusted it. "You got all your notes in order?"

Meyers glanced around the room. No one was paying any attention, thankfully. "Yeah, they're all here."

"Good," Brenda nodded. She proceeded to type up his three pages in five minutes. "There, it's all done. Now you can go home."

"I guess I can," Ron said with gratitude. He paused for a moment, gathering his courage. "Lieutenant, since you did that, can I... buy you dinner. I mean, it's the least I can do after you did that for me."

"Is this a date, Meyers? Because if it is, you know I don't go on dates," Brenda reminded him sharply.

"You did me a favor, Lieutenant," Meyers shot back. "I'm just saying 'thanks,' for helping me out. People do that for each other from time to time."

Brenda looked at him for a moment. "I guess they do. It's just no one ever thanks me for anything around here."

"Maybe they would if you gave them the chance," Ron said with defeat in his voice. "Let's skip it. We've had a long day, and I'm tired of fencing with you. I'll see you tomorrow." He put on his coat and started walking away.

"Hey Meyers: wait up," Brenda got out of the chair and caught up with him. "Look, I'm sorry. You were trying to be nice, and I bit your head off. There's a steak joint down the street that's really good. We can go there, okay?"

"All right," Ron said with a grin on his face. "It better have bad lighting and no cops around. Otherwise, people are going to start to talk."

"I don't care."

14

"Warren and her husband were here this morning, asking questions about Quimby," Decker told Haman Evans, the chairman of LuxVeritas. "I think they're becoming suspicious of our plans for that warehouse."

Evans' mobile face went dark with rage. "This whole operation has been bungled from the start! Kolov hired that imbecile Quimby, and then shot him when it looked as though he was going to crack. Now the police are investigating his death, along with our interest in that warehouse. Not to mention all of the homeless people he and his thugs have butchered over the past few months to scare them away from the dock areas. At this rate, they're going to have to open up a special wing at the City morgues just to handle the dead bodies Kolov's producing."

He reached for his intercom and punched a button. "Send Mr. Kolov in now, please."

Evans' lip curled. "I want this understood, Decker: we can't afford any more slipups in this matter. There are billions of dollars at stake, and timing is everything. Is that clear?"

Decker nodded meekly. "Yes sir."

Ivan Kolov entered the room. "Mr. Kolov, is there something wrong with your understanding about the need for secrecy in our operation?" The Chairman snarled, turning his wrath on Kolov. "I thought I made it clear that you and your people were to be careful about our operations. You came to us as a highly recommended operative who was discrete and got results. So far, I can't understand why. Your record right now is not very impressive, sir."

"Mr. Evans, please do not threaten me," Kolov replied, coming over to the man behind the desk. "I become rather disturbed when people do that."

"Save your intimidation tactics for someone else, Mr. Kolov. There are other people, powerful people, who want this job done right. One word from me, and you'll be found in the East River with a bullet in your head. We have the police swarming all over the place trying to find out about that building and those tunnels. What are we going to do about it?"

"Leave that to me," Kolov smiled unpleasantly. "I have plenty of tricks to throw them off."

His face darkened with rage, and he reached over the desk and grabbed Evans by the lapels of his jacket. "Do not, Mr. Evans, ever threaten me again. The last person who did that wound up scattered over several New England states." Kolov threw Evans back into the chair.

Decker held up his hand, trying to placate both of the angry men. "Gentlemen, please: let's try to get a handle on this. We are all reasonable men here. There's no need to indulge in petty quarrels. The stakes are too high."

Kolov turned to face Decker. He nodded his head after a moment. "I agree with your friend, Mr. Evans. We have come too far to let a few minor setbacks stand in our way. We have finally managed to get that old machine under the warehouse to work again."

Evans looked less than impressed. "So what did that prove?"

"That my sources in Germany were correct," Kolov replied with a slight smile. "The mission to America did indeed exist. We found intercepts by the computer that confirmed that part of the story.

"I have news about the other phase of our operation. We've finally managed to locate a Mr. Hans Schmidt. He is a retired teacher who taught physics at a small local university here in New York. My colleagues in Russia have told me he has a most interesting past." Kolov smiled ironically. "With some persuasion, I believe we will get the final pieces of information we need for the operation to reach completion."

"We have a time schedule, Kolov. Do you think we'll be able to get the information quickly enough?"

Kolov bared his teeth in an ugly grin. "Yes, I do. By the time I am through, the police will not know which way to turn. The tunnel systems under this island stretch for miles. It will be impossible for them to cover them all."

Evans was still skeptical. "What exactly do you plan to do?"

"You'll see. The police are stupid. They know nothing of our plans."

-0-

"What's this urgent page you got from Lucy Kelson, Charlie?" David asked as he drove their van back to Compton a few hours later.

"I don't know, David. Lucy's very levelheaded normally, but when I talked to her I could tell she'd been crying." Charlie said as they pulled into the Medical Examiner's parking lot. It was now after five, and most of the cars had left for the day. Lucy's car was still in the lot.

Lucy was waiting for them outside her office. "Charlie, I'm so sorry to bother you like this," she began, her eyes welling with tears. "I got a phone call from Regional Medical Center this afternoon. John was taken from prison today and has been placed in the hospital. They told me he was very sick."

Charlie gathered Lucy into her arms. "I'm so sorry, Lucy. What can I do to help?"

Lucy wept for a minute before answering. "I talked to John. He wants… he wants you and Angus and me to come to see him tonight. I told him I'd talk to you about it. Oh Charlie, I know you're going to England tomorrow, and it's already late, but could you come with me to the hospital tonight? You won't have to stay long."

"We'll stay as long as we need to, Lucy. Being there for you and John is what counts." Charlie said firmly, looking at David, who nodded in return.

Lucy dried her eyes. "You're so wonderful. Most people would have turned their backs on us, on John."

"Charlie, I'm going to leave you here with Lucy and drive over to the high school," David said as they walked back to the front door. "I'll head on home after rehearsal and get us packed."

"Sounds like a plan, David. All of my stuff is laid out on the bed. That beastly monkey suit is hanging up in a suit bag in the closet. Be sure that gets packed in the van," Charlie reminded him.

"Yeah, can't forget the monkey suit," David kissed her before he climbed into the van. "Hey, I'm really proud of you. Just don't be too late, okay?"

"Okay," Charlie kissed him as he closed the door. She waved as he drove off. Charlie turned back to Lucy. "All right, then: let's go over to the church and collect Angus."

The two women drove over to Trinity Church. Angus was sitting in his parlor dozing when they arrived. It took him thirty seconds to waken and answer Charlie's knock at the door.

"Charlie! It's good to see you! I'm sorry, but I was taking a bit of a nap in my chair. What can I do for you?" He rubbed his eyes to chase the sleep away.

Charlie's eyes narrowed slightly as she looked at her godfather. Angus did not look well. He was obviously exhausted. "Lucy Kelson called me this evening and told me that John Griggs has been sent to Regional Medical Center. John wants us to come see him in hospital."

Angus nodded. "Fine, my dear; I'll be with you in a minute. Would you mind fetching me the communion set? It's in the church office in the closet. And get me my stole; it's lying on the chair next to the cabinet. I have a vial of oil sitting on top of the prayer book on my desk. If you could get all of those items, I'd be grateful."

He started to get up out of the chair, but a wave of weariness overwhelmed him. Angus sank back into the chair as Charlie looked on in alarm. "I seem to have overdone things this afternoon with Katya."

"Quite, Uncle Angus: a masterpiece of understatement." Charlie took his wrist in her hand and felt it, looking at him with clinical detachment. "Did you have any chest discomfort this afternoon, Angus? The truth, if you please. You know you can't hide things from me."

A ghost of a smile flickered across his face. "I had some chest discomfort, my dear. I didn't want to alarm your sister. She's such an angel, Charlie."

"Yes, and she'd be crushed if you dropped dead in front of her." Charlie released his hand and bent down next to Angus. "You are loved by so many people. Please, Uncle Angus: please take care of yourself."

"I try, my dear," he nodded, stroking her face. "Give Lucy and John my regrets. Please tell them that I'm praying for them. I'll stay home tonight and rest."

"That sounds like a wise decision," Charlie said with approval. "I'll be back in a moment." She went over to the church office, and in a few moments returned with the items Angus had requested.

"I'm not sure I'm ready for this, Uncle Angus," she confided reluctantly. "I have a feeling that John Griggs is gravely ill."

"Then trust that God will lead you, Charlie. He always has in the past," Angus said with confidence.

He paused for a moment. "The bishop and I were discussing things this afternoon. He wants to proceed with your ordination whenever you are ready."

"Angus, I have not attended seminary. I am not qualified to lead this church," Charlie said, her voice trembling slightly. "You know I do not feel the call of God in this matter."

"I see God's hand in your life. Whether you like it or not, He is the one who calls His servants, willing or unwilling. You resist His call at your peril, Charlie," Angus said with sudden strength in his voice. "The particulars of that call will work themselves out, but you cannot escape it, any more than you can escape being a knight."

Charlie hung her head, unable to respond. Bending over, Angus kissed her cheek. "God is with you, dearest child."

Charlie rose and went to the door with the items. "Stay healthy, Angus," she whispered into his ear as she hugged him, "this church needs you for a long time to come. I need you as well."

A slight smile played across Angus McKendrick's lips. "I've been granted some time, child. How long, I don't know. We'll see."

-0-

Lucy told Charlie about John's illness on the way to the medical center. It had come upon him suddenly: rapid weight loss, along with gnawing abdominal pain and jaundice. The more she talked, the more Charlie was convinced of a terrible diagnosis that she knew was coming. It was not her place to deliver that blow, so she listened sympathetically as Lucy poured out her story.

"John hasn't told me much about his condition. He's actually been in the hospital for a day or so before he called this afternoon," Lucy paused looking at Charlie's face for a second. They were now almost at the medical center. "You know what it is, Charlie, don't you? I can see from your face that it's not good, is it?"

"Lucy, I'm not going to lie to you. From what you've told me, it doesn't sound good." Charlie busied herself gathering the items she'd brought from the church, trying to avoid looking directly at Lucy's face. "We'll know more when we get inside."

They went into the medical center and quickly found where John Griggs was being treated. "He's in the Medical ICU, Charlie," Lucy said in a small, frightened voice. "John didn't tell me he was that sick."

The two women reached the floor and were shown to the waiting room. After a few moments, a physician came out to talk to them. "Dr. Warren, Ms. Kelson: I'm Dr. Hassan," the tall, distinguished-looking doctor told them, his voice soft with sympathy. "I'm John Griggs' doctor. I specialize in cancers of the gastrointestinal system."

Lucy's face went white with shock. Charlie saw her face and put her arm around Lucy's shoulders. "I think we'd better sit down and listen to John's doctor, Lucy."

Everyone sat down in the waiting room chairs. "I'm sorry I upset you," Dr. Hassan began. "I was not aware that John had not told you of his condition. He has authorized me to tell you these things, so I am not violating any sort of confidences at this point."

"Please tell me what is wrong with John," Lucy whispered, clutching Charlie's arm.

Dr. Hassan reached over and took Lucy's hand. "John has cancer of the pancreas. It is advanced, and it is not operable."

Charlie held onto Lucy as he spoke those words. She knew there was no way she could soften the blow that was being dealt to Lucy at this moment. It was a diagnosis Charlie had half suspected when Lucy had started describing John's symptoms, but she had kept her peace.

Lucy's body trembled with grief. "No, no: it... it can't be happening," she looked wildly at Charlie. "Charlie, you're a doctor. Could there be anything else that could cause these symptoms? Please tell me!"

All Charlie could do is shake her head in agonized grief. Her own face was running with tears as she held her friend. Hassan sat by, allowing them their privacy. Charlie finally raised her head and dried her eyes. "How far along is he, Doctor?"

Hassan frowned. "It is difficult to say. Pancreatic cancer is almost invariably metastasized by the time it is detected. From the CT scans and other tests we have done, I believe his case is very far advanced."

Charlie nodded. "I see. Thank you." She stood up. It was time for her to provide comfort for Lucy and John. That was her duty and role. Somehow, for some reason, God had sent her there to comfort them, even though she was just as grief-stricken as they were.

She put her hand on Lucy's shoulder and looked at Dr. Hassan. "May we go see him? I've been sent by John's church to minister to him."

Hassan's face was a blend of admiration and bewilderment. "You are a physician as well as a minister?"

"Deaconess, actually," Charlie said with a slight smile, "more like a parish assistant than anything else. I would like to pray with him and serve him Communion, if it's not too much trouble."

"No, please. I'm very glad you came," Dr. Hassan paused for a moment. "It's sometimes difficult to find clergy who will see some of our patients. May I ask, after you finish with John, to see some other people as well? I have a number of people who have asked to speak to a minister and have not had the opportunity. Would you be willing to talk to them?"

Charlie hesitated before replying. She had already had an exhausting day. The news of John's illness had come as a personal blow to her as well. She remembered asking God to do His work that night. Apparently God had other people as well as John who needed her.

"Yes, Dr. Hassan. I will be happy to see those people as well," Charlie heard herself say in spite of her own weariness and grief.

-0-

It was well after midnight by the time Lucy dropped Charlie off at her house. The living room light was on, and David was waiting up for her. "I hope you've got me packed, David, because I don't think I can go another step," Charlie told him in an exhausted voice.

David came over to her and embraced her. "It's all right. Megan insisted on coming over after rehearsal and helping me pack things up for you. Between her and Katya, I think we've got everything ready for tomorrow."

Charlie nodded mutely, too tired to speak. "It's bad news, isn't it?" David asked gently, kissing her.

"John has pancreatic cancer. He only has a few weeks to live at the most," Charlie said as they moved down the hallway to their bedroom. "I... did the best I could, David, but I fear that I wasn't much help. The doctor asked me to see some other patients as well, ones who wanted someone to pray with them. I prayed with them, and I prayed with John. I gave John and Lucy Communion, and I administered Extreme Unction to him as well..."

Her voice trailed off as David picked her up and laid her down on the bed. Charlie was too tired to protest as he did this. He pulled back the covers and took off her shoes. Charlie was asleep before he pulled the covers over her.

-0-

It seemed to Charlie that she'd only closed her eyes for a moment when she felt David's hand upon her shoulder. "Charlie: it's time to wake up."

Normally, Charlie's response would be to pull the covers over her head and burrow deeper into the bed sheets. Today, it was different. They had a flight to catch.

"All right, David. I'm up." She threw off her covers and stretched luxuriously. "David, I don't even remember going to bed last night. I'm still dressed in my street clothes. What happened?"

"I think it's called exhaustion, love. Even you have limits," David came over to her and kissed her. "Come on: we have a breakfast engagement at Sophie's."

"Breakfast engagement? What are you talking about?" Charlie stared over at the digital clock face, which read 4:00. "David, you're insane! It's only four in the morning! Who's going to be up at this hour?"

"All of your friends," David replied smugly. "You're one to talk about early rising. I seem to remember someone pounding on my door back last September at five in the morning, remember?"

David was feeling immensely pleased with himself. Keeping secrets from Charlie was a major achievement, and he was proud he'd managed to pull one off on her.

"I'm coming too," a fully dressed and very wide-awake Katya called from the doorway. "I've missed seeing you so much, Charlie. I know it's been hard on you as well."

Charlie got up from the bed and hugged her sister. "Darling, I've missed you too!" She turned around and looked at David in mock anger. "You beast! I could skin you alive for keeping this from me!" She rushed over and hugged David's neck. "You dear, sweet man; I love you so much! I'll be ready in a few minutes."

Less than ten minutes later, Charlie was showered and dressed in clean clothes. The van was packed and they were headed into Compton. Katya and David filled Charlie in on what had happened at rehearsal that night, and Charlie in turn told them what she could about Lucy and John. She scrupulously omitted any details about how serious John's condition was, not wanting to upset Katya. They arrived at Sophie's to find the place packed with their friends.

"This is the most people we've had here at this hour since I opened the place back in 1970," the manager told Charlie and David as they came through the door.

"Look, Lenny: Compton's police department couldn't survive if it weren't for this place," Carl Davis pointed out as he kissed Charlie and shook David's hand. "Okay guys: your booth's ready.

There's coffee and the omelets are on the way."

He turned to Katya. "What are you doing up so early, young lady? I thought you had practice today."

"I do, but I wanted to see my sister off," Katya replied cheerily, sitting down across from Charlie and David.

"I'm taking her back to my house after this shindig and putting her down for a few hours," Joan Richards came up to the booth. She looked at Charlie with a stern expression on her face. "Look, little girl: try not to get yourself involved in any messes over there. You have until Tuesday, and then after that, I'm coming over to drag you back to America."

"Why Joan, I have no idea what you're talking about," Charlie's face was the picture of innocence.

"Uh huh. You'd better listen to me, Charlie. I WILL bring you back. Trust me on that," Joan finished with a wink as she turned and went back to her table.

Megan and Sean O'Grady came over to the table. "We just wanted to let you know that things are going to be okay while you're gone. We'll keep an eye on Angus for you," Sean said, smiling.

"I appreciate that so very much, Sean," Charlie said with gratitude. "Thank you."

Sean reached over and kissed her cheek. "Hey, you know you can count on us." He stood up and put his hand on Megan's shoulder. "Come on, Meg. We need to let these people eat."

They went back to their table just as the food arrived. Charlie and David ate quickly, saying little to each other. Both of them appreciated the send-off party, but they were anxious to get to the airport to make the flight.

"We need to go, Charlie," David drained the last of his coffee as he stood up. He turned and addressed the rest of their friends in the restaurant. "Thanks, all of you for coming. I promise you I'll bring her back, since I know that if I didn't, I'd never be allowed to set foot in this town again."

"Just make sure you don't get shot, Dave. Charlie, you need to keep him out of the bookstores." Megan called out.

"I'll do my best," Charlie laughed as they headed towards the door. They said goodbye to everyone, and Charlie held onto Katya for a few more moments before they left. The dawn was fast approaching, and a gentle breeze made the summer air seem cool and light.

David drew her close to him. "I know these next few days are going to be hard for you, Charlie. I'll do what I can to make it easy as possible on you."

"David, as long as we have people like this to come home to, I can face anything." Charlie replied, kissing him.

David started up the van. "Where are our raincoats, David?" Charlie asked as they started the drive out of town.

"I looked on the computer, Charlie," David frowned slightly. "The weather's supposed to be clear in London when we arrive."

"David, we're going to England, and it's summertime. I know English summers. We'll need those coats," Charlie rummaged around their luggage and got out their raincoats. "It will be raining cats and dogs when we get there."

"You're the expert." David said skeptically. "Are you sure you know what you're talking about?"

"On English weather? You'd better believe it."

15

Brenda walked into the precinct on Friday morning and found a surprise waiting for her. Someone had taken footage of the sparring match between Charlie and Brenda with their camera phone and had downloaded it onto all of the computers in the precinct.

She saw bank after bank of computer screens showing her flying through the air landing on her back. That scene had been looped so it kept repeating over and over. Everyone in the precinct had it downloaded onto their computer screens. The room was filled with laughter and giggles as a red-faced Brenda went to her desk to hang up her coat.

"Great," she grated through clinched teeth. "I'm going to get whoever did this!"

"Nice form, Bren," one of the detectives called out to her as she made her way over to Howard Vinson's office.

"Shut up, Gracie," Brenda snapped back.

The sound of chuckling could be heard in Captain Vinson's office as she entered. Vinson's computer was on, and he switched it off a fraction of a second before she came in through the door. Not quickly enough to stop Brenda from seeing that he had the image on his screen as well.

Reynolds controlled herself with an effort. "You wanted to see me, Captain?"

Vinson handed her a note. "You have a meeting at the Consulate this morning. Don't worry, Lieutenant; Warren's out of country right now, so you're safe. Minneli won the office pool on how fast Warren could take you down. You lasted two minutes. The FBI Academy record was five, in case you're interested."

"Thanks," Brenda took the note. "I could have taken her, Captain."

He looked at her for a moment. "Sure, Brenda; go ahead and think that. Warren could have really cleaned your clock at any time. I was there, remember?"

Brenda stomped out of the office without another word. Ron had arrived and was busy at his desk when she arrived. On her side was a large cup of steaming coffee.

"What's this?" she snapped.

"Coffee," Meyers replied, taking a sip of his own cup.

"I don't want this," Brenda shoved the cup across the desk with a violent motion. The hot liquid slopped over onto some of the night shift reports.

"Hey, take it easy, Lieutenant!" Meyers quickly snatched up the papers and blotted them off to prevent further damage. "What's eating you this morning?"

"Just stop trying to be nice to me, Meyers. I'm not going to turn into your girlfriend. Get over it." Brenda said, pulling on her jacket. "Let's get rolling. We need to get over to the British Consulate."

Meyers just looked at her. "All right, Lieutenant. I'm ready to go when you are."

-0-

They drove over to the consulate for several minutes without saying anything to each other. Brenda was still seething with embarrassment, and Ron was trying to make things better. If not better, then at least survivable.

"It was just a cup of coffee, Lieutenant, not a marriage proposal," Ron finally broke the ice.

Reynolds said nothing for a moment, concentrating on negotiating the New York traffic. "You forgot the cream."

"No I didn't. It was in the bag next to the coffee."

"I didn't look," Brenda admitted, her face softening slightly.

"No partner I've ever had has bought me a cup of coffee before."

"No partner I've ever had has typed up my reports before, so we're even."

"I hate going to that stupid consulate, Meyers," Brenda finally said as they drove towards the consulate gates. "I hate this whole case. At least we won't have to see that stupid little doctor today."

"Warren and Stone are on their way to the UK for that knighting ceremony, or whatever it was. They'll be back on Tuesday next week." Ron said in a carefully neutral tone.

"Good. At least we'll have a few days of peace without that twit nosing around," Brenda observed sourly as they arrived at the gates of the consulate. "So what are we supposed to do now? Bow or kiss someone's ring to get in?"

"No, I think we're supposed to roll down our window and present our IDs," Meyers said as he rolled down his window and presented his and Brenda's ID to the gate security officer.

The guard looked at the two cards and consulted his list. "Okay, go on. They're expecting you," he said in an unmistakable Bronx accent. Ron did a double take when he heard the man's voice.

"What part of England are you from?" Meyers asked incredulously.

"England? What are you talking about? I'm from the Bronx. Where else?" the guard shrugged elaborately. "I got four cousins working for PD down at the Ninth Precinct. This gig came open in January. I've got my name in for the Academy's next class. It's a living."

Meyers nodded, winking at Brenda, who was getting more and more irritated every minute with the delay. "Okay, thanks. We'll see you later."

The guard stood up and waved them through. "See? That wasn't so bad, was it, Lieutenant?" Meyers commented smugly as they located a parking spot.

"Right," Reynolds snapped. "Let's just get this over with."

They were shown into James' office. Rawlings was already there. "So glad you could make it," James held out his hand to the two detectives.

Meyers shook his hand warmly. Brenda took it briefly but

firmly. They both sat down in chairs next to Rawlings. James resumed his discussion with Rawlings. "You both came at just the right moment. Agent Rawlings was going over the results of the scans around that mysterious building over by the docks."

Rawlings brought out a series of photographs from an envelope he had. "We did these initial readings last night when the traffic cleared out of the dock areas." He handed the photographs to James, who looked at them for a minute or so.

James whistled, as he handed the photographs over to the two detectives. "Interesting: it's not your standard dockside building, is it?"

"No, they're not," Rawlings agreed with a wry smile. "They're amazingly modern, considering they were built almost seventy years ago. They have underground telephone and electrical connections, along with backup generators with enough underground reserve tanks of diesel oil to keep them operational for several weeks."

Reynolds was not impressed. "Okay, they have underground generators. So what?"

"It means that this isn't just any sort of warehouse, Lieutenant," Meyers pointed out eagerly. "This building was built with a special mission in mind."

"That's an understatement," Rawlings agreed. He pointed to another section of the photograph. "Look at the five hundred foot long section nearest to the dock. There's a concrete structure that runs the length of that part of the building underneath the roof. It takes up the entire part of that building."

"A roof within a roof," James mused, tapping his finger to his chin in thought. "Almost... I think I know what this is! I remember visiting the German submarine base at Lorient a few years ago. I saw structures like this at that base."

"What is it, Colonel Rosson?" MacKay asked.

"It's a submarine pen, a place where you could dock a submarine and have it protected from aerial attacks and observation." James replied excitedly. "It makes perfect sense! A structure like this would be invaluable for secret operations to be conducted. That's why it was so valuable and why it was protected so carefully."

Rawlings raised his eyebrows. "Even after the war ended?"

"Agent Rawlings, secret bases are valuable no matter who your opponent is," James said. "There are secret locations scattered throughout the world that have been used by British Intelligence as listening posts and bases for decades. Michael Warren was a servant of the British Crown. This was his mission and he executed it without question."

"That makes sense," Rawlings brought out a final photograph from his envelope. "I saved this one for last, guys." He handed it over to James, who looked at intently for a moment.

"You're sure this is from that warehouse?" he asked. "No mistakes?"

"Yeah, I'm sure. You know what it is?"

James nodded slowly. "I most certainly do. As far as I knew, the place machines like this existed was at Bletchley Park in the United Kingdom. When I saw it the other day, I started to remember touring Bletchley several years ago. This confirms my initial suspicions."

"What are you talking about, Mr. Rosson?" Brenda asked as she looked at the photograph.

"This machine we discovered in that warehouse is a *Colossus*, a code-breaking computer the British built back in the 1940s to decipher the German military codes." James replied in a hushed tone. "Ten of those machines existed at Bletchley Park. All of them were destroyed after the War."

"So why is this thing under a warehouse in New York?" Rawlings asked.

"It's obviously there because it was intended as a fall-back in case Britain was overrun. The British Intelligence service built numerous installations around the world to continue the fight against the Nazis if they captured the British Isles," James mused. "I wonder if it was ever operational?"

"Is this why this LuxVeritas corporation is so interested in those buildings? That's nuts," Reynolds scoffed. "Most handheld computers have more computing power than that big piece of junk. You could probably sell it to a museum for a few thousand bucks, maybe."

"Lieutenant, with all due respect, you don't know what you're talking about," James Rosson replied rather sharply. "*Colossus* was incredibly fast, even by today's standards. The information the Allies were able to decipher from German code traffic enabled them to win the War."

"I think it's not the computer that has value so much as what it might have stored," Meyers suggested. "Is there a way to get to that thing? Access its memory?"

"It's possible, but it would take time, time we may not have," James replied. "When Sergeant Major MacKay and I went over to those buildings the other day, it was obvious that someone had been there recently. Someone who was interested in getting that thing operational."

"The stair case leading down to the basement area where that machine is located is right next to the far wall of the submarine pen." Mackay pointed to an area on the scan.

Rosson sat back in his chair, tapping his teeth with the top of his pen. It was a nervous habit he'd developed over the years when he was thinking of something.

MacKay cleared his throat after a minute. "Sir, do you think Sir Leslie would be able to help us out with some cyberneticists who could access the machine?"

"What?" James looked up sharply. "Oh yes, forgive me, Sergeant Major. I was off musing in another world for a moment." He looked at Donald and blushed. "Of course we'll inform him of this development, but I'm not sure we have the time to engage in esoteric research."

"I agree with your assessment, Colonel Rosson," Rawlings said firmly. "Finding that old machine confirms that the site's important, but right now things are developing too quickly for an extended research project. We've established that it's there, and that's enough."

Rawlings said, looked at Reynolds and Meyers. "How are you two faring with your end of the investigation, detectives?"

We found Kolov's name on LuxVeritas stationary in Quimby's apartment," Brenda said. "We also got good descriptions from the landlady of the 'officers' who came by before we arrived on the scene. We're having her look through some mug shots to see if she can ID any. The slug used to kill Quimby was fired from a weapon implicated in several Russian mob hits."

"Well, things seem to be developing in an interesting fashion," Rosson said with satisfaction. "Have you any more intelligence information to share with us, Special Agent Rawlings?"

"My Task Force people are hearing rumblings that Kolov has been hired by this LuxVeritas for some sort of high-powered op. That piece of paper you guys found in Quimby's apartment is the first conclusive proof we've had linking those two. Nice work." Rawlings smiled at the two detectives.

"Thank you, Agent Rawlings," Reynolds smiled in return. The mood in the room brightened considerably. "We faxed the CSI reports and autopsy findings to the Consulate last night. Did Dr. Warren pick them up?"

"Yes, she did," Rosson replied. "She's taking them with her on this trip to Great Britain. She wanted me to pass along her thanks to you for all of your hard work."

"Oh yes, there's one more thing," Rawlings fished around in one of his pockets for a piece of paper. "Cartwright scrawled the word "Rache" on a piece of paper before he died. Do you have any idea what that might mean?"

"Only that it's the German word for 'revenge,'" Rosson replied. "I'm not sure why Cartwright would write that. Obviously it means something."

"Let us know if you find out what," Rawlings said.

"I will, Agent Rawlings," Rosson sighed and looked bleakly at the huge stack of paperwork on his desk. "I'm going to be tied up with administrative work for the balance of the day. Lady Margaret Wilson returns on Monday to rescue me from my temporary promotion," James said gloomily. He rose from his chair and held out his hand. "It's been a pleasure working with you, Special Agent Rawlings."

Rawlings stood up and shook his hand. "Thank you for all of your help, Mr. Rosson. We really appreciate having you lend your talent and resources to help us in this case."

James raised his hand. "Not at all. It's been my pleasure. A good deal of my job is rather unexciting. This case has been quite intriguing, and in my line of work, any kind of excitement is welcome."

He turned to Reynolds and Meyers. "I'm delighted to see you again."

Brenda grimaced slightly. "Right, Mr. Rosson." She turned to Meyers. "We'll be in touch and let you know what we find out."

"I'll look forward to that," James smiled, shaking their hands. Rosson saw his guests to the front door of the Consulate. After the door closed behind them, he turned to Donald, who had just returned from the communications section.

"I'm confused, sir," MacKay said. "That computer is hopelessly outdated by now. I can't figure out why Michael Warren would be so interested in making sure that the building housing that thing would be maintained so scrupulously."

"It is a bit of a puzzle," Rosson agreed. "He may have been ordered simply to maintain the building and that was the extent of his orders. We just don't know enough about his mission at this point to draw a conclusion one way or the other. All we have to go on is that scrap of paper with 'Rache' on it."

"Revenge is an ominous word to write when you're about to die."

"It is indeed." James said.

16

Sergeant Major MacKay decided to stop by Trinity Church that evening on his way over to the high school. James Rosson and he had discussed the need to notify Angus McKendrick about Richard Cartwright.

"There's always a chance that Father McKendrick might have some further information about the man that might be useful in our investigation. Any type of information about Richard Cartwright might be useful in helping us find out why he was here in America," Rosson pointed out. "Besides, the New York Medical Examiner has completed the examination of Richard Cartwright's body and is ready to release it to us."

"Father McKendrick will want to know about the lad, sir," Donald said. "If nothing else, he may be able to help us find some family over in Britain who will want to give him a proper burial."

"Yes, Sergeant Major; you're quite right about that," James nodded his head solemnly. "It's never an easy task letting families know about their loved ones dying in battle, is it?"

"You and I have done enough of our share, sir," MacKay replied. "I'll change into my dress uniform to deliver the news."

"I think that would be most appropriate," Rosson agreed.

Over the years, Donald MacKay had been tasked with the solemn duty of informing family of the loss of soldiers in battle. It was never an easy task, but it was a necessary one. Cartwright had no family in America, but Angus McKendrick was an old comrade.

"Donald MacKay! What a surprise to see you!" Angus' face lit up with joy as he answered Donald's knock on his door. "And dressed in your uniform. What brings you here this fine Friday evening?"

"Father McKendrick, I have been ordered by Her Majesty to inform you of the death of one of your brother soldiers," MacKay replied stiffly, drawing himself up to attention.

Angus' face became still and quiet. "Then please come in, Sergeant Major." He opened the door and ushered MacKay into his parlor.

"Father McKendrick, for the past few days, Colonel Warren and I have been involved in a case in New York City. The bodies of three men were discovered in one of the access tunnels under their tube system. One of the bodies had papers that identified him as Sergeant Richard Cartwright. His identity has now been confirmed. Colonel Rosson and I wanted you to know about the discovery of his body, since you knew the man."

Angus digested this news in silence for a moment. "Richard Cartwright was more than a fellow soldier to me, Sergeant Major. He was one of my best friends. Next to Michael Warren, he was one of the dearest people I had on this earth."

Tears formed in his eyes. "Richard lost everyone in the War. He has no family left on this earth to mourn him, except me."

MacKay nodded. "The Medical Examiner is set to release his body, Father McKendrick. What are your wishes?"

Angus stood up. "Sergeant Major, we will bury Richard Cartwright in Trinity's cemetery. If it is possible, I would like it done with full military honors."

MacKay stood up from his chair. "Your wishes will be obeyed, Father McKendrick. May I say on behalf of Her Majesty that the British Empire mourns your loss."

"Thank you, Sergeant Major, for telling me," McKendrick replied gratefully.

Donald paused before going to the door. "Colonel Rosson wanted me to ask you if Michael Warren ever mentioned why Richard Cartwright was sent over here to America. At this point, sir, we have no idea why he was over here."

Angus frowned. "I don't recollect Michael ever mentioning Richard Cartwright, except to say that he'd gone missing in New

York and had never been found. He was presumed dead a number of years ago. I'm sorry I can't help you any further, Donald."

"That's quite all right, sir," Donald said with a smile. "It was a long shot, but worth it. You'll be happy to know that Megan and I will be getting married in July as soon as this play is over."

"I'm happy for you, lad," McKendrick said sincerely. "I wish you all joy. Megan's a wonderful girl, and I know you'll be very happy together."

"Thank you, Father McKendrick," Donald suddenly became aware of the time. "You'll have to excuse me, sir, but I have to be off to the high school to meet Megan,"

"Of course: I understand completely, Donald. Thank you again for coming and telling me about Richard," Angus said as he opened the door. Sergeant Major MacKay passed through and walked down the sidewalk to his car. Angus watched him go, sadness filling his heart as he thought about Richard Cartwright's death.

"Now we know, laddie," he half-whispered to himself. "Now we know where you've been all these years."

-0-

Carl Davis stopped by the high school that night to talk to Sergeant Major MacKay. "I want you to know that we've got extra patrols going out to Charlie and Dave's place. I've also got an unmarked car following Katya when she goes for her daily skating lessons."

"That sounds prudent, Chief," MacKay nodded his approval. "I'm not sure Charlie and David would approve, but right now, they're out of the country, and we have the little girl to think about."

"These terrorists are cowards," Davis said grimly. "They bypass military targets for unarmed men, women and children. That's why we need to take precautions. We're not dealing with soldiers; we're dealing with scum."

"Who told you that you could have a break, soldier? Get back to work!" a very sweaty, Megan O'Grady came up to them. She had been working in the construction shop and was coated with sawdust.

"Lass, I've been meaning to talk to you about your dandruff

problem," MacKay started judiciously flicking off sawdust from the shoulders of his betrothed.

"Yeah? Well get used to it, buddy," Megan kissed his cheek. "Is this a private fight or can anyone join in?"

Davis nodded. "Sure. Pull up a pew. Watch out for the chairs. The wife of one of my cops cleans this place, and she'll have a fit if she knows you've been out in her auditorium with your sawdust, Meg." Davis, MacKay and Megan sat down in front row seats. "What's the problem?"

"It's not really a problem," Megan replied. "It's just something I've noticed in our parking lot for the past few nights. There's been a dark van sitting over in one of the far corners. I've never seen anybody go in and out of it. The van's always here when we arrive, and when we leave for the night, it's gone."

"Interesting," Davis' ears perked up. "Sounds like something we were just talking about, doesn't it, Sergeant Major?"

"Indeed it does," MacKay replied quietly. He looked at his watch. "It's about time for us to wrap things up, love. How did rehearsal go today?"

"Good," Megan nodded her head. "We open in about four weeks. The stage fighting scenes are coming along nicely. We'll be starting full run-throughs next week."

"I heard from Dad this morning. He said that they have tickets for the last week in July. Does that give you enough time for the wedding?"

"That's perfect, Donald. They've been saints about all of this craziness. Speaking of crazy, when are David and Charlie supposed to get back into town?" Megan asked.

"They come in Tuesday afternoon," MacKay replied. "They drove their minivan over to the consulate and parked it. Colonel Rosson and I took them into LaGuardia so they won't have to worry about airport parking.

"Besides, there are a number of rather sensitive items in that van that would attract undue attention if they tried to park it at the airport." MacKay added enigmatically.

"Things like guns and rocket launchers and high explosives?" Davis guessed.

"I'm not at liberty to say," MacKay replied, "but since I know the owners of the vehicle, that's a very good guess."

"Makes sense," Davis grunted. He looked at his watch. "Well, it's time for me to head back to the ranch. We'll see all of you later," he paused and looked at Megan. "Thanks for the tip about the van. We're keeping an eye on everything." He walked off.

Megan drew close to Donald and put her head on his shoulder. After a moment, she looked up into his face. "Donald, I never ask you about your business, but I need to know something: are we all in some sort of danger right now? You've been very quiet these past few days, and I'm worried."

Donald looked at her. "Lass, I will never lie to you, and I know you respect my need for being discrete. There is a danger, and it is real, but we are handling it."

"All right, I can accept that," Megan nodded. "Just stay safe, okay?"

"I'll do my best."

17

Hans Schmidt's phone rang early the following morning. It was unusual for that sort of thing to happen on a Sunday. Normally, his life at the retirement center was a series of predictable routines. This suited Schmidt, a former professor of physics at a local university. Routine suited his Newtonian sensibilities quite well.

The only persistent disruption in his ordered life was his encroaching kidney disease. Only recently he had been forced to start dialysis treatments, an ordeal of several hours in duration at the local dialysis center. Schmidt passed the time by chatting with the nurses and reading his physics journals.

Although he had retired from active university teaching, Schmidt donated several hours a week to tutoring students in physics. The stimulation of dealing with young minds was an immense source of pleasure for him, almost as much as keeping up with his very large, very spread-out family.

An early phone call was never a happy one, Schmidt had learned over the years. Usually they signaled unfortunate news, either for himself or for someone in his family. "Yes?" he said as he picked up the phone.

"Professor Schmidt, this is Rena Devon at the Dialysis Center," the voice on the other end of the phone said. "I'm sorry to bother you on a Sunday, but your latest chemistry levels came back, and they are not good. We are going to have to schedule a treatment for this morning."

A frown crossed Schmidt's face. "Rena, this is really a bad time for me. I go to church on Sunday morning, and I have a lecture to attend at the university later on this afternoon. Finally, my family will be picking me up this evening to take me to a reunion in New York City."

"I'm sorry sir, but Dr. Rankin was most insistent," Rena replied. "We'll have someone come by in a few moments to pick you up."

"All right then; I'll be ready. Goodbye," Schmidt hung up the phone and sighed. He turned his wheelchair around and headed for the bathroom. The wheelchair was the other major disruption in his life that was a constant source of irritation to him. Schmidt's arthritis had forced him into it six months ago, and he desperately missed his independence every day of his life.

A knock on his door twenty minutes later announced the arrival of the men assigned to take Schmidt to the dialysis center. Schmidt opened the door and let the two men in. They were not the same ones who normally picked him up.

"Good morning, Mr. Schmidt. We're here to take you for dialysis," one of them said as they moved him towards the door.

"Good morning," Schmidt replied. "You're not the same men who normally pick me up."

"It's a weekend," the other man replied pleasantly. "We're substituting for George and Kenny. They needed some time off."

The men wheeled Schmidt to the van and took him to the dialysis center. "There don't seem to be many people here today," Schmidt observed as he was rolled into the treatment area. A machine was already set up, with a nurse and a few unfamiliar technicians standing by to assist.

Rena Devon was there by her machine. She smiled as she saw Schmidt come through the door. "Hello, Professor: I'm sorry we have to do this on such short notice, but the doctor insisted."

"I understand, Rena; it can't be helped," Schmidt said tolerantly as he was wheeled up to the machine. Rena rolled up his sleeve and swiftly accessed the Gortex graft on his left arm.

"This will be a fairly quick treatment, Professor, so you shouldn't be here long," Rena said as her machine hummed to life. Her voice trembled slightly as she looked over to the two hulking ambulance attendants, who watched her stonily.

"It's all right; I've brought some of my journals to read," Schmidt said as he settled back into his chair to peruse the magazines he'd brought. As he did so, Rena reached down by her side and produced a syringe filled with a whitish liquid. She swiftly injected the substance into one of the intravenous lines running into Schmidt's graft. Hans Schmidt's head dropped swiftly down as he became unconscious almost immediately.

"Keep his head up," Rena said, connecting some oxygen tubing to an AMBU bag. She sealed the mask around his face and squeezed the bag, delivering oxygen to the unconscious man. One of the attendants took over ventilating Schmidt while Rena readied the machine. "The propofol will keep him under for a few minutes, but we need to support his airway and breathing until I get set up." She looked up at the attendants with raw fear in her eyes. "I've done what you've asked me to do, now can you let me go?"

"Of course we can," a bald headed man approached the machine. "Are things ready, Olga?" he asked in Russian.

"Yes, comrade Kolov," Olga replied. "The propofol injection will not disrupt the effects of our other medications. We will be ready in three minutes."

"Good," Kolov nodded approvingly. "I want this man drained of every bit of information about his last mission to the United States."

The ambulance attendants hustled Rena out the main entrance of the center. Kolov watched them go. One of the attendants came back into the building and asked him in Russian, "What about the woman?"

"Kill her when you take her home. Make it look like she was robbed." Kolov moved over to the recliner chair where Schmidt lay. "Now my friend: we will have a nice little morning chat about your experiences during the Second World War."

He picked up a case with a number of prefilled syringes and started to work.

-0-

Hans Schmidt drifted off into unsettling dreams. He dreamt of when he was a young man, an officer in the German Navy. He had forsaken his esoteric studies at the Berlin Institute of Advanced Physics to join in the defense of the Reich, becoming one of Germany's deadliest U-boat commanders. His training in physics, his abilities to think in multiple levels and to deal with the mathematics of chance and reason had helped him to stay one step ahead of an increasingly deadly and skilled opponent.

His training had borne fruit. The U-boat war had evolved into a war of science, of new and increasingly deadly technologies sparring over the hostile, unforgiving Atlantic. At the beginning of the war, Germany held the edge in submarine technology. It was an advantage that the U-boat commanders had used with deadly effect, almost starving England into submission before the tide had turned. Now the odds had tilted in favor of the Allies. The deadly coordination of surface ships and bombers drained the German submarine fleet every day.

He had welcomed the challenge of the deadly game. It was a war that challenged his abilities as a scientist, and as a warrior. Kepler was a scientist and a realist; he knew that the war had evolved into a contest that Germany could no longer win.

Strange how things had come full circle, he thought to himself. The Reich was dying, and he was now being called upon to use all of his training to save his country. No one had paid much attention to his branch of learning prior to the War in Germany, but now that particular branch of science was being called upon to save the country.

He had been summoned from his boat and whisked to Berlin, a city under Russian siege. Adolf Hitler's government was now confined to the underground lair complex known as the Fuhrerbunker. Above the complex, the city was in its death throws, the noose of the Russian forces drawing ever closer to the heart of the city. It was now problematic as to whether he would be able to leave the city and survive.

Schmidt was now standing before the Fuhrer. Hitler rose shakily from behind his massive oak desk to address him. They were alone in the Fuhrer's private study. The once dynamic and mesmerizing leader of the German nation had deteriorated over the years of war into a tottering wreck. Hitler still held his left arm uselessly at his side, a reminder of the near-fatal assassination attempt a year ago. His body had shrunken with age and infirmity.

But his voice still had the power to command, and Schmidt felt its power as he faced his leader. "Captain Kepler, I am addressing you as your supreme commander. You and your men have been chosen for this mission because of your loyalty, your tactical prowess, and your ability to follow orders without question."

"My name is Hans Schmidt, and I am a professor of physics," Schmidt wanted to scream at the apparition of Hitler before him. " I am not Kepler. Kepler is dead. He died when I came to America. I am an American now. This is some sort of hideous dream. I will awake and be back in New York."

But he could not awake. He was not dreaming. What he was experiencing was absolutely real to him. Hitler came closer to Schmidt, who stood rigidly at attention.

"You are ordered, Captain Kepler, to never reveal to anyone the details of your mission. Not to your superiors, or your crew, not to anyone. Is that understood?"

"Ja Wohl, Mein Fuhrer!" the young man snapped.

Hitler nodded. "Good. You are to leave for Bremen immediately. U-3551 is ready. She has passed all of her sea trials with flying colors. Her special modifications have been completed. You are to assume command of her after taking on stores. After you have completed that task, you are to submerge immediately and proceed on your mission.

"You are not to engage the enemy at any time, Captain. Your orders are to proceed to your target area and execute your mission. You are to maintain radio silence at all times. The enemy may attempt to fool you into believing that the War is over. Any radio transmissions you may receive which might attempt to convince you that hostilities have ended must be disregarded. The enemy has many ways to mimic official radio traffic. Radio transmissions are not to be trusted. Is that understood, Captain?"

Schmidt nodded, and Hitler continued. "If your ship is forced to the surface by enemy action, you are to scuttle your ship after killing all of your crew. You are not allowed to be captured alive, Captain. Your ship must succeed on its mission, or be utterly destroyed. There is no middle ground."

Hitler handed him a few sheets of paper. "These are the opera-tional orders, Captain. You are now ordered to commit them to memory. I have arranged for you to be taken to a small room where you may study them. After you have finished reviewing your orders, you will return to me and we will burn the papers. You will then recite the orders to me and depart for your ship."

"Thank you, mein Fuhrer," Schmidt replied with gratitude. "It is an honor to serve my country in such a glorious way. I will not fail you."

"Fail me," Hitler echoed the words bitterly. "So many of my trusted officers have failed me. Now our capital city is encircled, and our backs are to the wall. Your mission is the last best hope we have of breaking the enemy's back. If you succeed, you will strike a death blow to the enemy, a blow from which he cannot recover."

"I will not fail, Mein Fuhrer." Schmidt repeated the phrase with pride.

Adolf Hitler looked up at the young man's face, full of youthful bravado and arrogance. "We will see, Herr Kepler. We will see if your actions match your brave words."

He was led to a small room and given several sheets of informa-tion, along with a chart. It took him twenty minutes to digest all of the information. When he was through, he pressed a buzzer on the table. A staff member came and he was taken back to the Fuhrer's office.

"Now then, Captain," Adolf Hitler looked Kepler directly into his eyes. "You will tell me precisely the nature of your mission, including your final objectives..."

-0-

"I am truly impressed, Olga," Kolov said an hour later. "Our captain seems to have retained every detail of his mission to America."

"Indeed he has," Olga agreed. Schmidt had responded beauti-fully to the chemical interrogation. He had been given a blend of hypnotic sedatives, along with barbiturates. After he had completed the interview, his system had been totally dialyzed, removing almost all of the drugs. The whole process had taken less than two hours from start to finish.

Kolov looked down at his notepad, which contained at least three pages of closely written notes. "We now have the exact location of where Captain Kepler ended his voyage. I will relay this information to my associates, who will gather their teams of specialists to complete the mission."

"What about our brave U-boat commander?" Kolov indicated the sleeping form of Schmidt.

An evil look flashed across Olga's face. "It is unfortunate, but Professor Schmidt will inadvertently take too much of his heart medication later on today. His accident will cause him to go into a lethal, irreversible heart rhythm. It will be a slow process that will cast no suspicion on us at all."

"Are you sure there is no chance we can be implicated?"

"None, Comrade Kolov,"

-0-

"I'm so sorry. I must have dozed off," Schmidt said groggily, massaging his head. The dialysis nurse had just completed the treatment and was busy writing down the final information on Schmidt's chart. "What time is it? Where is Rena?"

"Rena had to be called away from the treatment center to deal with an emergency. I am Olga, and I stepped in to complete your treatment," the nurse replied. The two men who had transported Schmidt to the dialysis center reappeared with his wheelchair. "Now then, Professor: we will take you back home."

"Of course: thank you for everything," Schmidt replied gratefully. "It was so nice for you to make such a special accommodation for me."

"Not at all, Professor," the woman's hazel eyes flickered malevolently as the men wheeled him out the center door. "You are the one who's been most accommodating."

18

Sunday evening was usually a slow time at the dock complex opposite New York Harbor. Most of the ships docked there had already been unloaded, and the crews were away enjoying a few last minutes of leisure time before they left port Monday morning.

Pier 27 had nothing unusual to commend it. The tired-looking freighter moored next to it swayed gently at anchor, its ropes creaking as the ship rose and fell with the slight swell of the waters. Sun had long since set, and the dock was now deserted. The whole scene was lit with lights placed at infrequent intervals along the length of the pier.

No one was there to see the shadowy figures in rubber Zodiac boats coming up quietly to the side of the pier. The men in the boats were wearing scuba gear. After fastening their boats to one of the pilings supporting the pier, they quietly slipped beneath the dark water.

Once they were down about twenty feet, the divers switched on their high intensity underwater lights. Sweeping their lights carefully, the divers searched the shadowy bulk of the old pier. Suddenly, a glimmer of something metallic caught the light. The lead diver touched the arms of his companions, and together they focused all their beams in one direction.

The ghostly shape of a submerged submarine appeared before them. She was resting on her keel with silt mounded around her. The murky water diffused the light, giving the submarine a purplish green aura. The leader pointed towards the submarine and gestured for the rest of the team to follow him.

The divers swam up to the gray bulk of the old submarine, examining the hull of the submarine closely. Their mission was to examine the hull of the submarine to check its integrity.

"We need to find out if *U-3551* is seaworthy," Kolov had told his team of divers. "If she is, there is a chance her engines may be intact and able to move her on her own power."

Alexi Renov, a former Soviet submarine commander, was highly skeptical. "Comrade Kolov, it is highly unlikely that this submarine's hull is intact after sitting on the bottom of a busy harbor for almost sixty years. The traffic and buffeting of the ships above her alone will cause stress on her hull. Besides, it was standard procedure for submarine crews to scuttle their boats if they were abandoning them."

"I understand that, Captain," Kolov replied patiently. "However, our job will be much easier if the submarine is intact. An underwater salvage operation will be much more difficult and costly, not to mention more risky. It's worth finding out if we can sail her into the submarine pen."

Kolov's luck seemed to be running with their efforts, Renov decided as his crew slowly and meticulously tested the integrity of the submarine's hull. She was intact, and careful tapping on her pressure hull revealed that she had air inside of her.

Renov and his team worked their way over onto the deck of the submarine. He motioned for half of the team to continue its careful survey of the boat, heading towards the stern. Renov's section of the team moved up to the forward hatch. It was there that the escape trunk of the submarine was located. The hatch was open, indicating that the last crewmember had exited the submarine through the hatch.

Swimming down into the trunk, Renov tested the latch. Corrosion had frozen it shut. He grasped a wrench from his diving belt, and slipped it over the latch. Looking up at his team members, Renov made a gesture indicating that he wanted his companions to seal the hatch behind him. One of the members shook his head. Renov grasped his arm, squeezing it firmly and nodding his head. He then swam into the open trunk space and started to close the hatch behind him. Renov's comrades slammed the hatch shut.

Once the hatch was closed, Renov went to work on the hatch below his feet. Positioning the light in front of him, he turned the latch handle with all his might. The latch gave way slowly, and a great gout of bubbles poured out in front of his eyes. The water was escaping from beneath his feet, and the hatch integrity appeared to be holding.

In a few minutes, the water had drained to the point where Renov could open the inner hatch. He turned the wheel that unsealed the hatch and then pulled upward. The hatch hinges groaned as Renov opened the hatch. Renov focused the beam of his light downward into the heart of the ancient submarine.

He resisted the temptation to remove his mouth from the mouthpiece of his scuba gear. After decades on the harbor bottom, the atmosphere in the submarine was no longer breathable. Renov swept his light around the forward torpedo room. The bulkheads and inner frames of the submarine were in surprisingly good shape. Apparently the submarine's scrubbers had been left on, purifying the atmosphere until the submarine's battery supply had been exhausted.

Renov worked his way through the submarine. When he arrived at the conning tower, he checked his air supply. He only had twenty minutes left. Hastening through the rest of the submarine, he confirmed that the interior of the submarine was watertight. The batteries in the engine room were in particularly good condition. Captain Kepler had scrupulously kept his boat in superb working condition. *Comrade Kolov will be very pleased*, Renov thought to himself as he returned to the escape trunk for his outward voyage to the surface.

-0-

"*U-3551* is in superb condition, Comrade Kolov," Renov told Kolov enthusiastically an hour or so later. They were now inside the cavernous submarine pen nestled inside the abandoned warehouse that surrounded it like a shell. "This submarine pen is truly amazing. We can move the submarine into it and work at our leisure without detection."

"What is the next step, Captain?" Kolov asked.

"We must first get the batteries working, Comrade Kolov," Renov said, thinking quickly. "It is essential that the atmosphere inside the submarine can sustain life. We need to figure out a way to get the batteries operational in short order."

Kolov smiled. "There is a ship at anchor directly over the submarine. We can tie in electrical lines directly from that ship and feed them into *U-3551*. The ship generators will charge the batteries in no time."

"You are assuming, Comrade Kolov, that the ship will be deserted at the time we make this connection with the submarine," Renov observed. "How do you plan to do that?"

"Our little surprise will take care of that quite nicely," Kolov replied grimly. "Trust me on this, Alexi: there will be no one around on the docks to see what we are doing."

"The submarine is resting upon a relatively hard part of the harbor," another man told Kolov. "Our team found that her screws are only buried in half a meter of silt; that is not enough to impede the revolution of the screws when we attempt to free her."

"How much time do you think you will need to get the submarine fully operational? " Kolov said firmly. "We have less than three days left before the operation on the city is to commence. I want our movement of the submarine to be screened by the chaos caused by the operation."

"I believe we can have the submarine operational by Tuesday night, Colonel Kolov," Renov said with confidence. "That is, of course, if your plans for recharging the batteries proceeds accordingly."

"It will happen," Kolov said with a smile. "This is coming together much easier than I had ever planned."

19

"Didn't I tell you, David?" Charlie said as they emerged from Heathrow Airport into a torrential summer rain.

"Okay, go ahead and rub it in, Pest," David said in a resigned tone. He turned to Sir Leslie Gresham. "Miss I-Know-English-Weather-Better-than-Any-Forecaster said it was going to be raining when we got to London, Sir Leslie. How did she know that?"

"Charlie has a knack for those sorts of things," Sir Leslie said with an elaborate shrug. "I have no idea how she does it."

"Trade secret," Charlie said smugly.

They went directly to Sir Leslie Gresham's house for a few hours of needed sleep. Saturday morning, Charlie and David went to Buckingham Palace, where they received their knighthoods and honors from the Queen. They had lunch at the palace, and then did some shopping with the Greshams. Mary Ann accompanied them, and asked Charlie numerous questions about the wedding. Charlie was delighted to help out Mary Ann, who was one of her best friends from her days at the London Hospital.

"Jonathan has been absolutely no help at all with the wedding plans," Mary Ann complained to Charlie Saturday evening. "He's so busy right now getting ready to take over the regiment that he barely has any time at all."

"You're one for taking someone to task about time," Mary observed as her daughter gave her an exasperated expression. "Don't look at me like that, darling. You know it's true."

"I suppose you're right," Mary Ann conceded. She took

Charlie's hand. "I'm so glad you're here, even for a little while."

"I'm just glad to be out of that dreadful monkey suit," Charlie replied. "I can't for the life of me understand why we couldn't get the knighthood and awards ceremonies done on Monday instead of two separate days, Sir Leslie."

"I'm sorry, but tradition is tradition, Lady Warren. The Queen creates you a Lady of the Garter one day, and then you are formally installed on Garter Day in a separate ceremony," Leslie Gresham replied with a twinkle in his eye. He turned his attention to David. "You did splendidly this morning, my boy."

"Thank you, Sir Leslie," David said with a smile. "Now I'm at least noble like my wife."

Charlie nudged him. "More like a nuisance, Sir David."

"Does my being a knight mean that you're going to treat me with more respect?"

"No," Charlie rewarded his question by winking at him. "Are we headed over to St. Paul's tomorrow for service?"

"We most certainly are," Sir Leslie said. "I've been personally threatened with excommunication if you fail to put in an appearance tomorrow. Dean Groton was most insistent."

"I'm sure he was," Charlie said, stretching and yawning. "Forgive me, but I am absolutely exhausted."

"Perfectly understandable, my dear," Mary said indulgently, looking over at Mary Ann. "Are you free to go to service tomorrow, Mary Ann?"

Mary Ann shook her head. "I have to motor out to Hereford for some sort of beastly to-do with some general's wife in the morning. Jonathan insisted this was one I couldn't duck."

"The life of an officer's wife is not easy," Sir Leslie Gresham observed sagely.

"I agree with you, Leslie," Mary said archly. "Frankly, I'd rather face a tank regiment than some of those frowsy old biddies at those gatherings."

"David called me frowsy a few days ago, Mary," Charlie said, winking at David.

"I did not," David said in an outraged tone. "You were the one who used that term. Get your facts straight, Pest."

"I think that's enough out of all of you," Sir Leslie said, laughing. "We all need to turn in if we're going to be up to go to church in the morning."

-0-

Sunday passed all too quickly, and Monday was upon them before they knew it. The Greshams took Charlie and David to Windsor Castle early Monday morning. Garter Day was a major holiday in Britain, and the whole castle was arrayed in festal glory. Charlie, to her immense disgust, was once again the center of attention. She endured the ancient ceremonies with as much grace as she could muster, and was eternally grateful when the ceremonies concluded that afternoon.

"If I ever have to endure another ceremony like that, I think I'll shoot myself," an exhausted Charlie confided to Sir Leslie as she slumped into a chair in the Gresham's parlor.

"I'm afraid the Garter Day ceremony is an annual event, my dear," Gresham reminded her benignly. Charlie groaned and put her head in her hands in misery.

"Don't worry, Sir Leslie: I'll make sure she's not armed when we come over," David told him soothingly. His bride rewarded his statement with a look that shot daggers at him.

"I think you did splendidly," Mary Gresham said as she brought in some tea for everyone. "I think David actually has a whole host of pictures on that camera of his."

"Yes I do," David said confidently.

"Surrender your camera, sir, if you value your life," Charlie said in a threatening voice. "You know my rule about me and pictures."

"Of course," David handed her the camera. Charlie turned it on. "There's nothing here, David. What happened to the pictures?"

"I'm afraid I now have them, Charlie," Sir Leslie held up the memory stick. "Your power extends to your husband, but as your superior, I have now control over them."

"Fine," resigned, Charlie sank back into the chair. "At least all of this is over. Now we can go back to America and relax."

"It wasn't all that bad, my dear. You did a splendid job at the ceremonies today," Sir Leslie remarked. "You almost looked relaxed."

"Appearances are most deceiving, Sir Leslie, I can assure you," Charlie replied bleakly. "I will be very happy if I never have to undergo another royal ceremony for as long as I live."

"Come on, Charlie: you looked cute walking at Windsor Castle dressed in all your finery." David protested.

"Lady Margaret was quite upset that she couldn't be here for the ceremony. Unfortunately, the counter terrorism conference in Washington took precedence over anything else." Sir Leslie said.

"We need to go visit the Tower the next time we're here, Charlie," David said.

Charlie looked blackly at her husband and rewarded him with a nudge to his ribs. "I think I warned you about the Tower. If you must go, then you will do it solo. Another word from you, Sir David, and I'll send you back to America in a rowboat with one oar. Going to the National Gallery after church was enough of a treat."

"Enough, children," Gresham laughingly raised a hand. "We have some serious matters to discuss." He reached over by his chair and pulled up an impressive-looking satchel. "This file was given to me by Her Majesty this morning before the ceremony. It was your grandfather's, Charlie. The envelope on top has a note explaining what it is."

"Sir Leslie, I'm getting rather tired of unsolicited gifts popping up in my life. What sort of joy does this lovely parcel contain?"

"I haven't the slightest idea, my dear," Gresham smiled tolerantly. "I understand your hesitation, but you really have no choice. Her Majesty insisted that this be delivered to you."

"It's from the Queen, Charlie. If you refuse it, I think she can cut off your head," David said, earning another nudge from his bride.

Charlie opened the thick oblong envelope and pulled out the single heavy sheet of cotton fiber paper. Her face blanched as she read its contents. When she was done, she set the paper down and mutely pushed it across Sir Leslie's desk.

Gresham picked it up and read it. As he did, his face became quite still. "I have never seen anything like this before," he looked up at Charlie. "You realize, Charlie, that I had no idea what this message was about."

"What does the letter say, Charlie?" David asked. Charlie handed it to him without saying a word. David read it quickly. "I still don't understand. What is a royal warrant?"

"It's a type of formal commission granting the bearer certain powers," Sir Leslie Gresham explained. "In the case of your wife, David, she has been granted full authority by Her Majesty to use whatever means necessary and needed to complete the task outlined in that file."

"Whatever means necessary," Charlie repeated slowly. "What exactly does that mean, Sir Leslie?"

"It means, my dear, that all the assets of Her Majesty's government are now at your disposal. You, my dear Charlene, are the most powerful woman in England."

There was silence in the room for a minute or so. Sir Leslie's words had stunned Charlie into shocked silence. "I don't understand, Sir Leslie. Why me? I don't want to be the most powerful woman in England," Charlie finally said with tears in her eyes. "I want to go home and have children with my husband and live a quiet life."

Sir Leslie reached across his desk and grasped Charlie's hand. "My dear," he said with deadly earnestness, "you cannot escape who you are. I'm afraid that you will probably never have a quiet life as long as you live."

"That is the most terrible thing you have ever said to me, Sir Leslie," Charlie whispered.

"I know," Leslie Gresham nodded his head gravely. "It also happens to be the truth."

-0-

For the next several hours, Charlie, Gresham and David pored over the documents in the file. Michael Warren's work spanned the last decades of the twentieth century, stopping only with an entry dated a day or so before his death.

Charlie's initial shock and dismay had given way to fascination with the files and documents spread on the table before her. "I had no idea that my grandfather had a secret life. It's as if I never really knew him at all."

She looked up at Sir Leslie. "You had no idea about any of this, did you, sir? All of this was kept from you as well? How can that be?"

"British Intelligence as a discrete entity of the British Government has existed only since 1911, Charlie," Sir Leslie replied. "However, Her Majesty's Secret Service has existed in some form or another since the first Elizabeth. Your grandfather was an officer of the Crown, commissioned by George VI. He served in MI6 as a civil servant, but over and beyond all that, he served the Crown itself. He answered to a much higher authority than the civil servants appointed by Her Majesty. Does that make sense?"

"Yes it does, Sir Leslie," Charlie paused for a moment. She picked up the paper from the Queen granting her the royal warrant. "Does this mean that I've been personally appointed by the Queen to serve as a special agent of the Crown like Grandfather?"

"That's exactly what it means, my dear," Sir Leslie said quietly.

"What do all of these files mean, Sir Leslie?" David asked as he looked at all the documents spread across the table. "I see documents pertaining to all sorts of areas of the world."

"As near as I can tell, Charlie's grandfather was appointed by the Crown to investigate the possibility that the German atomic weapons program was further along than anyone had previously believed," Sir Leslie replied, rubbing his eyes.

"Why wasn't that job given to MI6? They could have done the work quite adequately," Charlie pointed out.

"As a student of military history, I can see several reasons," Sir Leslie chuckled. "You see, my dear, after the War, or actually just before its conclusion, the government changed hands. Churchill was dismissed by the British people, and Atlee took over. Atlee, you might say, saw things a bit differently than his predecessor. Intelligence establishments, like all human enterprises, have groups of people in it motivated by things other than love of Crown and country. They had their own self-centered agendas, and the change in regime allowed them to take over the intelligence efforts of Britain."

"So MI6 was compromised by political opportunists and could not be fully trusted," David observed.

"Excellent observation, my boy," Sir Leslie agreed. "In fact, it was much worse than that. Philby and his like actively wanted British Intelligence to be deflected away from finding out the truth about the German nuclear program. They did this on orders from their masters in the Kremlin.

"Churchill had a great fear of the Soviets, some say a phobia. History has, unfortunately, proved him correct, but at the time he was dismissed, his concerns were discounted."

"Except by the King," Charlie said with a smile. "The King trusted Churchill implicitly. They had fought a war together and understood each other's perspectives."

"Right," Sir Leslie nodded his head, peering at one of Michael Warren's notes. "The day Churchill was dismissed, King George summoned Winston to Buckingham Palace. He and Churchill discussed these concerns, and at that point, His Majesty granted Churchill a Royal Charter, giving him authority to carry out this mission. He would be answerable only to the Crown, and his operation would be carried on in utmost secrecy, out of the view of the public and prying eyes."

"Why didn't Grandfather come over to America and retrieve the message from the *Colossus* in New York?" Charlie asked. "That would have tipped off the British and Americans right away."

"It would have also tipped off the puppet masters in the Kremlin," Sir Leslie pointed out. "Michael Warren already suspected that MI6 was compromised. Besides, the entrance to the machine had been sealed up by order of the British Government. There was no way for Michael to access the machine. He was unaware of the tunnel entrance, though I imagine they sealed that off as well."

"So he pursued the evidence on the program from other avenues." Charlie said. "Grandfather also made sure that the warehouse never was allowed to be sold."

Exactly so, my dear," Sir Leslie said. "Michael kept things a family secret."

"So now that task has fallen to me."

"I'm afraid so, my dear," Sir Leslie said. "The timing of all of this seems to coincide with your current investigation over in America. The events described in your grandfather's file point directly to an incident that occurred in America just before the War ended, something that was never publicly revealed or discussed."

"Sir Leslie, if the Germans had developed a nuclear bomb, the Soviets would have been very eager to possess that technology," David said. "Roosevelt had informed Stalin of the existence of the Allied nuclear program, but declined to share the nuclear secrets with the Soviets. As Germany fell to the Soviets, they overran key German installations that had been involved in developing nuclear weapons."

"So someone in Russia has been working on finding out about the German program from their end all these years, pursuing it from their end of the puzzle." Charlie said, leaning across the table. "Grandfather was involved in a race against the Soviets to find out the secret part of the German plan."

"And that was what he was working on the day he died, Charlie," Sir Leslie pointed to the final entry in Michael Warren's journal. "The race, however, appears to be continuing in spite of his death."

"And time is running out," David said quietly.

"'Kepler is alive in New York City. He alone can verify my find-ings,'" Charlie read the entry slowly. "Who is Kepler, Sir Leslie?"

"I don't know, my dear," Gresham replied wearily, massaging his forehead and temples in an effort to clear his head. "I imagine you'll find out when you go through this file more thoroughly. However, it's very early in the morning, and you and David have a plane to catch. It's time to go to bed, at least for a while."

"Sir Leslie, I'm fine," Charlie said dismissively. "You and David go on. I need to check a few more things before I come up."

"Colonel Warren, you may be the bearer of a royal warrant, but I outrank you and as your superior, I'm ordering you to lay your work aside and retire," Gresham said with a mock frown.

"Come on, kid. You heard the Brigadier," David kissed her cheek gently. "We'll have seven long hours on that plane back to New York for you to look at all that stuff."

Standing up and stretching luxuriously, Charlie nodded her

agreement. "I agree, David. Let's get some rest before that flight back to America."

She looked down at the file. "Sir Leslie, why did Her Majesty appoint me to complete this task?"

"Because she knew that if anyone could finish the work of your late grandfather, you would be that person," Sir Leslie replied gently. "This task is something you were meant to do. I believe that God has called and equipped you to complete it. Don't worry or be afraid, Charlie. Rely on God, and you'll find your way."

David put his arm around her shoulders. "Let's get some rest, love. Morning is coming quickly."

-0-

Charlie went to bed, but spent the few hours tossing and turning. Mary Gresham crept up the stairs to their bedroom at five to waken them. "Charlie, David: it's five. Time to get up," she softly called out to the darkened room.

"Thanks Mary. Charlie's already up," David replied.

Mary went down to the kitchen and found Charlie already brewing coffee. The file was on the table alongside Charlie's notepad. "And what time did you get up, young lady?" Mary asked with mock disapproval. She softened her question by kissing Charlie's cheek.

"About four," Charlie replied, pouring coffee into two waiting cups. "Really, Mary; I'll get some rest later on when we're flying back to America."

Mary was skeptical. "Of course, my dear. You forget that you spent your medical training in London. I remember some of those all night sessions you and Mary Ann had studying for your examinations. I know how focused you get when you're on a task. Just try to take care of yourself."

Charlie nodded, taking a sip of her coffee. "I promise, Mary. What time did Mary Ann leave last night? We were rather busy in Uncle Leslie's study and missed seeing her off."

"She left at around eleven," Mary replied. "Mary Ann had rounds at five this morning. She understood you and David were busy with Leslie."

"I'm sorry this has been such a whirlwind visit, Mary," Charlie said regretfully. "David and I were so looking forward to spending more time with you."

Mary Gresham sighed. "We've all had to make adjustments. If you must know, this summer has been a bit of chaos from the very beginning. Even if you hadn't been pulled out of the wedding plans, things have been in a fair spot of turmoil since Jonathan's assumed command. I've had to move up wedding plans to accommodate his deployment."

"Life goes on at its own pace," Charlie looked down at her cup. "Sometimes things happen in spite of our best intentions."

"Yes, it does," a fully dressed David agreed from the kitchen door. "Charlie, you're suitcases are already packed except for the clothes you'll be wearing today. We need to be out of the house and over at Heathrow by seven."

"Thank you, David," Charlie got up from her chair and went over and kissed him. "Keep Mary company while I get ready." She left and went upstairs to shower and change clothes.

David shook his head after she left. "I don't know how Charlie does it. Life keeps throwing her all of these curves and she just keeps on going."

Mary handed him a cup of coffee. "Pretty much the way we all do, David. We just hang on and hope. I wish there was more we could do to help."

A few moments later, Sir Leslie made an appearance. Looking tired and drained, he accepted the steaming cup of coffee from Mary. "David, I'm so glad Charlie has you to lean on now. This latest task is going to be her greatest challenge yet."

"I'm just here to support her, sir. Charlie's the one who's had to do all of the heavy lifting," David replied. "Charlie once told me that molds were made to be broken. She's broken a lot of them these past few months."

"Indeed she has," Gresham nodded in affirmation. "She's smashed a fair number of them. Do you know that she's the first woman knighted by the Queen to be commanded to kneel and be dubbed with a sword? That's a tradition-breaking event then and there."

"Really?" David was interested, "I didn't know that. How is the knighting ceremony for a lady supposed to be conducted?"

"Female knights are normally led in and curtsey before the Sovereign, who announces their title. They are not required to kneel and be dubbed with a sword," Gresham said with a smile. "Your wife, David, won her title in combat. Her Majesty decided to break tradition by acknowledging that fact. Women have not been warriors in Britain from a historical standpoint. Our knighting ceremonies reflect that tradition."

"I have a number of Celtic ancestors who would probably dispute that claim," a freshly showered and dressed Charlie said from the door.

"Forgive me, my dear. I forgot your Celtic pedigree." Sir Leslie chuckled. "You receive a high mark for besting me in the history department."

"At least Charlie dresses in black when she's on duty, not blue woad." David said, kissing her.

"Indeed, wearing black is much more practical, especially at night," Charlie agreed. "Also, I prefer a machine pistol to a bow and arrow."

"You do have a disturbing taste for edged weapons," David pointed out.

"It's genetic," Charlie said with a bright smile.

Everyone sat down and had breakfast. They carefully avoided talking about Michael Warren's files, or the case in New York. Instead, they focused on the upcoming wedding and other domestic items. Sir Leslie excused himself and returned to the table ten minutes later fully dressed. "Now then, it's time to get you two off to the plane. It was delightful to have you over, even for a brief period of time."

"We'll have some time later on this year to come over for a visit," David promised.

"Only if it's not too much later," Charlie clarified, "the baby is due sometime in March."

"Just keep yourself in one piece, darling," Mary Gresham said, hugging Charlie one final time.

-0-

The flight from Heathrow was blessedly uneventful for the first few hours. Charlie and David busied themselves with going over the NYPD case file, as well as Michael Warren's satchel full of documents. The business pad on Charlie's lap filled quickly with pages of closely written notes as she pored systematically through her Grandfather's file. David reviewed the file on the case, working in a patient, methodical manner. They managed to make progress in both areas, and it was becoming increasingly obvious to both of them that the two cases were closely linked with each other.

Their work came to an abrupt end two hours before their plane was scheduled to land in New York. The plane suddenly made a pronounced turn to the south, accompanied by a sharp decrease in altitude.

"Whoa! That was quick!" David exclaimed as one of his stray pencils skittered off of his table onto the aisle floor. He looked out his window and his jaw dropped. Charlie was still intently scrutinizing one of her grandfather's papers and had decided not to notice the change in the aircraft's course and speed. David nudged her. "Charlie, look out the window."

"What, David?" she asked, slightly irritated. Charlie's irritation vanished when she saw what had gotten David's attention.

Fifty yards outside their window, two F-18's were flying next to their right wing. The fighters had long-range fuel tanks attached to their wings and they bristled with air-to-air missiles.

"They're long range interceptors from the *Kennedy*," David said grimly. "I recognize the tail insignia. Those are live warheads they're carrying. They mean business, Charlie."

"Ladies and gentlemen: this is the Captain speaking," the Captain's voice came over the cabin speakers. He sounded shaken. "I... we have some grave news to tell you. Apparently there has been some sort of terrorist incident in New York City. That is all the news I have at this time. The fighters outside our aircraft are there to escort us into the United States. Do not be alarmed by their presence."

There were several collective gasps as the captain made his announcement. Charlie gripped David's hand tightly. He nodded slightly as she did this. "I'm tracking you, Charlie," he said quietly. Both of them knew that the incident had something to do with their case.

A flight attendant came up to their seats. "Colonel Warren, Captain Matthews would like to see you, please." Charlie and David rose from their seats. The attendant looked over at David and shook her head slightly. "Alone, if you don't mind, sir."

David sat down, and Charlie reached for his hand, squeezing it slightly before she left. "I'll be back, David."

-0-

Captain Matthews was busy talking to the fighter escort as Charlie entered the cabin. "Roger, Bravo Six-Niner. We copy course change One Two Zero true and altitude vector Angels Forty."

"Roger, 257. This is Six Niner out," the terse response came from the lead fighter.

"Well, this is a fine way to end a long day," Matthews sighed as he replaced the microphone to its resting place on the instrument panel. He turned around to greet Charlie. "Ah, Colonel Warren! So good to meet you finally! You're rather a legend in our circles, with your Good Samaritan deed last January and all."

"Really, Captain: it was nothing," Charlie replied, blushing slightly. "You wished to see me?"

"See you? Oh yes, you have a message." Matthews said in an embarrassed tone. He had a tendency to gush at times when excited. "It came off the secure traffic line just before our friends from the *Kennedy* showed up." He handed her a sheet with a few lines on it.

Charlie read the message quickly. "Thank you, Captain," she said, carefully folding up the message and putting it into her pocket. "Do you have any more information on the situation in New York?"

"Nothing specific," Captain Matthews replied, his face growing solemn. "From the chatter we've heard over the American news networks, it sounds like some sort of chemical strike on New York City."

"I see," Charlie tried to hide her shock. "Thank you for the news, Captain."

"You're more than welcome, Colonel Warren," Matthews held out his hand. "Good luck and Godspeed, ma'am." Their eyes met, and Charlie nodded slightly. Charlie left the cabin, and the flight crew returned to the business of piloting the aircraft.

"I've got a niece who's about her age, Mick," the Flight Officer told Matthews after a few minutes. "She doesn't look a day over twenty."

"Looks are deceiving, chum," Matthews replied. "My friends in the Army say she's got quite a record. One of them told me she foiled some sort of plot in London in January."

"Do tell," the Second Officer said grimly. "I'm just worried about those Yank fighters standing off our wings. I hope they don't have itchy trigger fingers."

"Not to worry, Sid," Matthews said matter-of-factly. "All we need to do is follow orders. Besides, if they really wanted to shoot us down, they would have done that a long time ago."

"You always have a way of cheering me up, Mick."

Matthews shrugged elaborately. "What can I say? It's a gift."

-0-

Charlie returned to her seat next to David. She clasped his hand tightly and said nothing for a moment or two. "We're landing at LaGuardia, but it's going to take a little longer for us to get clearance into US air space. We'll be one of the only flights allowed to enter New York City."

"Good," David nodded, "our baggage has a chance of arriving with us on time for a change. We'll land just in time to get involved in a war."

Charlie stared out the window at the fighters. "The war has already started, David. It's been going on since September 11, 2001."

20

Tuesday morning in New York City had started out innocently enough. The highways and subways into the city were crowded with the usual flow of commuter traffic. Things proceeded along as they had for years. No one had any inkling that this day would be a day unlike any the city had ever experienced in its history.

The roar of the approaching subway train filled the tunnel. It was an outgoing train headed for the suburbs. A crowd of people awaiting its arrival reflexively moved towards the edge of the platform. Several people jettisoned items into trashcans stationed along the subway walls. Riding the trains was a crowded experience, and no one wanted to have the greasy remains of a donut or breakfast sandwich crushed into an expensive business suit.

An anonymous-looking man took a last bite of his muffin before putting it into a paper bag and throwing it into a trashcan. He joined the throng of people pressing into the train and finally found himself wedged uncomfortably into a tiny space with about fifty other people. A few minutes later, tendrils of white, almost colorless gas eddied upward from the bag the man had discarded.

The outbound subway train whirled away from the platform on its outward trek to the suburbs. Ten minutes after it left, an emergency sensor located on the subway platform sent a signal to a central relay center. At this point, several things happened automatically. The entrances to all subway stations automatically locked, and the ventilation systems to all tunnels sealed themselves from the outside world. All trains ground to a halt wherever they were in the system, stranding hundreds of thousands of people in various locations in the tunnels.

A warning alarm sounded in the command room of the New York City Emergency Operations Center. The sound alerted the technician manning that console, and she immediately pressed a button activating the network of trauma centers located in the city.

"Sir, we just had a nerve gas warning alarm go off on Route Seven near Madison Square Garden," the technician told the Watch Commander of the EOC, who had just been summoned into the command room by the activation of the alarm.

The Watch Commander nodded brusquely. "Have Dispatch send HAZMAT units twelve and two to Madison Square Garden. That looks like the closest area for a forward command post. I want ESU notified for crowd control and backup."

He turned and picked up a red phone. "Mr. Mayor? This is Captain Romano at the EOC. Yes, sir; it's not a drill. No, we haven't got units to the scene yet. It was an automated alarm. Yes sir, trauma units are standing by along with HAZMAT teams. Yes sir; I'll keep you posted."

Just then, four more alarms pierced through the hum of the command center. "Sir, I've got four more nerve agent alarms sounding in other tunnel locations!" The technician pointed to new red lights glowing on her console.

"Hold on, Mr. Mayor," the Watch Commander looked down at the console and the locations of the alarms. "Sir, the situation has just escalated. We have alarms sounding in four more systems. Yes sir, we've checked for malfunctions."

Another technician came up with a piece of paper. Romano took the paper and read it swiftly. His face blanched and he spoke again into the phone. "Sir, we're getting preliminary reports back from security personnel in the affected areas. They estimate... that we have at least fifty confirmed immediate deaths and several hundred people sick."

The Commander nodded slowly as the Mayor relayed his instructions. "Yes sir; I concur with your assessment." Romano went to his command console and picked up the phone. This phone put him through immediately to the Office of Homeland Security in

Washington. "This is Captain Romano at the New York City EOC. I want to report a level one release of nerve agent in the New York City area."

-0-

The emergency phone rang in Ken Rawlings' office two minutes later. "Special Agent Rawlings," he said tersely. "What? You're sure? All right, sir; we'll head to the areas immediately. Yes sir, this sounds exactly what we've been expecting. Right, sir; I'll keep you informed."

Rawlings put down the phone and looked up at Robin Dubek. "That was Captain Romano from the New York Emergency Operations Center. Looks like Kolov has just attacked New York City. We have reports of nerve gas in the subway tunnels all over the island."

Dubek gasped. "Casualties?"

"Fifty and climbing," Rawlings moved towards the door. "I want all agents to meet me in the briefing room in five minutes. The Mayor has been notified, and EOC is now coordinating first response efforts. As of right now, this city's just been sealed off from the rest of the world."

-0-

"Okay people, settle down, settle down!" Howard Vinson pitched his voice over the din of the crowed briefing room. "Here's what we know right now: at about eight this morning EOC nerve gas alarms were activated at these five subway stations," he pointed to a cluster of red areas marked on a map of New York City.

"Preliminary casualty figures are now at two hundred confirmed dead on the scenes and about two thousand people injured. This situation's developing hot. The city's locked down, and we've just had the terrorist threat level raised to Red. As of right now, no one's entering or leaving the United States of America unless on express orders of the President."

Vinson paused for a moment. "I'm having all department heads issue their emergency orders, so they'll brief you on your tasks during this situation. I just wanted to give you an overview right now on what's going on."

He left the podium and went over to Brenda Reynolds and Ron Meyers, who were discussing details of the situation with their immediate supervisor. "Sorry to barge in, guys, but I need to see you two in my office right now."

Reynolds and Meyers looked at each other and followed Vinson into his office. "Close the door," he told them as he sat down behind his desk. He tossed a folder across the desk to the two detectives. "I have another homicide linked to that LuxVeritas bunch you've been investigating. Woman who worked out in Huntington was found dead Monday evening. Looks like a home invasion, but the detectives on the scene aren't buying it.

"Rawlings got an anonymous tip from someone over in LuxVeritas that it's linked to this Kolov clown you guys have been tracking. That's why I'm sending you two over to Huntington."

"Why are we being sent to this, Captain?" Brenda asked. "Don't you need us here right now to help with this nerve gas thing?"

"This may be just as important," Vinson shook his head. "Rawlings let me know about it this morning. This murder has direct ties to your case. He says that this is your number one priority. Got any questions?"

The two detectives shook their heads. Vinson nodded his approval. "Good. I'll expect a report from you when you get back." He handed Brenda the case file the Huntington police department had faxed over.

He also gave them two green identification tags. "You'll need these to get back into New York City. Don't lose them, or you'll never get through the National Guard checkpoints."

Brenda took the tags from Vinson. "All right, Captain; we'll be back in a few hours and make our report." She glanced over at Meyers. "Let's go, Sergeant."

Meyers stared at her. It was the first time that he could remember Brenda taking an order without some sort of protest. "Okay, Lieutenant."

A bigger surprise awaited Ron out in the parking garage.

Brenda opened the passenger side door and settled into it. Meyers' jaw nearly fell onto the concrete floor. "What's wrong, Lieutenant? Don't you want to drive?"

"No, I want to read this case file. You go ahead," Brenda replied in a distracted tone. She was already deeply engrossed in the file.

First, she takes an order without question, and now she lets me drive. What's next? Ron thought as he turned on the car's ignition.

-0-

"Thanks for coming down, Lieutenant Reynolds," Al Marks, the chief detective said as Brenda and Ron came through the doors of his office. "I know you guys have your hands full with what's going on in the City."

"Not a problem," Reynolds said evenly. "We're here to help. What's going on?"

"We found the body of a dialysis nurse named Rena Devon in her apartment on Monday. Initially it looked like a home invasion gone bad, but once we took a closer look, we're not so sure. Nothing was taken. There were no signs of a struggle, which is what you generally find in situations like that."

"Do you have photographs of the crime scene?" Brenda asked.

"Here they are," Marks handed her some photographs. They showed the body of Rena laid out on her carpet, face down, blood seeping from a bullet hole in the back of her head, her arms splayed out at a grotesque angle.

It took Brenda only thirty seconds to figure out the situation from the photograph. "This was no home invasion, Detective. This was an execution."

"How do you know that?" Marks asked.

"The body is almost in the front entrance facing the stairwell." Brenda pointed to the photograph. "She was pushed through the door and shot in the back of her head. Her body came to rest with her head propped up against the stairwell. The people who did it didn't bother to arrange the body in a more convincing pose. They went in and tossed a few things around to make it look convincing. When was the body found?"

"Monday afternoon," the detective replied, obviously impressed with Brenda's analysis of the crime scene. "She didn't show up for work."

"Our captain said that this center is run by a LuxVeritas subsidiary," Ron said. "That's the principal reason we were sent out here today."

Marks scratched his head perplexedly. "Yeah, that's right. We have some witnesses who said they saw Devon at the center on Sunday with a patient. Trouble is, no one was scheduled to be dialyzed on Sunday. The center's normally closed."

"Does the center ever open up for emergencies?" Meyers asked.

"Not usually," Marks replied. "That's one of the things I asked the center director. He wasn't too interested in answering my questions. I think someone from higher up told him not to be cooperative."

"Do you have a list of clients who use the center?" Reynolds asked.

The detective made an irritated gesture. "I had to go get a warrant for it, but yeah, here it is." He handed Brenda a few sheets of paper.

"Thanks, Detective," Brenda put the sheets in her coat. "I guess our next stop is the dialysis center."

"Mind if I tag along?" Marks asked.

"Not at all," Reynolds replied. "I think it's time to have a talk with the guy who runs that place."

-0-

"One of your nurses is dead, Mr. Miller, and you don't seem the least bit upset about it," Brenda Reynolds leaned across the desk and glared at the director of the clinic. "I want to know who told you to not cooperate with the police in this matter, and why."

"Ms. Reynolds... I mean Detective Reynolds: I don't know what you're talking about," Fenton Miller stammered as Brenda continued to stare him down.

"We know this place was open on Sunday, and that Rena Devon was seen here. You don't seem to know anything about it," Al Marks chimed in. "Do you always have things happen around here that you don't know anything about? I'm sure the state licensing board would be interested in knowing about that. Now why don't you tell us what went on here on Sunday?"

Fenton Miller stared at the three detectives in his office. He felt like a cornered rat, with no place to go. He knew that if he cooperated, he would suffer a hideous, protracted death. His early morning visitors had promised him that.

He had wakened early in the morning to find two men in his apartment, standing over his bed. They had told him that Rena had been killed, and that if he failed too cooperate, then the two men would come back for him. To emphasize their point, they had dragged him to his bathroom and forced him to look at some photographs of people they had killed. Fenton knew that he would never, ever forget those photographs as long as he lived.

He swallowed again, and a film of sweat broke out over his face. "I... I don't. I can't..." he shook his head in misery.

Brenda's voice softened somewhat. "We know they threatened you, Miller. If you cooperate, we can protect you. But if you don't, we'll just walk out of here and let them take care of things. How about that? They know we're here in your office right now. They know we're talking to you. So what's it going to be?"

Miller stared at them and then decided. "All right; I... I was told by my district manager that a special patient needed to be dialyzed emergently on Sunday, so I contacted Rena to meet them down here at the center to open the place up."

"Who was the person who contacted you?" Ron Meyers asked.

"I think his name was Decker," Miller replied, blanching as he said the name.

"Now then, Mr. Miller; that wasn't so hard," Reynolds said with satisfaction. "Why didn't you tell Detective Marks this information earlier?"

"I... was told not to... release that information," Miller gulped, "or I'd lose my job and... other things."

"What was the name of the patient who was dialyzed here on Sunday, Mr. Miller?" Detective Marks asked.

"I wasn't told that information."

"Really?" Brenda turned and looked out at the busy dialysis

center. About twenty patients were hooked up to machines. The place was a beehive of activity, with nurses and technicians hurrying about. "I'm willing to bet that it was a regular client of yours. It will be easy enough to figure out who might not be here this morning."

"Why don't you go out and ask some of the nurses while Mr. Miller and I continue our little chat?" Al Marks suggested. "I'm going to make a few phone calls to Huntington Hospital to see if any renal patients checked in there in the last twenty-four hours." He looked at Miller. "I also have a few more questions to ask our little friend here."

"Good idea," Ron Meyers said as he and Brenda left the office. They went up to the receptionist's desk and identified themselves. "Good morning, Miss; we're detectives working the murder of Rena Devon, one of the employees here at the center. Have any of your clients not shown up for regular treatments today?"

"Let me see," the receptionist peered at her computer screen for a moment. "Yes, it looks as though Professor Schmidt didn't make it here today. He's very faithful. Let me see if I can find out why." She scrolled down the display a bit further. "Okay, it looks as though he was admitted to the Huntington Hospital yesterday evening."

"Do you know why?" Brenda asked.

"I can tell you why," Al Marks came up to them. "I just got off the phone with the hospital. Hans Schmidt is in ICU. He's not supposed to make it."

"You'd better bring that director in for further questioning, Detective," Brenda suggested grimly. "You'd better find out a way to hold him in custody as well. People who've been mixed up with this LuxVeritas bunch have a habit of winding up dead."

"I think we've got enough to hold him on right now," Marks replied. "Obstruction of justice, impeding a police investigation, not to mention conspiracy to commit murder: that's just for openers."

"Let's call up Rawlings and let him know what we've found," Brenda reached for her cell phone.

-0-

"You'll never guess who I've just finished talking to, Mr. Kolov,"

Robert Decker snarled at the Russian as he walked into his office. "Detective Brenda Reynolds of the NYPD, wanting to know how and why we opened a dialysis center on Sunday to dialyze a Professor Hans Schmidt. She also went on to say that this man is now in a coma at Huntington Regional Hospital and not expected to survive."

"Reynolds? That is a name that I have heard of before," Kolov chose to ignore Decker's remarks for a moment. "Oh yes: that's one of those meddlesome detectives sniffing at our heels these past few days. She and her partner have been trying to find out about our operation."

"Well, they've linked Quimby to us, and now Schmidt," Decker rose and looked at Kolov. "That fool Miller is now singing like a canary to the police. They said they'd be down here later on today to ask us some more questions."

"Please relax, Mr. Decker," Kolov attempted to be soothing. "Look outside your door for a moment. New York City is in a state of chaos. Traffic is paralyzed. No one can get in or out of the city. My people are now working on the submarine. Once it is operational, the final phase of this plan will be complete."

"I hope so, Kolov," Decker muttered. "I truly hope so."

"I have a feeling that those two detectives are not going to be able to make it to their appointment with you today."

"And how are you going to arrange that?"

Kolov smiled unpleasantly. "They are going to be sent off in another direction." He looked down at a picture of Brenda Reynolds he was carrying, along with a file. "She's rather attractive. It will be good to meet her, I think."

-0-

"I always knew traffic was bad coming in from Huntington, but this is ridiculous," Reynolds complained as they waited in traffic. The heat waves were eddying up off the surfaces of the cars, causing the buildings of New York City to dance and shimmer in the distance.

"National Guard's checking every single car going into the city," Meyers explained. "Anyone who's not on official business

gets turned around. Hey, cop!" Ron called out to a mounted policeman who was a lane over, walking his horse between the cars.

"Can I help you?" the patrolman said as he came over with his
horse.

Meyers showed him his badge. "NYPD on official business.
How long is this parking lot going to stay here?"

"You got me, man," the officer replied. "I've got people here
who've been waiting since seven this morning to get into the city.
They aren't letting anyone in who doesn't belong there."

"Is there any way we can get accelerated clearance?" Ron
asked. "We've got a murder investigation that's developing hot. Can
you call your section supervisor and get us into the city quickly?"

"I'll see what I can do," the officer spurred his mount and rode
away.

"I always thought that would be interesting duty," Brenda
commented.

"You and about 20,000 other cops in the city," Meyers said ironically. "The waiting list to be considered is about five years long.
You have to have a big time rabbi to get a spot on that detail."

They were silent for a moment, watching the summer sun glint
off the car roofs. "Meyers, I need to tell you something," Brenda
said after a few moments.

"What is it, Lieutenant?" Ron asked with secret dread in his
heart. There was a tone in Brenda's voice was all-too familiar. He'd
heard it from countless women over the years, so he knew what was
going to happen next: the brush-off.

"You and I have been partners for two years now," Brenda
began hesitantly. "I really don't think it's a good idea that we get
personally involved with each other.

"You've been a great partner to work with, and you've been
better to me than anyone ever has. I'd just feel better about working
with you if we keep our relationship on a purely professional level."

Meyers said nothing. He was trying to figure out how he should
handle this without making things worse. *I knew this was coming. I
guess I didn't realize how much it would hurt when it came.*

"That's all right, Lieutenant. I understand," he finally said in an
almost normal voice. "Look, I was just trying to be nice. No one

else in the Precinct gives you the time of day. I mean, you don't hang with the rest of the female officers, and I've never heard of you dating anyone. Everyone respects you, but nobody likes you.

"I want to be your partner, and your friend. Does that make sense?"

Brenda's face went red when Ron remarked about no one liking her. She was about to angrily respond to his statement when she looked at his face. Ron obviously did not agree with that opinion. She decided to make a concession. "Yeah, Meyers, it does make sense. We can be friends. Just don't expect things to go any farther than that, okay?"

A ghost of a smile appeared on Ron's face. "Okay."

The mounted patrolman appeared. "I just talked to the soldiers up at the checkpoint. They just got word from their higher-ups to get you through. Give me a minute to get traffic rerouted so we can get you up to the gate."

"Looks like we've got things finally moving off dead center." Brenda said, turning the car back on.

"You're right about that, Lieutenant." Meyers said, hoping Reynolds didn't pick up on the double meaning of his response.

It was late afternoon by the time Reynolds and Meyers finally reached downtown Manhattan. They were almost at LuxVeritas when Brenda's cell phone rang.

"Detective Reynolds? This is Rob Dubek. We need you to proceed to the Seventeenth Street subway station. We've just picked up intel that a situation might be developing there."

"That's where all of this nonsense started, Lieutenant, remember?" Meyers said grimly. "Seems like a thousand years ago."

"Yeah, it does," Brenda agreed. "Okay, Agent Dubek; we're on our way."

"All right," Meyers put the car into a tight, 180-degree turn. "Let's head a quarter of a mile back the way we came."

Half an hour later, they were back at the abandoned subway station. "I don't see any backup, Lieutenant," Meyers said as he looked around the deserted subway platform. All of the subways had been completely shut down since that morning. Usually the tunnels were filled with the sounds of trains, both distant and close.

Instead, the dark tunnels were full of an eerie, ominous quiet.

"Let's find out what's going on," Reynolds called Dubek's number at the FBI office. "Agent Dubek? This is Detective Meyers. We're here at the subway platform and we don't have any backup. What? Okay, I understand. We'll give you a call when we find out."

She closed up her phone. "We're to go in and find out what's going on, Meyers."

"That doesn't sound like a good idea, Lieutenant," Meyers observed skeptically. "Remember what Warren and that CSI found down in that place. We should at least call for backup."

The mention of Charlie's name set Brenda off. "Look, Meyers: I was a detective long before I met that meddlesome twit, and I don't need her advice on how to do my business. Now let's get this thing over with so we can get over to LuxVeritas and get this investigation on the fast track."

"Okay, Lieutenant, okay," Meyers said in a resigned tone, producing his flashlight. "CSI's probably taken down their lights, so I brought this along so we can see where we're going."

They moved quickly to the place where the access tunnel was located. The eerie quiet of the deserted subway station was unnerving. Far down in the blackness of the tunnel, they could here the moaning of the wind and the dripping of water.

The two detectives climbed down the ladder into the access tunnel. As Meyers had predicted, the illuminating lights had been removed from the crime scene. The only light came from the occasional grids from the subway overhead and Meyer's flashlight.

"Come on, Meyers: this place gives me the creeps," Brenda said, her voice slightly trembling.

They had only gotten about twelve feet from the ladder when someone came up from behind and threw them to the ground. Brenda felt her legs being kicked out from under her as she fell face forward to the ground. The fall knocked the wind out of her. A fraction of a second later her arms were pinned behind her back and fastened with a nylon quick-tie. A piece of tape was clamped over her mouth and she was hauled to her feet.

Looking wildly around, she could see that Ron was being held by two shadowy figures with guns. A flashlight blazed up into her face. "This is her," a voice said in Russian. "This is the woman Comrade Kolov wanted. Let's go."

What about this man?" one of the figures asked.

"Shoot him," his friend replied. Brenda found herself being half-dragged towards the black maw of the tunnel. She heard two shots behind her and the fall of Ron's body as he hit the hard tunnel floor.

21

Ken Rawlings met the aircraft in New York later that night. "Nice to have you back on American soil, Dr. Warren," he said perfunctorily as Charlie and David came off the airplane. He turned to a tall man in a military uniform standing next to him. "I think you know this man, don't you?"

"I should say I do," Charlie replied with a joyful smile on her face. She rushed up to the man and hugged his neck tightly. "Nathan Mason! It's so good to see you again!"

"I'm glad to see you, too, Charlie," Mason replied as Charlie released him. He turned and shook David's hand. "Glad you got her back to America in one piece, Dave."

"It isn't a job, it's a challenge. What happened, Colonel?" David shook his hand heartily and pointed to the stars on Mason's uniform. "Why on earth did you let them make you a general?"

"They forced me at gunpoint, Stone," Mason replied. "What's worse, they took me away from my unit at Bragg and sent me to the Pentagon. I hate that place. The food stinks and the place is full of nasty politicians, bootlickers and no-minds who think they know everything."

"General Mason's up from Washington to help us with the military aspect of operations," Rawlings explained. "He also said he's the only military man in the United States qualified to handle an op with Charlie Warren."

"I've got the scars to prove it," Mason said with a grin. "I'm using this crisis as a thinly disguised excuse to escape from the

Pentagon," Mason grinned crookedly.

The smile vanished from Charlie's face. "How are things going?"

"Bad," Rawlings shook his head. "They used VX and Sarin gas. The emergency ventilation and containment systems managed to isolate most of the contamination to a few areas of the subways, but HAZMAT's going to have to spend at least a couple of days decontaminating the whole system. We've had several near riots of people trying to break through the decontamination centers at the subways, but so far things have held. Most of the people are now out of the subways and in temporary shelters. Central Park's been turned into a giant tent city to house people who can't get back home."

"I know all about not being able to get back home, Agent Rawlings," Charlie said quietly. She had finally gotten in touch with Katya at Joan Richards' home. Katya was relieved to know that Charlie and David were all right.

"I have a rather selfish question to ask you. When do you think we'll be allowed to return to Compton?" Charlie asked.

Rawlings shrugged. "It depends on how fast we can get things up and moving in the city. Right now, things are pretty much at a standstill. The only vehicles allowed on the roads are those on official business." They continued to walk through the terminal, arriving at the front entrance. "We have a helicopter standing by to take you to the EOC."

"Have there been any more developments on that warehouse by the East river?" Charlie asked.

Rawlings shook his head. "We've had surveillance on the location ever since you left for the UK. No one's been near the place, and we haven't seen any activity in there. Things have changed since the nerve gas attack, and we've had to pull units off to help with the mess in the subways."

Which is precisely what they were counting on," Charlie half-murmured to herself. The Blackhawk helicopter came into view in front of them. "Oh jolly; I do so love helicopters," Charlie grumbled, looking at General Mason.

"Don't worry, Charlie. I'm not driving this one," Nathan said teasingly. "Besides, it's like riding a horse."

"Right," Charlie shook her head as she climbed into the helicopter, which bristled with several types of missiles and rockets. "Horses at least don't fall out of skies."

"Look at it this way, Charlie," David said, attempting to put a positive spin of things, "we don't have to fight the traffic out of the airport. Our car is parked downtown at the British Consulate."

"Yes, right in the middle of the chaos. How convenient," Charlie replied glumly. "At least we're not wearing web gear and weapons," David pointed out as he fastened his seat belt. Once they were all in the helicopter, the pilot quickly lifted off and headed towards the center of the city.

"I see we have company," David pointed out the window. In the dim light, the dark silhouettes of two attack helicopters flanked each side of their aircraft.

"Yes, we can't afford to take any chances. We have AWACs orbiting the city on a twenty-four hour basis," Mason replied. "We know Kolov has surface-to-air missiles. He's not afraid to use them. If he uses one, we'll have F-16's launching counter suppression strikes the moment they see a missile light up."

"I'm surprised he hasn't decided to attack the EOC," Rawlings said. "That's one of the places I'd hit if I were in his shoes."

"Too obvious," Charlie noted. "Kolov is a chess player. He thinks in terms of multiple strategies." A thought suddenly occurred to her. "Agent Rawlings, I believe this attack is simply a monstrous diversion, a ruse designed to draw us away from his primary mission."

The aircraft had finally arrived at the rooftop heliport of the EOC. "I'll let you explain yourself when we get to the command center," Rawlings yelled as they got out of the aircraft. They hurried over to the building and quickly went inside.

"I want to get you down to the Situation Room and get an update, General," Rawlings said quickly over his shoulder as they walked down into the center of the building. In a few minutes they were at the Situation Room. At the front, a huge computerized map of New York City was projected. The contaminated areas were highlighted in a ghastly orange-red. Over to one side were the casualty figures broken down into sectors, along with the trauma centers treating the casualties.

"This just keeps getting worse," Rob Dubek walked up to them with a worried expression on his face. "We've just completed primary surveys of the tunnel systems. All of the major lines into the city have been contaminated. Even with our primary isolation procedures, the gas was able to penetrate a substantial percentage of the downtown subway areas."

"In other words, they knew where and how to hit us," Mason summarized grimly. "What are the latest casualty figures?"

"They've stabilized somewhat," Dubek looked down at his notes. "So far, we've had no more fatalities, but all of the ICU's in downtown New York are packed. We've had to divert non-nerve illnesses and injuries out to outlying hospitals. EMS has its hands full, but we've been through this drill enough that everyone knows what they need to do."

"That's good news," Charlie said, looking at Rawlings. "Have there been any people willing to come forward to claim responsibility for this?"

"Actually, it's been the reverse," Mason answered. "Most of the major players have backed away from this event. In fact, before we left Washington, the Secretary told me that he's gotten offers of assistance from every nation you can think of to help in this situation."

"Speaking of help, Dr. Warren, I was told to give you this from the British Consulate." Dubek handed Charlie a piece of paper.

"It's from Lady Margaret. James and Sergeant Major MacKay weren't able to get into New York City at all today," Charlie said, reading the note. "She wants me to call her as soon as possible."

"Dr. Warren, you were about to tell me a theory about this attack," Rawlings glanced towards one of the conference rooms. "Would you like to elaborate now?"

Charlie looked over at Dubek, who was busy talking to Mason. "Yes sir; if I can have a word with you alone, please. You're invited, David."

They went over to the conference room and closed the door. "Sir, for the past few weeks, you've been focused on the East River area. Your whole operation has been dedicated to finding out what's going on down there. Now comes this attack, and suddenly the focus is drawn away from there."

Rawlings was not convinced. "Charlie, we've known something big was coming down in the city. A major chemical attack is definitely a big league operation. This may be it. We were expecting something like this. This has Kolov written all over it."

"That's right sir, it's what you've been expecting. That's exactly what Kolov wants you to believe," David said quickly. He was following along Charlie's line of reasoning. "What better way to put you off your guard than to stage a major attack in the opposite direction? He may be diverting you away from the real threat that's coming down the tubes."

Rawlings looked at them for a minute. "All right, if that's what's really happening, then put all of this together so we can meet the real threat. Do you think you can do that?"

"Agent Rawlings, I've just spent most of two days going through my grandfather's notes, along with this investigation," Charlie said with conviction. "I believe I know exactly what Kolov is up to and why."

Rawlings was about to answer Charlie when his cell phone rang. "Hello? No, Captain Vinson, I haven't seen Meyers or Reynolds since this morning. What? I didn't tell them to go to the Seventeenth Street station. The last thing I told them was to go to LuxVeritas and talk to a Mr. Decker. Okay, if I see them, I'll have them report in to you. Bye."

He closed his phone. "It's the worst terrorist incident since 9/11, and a precinct captain calls me up and tells me two of his cops are missing. What a world."

"Wait a minute, Agent Rawlings," Charlie said. "Did you say LuxVeritas? How long ago was that?"

"Four hours ago. Traffic's a nightmare out there, so I wasn't worried," Rawlings frowned. "What's the problem?"

"The problem is that I think those two detectives are in grave danger," Charlie turned and started to walk towards an exit. "I think they were sent into a trap."

"Hold on a minute, Dr. Warren!" Rawlings called after her. "Just where do you think you're going?"

"I'm going to find out where those two people are," Charlie said, not slowing down at all.

"Charlie, you can't just run off like that and leave everyone hanging," David said, catching up to her. "We've got to sort things out around here."

"All right, I'll explain things to you," Charlie stopped and faced the three men. "That tunnel is the direct route into the heart of the dock area. I'm certain it leads to my grandfather's warehouse. There are people down in those tunnels right now, people of Kolov's who are searching for something. I'm certain Meyers and Reynolds were sent there for a reason, and I think they've been captured."

"Captured? Why?" Rawlings asked.

"Because they're getting too close to the truth about LuxVeritas and what's down there in those tunnels, that's why," Charlie replied sharply. "I know you're busy dealing with all of this current disaster. I'm willing to go and find out what's going on with those two detectives. You can't just simply brush off their disappearance."

"Charlie, this sounds like November again," General Mason warned. "Are you going off on some sort of half-baked mission again?"

"No sir, I'm not," Charlie replied, glancing at David. "David's coming with me. If we get into trouble, we'll signal for help. I'm no fool, but your system is completely overloaded with this current crisis. Let me have a chance to look into this."

"Colonel Warren, I respect your opinion, but you're needed here and now," General Mason said firmly. "We have other resources who can check this out. Resources who are far more expendable than you are, I might add."

Charlie's face became cold and set. "General Mason, I am an SAS operative. You know what kind of training I've been through. I know the tunnels, and I know my adversary. Right now, I am your best option for finding out what is going on down there. All of your resources are currently being used to combat this crisis. I'm the only one right now who isn't currently dedicated to a mission. I'm free, and I'm available. Logic, sir, dictates that David and I are the ones to handle this."

Her voice took on a note of urgency. "Kolov is ex-KGB. You know what that means, General Mason. I've seen records of what he did to men, women and children in Afghanistan. No one deserves a death at his hands, especially a death by slow torture. They've been out of the net for four hours. Heaven knows what's going on with them right now."

Mason looked at her for a moment. "Flawlessly reasoned, Colonel. Unfortunately you make a lot of sense. I know what kind of soldier you are. Your request is reluctantly approved."

"I hate the whole idea of sending you two down there, but I have to agree with General Mason," Rawlings said slowly. "You two go and find those detectives. I'll put ESU on notice, so that if you need backup, it will be there for you. Don't be heroes, okay?"

"I promise," Charlie said, looking at David. "We need to get to the British Consulate. I have equipment there that I need to accomplish this mission."

"That I can help you with," Rawlings reached for his cell phone and dialed a number. "I need a chopper down here ASAP to take Dr. Warren and her husband to the British Consulate. Okay, thanks," he closed his phone. "There will be a chopper here in five minutes. You two take care of yourselves."

"We will," David promised.

Rawlings and Mason watched them go out the door. Once they were alone, Rawlings turned to Mason. "Nate, I'd never pull rank on you or criticize you in front of anyone, but I've got to tell you: sending those two out there is a crazy idea."

"No Ken, it's not," Mason shook his head. "I've read the full file on Charlie Warren. I know things about her that her husband doesn't know, things that would make him not want to sleep next to her at night. You wouldn't believe me if I told you either, so I won't even try."

"You make her out like she's some sort of monster, Nate," Rawlings said with a hint of nervousness. "She's taught at Behavioral down at Quantico. I've seen her psych scores. She's completely well-adjusted."

"Charlie Warren's not a monster; she kills monsters. That's what she's been trained to do, Ken." Nathan Mason countered. "She is going to rescue Brenda Reynolds, or she's not coming back alive. Anyone who tries to stop her will be dead, period. She will not stop until she brings that woman back."

Rob Dubek came up to them as they left the conference room. "Where are Warren and Stone going?" he asked. Rawlings and Mason looked at each other.

"They're going to the British Consulate, Rob," Rawlings replied evenly. "Warren's got some work to do over there. By the way, do you have the latest hospital occupancy rates for me? I'd like to know if we're going to have to start shipping nerve agent casualties to some of the hospitals in New Jersey."

"Not with me, but I'll get those figures for you in a minute," Dubek turned and went back to the main EOC control room.

"You're sure it's him?" Mason asked quietly.

Rawlings nodded. "Yeah, I'm sure. If I wasn't sure before this afternoon, I am now."

22

"It's good to see you again, Charlie," Lady Margaret said as she and David arrived in her office. "We already know you're going to be busy down at the Emergency Operations Center. Special Agent Rawlings has already told us that he needs you."

"Right now Lady Margaret, we're off to rescue the two detectives who've been helping us with our case," Charlie said, looking around. "Where are James and Sergeant Major MacKay?"

"Stranded on the other side of the Hudson River, I'm afraid. I came in early this morning to get caught up on work, but as it stands right now, I'm the sole representative of Her Majesty's government in New York," Lady Margaret replied. "I've been trying to reach them for the better part of the day, but communications have completely broken down. The system is completely overloaded. I can't even reach them by cellular telephone at this time."

"It's understandable," David nodded. "New York is one of the best cities in the world to deal with terrorist attacks, but the system's still not perfect."

"Lady Margaret, I need to know if there are any SAS detachments that can be deployed to New York if need be," Charlie said quickly. "We may have need of them."

"I will contact our offices in Washington to find out, Charlie," Lady Margaret replied. "Is there anything else you need right now?"

Charlie put her hand on Lady Margaret's shoulder. "Prayer, Lady Margaret. Pray for us with all your heart. Please have James contact us as soon as he comes in. I'm sorry, but I have to do the best I can under the circumstances."

Lady Margaret nodded. "Sir Leslie has informed me about the royal warrant Her Majesty has given you. I'm afraid you don't fully understand the implications of that document, Lady Warren. What it means, my dear, is that we are at your command, not the other way around."

"What do you mean, Lady Margaret?" Charlie blinked in astonishment.

"I believe I spoke plainly enough, child," Lady Margaret replied, looking at Charlie with a maternal expression. "I will inform James of your request for military resources. You can expect to hear from us as soon as possible."

"David and I are going to rescue Brenda Reynolds and Ron Meyers," Charlie told her. "I will call you again when I can."

"Of course, Lady Warren," Lady Margaret said quietly, a look of concern coming over her face. "I wish you success in your mission. Godspeed to you."

Charlie stood at attention and bowed her head. "Ma'am." She turned and walked with David out of Lady Margaret's office.

-0-

"All right, David; it's time to open up our picnic basket," Charlie said as she opened up the rear storage compartment of their minivan. They had changed into their tactical jumpsuits while at the consulate.

"Oh goody, I've been waiting for this. We are so lucky you didn't get pulled over when we came into the city." David remarked, peering into the compartment. Inside was an assortment of odd-shaped black bags, none of which looked like containers for food. Charlie opened one up, taking out three machine pistols and two bandoliers of ammunition.

"You forgot the surface to air missiles, Charlie," David noted as he looked at the array of gear in Charlie's bag. "That seems to be the only thing missing, though."

Charlie slung two MP9 machine pistols around her neck. "I'm not shooting down aircraft today, David. I'm going on a raid to rescue Brenda Reynolds from terrorists. Here, pick up that medical bag for me." She indicated a hefty-sized bag in the rear of the compartment.

"Why do you need this? I thought you were going to kill the terrorists, not treat them," David said as he picked up the bag. It was very heavy. "This thing weighs a ton. Have you got a heart-bypass machine in this bag?"

"I may have to treat Ron or Brenda, silly," Charlie said as she strapped on her flak jacket and put her commando knife in its sheath. "I want to be prepared for anything."She busied herself with screwing a silencer onto her Glock.

"Knives and silencers, the trademark of SAS," David observed as Charlie holstered her pistol and secured five grenades to her vest. "You look like a commando, Charlie. It's a good look for you: cute, but lethal."

"That's what I am, David," Charlie replied with a fake smile. "Never, ever forget that."

"I never do, Charlie. I wouldn't have you any other way," David said, closing the hatchback. "What now?"

Charlie glanced down the street and then at her watch. "It's ten blocks to the subway station. With the traffic the way it is, we can foot it to there in less time."

"Not a good idea, Charlie. We go into downtown dressed like this, and some trigger happy cop's going to nail us before we have a chance to explain ourselves," David cautioned.

"David, we have no choice," Charlie shouldered one of the bags. "Brenda's and Ron's lives are on the line. We'll just have to risk it."

"All right, Charlie; if we get killed, don't say that I didn't warn you," David picked up the medical bag and the other bag of equipment. "I still think walking around in New York City dressed like this is a dumb idea."

"It's not a dumb idea. I never have dumb ideas."

"Right."

-0-

Forty-five minutes later, they were at the subway entrance. Charlie was correct in assuming that by walking they would make better time. The streets were clogged with cars and people. Traffic was going nowhere. David and Charlie drew stares from people as they jogged along in their black outfits carrying their equipment bags. Fortunately they were wearing badges and the backs of their suits had POLICE written in bold white letters. People saw them and started cheering and yelling as they passed.

"Charlie, they're cheering us," David told her as they passed people on the street.

"Yes, David, they are," Charlie said softly as they jogged along. "I guess it wasn't a dumb idea, was it?"

"We're not there yet," David puffed, starting to tire slightly. "Never underestimate the power of dumb, Charlie."

They reached the subway, which was guarded by a cordon of uniformed police officers. "You guys Warren and Stone?" one of them asked, his eyes narrowed slightly as he looked David and Charlie over. "Hey, wait a minute! I remember you! You're the donut girl!"

"Hello, Sergeant," Charlie replied with a smile. "I'm afraid I don't have any donuts for you today."

"Don't worry about that, Dr. Warren," the sergeant replied, eyeing them doubtfully. "What's with the tactical gear? You look like something out of a bad Hollywood movie. Who's this guy with you, another Brit?"

"I'm her husband, Dave Stone, Sergeant. Charlie's the expert," David said, attempting to catch his breath. "I'm just along for the ride."

Charlie and David produced their ID's. The officer eyed them and looked at their cards. "Okay, I've got orders from Headquarters to let you proceed. Call us if you need backup," the officer said reluctantly as he returned their ID cards. He looked at David dubiously. "You gonna make it, Mac? You don't look so good."

"Don't worry; I'll holler if we need help. I can promise you that. Besides, she's a doctor, so she can treat me if I have a heart attack," David assured him as they started down the stairs.

"Actually, darling, I'd simply put a bullet through your head and be done with it," Charlie said as they went to the entrance. The levity vanished from her voice as she looked at her watch. "Let's hurry up, David," Charlie fairly sprinted down the stairs. "There isn't much time."

"I'm right behind you, Charlie." David said.

The cops watched Charlie and David disappear down the stairs. "Did you get a load of that chick with all the tactical gear?" one of the officers asked the sergeant in charge. "I wouldn't want to run into her on a dark night."

The sergeant shook his head. "Guys, I've been around for a while. Unless those creeps are better than I think they are, they don't stand a chance against that girl."

-0-

They found Ron Meyers lying face down a few feet from the ladder leading up from the tunnel into the subway. His pose on the ground was so familiar that for a brief instant Charlie thought that they had forgotten to remove the body of Richard Cartwright.

Charlie knelt down by his head and felt for his carotid pulse. His pulse was weak and thready.

"David, he's alive!" she exclaimed. "Quick, we need to turn him over carefully. I'll hold his head and neck while we turn his body as a unit. I need to palpate his head and neck before we move him." Charlie slowly and carefully felt along Ron's skull, checking for deformities and obvious signs of fractures or dislocations. "His head and neck are stable. We can turn him over as a unit."

"Okay, Charlie," David gently pulled Ron's body over as Charlie stabilized his head and neck. The front of Meyers' shirt was covered in blood. There were two bullet holes in his chest. They had stopped actively bleeding.

"What incredible luck," Charlie murmured as she did a quick cursory exam. "Looks like both slugs skittered along his rib cage and went into his abdomen."

"Luck? What are you talking about, Charlie? The man's been shot," David observed, quickly looking over Ron's body to see if there were any other injuries.

"He's stabilized enough for us to work on him," Charlie replied brusquely. "If he hadn't, he'd be dead by now. At least we've got some chance of saving his life."

She got out a stethoscope from the medical bag and listened to his chest. "I can hear lung sounds in all lobes. He doesn't have a pneumothorax. David, start two large bore IVs on him. Run normal saline, please. Connect them to pressure bags while I dress his wounds."

David started the IVs. After they had given him about two liters of fluid, Meyers started to regain consciousness. He groaned and tried to talk. "Ron, rest easy," Charlie soothed. "It's Charlie Warren. David's here with me. You've been shot and we're treating you."

Ron reached up and squeezed her hand. "Charlie," he croaked. "I knew you'd come. They've got Brenda. They took her."

"I know, Ron," Charlie said, her voice filling with emotion. She tried to control her voice and make it steady. "We're going to get you to a hospital and I'm going to go get Brenda. I'll bring her back to you, Ron. I swear it."

"Charlie," Ron's voice became stronger, and a note of desperation came into it. "Charlie, please save her. I... I love her, Charlie."

Charlie drew close and whispered to him. "I knew it the day I met you both. You will see her again."

"I know I will, Charlie, I believe in you," Ron looked over at David. "You're a lucky guy, Stone. You know that?"

"Yeah buddy, I know," David looked over at Charlie. It was obvious to both of them that time was running out.

"We've got to get him out of this tunnel, David. Right now." Charlie said in a decisive tone. "Get the medics on line."

David tried a few times to raise EMS on his radio. "Reception in this hole is lousy. I can't get a hold of anyone." He looked at Ron. "What about his neck, Charlie? We don't have a stretcher. Shouldn't we radio in for some medics to back us up?"

Charlie glanced over to the dark, gaping maw of the tunnel. "We need to get him out of here. You just said we can't raise them on the radio. Besides, there's no room for them to send down a rigid litter. It's also too dangerous to leave him in this place. We've got to get him up onto the subway level."

"You want to move him? Charlie, his neck may be broken."

"We'll have to risk it," Charlie got out a rigid C-collar. "Here, put this on his neck. I've completed my primary and secondary surveys. I think his spine is cleared. In either case, we need to get him up to the subway platform."

They carefully moved Ron over to the ladder. "David, you go up first," Charlie directed. "Keep his body in alignment and hold him steady. I'll push from below."

Together, they managed to get Ron up the ladder and out onto the level ledge that led to the subway platform. Fortunately, there were no trains coming, so they were able to get his body onto the platform with little trouble.

"Okay, now we can call for backup," David said as he keyed his police radio. "Dispatch this is Delta-312. Request Medics and ESU Seventeenth Street Subway platform. Request Medics trauma stat. Officer down, over."

"Roger 312-Delta," the dispatcher replied. "We copy your officer down. Medics and ESU on the way, code two."

"Roger, Dispatch. 312-Delta, out." David looked over at Charlie, who was busy gathering additional clips of nine-millimeter ammunition for her machine pistols. "Where are you going, Doctor? You have a patient."

"Correction, David: you have a patient. I have a hostage to rescue," Charlie said, pulling back the actions on her pistols and safteying them. "Every second we wait plays into those people's hands." She put the night vision goggles on her head.

"Charlie, ESU is five minutes out. You can wait five minutes until they arrive," David protested. "Come on, now. Meyers needs you here."

"Five minutes from now Brenda Reynolds may be dead, and I'll be arguing with more people about my decision. Nothing or no one is going to change my mind in any case. You were trained as a medic in Special Forces, David," Charlie snapped back, shouldering a bag of grenades and explosives. "You're every bit as qualified as I am to treat him. What you haven't been trained in is hostage rescue. That's my bailiwick."

David rose to his feet. "No, Charlie; you're not going back down into that tunnel."

Charlie came up to him, her face cold and set. "I've killed half a dozen men bigger than you with my bare hands, David. I am quite capable of taking care of myself. The only way you can stop me from going down into that tunnel right now is to shoot me in my tracks."

"Charlie, I…" David started to reply.

"I mean it, David. This discussion is over," Charlie turned and headed back towards the entrance to the tunnel. Ron coughed and moaned. David turned away from Charlie for a second to see what was going on with Meyers. When he turned back, Charlie was gone.

23

The salvage mission was going perfectly, Ivan Kolov decided. The dock areas had been completely evacuated that morning, enabling Renov and his crew to run cables from the ship anchored at the dock down to the submerged submarine. The batteries had charged up quickly, and fresh air was now circulating inside the old submarine. Kolov's thoughts now turned to Brenda Reynolds.

"Where did you put the woman, Valentin?" he asked his second-in-command.

"She's in a room about halfway down the main tunnel, Ivan, We tied her to a chair very securely," Valentin Karpov replied. "She's not going anywhere."

"Good," Kolov nodded. "It will take Alexi's crew some time to check the submarine out to determine if she can reach the pen on her own power. We have time now to question the detective. Bring her to our operations center. We have more sophisticated tools to question her there."

"Yes sir," Karpov grinned wolfishly.

-0-

Charlie crept noiselessly but swiftly into the tunnel. Her whole mind was completely focused on the mission and her surroundings. Darkness was her ally, and she followed the contour of the old passageway as closely as possible. Her night vision goggles enabled her to move through the blackness of the tunnel with relative ease. Charlie constantly swept from side to side, alert for any signs of people ahead or behind her.

The floor beneath her showed signs of more footprints. She saw a fresh set of two male footprints walking close together into the tunnel. In between them was a smaller set of prints, irregularly spaced. *They were dragging you into the tunnel, weren't they, Brenda?* Charlie thought to herself.

The thought of what Brenda might be suffering at the hands of Kolov and his people redoubled Charlie's resolve. The tracks on the floor confirmed Charlie's suspicion that Brenda had put up a fight. There were frequent areas where Brenda dragged her feet or had caused her captors to be thrown against the wall. *Good for you, Brenda,* Charlie thought to herself. *You're leaving me a trail that I can follow.*

After a hundred yards, Charlie arrived at the major intersection that had two branching tunnels. Instead of an iron door barring her way forward, the door had been removed and cast aside. A cold blast of air carried the distant sounds of traffic to

Charlie's ears. The trail continued straight on through the opening to Charlie's front.

She inched cautiously across the intersection, ever alert for sounds of anyone following her. Charlie held her pistol outstretched, ready to fire, waiting for the sounds of approaching feet. Nothing happened, and the only sounds she heard were the squeaking of rats and the far-off dripping of running water.

Moving swiftly across the intersection, Charlie saw a dim glimmer of light in the distance, about fifty yards ahead of her. The light was to the right, and she could see it reflected on the tunnel wall. It was coming from a side passage or room.

Charlie quickly moved along the tunnel, reaching the light source after a minute or so of careful, rapid movement. The light was coming from a side passage, from a nearby room.

Her night vision goggles were no longer useful in brightly lit areas. She pushed them up out of her eyes onto her forehead. Charlie inched carefully over to the doorframe, using the inky black shadow as cover. Peering around the frame, she looked inside the room.

A single bulb dangling from a wire illuminated the room. In the center of the room was a figure, bound to a chair. The head of the person was bent forward, as if the person was sleeping. Suddenly, the figure stirred, and the person's head raised up.

Charlie's heart silently leapt with joy. Brenda Reynolds was alive.

-0-

Brenda Reynolds had forced herself to remain calm, concentrating on keeping her breathing even and steady. This was essential, since her mouth had been covered with strips of adhesive tape. Her captors had dragged her down the tunnel for a seemingly endless distance before stopping at a small room lit by a single overhead bulb. They hustled her into the room and shoved her down into an old chair.

Once she was in the chair, they bound her arms and legs to the chair using some more nylon quick ties. "If you start to cry, your nose will plug up, and then you won't be able to breathe," one of the men said, chuckling sadistically as he put more tape across her mouth.

They had been gone for several hours now. From time to time, Brenda could hear voices of men passing by the room, speaking in Russian. No one came in to see about her. There was no reason, since she was absolutely alone and helpless.

It was useless to struggle. The ties binding her to the chair were too tight. Brenda kept thinking about Ron. The two shots she had heard behind her and the sound of his body falling kept echoing through her mind. *It's all my fault*, she thought, her eyes filling with tears.

A small sound caught Brenda's attention, and she lifted up her head. A slight figure dressed in black wearing a set of night vision goggles carrying a silenced pistol crept into the room.

Brenda saw her, and moaned slightly. Charlie motioned for silence and came swiftly over to the chair where Brenda was tied. She carefully peeled the tape from Brenda's mouth. "Charlie!" she breathed in a low voice filled with gratitude, "I'm so glad to see you. How's Ron?"

"He's alive," Charlie concentrated on cutting the nylon ties with her commando knife. "We need to get you out of here." Suddenly, she heard heavy footsteps at the doorstep. Brenda's eyes went wide with fright as the shape of Valentin Karpov framed the door.

Charlie had been thoroughly trained by the Special Air Service in hostage rescue operations. She was trained to kill instantly if necessary without hesitation if the situation warranted. This was one of those situations.

In one fluid, lightening-quick motion, Charlie whirled around and threw her commando knife at Karpov. The knife struck him in the chest, burying itself up to the hilt. Valentin Karpov stared at the knife, and looked up at Charlie with astonishment. His eyes glazed over, and his dead body took one last reflexive step into the room. Karpov's corpse pitched face forward, falling with a crash. A dark pool of blood spread from his prostrate corpse.

"Valentin? Valentin, are you all right?" the sound of a second man's voice came closer to the room. Charlie swept out her silenced automatic. As the second man crossed the threshold into the room, two soft "plops" were heard as Charlie's pistol fired.

Two dark holes appeared in the man's chest. He pitched forward into the room. Charlie caught him, lowering his dead body to the ground. The whole incident had taken less than ten seconds from start to finish.

"Let's get out of here before more of them show up," Charlie moved the second man's body and retrieved her knife from Karpov's chest. She finished cutting the ties that bound Brenda to the chair. Brenda got stiffly up from the chair, flexing the muscles in her sore arms and legs.

Charlie pulled out an MP9 from her bag and gave it to Brenda. "You know how to use this?"

"Are you kidding? I'm the precinct champ. The MP9 and I are good friends," Brenda replied grimly, pulling the action back on the pistol. "You don't have a second set of NVGs, do you?"

"No, but I have some early Christmas presents for you," Charlie placed a bandolier with couple of flash grenades and some extra clips of ammunition around Brenda's neck. "Here's the plan: we run down this corridor as fast as we can. I'll lead the way since I've got the NVGs on. If you hear anything behind us, shoot it. Shoot low; the MP9 will keep whoever's behind us from getting too close. If they start shooting back, throw a flash grenade. That might slow them up for a while."

"Sounds good, Charlie. What about our playmates here?" Brenda asked as she looked at the two very dead men in front of them.

"Don't worry about them. Let's go now." Charlie put on her NVGs. She crept to the door and peered out to he right and left. She motioned to Brenda that the way was clear. The two women silently left the room, leaving the two bodies on the floor in an ever-widening pool of blood.

-0-

"Valentin and Igor have been gone for a long time, Comrade Kolov," one of the men with Kolov said as they waited in their command center. "Do you want me to go and find out what is going on?"

Kolov looked up from a set of plans he was studying. "Yes, find out." The man left the room, leaving Kolov to study the drawings and diagrams strewn all over the table.

Two minutes later, the man came running back into the room. "Comrade Kolov! I found Valentin and Igor in the room! They are dead, and the woman is gone!"

Kolov's face became purple with rage. "Find whoever did this! Kill them and bring their bodies back to me!"

The man nodded quickly and fled the room, calling to others to follow him. Kolov turned back to the plans. "I know this is Warren's daughter's doing," he ground the words out in rage. "I will make her pay, and pay dearly." His hands were shaking with rage as he punched in a number on a cell phone. A voice on the other end answered him quickly.

"Valentin Karpov is dead. Warren killed him and Igor. I want you to find that half-Ukranian brat of John Warren's. I know that she is living in Compton with her sister. Make arrangements to have her abducted. Do it now!" He closed the phone and stared at the plans for a moment. "I will make you pay, Warren. I will show you what it means to cross me."

He turned to Alexi Renov. "Alexi, I want you to get the submarine ready as soon as possible. The clock is running, and I know the Americans will try to stop us. Make sure that all access tunnels are guarded and the approaches booby trapped."

Renov smiled. "Yes sir. We'll make sure that the Americans will regret it if they try to go down into our tunnels."

Kolov nodded. "Good. I don't want any more slipups."

-0-

"You did WHAT?" the Emergency Services Unit commander asked David in an outraged tone. "You let that girl go down into that tunnel all by herself? Stone, you're an idiot, and that wife of yours is an even bigger idiot!"

"Look, Captain: we can spend time debating on what Charlie did and why sometime later," David said in an irritated tone, glancing as the medics loaded Ron Meyers onto a waiting gurney. "Right now, we need to stand fast and let the lady work."

"I don't believe this," Hank Blevins muttered as he dialed up the EOC. "This is Blevins. I need to talk to the Watch Commander now. Stan? This is Hank. Yeah, I'm at the tunnel. Look, that British girl and her dopey husband went into the tunnels without authorization. Yeah, they couldn't wait five minutes for us to get here. What? She is? You're kidding; I've seen pictures of her. I have teenage daughters who look older than she does. Okay, if that's what the honchos want us to do, then we'll do it. This whole thing stinks, Stan. Yeah, I agree, but what do we know. Okay, I'll let you know what happens. Bye."

Blevins put away his phone and glared at David. "Okay Stone, we've been told to stand fast for thirty minutes. If your wife and Reynolds haven't shown by then, we're to go in and get them out. The powers that be told me that Warren knows what she's doing. I hope and pray that they're right, and let me tell you that if this goes down wrong, you're going to be lucky to pull security guard in a mall."

This was too much for David to take. "Captain, with all due

respect, if one of your people was down that tunnel in the hands of psychotic perverts who torture people for fun, wouldn't you be one of the first ones down that tunnel?

"Right now, there is an SAS operative down in the tunnels rescuing an NYPD cop. She just happens to be my wife. Charlie's a pro, Captain Blevins. If I didn't think she was up to the job, I'd be down there with her right now."

Blevins looked at David for a moment. "Must have been tough for you to watch her walk into that tunnel by herself."

"You have no idea, Captain," David replied. "I got stuck playing doctor while my wife goes off to rescue one of our own from the bad guys. Talk about role reversal."

"Okay Stone; I'll cut her some slack," Blevins said as they walked down to the entrance that led to the tunnel. "Let's hunker down and let the lady work." He glanced at his watch. "She's got twenty minutes left, by my reckoning. After twenty minutes, we're going in."

"I'll be five minutes ahead of you," David said grimly.

-0-

Charlie and Brenda had made it halfway down the tunnel before they heard voices behind them, calling to each other in Russian. Brenda swung the MP9 over her shoulder, not breaking her stride as she jogged down the tunnel. She fired a short burst, the weapon echoing with deafening power in the confined spaces of the tunnel. Two screams of pain greeted her ears.

"Nice snap shot, Brenda," Charlie said with admiration in her voice as they ran. "That will keep them busy for a while."

The sound of shots in reply echoed down the tunnel. "They're firing blind, Brenda." Charlie said, not slackening her pace. "Okay, we're coming up to the main junction. We may have trouble up here."

"Right," Brenda puffed, slightly out of breath. Although Charlie was wearing her tactical vest loaded down with extra clips of ammunition and grenades, she was setting a killer pace. She abruptly slowed down and stopped as they came to the intersection.

Brenda stopped behind her and waited. Coming up close to

Charlie, she stopped as Charlie peered to the right and left of the intersection. Charlie reached back and silently squeezed her hand three times and moved her hand to the right. The gesture communicated to Brenda that there were three men waiting in ambush in the tunnel branch to the right of them.

Charlie jumped up and sprayed the right hand tunnel with machine gun fire. Screams of pain answered them, along with a few shots, then silence punctuated by a few moans.

"Let's foot it!" Charlie sprinted across the tunnel intersection. Brenda followed her, breaking into a dead run. More voices echoed up the corridor behind them as they ran.

Suddenly, Charlie stopped in her tracks. "Hold it, Brenda! I need to do something." She stooped down and busied herself with several oblong objects scattered on the tunnel floor.

"Charlie, what are you doing?" Brenda asked nervously, peering into the blackness. The sound of their approaching pursuers grew closer. "They're almost on us!"

"Right," Charlie stood up. "That's done. Okay, Brenda, spray the tunnel!"

The two women opened up with their machine pistols, the tunnel echoing with the sound of gunfire. "Let's go!" Charlie said, grasping Brenda's shoulder. She tossed a couple of grenades over her shoulder for good measure. A few seconds later, two shattering blasts roared behind them. The light of the tunnel entrance ahead of them grew ever brighter.

Two minutes later, they arrived at the tunnel entrance. As they burst out of the tunnel, a dozen voices greeted them. "Hold your fire, people!" a Captain Blevins commanded the officers massed in covered positions around the tunnel. "We have officers coming out!"

Charlie and Brenda lowered their weapons. The officers rushed up to them as they stood there. The tunnel erupted with the sound of cheers and whistles as David came up to Charlie and crushed her in an embrace. "Charlie! I'm so glad you're back in one piece!" He shouted over the din as he smothered her with kisses.

"It's good to be back," Charlie said, kissing him back. She glanced over at Brenda, who was standing desolately by herself. "How's Ron?"

David released Charlie and looked at Brenda. He came over to her and put his hands on her shoulders. "Brenda, Ron's in pretty bad shape. I stabilized him as best I could. Captain Vinson called a moment ago to let me know he's in surgery now."

Brenda hung her head and her shoulders started to shake. Charlie came up and hugged her. "Brenda, it's okay. We'll take you to him as soon as we can."

The cheering went on for a few minutes until finally subsiding. Captain Blevins

came up to them. "Okay, people. We need to clear this area. I don't mean to be rude, but this area is not safe."

He turned to Charlie. "It sounded like a war down there."

"It is a war, Captain," Charlie replied solemnly. "This was just the opening skirmish."

Blevins nodded. "Colonel Warren, you and your husband are ordered to return to EOC immediately. I have a unit standing by to take you there, along with Lieutenant Reynolds."

"All right, Captain," Charlie replied, glancing at the tunnel they'd just come out of. "You and your men need to establish this area as a secure base. We're going to need to go down this tunnel again very soon. They took down a steel door on the main tunnel. It must be the direct route to the dock areas."

Blevins stared at Charlie and shook his head slightly. It was obvious that he was still having a hard time taking Charlie seriously. Brenda Reynolds caught the look and spoke up for her. "Captain, Colonel Warren killed one terrorist with a knife, and then shot another. We just finished fighting a running gun battle underneath half a mile of tunnels. I strongly suggest that you take her and her analysis seriously."

"All right, people: set up a perimeter around this entrance," Blevins directed. "No one goes into that tunnel without my orders. Anyone who comes out of that tunnel, shoot them first and arrest them if they're still alive after that."

Charlie turned to the Blevins. "Captain, Detective Reynolds has some valuable information that Agent Rawlings needs to hear. We need to have her accompany us to the operations center."

Blevins nodded and turned to Reynolds. "Lieutenant, as soon as you're done with the debrief at the EOC, I've been instructed to take you to University Hospital where your partner is being treated."

Brenda was too exhausted to do anything except nod. Tears ran down her cheeks as Charlie came up to her and held her shoulders. "Come on, Brenda. Let's get this over with so we can get you to Ron."

"Why did you stop in the tunnel, Charlie?" Brenda asked as they climbed the stairs up to street level.

"I arranged a little surprise for our friends in a tunnel." Charlie replied enigmatically.

"What kind of surprise?" David asked.

"If I told you, then it wouldn't be a surprise," Charlie explained with a smile.

"Okay, I guess we'll find out later," David looked at Brenda and winked. "Most of the times, when Charlie arranges a surprise, someone gets hurt, worse."

A faint smile came onto Brenda's face. "Yeah, I just saw two very surprised people down in those tunnels."

-0-

General Mason and Special Agent Rawlings were waiting for them in the EOC. Rawlings' face was a mixture of rage, astonishment and admiration. "General Mason was filling me in on your little adventure back in November, Dr. Warren," he said, shaking his head. "I'm still trying to find out exactly what to do about you. I'm toying with either giving you a medal or having you shot."

Charlie was too tired to reply. Mason sized up the situation immediately. "Colonel Warren, you and Mr. Stone are going to be placed in some rooms close by. You are going to sleep for at least four hours. After that, we're going to debrief you. If you stick your head out the door before four hours is up, I'll have the medics sedate you. Is that clear, Colonel?"

"Crystal, sir," David answered for them both.

Rawlings turned to Brenda. "Lieutenant, we can pick your brain now, if you don't mind. I know you want to get over to the hospital and be with Sergeant Meyers, but we need to get whatever information you have right now. As soon as my Intel people are done, we'll get you over to the hospital. Is that all right with you?"

"Yes sir, that's fine and thank you," Brenda said gratefully. She paused for a moment. "Sir, before we begin, I'd like to talk to Dr. Warren and Detective Stone for just a moment in private. Is that possible?"

Mason and Rawlings exchanged looks. "Just for a moment," Rawlings said, indicating a door a few feet away from them. "After that, I'm sending these two soldiers to bed. That's the room, by the way."

Charlie and David went into the room, and Brenda closed the door behind them. "I want you both to know how sorry I am for the way I've treated you these past few days," Brenda began, her voice shaking with remorse. "David, I'm sorry for the way I was at Karen's funeral, and for the way my family behaved towards you and Karen. I... I don't know what else to say, except that I'm sorry."

"It's okay, Brenda," Charlie said gently. "It's over now; all of it. We're just glad we got you back safe."

David put his arm around Brenda. "Come on, kid. I'm just glad Charlie had you covering her back when you were coming up that tunnel. I know what a good shot you are."

Brenda laughed and wiped her eyes. "Dave, you should have seen the way Charlie threw her knife at that guy! I mean she looks... well, she just doesn't look like the sort..."

"That could kill a big hulking man with a knife and then turn around and shoot another man dead with a gun. I know, Brenda; I couldn't believe it either," David hugged Charlie. "My little killer." Charlie smacked him on the arm and glared.

"Stop it, you beast," she said, blushing. "Brenda, give our love to Ron. We'll be thinking about him and praying for him."

"I will," Brenda nodded as she went out the door. "Thank you both for saving my life," she whispered as she closed the door.

David let out a sigh as the door closed. "Well, Charlie," he said, looking about the room. It was softly lit, with a queen-sized bed and a door leading to a small bathroom with a shower stall. "It's not luxurious, but the bed looks nice."

Charlie sat down on the bed, too tired to talk. David helped her out of her web gear and laid her down onto the bed. By the time he did this, she was already asleep. He took off his own web gear and boots and lay down beside her. David listened to the gentle sound of her breathing; in a few minutes, he was asleep as well.

Outside the door, the EOC's tempo had increased dramatically. Brenda's information was immediately acted upon. "Send recon teams into those tunnels at once. Get every scrap of information you can. I want Warren and Stone debriefed as soon as they wake up," Rawlings told Mason. He looked up at the situation map.

"What's down in those tunnels, Nate?" Rawlings asked.

Mason turned to Rawlings. "We're about to find out. Whatever it is, it's major league."

-0-

Ron Meyers was out of surgery by the time Brenda got to University Hospital. She was directed to the waiting area outside of the recovery room. After a seemingly endless wait, a weary surgeon in scrubs came out of the double doors to talk to her.

"Lieutenant Reynolds, I'm John Klein," the surgeon introduced himself, shaking Brenda's hand. "I want to talk to you about Sergeant Meyers and what I found."

"Go ahead, Doctor," Brenda said quietly, dreading the worst.

"Your partner lost a lot of blood. Fortunately he got excellent medical care on the scene, otherwise I'd be out here telling you he died." The surgeon looked at her, trying to be as objective as possible. He knew that his words were going to be hard for her to bear.

"He's on life support, and he's going to spend the next day or so in Intensive Care. I'll let you go in to see him for a little bit. We've got him sedated, so he can't respond to you. I'm going to let you know up front that there are a lot of bandages and tubes coming out of him. He's got all sorts of invasive lines. That's pretty much standard for critically ill patients."

Klein paused for a moment. "Lieutenant, I'm not going to lie to you. Your partner may still die. The next twenty-four hours are going to be absolutely critical. If he starts to improve after that period, and doesn't develop a fever, we'll be in good shape. If things don't improve after that, it won't look good. Do you understand what I'm telling you, Lieutenant Reynolds?"

"Yes, Doctor; I understand," Brenda said heavily. "Thank you."

"You're welcome," the doctor turned and went back into the Recovery Room. Brenda sat down and waited for the chance to go in to see Meyers. A few moments later, Captain Vinson came down the hallway.

"How are you doing, Lieutenant?" he asked softly. Normally, he would have put his arm around her shoulder, but since it was Brenda Reynolds, Vinson wasn't sure how to proceed.

Brenda looked at him for a moment and opened her purse. Finding her wallet, she opened it and handed him her badge. "They took my gun, Captain, so I guess that will have to come out of my severance pay. Sorry." Her voice was shaking with grief and remorse.

Vinson looked at the badge. "What's this for?"

"Ron Meyers is in there, fighting for his life, because I screwed up," the words came pouring out of her mouth in a rush of grief. "It's my fault that we got jumped. I should have followed procedure. We should have called for backup. I should have..." Her reserve completely disintegrated and she started weeping uncontrollably.

Vinson sat down next to her and put his hand on her shoulder. Brenda leaned into him and cried for a few minutes into his shoulder, then composed herself.

"He's... he's really bad, Captain," Brenda said, drying her eyes. "The surgeon said that if Warren and Stone hadn't gotten there when they did, he would have died. They saved his life, sir. They saved my life, too."

"I know, Brenda," Vinson said, his voice cracking slightly. "Listen, for right now, your place of duty is right by that man's bedside. Is that clear? You set foot outside this hospital, and I'll personally come and handcuff you to the rail of his bed, understand?"

"Yes sir; I understand." A faint smile appeared on Brenda's lips.

A nurse in scrubs came out of the Recovery Room doors. "I'm here to take you back, Lieutenant," she said, looking at Vinson. "You can come back, too, Captain Vinson."

"Hey listen: everyone down at the Precinct thinks you and Ron did a great job today," Vinson said. "We all think you're the best."

Brenda looked at him in astonishment. "Is that a compliment, Captain Vinson?"

Howard Vinson grinned crookedly. "Yeah, I guess it is. Don't spread it around. I've got a reputation to keep up."

He handed her badge back to her. "You'll need this, Lieutenant. You're still on the clock until this man gets out of this hospital. Is that clear?"

"Crystal, sir," Brenda replied, looking at the doors of the recovery room. Her eyes started to fill with tears again.

Vinson put his arm on Brenda's shoulders. "Let's go back and see our Sergeant, Brenda."

24

A knock on the door came four hours later. "Colonel Warren? Mr. Stone? General Mason wants to see you."

Charlie turned over at the aide who opened the door a crack. "Thank you. We'll be up in a minute or two."

David turned over and groaned. "I'm up, Charlie. What time is it?"

Charlie squinted at her watch. "It's five in the morning, I think. I feel like someone ran me over with a truck."

"Make that two trucks," David massaged his neck and stretched. "I hope someone has some shaving gear, because mine's still out at LaGuardia."

"Look's like someone heard you, David," Charlie's voice came from the bathroom. "There's soap and towels and everything else we need in here."

"Good," David said, stretching himself. "At least we can start to feel human again."

They emerged from their room a few moments later, feeling considerably better. "Glad you guys got some rest. It's going to be a busy day for us," Agent Rawlings said. "We are going to have a briefing shortly after you two get something to eat."

"How's Sergeant Meyers doing, Agent Rawlings?" Charlie asked as they walked down to a cafeteria.

"He's listed as critical, but my last reports said his vital signs are stable," Rawlings replied. "Lieutenant Reynolds has been ordered to stay at the hospital with him."

"I don't think you need to worry about her disobeying that order," David observed with a smile.

"I don't either," Rawlings agreed as they came through the cafeteria doors. "I got your carry-ons off of the airplane and had them sent to your room, so you can get out of your tactical gear when you want. Both of you are out of the field right now, by the way."

"You mean you're sending us home?" Charlie asked incredulously.

"Oh no, my dear Colonel, not by a long shot," Rawlings said, looking at Charlie bleakly. "You don't get off that easy. By this afternoon, you'll be longing for being back in that tunnel slugging it out with bad guys."

"Lovely," Charlie said gloomily. "What does that mean?"

"You'll find out."

-0-

After breakfast, Charlie and David spent the next few hours being debriefed by Rawlings. They went over Charlie's grandfather's files exhaustively, piecing together his research and marrying it up with their own findings. Rawlings brought in experts from his task force and collated their intelligence. By noon, a coherent pattern of action was beginning to take shape.

"Cartwright's part here seems to have been the missing link to all of this, Agent Rawlings," Charlie explained. "The *Colossus* here in New York picked up *U-3551's* last transmission. That was the confirmation message it was ordered to transmit to German High Command once it had arrived at its target destination."

"Only Germany had surrendered by then, and no one was there to receive the transmission." David added.

"Correct," Charlie nodded. "Cartwright got to the warehouse where the computer was located, retrieved the message and was trying to reach the British Consulate to let them know about the arrival of the submarine. The German agents intercepted him and killed him in the tunnels before he could complete his mission."

"Well, the message has now been received," David said, stretching his aching body. "It's taken almost sixty years for the mission to be completed, but now it's done."

"Okay people," Rawlings rubbed his neck. "I think we're ready to put this all together."

"I agree," Charlie nodded her head, taking a sip of coffee. "What's next, Ken?"

"A promotion for you, Colonel Warren," Nathan Mason walked in through the door. "I'm appointing you as ground tactical commander for this operation."

Charlie looked as though someone had just dropped a safe on her. "What?"

"I think you've rendered my wife speechless, which ranks as a minor miracle, I might add," David said, earning a smack on the arm from his wife. "What do you mean, she's the ground tactical commander?"

"Look, I need someone who understands the ins and outs of this operation," Mason explained in a professional tone. "You're the most qualified to lead this mission, that's why you get the job."

"The job?" Charlie blanched. "I've never commanded anything larger than an SAS team. You're putting the lives of thousands of people into my hands? How can you possibly think I can handle an operation of this magnitude?"

"Because I think you can. Actually, you have the lives of millions of people in your hands, Charlie," Rawlings corrected her. "I've seen you work, and so has General Mason. I trust his judgment, and you should too. Besides, you're not doing this solo; you'll have plenty of help."

"Just bone-crushing responsibility, that's all," Charlie groaned, sitting down in a chair. "All right," she sighed, "I guess I need to draft up an operations order and prepare a briefing."

"Good move, Colonel," Mason said with satisfaction. "See? That wasn't so hard. You just made two excellent decisions, the first of many."

"We'll expect a briefing by 1600 local time," Rawlings told her. "The op is laid on for tonight, so there's not much time."

"Right," Charlie shrugged. "What else is new?"

Rawlings got up and stretched. "We've been going at this for a good five hours. It's time to take a break."

David looked at his watch and decided it was time for a change of pace and perspective. "Why don't we try to talk to Joan?" he suggested.

"Good idea," Charlie dialed Joan's number on her cell phone. "Joan, it's Charlie!"

"Glad to hear your voice, Charlie," Joan's voice was flooded with relief. "Katya's been frantic about you. She's here right now and she wants to talk to you."

Katya came on the phone. "Sister! How are you? I've been so worried! Are you and David all right?"

Charlie struggled to keep the tears from her eyes as she talked. "I'm fine, darling; we're okay, just very busy right now. We'll be home as soon as we can. How's your skating coming along?"

"I'm doing well, Charlie," Katya replied, her voice becoming calmer as she talked. "Megan is coming by to take me to the rink this morning. Ms. Robeson says I am making excellent progress. She is very pleased."

"That's good, darling. Let me talk to Joan again," Charlie waited until Joan came back on the phone. "Joan, watch her carefully. I have a feeling these reptiles might try to go out to Compton and try to do something to her."

"We're way ahead of you, little girl," Joan replied, her voice filling with anger. "They'll have to climb over my cold dead body before they get to your sister, Charlie. Carl's got everything in this town locked up tight, and anyone who comes into this place looking for trouble is going to wish they hadn't."

"That's good," Charlie relaxed, knowing that Katya was going to be safe. "Give my love to everyone, especially Uncle Angus, okay?"

"Okay. Stay in touch, Charlie. We love you."

"Love you too. Bye." Charlie hung up and looked at David. "Kolov's not above kidnapping people. I'm worried that something might happen to Katya."

"We're just going to have to trust that Carl and the rest of the force in Compton are up to the task of protecting Katya, Charlie," David said, pulling her close for a moment.

"Just as all of New York is hoping we're up to the task of protecting them," Charlie whispered.

-0-

"Comrade Kolov, Captain Renov reports that his crew aboard the submarine has now restored full electrical power. The electrical cables connecting the submarine to the ship on the surface have been disconnected," a radio technician reported. Kolov acknowledged the report with a cursory nod.

"Excellent. Let Alexi know that we will have the facility ready to receive him by 2000 hours tonight. What is the status of the devices?"

The technician relayed Kolov's question to the submarine commander. "Comrade Kolov, Renov states that the devices are in excellent shape. They should be easy to dismantle and the core materials can be transferred to our devices once they dock."

Kolov looked at his watch. "We should have our devices fully configured and operational by midnight. Are there any signs that the Americans are aware of our intentions?"

"We haven't heard from our source inside their operations center for a number of hours," the man replied. "But that is not unusual, given the fact that the Americans are trying to cope with the aftermath of our attack."

"We've been monitoring police tactical and military bands. So far, we've picked up nothing unusual." Another man replied, handing Kolov a report. "Our listening posts report that no further incidents involving the police have happened since Karpov died."

The mention of Karpov's name sent Kolov into another black fury. "What is the word about abducting the child of John Warren? Are our people out in Compton ready to move?"

"We have them watching where the child is, Comrade Kolov," the man said. "She is at a local skating rink taking lessons from an instructor."

"Good, let the brat have her lesson," a wolfish grin spread across Kolov's face. "She will have another, more painful lesson to learn later on today."

-0-

"Mr. President, Mr. Director, Mr. Mayor, ladies and gentlemen:

welcome to our final operational briefing," Ken Rawlings grasped the podium with both hands as he leaned out, addressing the packed room filled with men and women in uniforms and business suits. The afternoon meeting had convened on time, and in the audience were representatives of the military, FBI, and various law enforcement groups. The meeting was being live-streamed to the Pentagon and the White House.

"Before we began, let me give you a summary of the events that have happened in New York City in the past thirty-six hours. At 0800 local time yesterday, four devices containing a mixture of nerve agents were detonated in the subways of New York City. As of this afternoon, there have been six hundred fatalities and over three thousand people injured in this attack. New York City has been virtually shut down as the result of this terrorist act. We have contained and isolated the affected areas, and decontamination by HAZMAT teams is proceeding ahead of schedule. We should have the transportation system of greater New York City operational by the end of this week."

Rawlings paused for a moment, gathering his strength. "Over the past few months, the FBI had been aware that a major terrorist attack of this magnitude was in the offing. We did not know where, and we did not know when, but we knew it was coming. The EOC and emergency resources of this city responded magnificently to this threat, and they are to be commended. Unfortunately, what we have just been through these past few days was NOT the main threat facing this city."

A murmur of disbelief rippled through the assembly as Rawlings made this statement. He waited until the audience settled down before he continued. "We know now that the chemical attack was a diversion designed to throw us off track and tie up our investigative and tactical resources. It was designed to blind us to the more terrible threat that we now must face.

"We have conclusive proof that there are now four operational nuclear weapons in the hands of terrorists in New York City. Our purpose today is to appraise you of this threat, and to tell you how we are to deal with it."

There was a deafening silence in the room. "At this time, I am going to turn this briefing over to Brigadier General Nathan Mason, Deputy Assistant to the Army Chief of Staff. He will brief you on the operational aspects of this mission."

Rawlings sat down and Mason came up to the podium. "Good afternoon. As Special Agent Rawlings has just said, I'm Nathan Mason, the military coordinator of this operation. This is an extraordinary threat facing this country. No nuclear device has been exploded in a city since Hiroshima and Nagasaki. Various computer models using New York have been done, and the results of even a modest-sized nuclear explosion in the New York area will produce horrendous casualties."

"An atomic blast in a metropolitan area has been the world's nightmare scenario for the past sixty years," Mason's voice took on a grim edge. "Ladies and gentlemen, the nightmare is here, and it is now.

"It is my responsibility to lead a multi-agency task force of military and law enforcement agencies to combat this threat. I have chosen a person to lead the ground forces in this operation. My choice may surprise some of you, but not all. It is my pleasure to turn over the operational aspects of this briefing to my second-in-command, the ground commander of this operation, Lieutenant Colonel Charlene Warren.

"You may ask, why have I chosen someone who isn't an American to lead us in this effort? My reasons are simple: Colonel Warren has tactical experience and a thorough familiarity with all aspects of this situation. She's the best qualified officer for this position."

Mason sat down, and Charlie came up to the podium. She was glad that the spacious desk where she placed her notes was wide enough to conceal her trembling legs.

"Good afternoon, as General Mason has said in his warm and overly-generous introduction, I am Lieutenant Colonel Warren of Her Majesty's SAS," Charlie began, her voice gaining strength by the moment. "I want to first lay out for you the extraordinary history behind the threat we are now facing. This is not a dry exercise in military history. It is essential that we all know where this threat originated so we can mount an intelligent and reasoned response to the crisis now facing us."

A picture of *U-3551* flashed on the screen behind where Charlie was speaking. "This submarine, *U-3551*, was one of the last, most technically advanced submarines constructed by the German Navy in World War II. It was one of the class of U-boats known as an *elektroboat*, a fast, stealthy type of submarine with many advanced features that rendered it highly difficult for Allied ships to detect.

"This submarine set sail for America on April 23, 1945, a few days before Berlin fell, and Adolf Hitler shot himself. It was commanded by this man, Hans Kepler."

Charlie paused while Kepler's picture came on the screen. "Kepler was not only one of Germany's top U-boat commanders; he was also a brilliant nuclear physicist. His submarine had orders to sail to New York Harbor, penetrate the harbor defenses, and detonate the devices that she carried."

Taking a deep breath, Charlie braced herself to tell these people something that she knew they would not believe, but had to accept. "*U-3551* was carrying four twenty-kiloton nuclear weapons."

The reaction was immediate. "That's impossible, Colonel Warren," a man from the Nuclear Emergency Response Team stood up. "Germany never had more than a primitive nuclear weapons program." Scores of other people echoed the man's sentiments. Charlie waited for the room to quiet down before she responded.

"I'm afraid your supposition is not correct, sir," Charlie smiled gently at the interruption. "My grandfather, Michael Warren, spent his life tracking down the evidence for Germany's secret nuclear weapons program. The evidence he collected, including information about this U-boat, demonstrates that Germany not only had a vigorous and advanced nuclear weapons program by the end of the War, but that they had produced and had detonated at least two nuclear weapons a full year before the Manhattan Project."

The man refused to be put off. "Your evidence, Colonel Warren?"

"Excuse me, sir. This is a tactical briefing, not a lecture," General Mason interrupted. "The existence of these weapons is not an academic issue. They are real and so is the threat to this city. Colonel Warren is trying to present our response to that threat. I'm sure she will be happy at a later date to give you the information you requested. Please continue, Colonel Warren."

"Thank you, General Mason," Charlie smiled and nodded at Nathan. "*U-3551* arrived in New York Harbor at some unknown location. For some reason, Kepler failed to complete his mission. He and his crew abandoned the submarine and escaped into the city. We're not sure why this happened, but fortunately it did. The ship with its weapons remained on the bottom of New York Harbor undisturbed for the better part of sixty years until this man discovered their existence."

A picture of Ivan Kolov appeared on the screen. "Ivan Kolov, former Soviet Colonel and nuclear physicist-turned terrorist, discovered through extensive research the existence of *U-3551* and its cargo. He has spent the better part of a year putting together an operation designed to raise *U-3551* and salvage her weapons. We know that he has located the submarine and is currently engaged in operations to salvage her."

Charlie paused for a moment. "We do not know where the submarine is, or what Kolov will do once he and his team finds her. There are several possibilities. If the submarine is intact and the devices still operational, he may keep them in place, set a time delay on the devices, and detonate them at his pleasure.

"An alternate scenario, and the one I believe will happen, is that he will attempt to tow or move the submarine to a secure location, where he can dismantle the devices into a more compact and portable form so that he can use them at will.

"My reason for believing that this is the most likely course of action is that Kolov is a creature of profit, not ideology. He has no dream of a terrorist martyrdom. Rendering the devices into more portable units affords him the greatest chance to exploit the profit possibilities in the terrorist market.

"Nuclear weapons are the Holy Grail of terrorist weapons. With four operational devices under his control, located in a strategic target like New York City, Kolov could ask for and receive billions of dollars from terrorist organizations."

General Mason stood up. "This concludes the general information portion of this briefing. The tactical portion follows, and I am going to ask all those personnel not directly involved in the tactical aspects of this operation to leave this auditorium. Let me remind you that this briefing is classified as 'Top Secret.' Thank you for your time."

There was a stirring and murmuring in the room as several dozen people left the auditorium. Ken Rawlings came up to Mason and Charlie. "Before you begin, I need to see you both in my office."

"All right, Ken," Charlie said as she followed Mason and Rawlings down a side corridor to the room that served as his temporary office. Robin Dubek was there, along with two security guards. He was handcuffed and sitting in a chair.

"I'd like you to meet our security leak who's been feeding Kolov high-level intel on our operations," Rawlings said as they walked into his office.

"Dubek? How did you know? Why did he do this?" Charlie was thunderstruck.

"The how is simple, the why may be a bit more complex," Rawlings glared at Dubek. "Okay, Robin: why did you do this?"

"The same reason Kolov is looking for nuclear weapons," Dubek replied bitterly. "He promised me millions for information. He's going to succeed, Rawlings, regardless of what you do. I already have several million stashed away in some Swiss accounts. Even if you put me away for decades, I'll still be a rich man."

"That money won't do you any good if you're dead," Mason said coldy. "You're at Ground Zero right now, buddy. If Kolov detonates just one of those nukes, you're going to be nothing but a handful of ash and charred bones."

"I want my lawyer," Dubek said sullenly.

"A lawyer? We can get you a lawyer," Rawlings said brutally. "Oh, wait a minute: this is an ongoing classified operation, and I'm so sorry, Dubek, but I can't seem to spare the time to get to your request. You can't leave the building, and there's no phone service right now. But don't worry; we'll get you a lawyer sometime soon. Get this piece of trash out of my office."

After the guards took Dubek away. Rawlings sat down at his desk. "Here's the deal, guys: Dubek's been under surveillance for a number of months. Hard intel we had on Kolov was going out of here and useless information was coming in. The final straw was the situation with Reynolds and Meyers.

"I'm sorry that that traitor put those two detective's lives on the line. We nabbed him and now we can put him away."

"What about the operation and its security?" Charlie asked. "We've got hundreds of men and women out there right now ready to go."

Rawlings raised a hand. "Don't worry, the op's airtight now. I've had dozens of tactical patrols gathering real-time intel on the tunnel systems. It's been a huge job, but we've got all of that information fed into our tactical plans. These are experts, Charlie; these are people who infiltrate and blow up tunnels for a living, so don't worry."

"Let's get back out there and conclude the briefing, Charlie," Mason smiled at her. "By the way, you're doing great. Everyone's impressed with how you've handled things so far."

"So far, General, I haven't done anything," Charlie pointed out. "We've not recovered those weapons, and millions of people's lives are at stake."

An aide came up to them. "Colonel Warren, I have Sergeant Major MacKay on the line for you."

"Finally," Charlie said, looking at Mason. "Communications have been in a terrible mess. I've been trying to get in touch with him and Colonel Rosson all day."

They walked over to a desk. Charlie picked up the phone. "Hello? Yes, Donald, it's been a dreadful day here. It's much worse than that; they've put me in charge of the whole field operation. What? Well, you're entitled to your opinion, Sergeant Major. Listen, I need you to get over to Jane's house and let him know I need you both to lead a team. You need to get to Newark airport. We'll have information on the operation for you there. All right, see you soon. Goodbye."

She hung up the phone. "Donald wasn't the least bit surprised that I got put in charge of all this. He said it was about time I did something useful."

"Okay, Colonel, I get the point," Nathan laughed. "Let's get out there and talk to our troops."

-0-

James Rosson was stuck like millions of New Yorkers outside the city, unable to enter due to the security lockdown caused by the nerve gas release. He had called the Consulate and talked to Lady Margaret Wilson, who had managed to get into the Consulate and was trying to conduct business with a skeletal staff. Rosson spent most of the day fuming in front of the television set, listening to the not-so-informed guesses of news commentators and "experts."

"James, you might as well go with me and the children to the softball game," Jane suggested. "At least you'll be able to vent some of that frustration you've been feeling by screaming at my opposition."

Her husband looked up at her with a face of quizzical frustration. "What ever are you talking about, Jane? I've been perfectly calm and rational through out this whole mess."

Jane walked over to the television and turned it off. "Good, then you won't mind if I turn this wretched thing off."

"It's just as well. Markham was practically cashiered out of the service. I can't for the life of me figure out why anyone with half a brain would listen to him. Bloviating imbecile," he muttered at the television, picking up the phone for the fifteenth time and dialing Donald MacKay's number. The phone rang several times, then MacKay's answering machine answered. "Donald? It's Rosson. Please ring me up when you get this message. We've got to figure out a way to get into that city. Goodbye."

James slammed down the phone. "Blast that man! I feel so helpless, just sitting here!" He sat down on the couch heavily in a flaming blue funk.

"Lord, please, if you can; get this man out of my house before he drives all of us stark raving mad." Jane raised her eyes heavenward in sincere prayer.

There was a knock on the door. Jane answered the door. "Thank Heaven's it's you," she said in a relieved tone as Donald MacKay entered the house. He was dressed in his black fatigues. "James: it's Sergeant Major MacKay. I think it's a business call, right, Donald?"

Rosson came to the door. "It's about time you showed up. What kept you?"

MacKay raised an eyebrow. "Bad day?" He turned to Jane.

"Begging your pardon, Ms. Rosson, but we have need of the Colonel's services. Colonel Warren needs his assistance."

"Assistance? Must be a mission. Good, I'll be down in a moment." James bounded up the stairs. MacKay and Jane looked at each other and shook their heads.

"For Heaven's sake, take him away with my blessing," Jane said with relief. "He's been absolutely impossible all day."

Rosson reappeared a few minutes later dressed in his black fatigues carrying a large rucksack. "I'll see you later, love," he said as he kissed his wife and children goodbye.

The door closed behind him. Jane sighed and looked at her children. "Is Daddy going off to help Aunt Charlie?" Amanda asked.

"Yes dear," Jane sighed, shaking her head.

"We're on our way to New York City?" James asked as he and MacKay went to Donald's car.

"You might say that, sir," MacKay replied cryptically. "We need to get over to Newark airport. We have a mission."

-0-

David was excused from the briefing to go over to the hospital to check on Ron Meyers. He found Brenda Reynolds asleep in the Surgical ICU waiting room. "Hey, sleepyhead: wake up." David gently shook her shoulder.

"What?" Brenda bolted awake, staring wildly. "What's wrong, Ron?" She blinked a few times and shook her head. "Oh, it's you, Stone. Why are you here?"

"I'm taking you to dinner, Brenda. My treat," David said, looking at her with some concern. "Have you gotten any kind of rest at all?"

"Some," Brenda said quietly. "I've been in to see Ron every couple of hours or so. He seems to be getting better."

"Good," David nodded. "Now I know that your job is to watch over him, but I also know that he'd want you to take care of yourself. Let's get some grub."

"I've eaten here before, Stone. The hospital cafeteria's food is pretty bad," Brenda got up and stretched. "I'd like to go out and get some decent food, but the way things are, that's not an option right now."

She stared out the window. It was another hazy New York day. The city looked normal, except for the almost total lack of traffic in the streets. "It seems so strange to see practically no one on the roads." Brenda paused for a moment. "What's Charlie up to?"

"She's been appointed ground tactical commander for the operation," David said with obvious pride. "Charlie didn't want to do it, but Mason pulled a gun on her and she had to accept."

Brenda laughed. "I doubt if it happened that way."

"You're right, but it makes a good story. Let's go eat." David said as they left the waiting room. They went down to the cafeteria and ate. Brenda had not eaten or left the waiting room since arriving at the hospital. She picked at her food listlessly.

"Hey, Ron's going to pull through this," David said quietly.

Brenda put down her fork and put her head in her hands. "I feel so worthless, Dave. Ron's in there hooked up to all of those machines because I goofed. I let him down. I wasn't watching his back."

"That's not true, Brenda, and you know it," David said sharply. "You're a good cop. Ron knows it; everyone does. You were ambushed. You had no idea you were walking into a trap."

"Why did you come after us, Dave? Why did Charlie risk her life to save me?" Brenda asked with wonder in her voice.

David thought for a moment. "Brenda, that's just the way Charlie is. She does stuff like that all the time. She could have spent her life in a crime lab or medical examiner's office processing cases and doing autopsies, but I don't think she would have been happy doing it. Charlie just cares about people too much to stand on the sidelines. That's why she jumps in with both feet into everything she does."

He chuckled. "She also has the habit of pulling everyone in after her. I could have killed her yesterday, taking the chance that she did by going in after you solo. I thought that was my job, but Charlie was the one best qualified to do it, so I let her."

"It must have killed you to stay behind, Stone," Brenda observed with a smile.

David shrugged. "Yeah, it was. I mean, I'm a guy, and that's what guys generally do. You know: being a hero and all that nonsense. It's been tough for me to realize that sort of thing doesn't work with Charlie. She can take care of herself. Anyway, that's just the way it is."

Brenda took a sip of coffee and stared at her plate for a moment. "Dave, you and Charlie seem so happy together. I haven't seen you like that since…"

"Since I married Karen," David finished Brenda's sentence for her. "Yeah, Brenda, meeting Charlie saved my life. Everything changed when she came to Compton. I didn't think anyone could ever replace Karen, but God had other plans."

Brenda looked at her coffee. "You and Charlie have something special, Dave. Something I never had. I mean, Karen was religious and all that. I never understood all that stuff she talked about. It made no sense to me. You and Charlie seem to have a relationship with God that's, well, real."

"That's because it is real, Brenda," David replied quietly. "God is real. As real as anyone else I know." He paused for a moment. "Charlie's better at explaining this stuff than I am. You can ask her some time."

David looked at her curiously. "You never talked about this sort of stuff before, Brenda. Why are you talking about it now?"

"Being tied to a chair for a couple of hours gave me plenty of time to think," Brenda said with a half-hearted grin. "Not knowing whether I was going to live or die. Then Charlie shows up like some sort of angel. It was like a miracle, totally amazing. You guys put everything on the line for me and Ron. I just can't get over it."

They got up from their table and went back to the waiting room. "Is there anything I can get for you, Brenda?" David asked before leaving.

"I don't think so," Brenda said, sitting down in her chair. "Thanks for dinner. It was really nice of you."

"No it wasn't, Brenda," David replied in a joking tone. "Dinner was lousy. Don't lie to me. We'll do it up right after all this mess blows over. You and Ron and Charlie and me, okay?"

"Okay." Brenda got up and hugged David closely. She kissed

his cheek. "Thanks, Dave. Thanks for bringing us back."

"Okay, Lieutenant. Take care of your partner," David said, releasing her.

25

The briefing was still underway when David arrived back at the EOC. Charlie was up on the stage with a picture of her grandfather's warehouse behind her. "This structure is the most likely place that Kolov will take the submarine, assuming that she is capable of sailing there under her own power. Surveillance teams report that there has been activity both in and around the building. It is obvious that Kolov is readying the building to receive the submarine."

"Then it follows that the submarine is operational," a Delta Force NCO pointed out.

"That's correct," Charlie agreed. "We believe he will attempt to move the submarine tonight after the sun goes down. If you've noticed, the harbor has been closed to traffic since the incident in the tunnels. All dock facilities have been evacuated by Harbor Patrol units. We have not increased surveillance by harbor patrols or any other activities. The reason for this is simple. We want Kolov to play out his hand. Once the submarine is in this location, his operation is on a strict time schedule. It is at this point that he's most vulnerable."

"Don't you think he's anticipated that aspect of his operation and has planned accordingly?" An ESU officer asked.

"He probably has, and that's why when we go in, we're going in full force," Mason interjected. "We're going to hit him from every direction conceivable: Air, sea, and land. If he tries to evac through the tunnels, we'll be waiting for him."

A wave of cheers and shouts erupted in the auditorium as he

said this. Mason held up his hand. "Okay people: settle down. We've got a few more operational details to discuss before we head for our staging areas. Forward tactical control of this operation is going to take place down by the waterfront. We'll give you tactical frequencies and procedures once you get to your staging are as."

Mason's tone took on a grim edge. "Let me talk for a minute about rules of engagement, people. This is NOT a standard police operation. Your opponents are to be treated as enemy combatants, not criminals. You are to use whatever level of force necessary needed to neutralize the threat. If they choose to surrender, then treat them in accordance with the rules governing prisoners of war. These people are playing for keeps, and so are we, so stay safe. We'll sort out the legal details later when the threat is passed."

He turned to Charlie. "Do you have anything to add, Colonel Warren?"

Charlie shook her head. "I'm not good at noble speeches. Let's just get out there and get rid of these people. Be safe and Godspeed."

Everyone snapped to attention as Mason and Charlie left the room. "Okay," Charlie said, letting out a gust of air, "now the hard part begins."

"I'm briefing the SEALs over at the Navy yard in an hour," Mason said. "They've got to get across that harbor quickly, and they've got the toughest job as far as distance and travel. Good job on the presentation, by the way."

"I've got your HALO team in a staging area at Newark airport," Mason said with a smile. "per your request, the NCOIC is Sergeant Major MacKay, and the CO is Colonel Rosson. They'll be leading the joint Delta-SAS strike team that's tasked with landing on the roof of the building."

"I'm glad James and Donald will be involved in this," Charlie said. "I just hope this whole thing works," she added reluctantly.

-0-

"Nice briefing, Charlie," David said approvingly as she came into the room where they had slept that morning.

"Thank you, David. How are Brenda and Ron doing?" Charlie

asked as she put on her flak vest and pistol.

"They're doing fine," David replied. He was now dressed in a tactical jumpsuit and flak jacket. "Since I don't have anything to do here while you're playing Eisenhower, I've asked to go out with one of the ESU outfits. I hope you don't mind."

"No, David, I don't mind," Charlie said softly, coming up to him and kissing him. "You've been an angel through all of this. I don't think I could have gotten through all of this without you."

A knock came at the door. "Yes?" Charlie answered.

An aide opened the door. "Colonel Warren, there's a phone call at the command desk for you."

"Okay, I'll be out in a moment," Charlie turned and kissed David again. "You be careful out there. After all, I'm not going to be out there to watch over you."

"I think I'll manage, Pest." David said with a smile as she left the room.

Charlie went over to the command desk and picked up the phone. "Hello?"

"Dr. Warren, my name is Joseph Schmidt. I am the son of Hans Schmidt," the voice at the other end replied. "My father is involved in the murder investigation in Huntington, New York. He is... dying, and he regained consciousness this morning. My father wants to talk to you, Dr. Warren. He says it is very important that you come to him. Can you come?"

Charlie looked at her watch. "I need to check on something, Mr. Schmidt. Can you hold on for a moment?"

She put her hand over the receiver. Ken Rawlings came up to her. "I have the son of Hans Schmidt on the line. He says that his father wants to talk to me."

"You've got time before all this kicks off, Charlie," Rawlings said. "Do you think this could be important?"

"Yes I do," Charlie replied. She spoke into the phone. "Mr. Schmidt, I will be out there in half an hour. Please thank your father for me."

"I will, Dr. Warren. Thank you. Goodbye." Charlie hung up the phone.

"Okay, so what does that phone call mean?" Rawlings asked.

"We may have just gotten a major break in our case," Charlie said excitedly. "Do you remember that U-boat commander, Hans Kepler? I've been doing some cross-referencing on Grandfather's files, checking employment records with the Immigration database. This Hans Schmidt and Hans Kepler have identical birth dates, as well as identical towns of origin in Germany. Schmidt taught physics for years at a local university, and Kepler was a physicist. I'm almost positive the two men are one and the same."

Rawlings looked at Charlie. "That comes in the class of a major miracle, kiddo. If we've found the commander of that sub, then we can find out where it is."

"It most certainly does," Charlie said with relief. "If we can pinpoint the location of that sub, we can stop this in its tracks without firing a shot. That would be a blessing."

"Amen to that," Ken Rawlings agreed. "Let me know how things pan out. Take a chopper; it'll be faster. Traffic's still a nightmare out there."

"Okay," Charlie was already headed for the door.

-0-

"Good afternoon, gentlemen, and I use that term loosely," Mason said to the seven men assembled in a warehouse at the Navy yard located across from New York Harbor. "We have an assignment that's uniquely suited for your special skills."

A chorus of howls and hoots greeted him in reply. "Okay, people: pipe down! That's good news, Colonel. We've been rusting away in dry dock ever since we came back from the Middle East," the team leader, Commander Simpson, said with anticipation in his voice.

"Well, this op will rock your world, Commander," Mason unfolded a map of the harbor and spread it before them. "We need you and your team to position yourselves in a concealed location along the docks here." He pointed to a location on the map a quarter of a mile from the warehouse. "This warehouse is your target. It's an abandoned submarine pen left over from the Second World War. The bad guys are going to raise an old sub in the harbor and sail her into that pen tonight."

"A sub? You mean like an old World War Two submarine?" the Master Chief in charge of the team asked.

"Yeah, Master Chief," Mason replied. "More specifically, a U-boat carrying four nuclear weapons."

"I thought we were the only ones who had the Bomb," Simpson said with a frown.

"Well, the history books were wrong," Mason said grimly. "The bad guys want those weapons, and we've got to stop them. You guys are going to capture the warehouse, along with a Delta team/SAS detachment who's going to parachute onto the roof."

"Combined seaborne and airborne assaults: that's way cool," Simpson said with admiration. "Who thought that one up?"

"A British lieutenant colonel by the name of Charlie Warren," Mason said smoothly.

"I like his style," the Master Chief said with respect. "It's sneaky and bold. Almost like an op we'd come up with. Is this guy SAS or something?"

"Yeah, she is. I'll pass your comments along to her," Mason said with a smile.

"Her? You mean a girl thought this up?" Simpson's jaw dropped.

"Yup," Mason folded up the map. "Warren's also running the show, by the way."

"Excuse me, sir, but what does some female know about spec ops?" Master Chief Dobbs asked with profound skepticism.

"This one knows a lot," General Mason replied. "Did you guys hear anything about that op out on Long Island in November?"

"I did, sir," Simpson replied. "Wasn't that the one where you got hurt?"

Mason grinned crookedly. "That's right, Commander. After our aircraft got shot down, that 'girl' set up a perimeter defense around our aircraft and then took out an enemy ambush, all by herself. Is that good enough for you?"

Dobbs emitted a low whistle. "Strike my last comments, sir. The lady knows her stuff."

"That's what the Brits thought," Mason replied. "Not only is she a member of SAS, she won the VC for her efforts. I think Warren's up for the job."

"Works for me," Dobbs replied, an unpleasant grin spread across his face. "When do we get things rolling?"

"You're due to head out in two hours, gentlemen," Mason said as he gathered up his folders. "H-hour is at 2400 hours local. Good luck, and good hunting."

"Aye, aye, sir," Doug Simpson said, rendering a sharp salute. The SEALs snapped to attention as Mason returned the salute and left the warehouse.

-0-

Half an hour later, a military helicopter with Charlie on board touched down at the helipad at Huntington Hospital. Charlie was led to the ICU where the Schmidt family waited.

"I'm so glad you came, Dr. Warren," Joseph Schmidt said with gratitude as Charlie greeted him and the family in the waiting area. "My father is now awake and expecting you."

"Thank you for calling, Mr. Schmidt. You may be responsible for saving millions of lives today," Charlie told him quietly. She glanced around the room. It was filled with Schmidt's relatives. They looked like any other family: full of grief over the loss of a loved one, holding onto each other, some weeping quietly, others sitting in shock.

A nurse came to the door. "He's ready to see you now, Dr. Warren."

Hans Schmidt lay in his bed, his face drawn with pain and grief. "Dr. Warren, I'm glad to finally meet you." He held out his hand, and Charlie took it warmly and gently.

Schmidt looked at his son. "Joseph, Dr. Warren and I need a few moments in private. Would you indulge me, please?"

"Of course, father," Joseph Schmidt left the room.

Charlie waited until they were alone. "I'm glad to meet you, Herr Schmidt," Charlie replied in fluent German, "or should I say, Captain Kepler?"

There was a long silence in the room. Schmidt looked at her and nodded his head. "I prefer English, if you don't mind," he finally replied, "though your German is quite excellent. My compliments, and you honor me with the use of my military title."

"You were a brave warrior, Captain," Charlie said. "I've seen your record. You fought with honor and fairness, and you earned the respect of the English and American sailors you fought against."

Schmidt nodded slightly. "It is good to be honored by one's opponents." He paused for a moment. "I have not summoned you here to be reminded of my record during the War. I have some things I must tell you before I die."

"We know about the U-boat, Captain," Charlie said softly. " A terrorist has located your submarine and is attempting to raise her and steal the weapons on board her."

A look of pain washed over Schmidt's face. "I was afraid of that. I should have set off the scuttling charges, but I was afraid that the radiation would poison the city. We did not know very much about nuclear bombs back then."

"Why did you not complete your last mission?"

"I hated Hitler and the Nazis," Schmidt replied. "When I volunteered for U-boat service, I was defending my country. That was different. By the time I was summoned to Berlin, I knew that the war was lost. Hitler knew that as well. Sending those bombs to America to murder millions of innocent people was not the act of a soldier; it was the act of a butcher. It was an illegal order.

"Since the order was illegal, once we were at sea, I disclosed Hitler's plan to my crew. I convinced my crew, and we agreed to dock the boat next to one of the piers and escape into the New York City. We vowed to each other never to meet again, and never to reveal the location of the submarine. Until Sunday, I kept my vow.

"Those people gave me drugs to make me talk. I revealed the location of the submarine, along with other details of the mission. Now they will kill millions of people, and their blood will be on my hands as I go before God," Schmidt's voice broke and he started to weep silently.

"That's not true, Captain," Charlie drew close, holding onto his frail hand with both of hers. "Tonight, special forces are going to capture that submarine and its weapons. You will be part of that. Your information will help us accomplish that mission."

Schmidt looked up into Charlie's eyes, and slowly his grief

went away. He nodded slowly, tears welling up in his eyes and streaming down his cheeks. "My name was Hans Kepler, but Kepler died when I set foot in this country. My family did not know who I was, or what I did until a few days ago. I told them everything, and they understand. That is why they called you."

Charlie handed him a chart of New York Harbor, "Can you show me the location of your boat, Captain?" Schmidt pointed to a location directly across from New York Harbor.

"She is there," he said, his voice gaining strength. "There is about ten meters of water over her conning tower at that point. There was very little room to maneuver her."

Charlie produced her cell phone, called the EOC and relayed the information. "Thank you, Herr Schmidt, for helping us," she said when she finished talking on her phone. "Your country thanks you as well."

"America is my country now," Schmidt told her. "My family is here, and I will be buried here when I die."

He looked at Charlie more closely. "You are dressed as a soldier, Dr. Warren. You are a soldier as well as a physician?"

"Dr. Schmidt, I am a British Army officer," Charlie told him quietly. "I came to America, just like you. America is now my home as well. I will be leading those forces as we go into battle."

"Someone told me that you were knighted by the Queen of England. Is that true?" Schmidt asked.

"Yes, Professor Schmidt, I was knighted by the Queen. Twice, as a matter of fact," Charlie said, acutely uncomfortable at the mentioning of her titles.

"You are a physician as well as a soldier and a knight," Schmidt nodded. "I understand now. I am glad I have had the honor of meeting you, Dr. Warren. You are a brave warrior, I can tell that. We will both be fighting for the same side today," Schmidt pointed out. "That is good. It is good to fight with warriors like you in a just cause. It makes life worth living. Good luck to you and your soldiers tonight, Dr. Warren. God go with you."

"Go with God, Captain," Charlie replied with tears in her eyes.

-0-

"Now that we have a bead on that sub, we can fine tune our operation," Nathan Mason said with satisfaction as Charlie entered the command room. "Nice work, Colonel."

"Thank Herr Schmidt," Charlie replied. "He is a fine man who wanted to do the right thing."

Mason nodded. "My grandfather served in World War II. He always made a point of telling me that there were men of honor on both sides, and that you couldn't always judge a man by what uniform he wore."

"That's true," Charlie sighed. "Speaking of uniforms, I take it that my husband has run off to the war."

"Yes he has," Nathan replied. "He said it was his turn to go out and fight the bad guys. According to him, you have the hard duty tonight, being stuck in a command center watching all the action. Dave said it's payback for last November when he was stuck in an ops center and you were out shooting bad guys and having fun."

"I can see his point. Turnabout and all that," Charlie agreed. "What do you want to do, now that we know where the sub is?"

"Well, there are two options, as I see it," Mason scratched his head. "We can send in the Navy and blow the thing out of the water. It's quick, but messy. We'll have a radioactive mess to clean up, plus it's rather barbaric. Some of the guys want to do it because it will save the lives of our people."

"The problem is that Kolov will most likely get away. You know he's not on board that submarine," Charlie pointed out.

"That's what I told the people who wanted that option," Mason said. "Besides, I want to capture these people alive so I can find out all I can about who's bankrolling them, and who their buyer is. We can't do that if they're fish food."

He grinned. "Besides, I'd have a bunch of angry SEALs after me. They are dying to get going on their part of your plan."

"So we're going with the second option, which is keeping an eye on the sub and trailing it to that sub pen, right?" Charlie said with a smile.

"Oh yeah," a gleam of excitement appeared in Mason's eyes. "You should have heard the SEAL team commander when I briefed him on your plan. He went wild, thought it was the greatest thing he'd ever heard. He said he couldn't believe an Army guy thought it up. When I told him it was you, his jaw nearly dropped on the floor. He wants to know if you'd like to go through SEAL training some time."

Charlie smiled and shook her head. "I'm flattered, but I'm going to be busy for the next few years. Besides, I thought it was against the law for females to go through that sort of training. But I really wouldn't want to let the SEALs down. I have a soft spot in my heart for pirates, you know."

"I knew that the day I met you," Mason pointed out. "Oh yes," Mason suddenly remembered. "The commander of the HALO detachment wants to speak to you personally. He's on the line right now."

He handed the phone to Charlie. "Hello?"

"Good evening, Colonel Warren," James Rosson's voice came over the line. "I wanted to let you know that Lady Wilson relayed your request to us. A detachment of SAS and Delta commandos will be parachuting onto the warehouse at 2400 hours tonight. I am the commander of the team. Sergeant Major MacKay is my NCO, and I, my lady, am at your service."

Charlie was at a loss for words. "James, I... it could be dangerous."

"You of all people should know better than to lecture me about danger, ma'am." Rosson replied, a deep note of respect in his voice. "It's an honor to serve with you on the field of battle."

"James... Colonel Rosson: thank you for your help. Give my best to your team," Charlie heard herself say. "God go with you tonight."

"And with you, my Lady Knight," Rosson said softly. "God be with us all."

Charlie put down the phone receiver slowly. Her hands trembled slightly. She said nothing for a moment, and then looked over at Mason.

"You can do this, Charlie," he said quietly. "I know you can. I've known it ever since you took charge that night in November when our chopper crashed. This is your mission, Colonel; that's why you're here. You're the battlefield commander I need to do the job." He looked at his watch. "It's time for you to get to your post, Colonel Warren."

"I understand, sir," Charlie paused for a moment. "General, is there a chance I can talk to my godfather before I leave?"

" Absolutely," General Mason replied. "Give him my best when you do." He left Charlie to go see about other matters in the command room.

Charlie dialed Angus' number and got him immediately. "Hello, Uncle Angus? It's Charlie."

"Charlie, love! It's good to hear your voice." Pure joy filled Angus' voice as he talked to her. "Where are you now, lass? Are you safe?"

"I'm here in New York City, Uncle Angus," Charlie's voice broke a bit. "I'm... I'm going to need your prayers and your blessing tonight."

There was a very long pause at the other end of the line. "You need my blessing, child. I understand. You're going into battle again, aren't you, Charlie?"

"Yes, Uncle. I am going into battle again. Not only myself this time. I am commanding troops in the field. I am in charge of a major operation."

"I understand, Charlie. I know that God will go with you, lass. The church has been open since all of this began. People have been praying round the clock for you, and for everyone else in New York."

"James and Donald will be parachuting into the battle zone tonight, Uncle Angus. Please remember them especially."

"I will, Charlie," Angus replied softly. "You know your father and grandfather are proud of you, as am I."

"I know, Uncle Angus," Charlie said, tears in her eyes. "I will see you soon."

"God bless you, child."

-0-

"She's certainly not an *Akula* class submarine," Alexi Renov commented to his second in command as he looked at the cramped conning tower.

"No sir, but she's in amazingly good shape, considering her age," Boris Radek nodded, looking at the power gauges before him on the hull of the submarine. "Captain, we have full charge on batteries. We are running on full internal power."

"Very well," Renov replied. "It is time to begin. Engine room: stand by to engage engines."

A reply crackled over the speakers. "Engine room aye."

Renov turned to his executive officer. "Inform Colonel Kolov that we are headed towards the submarine pen. Engine room: give me sixty revolutions per minute on the screws."

"Aye, sixty revolutions per minute on the screws."

Radek relayed Renov's message to the communications specialist. There was a slight shudder as the submarine freed itself from the harbor bottom. He turned to another man who was standing behind the two people manning the diving controls. "Diving officer: give me two degrees up angle on the bow planes. Rudder amidships. Proceed slowly, gentlemen. This is a harbor full of ships, not the open sea."

There was a slight, almost imperceptible rise in the submarine's attitude as she gently and slowly moved past the dockside berth where she had rested for almost sixty years.

"She handles well," Renov remarked approvingly. "Our German friends did a splendid job in building her. She reminds me of my first command out of sub school."

"Captain, we are free of the dock and ready to maneuver," Radek told him a few moments later.

"Very well," Renov replied. "Make your course 270. Diving officer: level her off. What is our current depth?"

"We have ten meters above our conning tower, Captain," Radek said, looking at one of the gauges. "We have four meters clearance from below our keel."

Renov nodded his approval. "Good, then let us head to the submarine pen. Give me four knots on the engines, please."

"Four knots, aye," Radek said, repeating the command to the engine room.

The submarine glided slowly along the harbor bottom. Renov brought up the periscope and did a 360-degree sweep of the harbor.

The moonlight glimmered brightly on the water.

"The harbor is almost deserted," Renov observed. "Comrade Kolov was sure that the Americans would shut down the harbor after the nerve gas attack. Things are going exactly as planned."

"Sir, Colonel Kolov sends his compliments on your achievement. He wishes to inform you that the submarine pen is ready to receive you." The communications specialist said over the intercom.

"Thank you," Renov acknowledged, peering into the periscope. "The pen is one hundred meters away. Diving officer: surface the ship. All hands, prepare for surface action. Lookouts to your posts. Steady on course 270. Engine room: slow to one knot; prepare to reverse engines on my command."

Slowly, *U-3551* broke the surface of New York harbor. Her hatches opened and bristled with men armed with weapons as she slowed to a crawl. The side of the warehouse rumbled open, revealing an opening that stretched from the roof to the surface of the water. The submarine glided effortlessly into the opening, her rust-streaked hull gleaming dully in the moonlight.

"Reverse engines!" Renov commanded as the bow of the submarine pierced the inky darkness of the submarine pen. The submarine slowed almost to a stop as her engines went full reverse, slowing her momentum as she advanced.

When her stern had cleared the doors, Renov issued his final command. "All engines stop." The submarine, now barely moving, inched gently forward into the bay. Waiting men on the sides of the bay caught the lines thrown to them by men on the submarine's deck. The ropes were made fast to the cleats on the dock, and the submarine stopped. The doors to the submarine pen rumbled closed.

The submarine pen echoed with cheers as Alexi Renov came out of the conning tower and down the ladder onto the deck of the submarine. He stepped off onto the dock and was greeted by Ivan Kolov. "Well done, Alexi. Well done," Kolov embraced him. "Now we need to look at those devices. Are they in good shape?"

"Yes, Comrade Kolov," Renov replied. "I am not an expert in this field, but they appear to be sound. There are no signs the crew tampered with them before they left. My people found no evidence of sabotage."

"Strange that they failed to activate the scuttling charges if they had decided to simply abandon her," Kolov mused. "Perhaps Kepler was afraid the explosions might somehow activate the weapons or cause contamination."

He stepped onto the submarine's forward deck and climbed down the forward hatch. Kolov went down the narrow corridor to the forward torpedo room. Instead of rows of torpedoes resting in cradles, the whole forward section of the submarine had been cleared out. In the place of the torpedo tubes, four large spherical devices squatted on the gray deck. Renov followed Kolov into the room. "There they are, Alexi," Kolov's voice was hushed with awe. "These will make every one of us rich as czars!"

Renov nodded and looked at his watch. "Ivan, we need to hurry. I am sure the Americans are aware of where we are right now."

"You may be sure, Alexi, but I am not," Kolov replied, his voice heavy with contempt. "The Americans are blundering fools. They are too busy right now cleaning up the mess from the nerve gas attack to worry about us. Besides, I have more surprises in store for them should they try to attack."

-0-

"There she goes," Lieutenant Commander Douglas Tecumseh Simpson said as he peered through a pair of night vision goggles. He was in the lead Zodiac boat carrying the SEAL team as they moved carefully and slowly across New York harbor. The submarine's stern had just cleared the submarine pen.

"Man, this plan is going to be fun," one of the sailors named McNally said to one of his friends. "We haven't had anything like this since we busted in on those goons outside of Baghdad."

"Pipe down, McNally," the Master Chief in charge of the team ordered. "Save it for later, okay?"

Aye aye, Master Chief," McNally said, hunkering down in the raft. He was in charge of placing demolitions and had a tendency to get a little too excited at times.

Simpson looked at his watch. "Let's get across this pond and get into position. We'll follow the docks to about fifty meters from the pier. At H-hour, we'll switch on the engines and get across to the front of the pier. We got a ten-meter climb up onto the pier level, then we'll bust the place open. Clear?"

"Clear," the team members replied.

-0-

"Ops, this is Watch 12: submarine is now inside the warehouse," a dark figure said as he peered over the edge of a building located a quarter of a mile from the warehouse. He was not alone. Beside him were four men positioned at intervals along the roof, each of them armed with sniper rifles. Their mission was a simple one: they were to shoot any individuals who might interfere with the expected landing of troops on the warehouse roof.

They were police snipers, all of whom had military backgrounds. Normally, they were trained for hostage rescue situations. Tonight, they were on a military operation. The people they were going to kill on that roof were not criminals; they were enemy soldiers. New York City had been attacked and invaded by enemy troops, and they were at war.

"Roger 12," a voice replied. "Be advised that we are X minus 200 minutes. Ops out."

The man relaxed and signaled to the other men in his group. They came up to him. "Okay guys: stand easy. Watch for activity on that rooftop. That's where Delta and the Brits are going to land. When we get the word, we're to neutralize any targets on that roof. It's our job to sweep the LZ."

"What about the SEALs, Joe?" one of the snipers asked.

"They're going to come up along the sides of the warehouse and breach it," the team leader replied. "We'll provide cover fire for them as well."

"Friend of mine down in ESU says that they have a couple of surprises in store for those idiots in the tunnels." One of the snipers told the team.

"This kinda reminds me of the sort of stuff I used to do in Afghanistan," a sniper named Chris told the rest of the team. "We'd hunker down behind some rocks and wait for the bad guys to poke their heads out and then we'd whack 'em good."

"Okay guys: cut the chatter and lets get back to our posts." The team leader told his people. "Those clowns in the warehouse have NVGs as well. You can bet they're watching for us to show up."

"They aint never gonna have the chance, Joe." Chris assured him.

26

I *haven't felt this nervous since I took my entrance exams to* *medical school,* Charlie Warren thought to herself as she looked around the busy Ops Center. It was a collection of expandable units on several tractor-trailer vans that married together to form a complex of rooms. It was a buzzing hive of glowing consoles, scurrying technicians, and hushed voices as people spoke to each other.

Charlie stared up at the plexiglass command map showing the target section of the East River docks. Her grandfather's warehouse was marked in red. Clustered around it were various cryptic symbols indicating the position of units involved in and supporting the operation.. To the immediate right of the map were screens displaying data on the units as well as a countdown clock indicating the time left before the operation was to start. *People are looking to me to run this whole operation. I've never done anything like this before in my entire life.* Charlie shook her head in disbelief.

"This place looks more like the launch center for the Space Shuttle than a battlefield command center," she told Nathan Mason.

"Welcome to the twenty-first century battlefield," General Mason said with a smile. "Actually, it's got more gizmos and whiz-bangs for you to see the battlefield, it's still a nerve center where a commander runs the battle. That's a time tested principle, Charlie."

Mason looked at Charlie's anxious face. "I recognize the look. I've been there, and I've seen it on my face and the faces of my commanders. Don't worry, Charlie. Once things start, you'll be too busy to be scared. It's the waiting that drives people nuts."

"All of these people are counting on me, General," Charlie said quietly. "They're counting on me to do the right thing. I have their lives in my hands. It's terrifying." Charlie looked at her watch for the fifteenth time in the past thirty minutes. "I keep wondering what all of those people are thinking as they wait in boats and planes and in tunnels underneath this city. I just hope and pray that this plan of mine works."

"I think it will, Colonel," Mason smiled. "It's gutsy and bold. You were able to sell the Joint Chiefs and the President on it, and that's the hardest crowd to sell on anything. We have combined airborne and sea borne assaults with simultaneous advances through the tunnel systems. We'll be hitting them with overwhelming power from every direction. We've got enough firepower concentrated in key spots to keep the enemy's head down."

"Are you sure they haven't already removed the weapons from the submarine?" Charlie asked. "My biggest fear is that we're going to go through all of this to find out that the weapons are gone."

"I doubt it," Mason said confidently. "The people from the Nuclear Emergency Search Team told me these old devices were bulky and cumbersome. It will take Kolov and his technicians time to dismantle and remove the plutonium cores."

Charlie's plan was simple: the warehouse was to be secured by SAS and Delta forces landing on the roof, combined by a sea borne assault by a SEAL team. Once the warehouse was secure, the nuclear devices would be inspected and disarmed by the Nuclear Emergency Search Team. Kolov's underground complex was to be assaulted and captured in a simultaneous series of attacks launched by Emergency Services Unit teams.

"Zero minus fifteen," an automated voice announced throughout the complex. Charlie started when she heard the announcement.

"I'm sorry, sir," she said regretfully to Mason. "I guess I didn't realize how nervous I am. I'd rather be down on the docks with the rest of the pirates and cutthroats."

"I understand, Charlie. Unfortunately, someone has to coordinate all of this. No one questions your courage or willingness to do the heavy lifting. That's why you're here right now," Mason put a hand on her shoulder before he left for the EOC. "I'll be located in the EOC. If there's anything you need, just let me know."

"Colonel Warren, we're coming up on Minus-ten readiness checks," Lieutenant Sydney Hobbs told her. Hobbs was an Army Intelligence officer assigned to Charlie as her executive officer. Sydney had jumped at the chance to work with Charlie, and the two had become instantly close in an astonishingly short period of time.

"Thank you, Lieutenant," Charlie replied, hoping her voice didn't betray her nervousness. "Is the HALO flight in the air yet?"

Hobbs looked at her clipboard. "Yes ma'am, it is. Do you wish to contact the commander of the team? I thought you might."

"Yes, please." Charlie replied. "Thank you, Sydney. You're reading my mind."

"That's what a good XO does," Hobbs said, smiling. She went to a nearby desk and made the necessary arrangements. When Sydney was ready, she handed the phone receiver to Charlie. "George this is Michael: status check, over."

James Rosson's voice came over the phone. "Michael this is George: we are green. X minus-twelve. Weather over objective is good, over."

"We copy X minus-twelve," Charlie paused for a moment, controlling the emotion in her voice. She realized it was possible that this was the last time on earth she would hear James' voice. "Godspeed, George. Good hunting."

"Good hunting to us all. George out."

Charlie lowered the phone receiver to its cradle. Sydney came up to Charlie with a cup of coffee and handed it wordlessly to her. "My best friend is on that plane, Sydney," Charlie told Hobbs as she sipped the coffee. "My husband is down in one of those tunnels."

"I know, Colonel," Hobbs said quietly. "We're ready to test communications and readiness status checks on ten."

"All right then, let's go through this checklist," Charlie replied, her confidence growing steadily. She knew that everyone was ready, that everything had been done to assure the safety and success of the operation. It was time to go to work.

-0-

"I wish I could be there for her, sir," Donald MacKay shouted over the din of the aircraft engines as they sat in the cargo bay of the C-141. Their aircraft was now in a pattern orbiting New York City. At five minutes to midnight, the tailgate to the giant aircraft would drop, and their team would drop ten thousand feet down to the warehouse located in the harbor. At five hundred feet, their chutes would open, slowing their descent to a gentle speed. The plan was for the team to drop silently down onto the warehouse rooftop.

Rosson nodded. "I know she's nervous, Sergeant Major. But she's ready. You're where she needs you right now. You trained her well, and now it's her time to be in command."

MacKay was silent for a moment. "She was one of the best officers I ever trained. Very thorough, looked out for her men; she never did anything without thinking about them first. She reminded me of you. I guess that's why I was so hard on her. I wanted to make sure she was up to the task."

"I think we've seen that she was, Sergeant Major." Rosson agreed. "How are the lads holding up?"

"They're ready, sir," MacKay told him. "They've been training with this Delta team for the past few weeks. They jumped at the chance to come up and help out."

The Delta team leader came up to MacKay and Rosson. "Sir, the pilot reports wind patterns at the drop zone favor insertion two kilometers to the north. We've set chute deployment at five hundred feet to allow for possible thermal activity above the city to give us room to maneuver. It was a hot one in New York City this afternoon."

"Very well, Captain," Rosson looked at MacKay. "Pass the word along to the men, Sergeant Major."

"Yes sir," MacKay left and went to brief the team members and conduct the final equipment inspection before the drop. Rosson was left alone with his thoughts.

"Good luck, Charlie," he murmured, looking at his watch.

-0-

"Comrade Kolov, the first weapon has been extracted from the submarine," Alexi Renov told him over the cell phone. "We are proceeding to dismantle the other three devices."

"Good; have the device brought to the command center immediately," Kolov directed, looking at his watch. He dialed up another number. "Are you in place yet? I want you to take the girl now. Do not kill anyone unless they resist."

27

The van moved quietly along the darkened Compton streets. There was little traffic. Only an occasional car passed by as the van made its way over to the Richards house.

Kolov had been explicit about his instructions. No one was to be harmed as long as the family did not resist. The three people inside the van all hoped that the family would put up a struggle when they took Katya.

"There's the house," Illya pointed to a white two-story frame house with gray shutters. There was only one car in the driveway. The driver turned off the lights as they pulled into driveway by the house.

The side panel slid open, and the two men got out of the van. Before they could take another step, their van was lit up by a bank of floodlights. "Freeze!" a voice shattered the peace of the summer night. The van was instantly surrounded by men in black pointing automatic weapons at their heads.

"Good evening, gentlemen," Joan Richards sauntered up to them, shoving a very large pistol in their faces. "I take it you're not here to deliver pizzas."

Her statement completely went past the two terrorists, who had only a nodding acquaintance with English. "I... we are lost and looking for directions," Illya stammered, looking at Joan's gun with horror. There was no doubt in anyone's mind that Joan would shoot them at the slightest provocation.

"All right, Joan," Carl Davis came up. "We'll take these two pixies down to the station. We'll let the FBI know we've snagged some of their playmates."

"Aren't you going to read us our rights?" One of the terrorists asked. He had been raised on a steady diet of Hollywood crime shows.

"Rights? You are enemy combatants," Joan gritted through her teeth as she not too-gently handcuffed the man. "You are not American citizens, and you have no rights, except the right to shut up until I say you can talk."

She turned to Carl. "Can I kill them just a little?"

"No, Joan; you may not. You broke the last ones you played with, and you're much too messy," Carl shook his head. The terrorists' eyes went wide with fright as he said this. "Okay, guys: this is the drill. You cooperate with us, and I'll keep my chief of detectives on a very short leash. Do we have a deal?"

"We will never cooperate with you, you American pig," Illya said with shaky defiance.

Joan came up to him and looked at him appraisingly. "You know, Charlie told me the other day that a human being can survive after having their face blown off. It's a painful and messy way to live, but it can be done. I'd like to find out myself." Joan slowly pulled out her pistol and fingered it lovingly. She pressed the barrel up under the man's chin. "Do yourself a favor, chum. Make the call to your boss and tell him you've got the girl. If you don't, then I'm going to make a lot of plastic surgeons real rich reconstructing your face for the next several years."

"You... you are joking, right?" Illya said in stuttering English. "This is all a joke. You are an American woman. Americans would never treat anyone like that, would they?" He tittered nervously in a nervous falsetto.

Joan picked the man up and held him close to her, her face only inches from his. "You nearly killed one of my friends and tried to kidnap her sister. They are my family, and no one does that to my family and gets away with it. Do you understand me?"

The man's face broke out in a cold sweat as he stared into Joan's face. He knew she was not joking. He made gargled, strangling noises. Joan shoved him away from her.

"That's enough, Joan," Carl said quietly. He looked at the terrorists. "Well, gentlemen, I think you can see the lady means business. What's the verdict?"

"We... we will cooperate," Illya finally gasped. "Just keep that woman away from us."

"Wonderful," a big smile broke out over Carl's face. "All right, Joan: we're going to take our playmates down to the station. You have a family to take care off, so go back in your house and get some sleep."

"You never let me have any fun," Joan looked crushed, and the three terrorists, who managed to follow every word of that conversation, looked profoundly relieved.

"Come on, Joan: you heard Carl," Sam Richards came up to his wife and put his hand on her shoulder. "There won't be any more excitement tonight."

He gave her a look that meant business. "We have a bunch of teenaged girls inside who need to get some rest. You do too."

"All right, Sam: let's go back inside." As the patrol car drove off to the police station, Joan sighed, looking to the west. "I won't rest easy until Charlie and Dave are back."

"None of us will," Carl agreed. He looked at Sam. "This isn't over yet, Sam. I want double patrols on the street tomorrow, and make sure the SRT guys are ready to move. These clowns didn't come here solo. I'm sure they'll be more of them crawling into town tomorrow morning."

"Don't worry, Carl," Sam promised. "We'll be ready." He glanced at Joan. "Nothing's going to happen to any of us on my watch."

-0-

"Sir, Colonel Warren reports all units are green at Zero Minus Five," Rawlings said to General Mason. They were in the Command Center of the EOC, staring up at the situation board. The symbols marking the locations of all units were marked green.

"Good," Mason nodded. He turned to a desk marked MEDI-CAL. "Are the local hospitals ready to receive casualties?"

"Yes sir," the technician manning the desk replied. "I've received confirmation of ready status from all emergency department medical officers and hospital administrators. We have trauma units on the streets as well as forward emergency surgical teams standing by at various points throughout the city. We also have HAZMAT standing by in case Kolov attempts to use chemical or biological agents."

"Good move, General," Rawlings said appreciatively. "He's already used them once. No sense in taking any chances that he won't do it again."

"I'm just thinking about all those troops down in those rat holes under the city," Mason shuddered. "I want to make sure we've prepared for all contingencies."

Rawlings nodded. Both men were silent for a moment. They were both aware that casualty rates for the planned assault could be as high as forty percent. Mason had also sent a significant part of the EOC staff out of the city to a secondary base in New Jersey. This base was out of range of the projected blast area if the nuclear weapons were to detonate. The tactical situation was being projected on similar boards located in the White House, the Pentagon, the Department of Homeland Security, and the secondary base." All stations, all units: final communications check," the technician at the communications center called out. "Give me a 'Go' or "No Go' status. "White House?"

"We are Go."

"Pentagon."

"Go."

"Homeland?"

"We are Go, EOC."

"Fallback?"

"Roger, EOC, we are Go."

"Forward Ops?"

"We are Go, EOC," Charlie's voice replied.

"Sir, all stations are go at this time," the communications center reported.

"Very well," General Mason picked up the phone connecting the EOC with the forward base. "Colonel Warren, we are ready."

"We are as well, General," Charlie replied.

28

The field units spent the last few moments before the operation started checking their weapons and testing their equipment. All preparations had been made and all contingencies planned. There was nothing more anybody could do except wait for the "Go" signal.

Charlie looked up as the digital clock headed down the final ten seconds to zero. *Time to get things started,* Charlie thought to herself. "All right, Sydney: it's time to send in the pirates and cutthroats."

Sydney Dobbs nodded and keyed her microphone. "All units: this is Command. Execute. Execute. Execute."

In the C-141 orbiting New York Harbor, a green light went on in the cargo bay of the giant aircraft. The tailgate dropped open, and the noise in the aircraft assumed hurricane levels. Below the plane, the clustered city lights of New York spread out like a great galaxy in the inky blackness.

The jumpmaster assumed his position next to the door. James Rosson walked out of the aircraft along with the rest of the team. The twenty-four members of the HALO team exited the aircraft, and streaked down silently towards the harbor.

"Colonel, the HALO unit has deployed," Lieutenant Hobbs told Charlie.

"Very well," Charlie nodded her head, her eyes riveted to the display screen in front of her. "God be with us all," she whispered.

-0-

"Command, this is Watch 12; we have six targets on the roof," the sniper team leader reported. His team was now deployed along the edge of their building, their rifles ready and sighted.

"Roger 12. Neutralize."

The team's rifles flashed briefly. The leader checked through his night vision device. There were now six sprawled bodies on the top of the warehouse. "Command, targets have been neutralized."

"Copy, 12: HALO ETA X-minus one mike."

"Roger, Command. Drop zone is secure." The team leader relaxed a little. They had cleared the drop zone so that the HALO team could now land unobserved. "Okay guys, stay sharp. We need to provide cover fire for the SEALs."

-0-

The two Zodiac boats raced towards the warehouse at forty knots. Designed for speed and stealth, the craft bristled with SEALs and automatic weapons. So far, their approach to the warehouse was undetected; no fire came from that location. The craft swung around to the sides of the warehouse, and the team threw grappling hooks up at the sides of the pier. The hooks caught and held fast. The team swarmed silently up the ropes and poured out onto the pier, racing to the sides of the warehouse wall.

Flattening themselves against the warehouse wall, the SEALs crept up to the warehouse doors and set breaching charges made out of C4.

"Command, this is Team Leader, the commander of the SEAL team reported into the small radio attached to his shoulder. "Doors secure. Ready to breach on signal."

"Acknowledged," the reply came from the Command Center. "Execute."

At that moment, the SEALs blew their charges, blowing the warehouse doors off of their hinges. The doors went sailing into the water below the warehouse.

Simultaneously, the SAS and Delta force commandos stormed

down the narrow staircase into the bowels of the warehouse. Both groups were wearing night vision goggles that enabled them to select targets in total blackness. The commandos streamed into one side of the warehouse shell covering the sub pen, while the SEALs took control of the other.

The shock of the two-pronged assault was overwhelming. The two forces encountered virtually no resistance from the people inside the warehouse. The Russians threw down their weapons and flattened themselves against the concrete floor. Rosson's team raced the sub pen entrances.

Instantly they were greeted by a storm of gunfire from Russians on the U-boat. There were only four entrances through the thick concrete walls on either side of the sub pen. The Russians on board the submarine swept the entrances with a hail of machine gun fire.

"Get your heads down!" Donald MacKay shouted as the bullets whined overhead.

"George, this is Fox one," Rosson's earpiece crackled. It was a message from Team Leader Simpson. "We are going to throw some Easter eggs."

"Copy, Fox One," Rosson replied, glancing over at his team of commando's poised to burst through the sub pen entrance. "Get down, lads: this is going to be loud."

Two seconds later, the SEALs fired four grenades from their M-203 grenade launchers into the pen. The grenades sailed onto the deck of the submarine next to the hatches. The whole building shook from the four blasts that went up almost simultaneously.

The dust had barely settled when Rosson's commando's swarmed onto the dock next to the sub. Part of the SEAL team took up covered positions on the opposite side.

"Colonel Rosson: Commander Doug Simpson," the black-faced SEAL team leader came up to Rosson and identified himself. "The warehouse is secure, and I've notified command that we're having some problems with the people in the sub."

"Looks like a job for the Navy, Commander," Rosson said.

"I'm on it," Simpson turned to a group of SEALs behind him. "Okay people, you heard the Colonel. They want to play rough. Let's give it to them."

Without another word, the SEALs swarmed onto the deck of the submarine. They went up to the forward and rear hatches on the main deck, as well as the hatches on the conning tower. They set generous charges of C4 at each hatch and then jumped off of the sub, finding covered positions along the wall of the pen.

"Okay Colonel: this is going to be loud and messy," Commander Simpson nodded to a man who was carrying the detonator. Everyone hunkered down and covered their heads.

The three hatches were blasted to bits simultaneously, fragments of metal spraying everywhere, ricocheting off of the concrete sub pen walls. The SEALs did not wait for the smoke to clear, or the fragments to stop falling. They were immediately onto the sub, positioning themselves at the hatches. Dropping fragmentation grenades into the hatches, the SEALs stepped back. A series of blasts shook the submarine once more.

"Very efficient, Commander," Rosson said with approval. "My compliments."

"It's what we do," Simpson replied modestly. "Now then, Colonel. We can sit back and be humane about this and let these poor idiots realize that we're up here and can blast them into eternity if they continue to resist, or we can go in and get them. What's your pleasure?"

Rosson looked at his watch. "Commander, we have other things to do tonight. Let's get this over with."

"You're the boss," Simpson directed the SEALs to begin entering the submarine. The Delta and SAS teams followed them in. There was a series of gunshots and explosions, and a few minutes later, Simpson was back with his report.

"Most of the bad guys decided they'd had enough. The boat is now secure."

"You said most, Commander," Sergeant Major MacKay raised his eyebrows. "The others?"

"They're in no shape to object one way or the other," Simpson grinned.

"All right then," Colonel Rosson sighed. "It's time to call in the atom bomb people." He keyed his microphone. "Command this is George. Boat secure. I say again: boat secure."

"Roger, George. Well done."

"How many of the Russians surrendered to you, Commander?" Rosson asked as the group of Russians came out of the submarine with their hands up.

"Twenty in the warehouse, ten in the sub," Simpson replied. "We had a few unbelievers in the office part of the warehouse, but we've convinced them as well."

"Nothing like a few conversions to warm the soul," Rosson said with satisfaction.

"Sir, do you know this chick who dreamed this up?" Doug Simpson asked. "I heard she's really hot. Is that true?"

"I do, she is, and she's married, sailor," Rosson grinned. "However, I'll be sure to pass along your compliments. She has a soft spot in her heart for pirates and cutthroats."

"That's us," the SEAL team commander replied with a wink.

"All right then," Rosson got out his map. "We need to proceed along this route and attack the enemy command center. Leave a section to secure the prisoners until ESU and NEST arrive, then have them proceed up to join us once they're relieved."

"Aye, aye, sir," Commander Simpson replied. "Okay, people: you heard the Colonel. Lyons: take the forward element and head up along the route with the Colonel. The rest of you guys secure the prisoners and stand fast until the police arrive, clear?"

"Crystal, sir!" the SEALs snapped back.

"Very well, Commander," Rosson said grimly. "Let's finish the job."

-0-

"All right people, it's our turn. I've just gotten word that the warehouse is secure," the leader of the Nuclear Emergency Search Team told his section as they loaded onto their trucks. They had been kept back from the warehouse until it was secure. "NEST to Command: we are now moving into position. We will advise status of the weapons when we arrive on site."

"Roger, NEST." Charlie acknowledged over the microphone at her console. She looked up at the map. The warehouse was now blue, indicating it was now in friendly hands. "George, this is Michael: I need you and your teams to advance into the tunnels as soon as the ESU teams arrive with NEST. Do you copy? Over."

"Roger, Michael," Rosson replied. "My fellows are most anxious to get on with business."

"Yes, I'm sure you're all getting on famously, George," Charlie said. "You're all pirates and cutthroats, the lot of you."

"That's the nicest thing a lady's ever said to me," Simpson broke into the transmission.

Charlie laughed. "Off you go then. Stay safe and good hunting." She turned to Hobbs. "Looks like things are going pretty smoothly right now. We've captured the submarine and the nuclear devices. All that's left is to capture the Russians in the tunnels."

Hobbs nodded. "That's going to be the tricky part, Colonel." She pointed to the board. "We've already encountered heavy resistance on most of the main corridors. It's going to be a long, slow process to get those people out of their positions."

-0-

The teams in the tunnels crept forward slowly, inching their way through the narrow corridors and abandoned rooms that constituted the tunnel complex underneath the city streets. It was slow, dangerous work. Even though the areas had been thoroughly mapped and scouted by ESU a few days before, there was always the danger of booby traps and listening devices.

The underground system was not just simply a network of tunnels, but a whole group of underground rooms and storage areas interlaced with narrow passages and abrupt changes in direction. No maps existed for this labyrinth. It had grown over the course of several decades into a confusing array of rooms and cul de sacs.

At first, the ESU teams made good headway, advancing the first hundred yards or so with comparative ease. Then the tunnels would branch out into a series of underground rooms. An ambush would be set up at that point, and a vicious firefight would erupt.

The police units moved quietly and carefully, trying whenever they could to surprise and arrest Russians left at listening posts. It was hard, dangerous work.

David was assigned to the team moving through the main tunnel where Cartwright's body had been found. Hank Blevins was in charge of this team. They had moved quickly up the main corridor where the tunnels branched off. The Russians had set up a fortified position and started shooting as soon as the ESU team had gotten within range.

The advance slowed to a crawl as the team was pinned down. Blevins was in no mood to wait. "Command, this is Four Alpha," he snarled into his radio. "I want heavy reinforcements sent to Route Red. We're taking heavy fire and my people are pinned down. Do you copy? Over."

"Roger Four Alpha. We're getting requests for backup from all sectors. Help is on the way. Command out."

Blevins glared at David, who had crawled up to where the ESU commander was located. "Okay, Stone. I'm officially not impressed. Here we are, pinned down in this rat hole. Got any suggestions?"

David thought for a moment. "Let's just mow through, Captain. We've got the manpower. Everyone throw a fragmentation grenade towards the intersection and then charge the position. The combined force of the explosions is bound to knock them off their feet for a second or so. By the time they recover, we'll be on top of them."

Blevins stared at David for a moment. "You know, Stone, that's the stupidest thing I've heard in a long time. It's so stupid in fact that it just might work. All we're doing right now is using up ammo and wasting time. I like it. Pass the word down."

David relayed the plan to the rest of the ESU team. All of them crept forward as far as they could. Before they went more than ten yards, a huge blast knocked them to the ground.

"What was that?" Blevins sputtered as he picked himself off the ground.

"It must have been Charlie's surprise," David said, trying to clear his head of the ringing in his ears.

"Okay, I'll pretend I know what you're talking about," Blevins said, peering ahead, trying to see into the cloud of dust filling the tunnel. "Whatever it was, the dust cloud works to our advantage. Let's move in and get ready to assault that machine gun nest."

The team moved down into the tunnel for fifty more yards. At a prearranged signal, they hurled their grenades down the tunnel towards the main intersection.

The grenades sailed through the air and bounced directly into the front of the machine gun nest. The grenades went off simultaneously in a devastating ROAR! The entire tunnel shook with the force of the explosion, and huge clouds of dust and debris rained down.

"Okay people, charge!" Blevins yelled at the top of his lungs. The entire ESU team rose up, and advanced down the tunnel, firing their weapons on full automatic. They reached the junction twenty seconds later. All that was left was a broken machine gun and seven shattered bodies.

"Looks like there's no one around to arrest," David said cryptically. "Captain, we need to move up there quickly. I hear shots in the distance."

"Captain, I think I know what caused the explosion," an SRT member came up to where Blevins was standing with David. "We found some portable mines similar to Claymores arranged in a chain pattern across the tunnel. Someone turned them around to face the Russians."

"That was Charlie's surprise," David observed, looking at Blevins. "It's a trick we learned in SF. Guess the Brits taught Charlie how to do it."

"Those bad guys were already dead when we threw our grenades. Score another one for the SAS." Blevins smiled. The sounds of gunfire intensified ahead of them.

"Probably the SEALs and Delta mixing it up," Blevins said, keying his radio. "Command, this is Four Alpha. We've breached our obstacle and are continuing on Route Red. Give me a sitrep, over."

"We copy your breach, Four Alpha. Units from White Two are advancing on central complex two hundred meters to your forward. Be advised we want you to hold at present position and pick up any strays coming your way."

This order did not suit Blevins one bit. "Command, say again your last transmission. You wish for us to hold at present position?"

"Affirmative, Four Alpha."

"Roger, Command. Four Alpha out." Blevins looked again at

David. "Blast it, Stone! Now we're supposed to sit and wait for the bad guys to run to us while those soldiers and sailors have all the fun!"

"Hey Captain, don't blame me, okay?" David held up a protesting hand. "I'm down here with you. I've got no control over how she's running this operation. It's her show, not mine."

"At least we managed to blow through that machine gun nest," Blevins admitted grudgingly. "That was good work, by the way."

"Is that a compliment, Captain?"

"It was, but don't let it go to your head," Hank Blevins grinned. "Okay people: we're going to hold here and catch any of the bad guys who have the misfortune to run our way. We're going to mutate back into police officers and arrest them, if they'll let us."

"What does that mean, Captain?" one of the ESU officers asked.

"It means we tell them to throw down their weapons and surrender, we'll arrest them. If they fail to comply or start shooting, we'll make them comply. You get the point."

"Yes sir," the officer replied.

29

Ivan Kolov's life had disintegrated in the space of two minutes, starting just after midnight. He had been gleefully thinking about all of the billions of dollars the four nuclear weapons were going to bring to him when the lights dimmed and then flickered out in his command center.

"Renov, what has happened to our power?" Kolov asked. They had never had problems with power before, having tapped into the generous supply of underground electrical cables from various businesses scattered throughout the New York district.

"I do not know, Comrade Colonel," Renov replied. "I will see about activating the emergency generators."

As Renov went off to find out about the generators, Kolov's phone rang. It was one of his section leaders in charge of the dismantling of the bombs on board the submarine.

"Comrade Kolov! We are hearing shots and explosions outside the submarine! It sounds as though the building is under attack we…" The transmission was abruptly cut off.

Kolov stared at the dead phone in his hand. The lights flickered back on fitfully, and Renov returned to the command center. "Renov, Stefan from the submarine just called and said that the warehouse is under attack. Raise the listening posts in the tunnels and see if they hear anything. Have any of the observers on the roof of the warehouse reported in?"

"No one has reported any activity, Colonel Kolov," Renov replied. He contacted the listening posts and spoke to the teams manning them. "Comrade Kolov. No one has reported any movements in the tunnels. Everything is quiet."

Kolov's phone rang again. It was Stefan. "Sir! Commandos have overrun the warehouse! We are now sealed up inside the submarine! We have locked the hatches, but we know that there are enemy forces walking on the deck of the submarine..."

Kolov heard the phone drop to the floor and suddenly there was the sound of a deafening explosion. The phone went dead, and the entire center shook violently.

"Renov, send reinforcements down into the tunnel complex towards the warehouse. I want that position held," Kolov ordered. Suddenly the central communications board started lighting up.

"Sir, we have reports from all sectors indicating large numbers of enemy soldiers in the tunnels," the communications specialist said, his voice tinged with hysteria. "They are advancing rapidly with massive firepower, sir!"

"Send word to all posts to hold out," Kolov directed, turning to Renov. "I want all reserves sent up into the tunnels to reinforce our positions."

"Yes sir," Renov ran off to issue directions to the teams. Kolov's phone rang again.

"Ivan Alexyevich, this is Colonel Warren calling," Charlie's voice came over the phone in Russian. "I am your opponent, Colonel. As you undoubtedly know by now, your forces are under massive and overwhelming attack. I am giving you and your people the opportunity to surrender now. Lay down your weapons, or we will annihilate you."

"I... you... I will not negotiate with you, woman!" Kolov spat into the phone.

Charlie was unfazed by his reply. "The choice is yours, Colonel. By the way, all of your listening posts have now been overrun. Surrender now, Colonel, while you have the time.

"One more thing, Colonel: your friends who attempted to kidnap my sister have been captured. They are at the Compton police station now, providing us with all sorts of useful information." Charlie continued in a conversational tone.

"Colonel Kolov, I was the one who killed your two friends. I left those wounds on their bodies. They seemed surprised to be killed by a woman, most surprised. Pity that. I also reversed the mines your people had placed in one of the subway access tunnels. It was most unfortunate that they failed to be more careful."

Kolov hurled the phone at the wall of the room. The phone shattered into a mass of broken fragments. The sounds of explosions and machine gun fire grew nearer and nearer.

Alexi Renov came back an hour later. His face was grim and set. "Comrade Colonel, our defenses are collapsing on every front. Our positions are being overrun faster than I can get reinforcements up to them. We have whole units throwing down their arms and surrendering rather than defending their positions. What do you want us to do, Colonel Kolov?"

Ivan Kolov pondered for a minute. He looked down at the single nuclear device that had been completely recovered from the submarine before the attack started. "We still have options open, Alexi. There are always options when you have the winning hand."

He looked up at Renov. "Alexi, have our forces disengage contact with the enemy. Have them scatter into the tunnels and evacuate immediately. We have predetermined rally points scattered throughout this city. The enemy has no knowledge of them at this time. We will rally and regroup once everyone is safely out of the tunnels."

A malevolent look crossed his face. "I know that the American command center is located somewhere close by on the riverfront. We will locate it and send the Americans a little present."

"We have a few RPGs left in reserve, Colonel," Renov said. "They will probably be most useful."

"They will indeed, Captain Renov. They will indeed." Kolov looked around. "I need another cell phone, Alexi."

Renov handed him another cell phone. Kolov dialed a number. "Hello, Decker? This is Kolov. The police and Army are on to us! I'm surprised you can't hear the gunshots and explosions over in New Jersey. I will contact you when I am in a safer location. Yes, I will make sure all the documents are destroyed before we leave. Goodbye."

Kolov closed the cell phone and looked at Renov. "Alexi, make sure all of the documents implicating that stupid Decker and that LuxVeritas organization are in plain view for the Americans to find."

"What about the buyers for the bomb?" Renov asked.

"There are dozens of organizations who will be willing to purchase our bomb," Kolov said confidently. "Many of them will give us a far higher price."

A man came up to them. "Colonel Kolov, we have pinpointed the command center where this operation is located. If we go through the tunnels now, we can destroy the center and leave the city."

"Good," Kolov nodded. "It's time to reward the Americans for their efforts."

Renov put his hand on Kolov's shoulder. "Ivan, let's leave the bomb and get out of here. Every second we delay plays into the Americans' hands."

Kolov knocked away his hand. "Every second you talk wastes time. We take the bomb."

-0-

There was jubilation in the forward command center as the positive reports started rolling in. So far, casualties had been minimal: a few minor gunshots and shrapnel injuries, but no one seriously hurt or killed. Most of the Russians had surrendered once they realized there was no escape from the massive force being applied to their positions.

"We've managed to secure all of the tunnels very rapidly, Colonel Warren," Lieutenant Hobbs told Charlie. "By the way, your surrender ultimatum to Kolov was brilliant!"

"I couldn't resist that," Charlie replied, an impish light playing in her eyes. "I rather like twisting the knife a bit at times. What's the word from NEST?"

"Three of the four devices are accounted for, which makes all of us very happy," Hobbs looked at her clipboard. "NEST says that these devices were very sophisticated for their times, and they definitely posed a real threat to the city."

"What about the missing device?"

"The captured technicians told us that Kolov dismantled the plutonium core and married it up with his own system."

"So it's now definitely portable," Charlie's face turned grim. "It could easily be transported by anyone in a backpack or a suitcase."

"That's what NEST thinks. From what you've told me about Kolov, he'll take the device with him and will try to leave the city with it."

"That makes sense, unfortunately," Charlie nodded. She dialed up the Emergency Operations Center. "General Mason, we have secured the submarine, along with three of the four devices. We believe Kolov has one of them with him and will probably try to leave the city with it in his possession."

"If he tries that, he won't get far," Mason replied. "We have radioactive detection units saturating the city right now. He'll never be able to shield the device properly. It's only a matter of time before we find him."

"Sir, we've penetrated all of the tunnel areas successfully. My latest reports from forward units indicate that the enemy is now in complete disarray and is surrendering to us."

"That's good, Colonel," Mason said with pride in his voice. "I knew you could do this, Charlie."

"Thank you, General, but it's been the people on the ground that have achieved the victory," Charlie replied, blushing. "Anyway, I just wanted to give you an update on our progress."

"It looks excellent from our end, Colonel. Keep us informed." Mason hung up.

Charlie put down the phone and rubbed her neck. It had been an exhausting night. "Sydney, is there a place where I could get some coffee? I'd like to step out of here for just a moment. Do you think you can handle things while I step out?"

"Sure, no problem, Colonel. There's a place just down the street where you can get some coffee," Lieutenant Hobbs replied. "You've earned a break. We'll see you in a few minutes."

"Okay, I'll be back in a minute or so," Charlie picked up her purse and walked out of the trailer complex that comprised the forward command post. It was located right next to the water on an open section of a pier. It was now early morning, with a breeze blowing in off the harbor. The moon was now setting, and the sun was finally peaking over the edges of the buildings across the harbor.

Charlie turned and headed down the street towards the lights of the small diner that Sydney had mentioned. She had gotten within fifty feet of the diner entrance when the world behind her erupted in a shattering holocaust of blast, flame and smoke. Charlie had no time to turn to see what had happened, as the blast wave from the exploding command center threw her down to the ground, knocking her senseless.

-0-

"Sir, we've just lost contact with the forward command center!" the technician manning the communications console told General Mason.

"Try an alternate band; we've had trouble like that before," Mason said, coming over to the communications section.

"I've already tried it, sir. There's no response," she said, trying to type in alternate frequencies.

Mason looked up at the board, stunned. Instead of the blue icon which marked the location of the forward command center, there was now a dull orange marker in its place. The marker had appeared the second communications from the center had been lost. Few people other than Mason knew what that marker meant. It came from a special sensor located in the forward center that would automatically activate if the center were to be destroyed.

"Sir, I have the New York Fire Department on line," another technician held up a phone, "they want to talk to you directly."

Mason came over and picked up the phone. "General Mason speaking."

"Sir, this is Patrick O'Hara. I'm the commander of Station 24 located on the East River. We've… we've just received word that there was an explosion at your forward command center. Our engine company is responding along with medics and ESU."

For a moment, he didn't know what to say. "I see. Thank you, Chief. Keep us posted." He sat down in a chair. Ken Rawlings came up to him.

"What's going on, General?"

General Mason looked up at him. "There's been an explosion at the forward command center. That was the Fire Department. They're now responding."

"No," disbelief colored Rawlings voice. "No, that's not possible. It... they were fine just a moment ago. I talked to them."

"Things seem to have changed," Mason got up, his face set with cold fury. "Put me through to all command units," he directed the communications specialist. He picked up the microphone after she had completed the connection.

"Attention all units, all commanders: this is General Mason. The forward command center has been destroyed by enemy action. We have no word at this time concerning the extent of damage or casualties. Communication was lost with the center approximately five minutes ago. I just received word from NYFD that an explosion was reported at the center.

"All command and control activities have been transferred to this location. I am ordering all units to complete their missions and standby for further orders. Mason out."

Mason put down the microphone and looked at Rawlings. "Which unit is Colonel Warren's husband with?"

"The unit working the main tunnel, sir," Rawlings replied. "The man in charge's name is Blevins."

"Get me the commander of that unit on the horn. I want to speak to him." Mason directed. Once the connection was made, Mason spoke into a telephone. "Captain Blevins? This is General Mason. Is David Stone with you?"

"Yes sir, he is."

"Please put him on for me."

"This is David Stone," David's voice came over the phone half a minute later. "General, do you have any idea... about casualties?"

"Not at this time, Detective," Mason forced his voice to remain level. "We'll know more about the situation when I get a report back from the Fire Department."

"Yes sir," David said slowly, "I understand."

"We've been through this drill before, Dave," Mason said, trying to convey optimism and confidence that he did not feel. "I'm pulling you out of there and bringing you back to the EOC. I've got some work for you to do here. Let me talk to Captain Blevins again."

A technician came up to Mason as he was speaking. In his hand was the latest report from the fire chief conducting the fire operations at the forward command center.

"Yes sir?" Blevins came back on the line.

Mason stared at the paper, not wanting to believe what it said. "Captain, pull Stone off the line and get him back to the EOC. I just got a report from Chief O'Hara; there are no survivors at the command center."

30

Patrick Joseph O'Hara was fifty-two years old, a fifth generation firefighter. All O'Hara had ever wanted to do was fight fires. He had spent a lifetime fighting fires, all types and descriptions: structure fires, apartment fires, dockside fires and so on. O'Hara had developed a healthy respect for fire. For him, fire was a cunning and deadly enemy, one he never underestimated. He had seen too many people who had become complacent on the job, and had paid for their lack of concern with their lives.

Like all NYFD firefighters, 9/11 had changed O'Hara forever. The terrorists had killed three of the closest people O'Hara knew on this earth: two cousins and his best friend. As a firefighter, all of his fellow firemen were his family. He had attended every single one of the myriads of funerals of his brothers that had occurred in 9/11's wake.

If O'Hara had a respect for fire, he had none for politics and political causes. One of his distant relatives from Northern Ireland made the mistake a few years ago of trying to talk to O'Hara about the IRA. O'Hara punched him in the face and walked off, never saying a word. No one in the family ever talked to him about politics ever again.

Their engine company had been held back in reserve. Even with the massive destruction caused by the nerve gas attack, New York City still needed protection from conventional sources of destruction.

The firefighters were busy cleaning their equipment with the all-too familiar tones sounded throughout the engine house. "Engine Company 47, Rescue 89: respond to explosion and fire at location 23rd Street Docking Terminal."

"Roger, Engine 47 responding," O'Hara said into his radio. His company was already climbing into their suits and manning the trucks. The doors of the station were almost completely opened by the time the trucks thundered to life. O'Hara prided himself on his company's quick response time.

"Nice job, lads," he said warmly to his crew as they pulled out of the station. "Two minutes from alarm to rollout. We'll be there in no time."

They arrived on the scene in less than five minutes. The police had already started cordoning off the area when the trucks rolled up. The scene was one of complete devastation. Here and there, small pieces of debris smoldered sullenly.

"Not much fire to put out, Pat," one of the patrolmen said grimly as O'Hara climbed off the truck.

"This looks like a bombing, Evan," O'Hara replied. "What in the name of Heaven went up?"

"This is where EOC had their forward command center," the patrolman said as they walked slowly towards the grotesquely twisted masses of metal and steel.

O'Hara turned around. His second-in-command came up to him. "Pat, we've got connections to the mains. How do you want to handle this?" Jim Wilkins asked.

"Put out the secondary fires, Jimmy," O'Hara directed. "Try not to wet too much down. We need to preserve as much of this as possible for the CSI people. Tell our guys to search for survivors."

"You won't find any of those, Pat," Evan Wychek told him. "We saw the place go up. No one could have survived it."

-0-

The hideous masses of burned, twisted metal that had been Charlie's forward command center brought back searing memories of the Twin Towers to O'Hara. *No survivors*, his initial report to the EOC had been. So far, nothing he had seen had changed that initial assessment.

A few of the younger firefighters were now moving into the center of the blast, trying to put out stubborn hot spots. O'Hara had briefed them on what they would find. What they saw still shook them. Some of the rookies had gotten sick, which was understandable. The veterans didn't give them a hard time about it; everyone was feeling sick right now.

A solitary woman's body lay face down away from the center of the wreckage. *Probably someone walking away from the center*, O'Hara thought, stooping next to the body for a closer look. His heart stopped for a moment. The woman looked a good deal like one of his daughters. She had short, reddish-golden hair, and her still white face had a dusting of freckles on it.

You look like my Katie, O'Hara thought, tears rising to his eyes. *Someone's lost a daughter today*. He reached out and touched the woman's cheek. It felt warm to his touch. Suddenly, the woman's head jerked up and she opened her eyes.

O'Hara stepped back and blinked. Sometimes firefighters would come on to a dead body and swear they saw signs of life. It was a natural reaction to want to find someone alive in the midst of a disaster. This was different.

The woman started to cough and choke. O'Hara sprang to her side and turned her gently over. "Rescue!" he roared. "I need Rescue over here now! We have a live victim!"

-0-

"I'm.... I'm fine. Really," Charlie Warren said shakily. She identified herself and haltingly took a sip of water from a cup offered to her. She shivered involuntarily as she gazed about the explosion site. "Captain, I must contact the EOC," she said, looking up at O'Hara's concerned face.

"Colonel, I'd really feel a whole lot better if you'd allow the medics to take a look at you." O'Hara replied. "You're in shock right now."

"I suppose I am," Charlie said. She knew the chief was trying to be kind, trying to soften the blow of the disaster. "I promise you I'll have them take a look at me later, Chief. Right now I need that phone, please."

"You're as stubborn as my Kate," O'Hara shook his head with a smile. "I have to tell you, Colonel, when I first came up on you, I thought you were my own daughter lying there. Here's the phone." He handed a cell phone to Charlie.

"Thank you, Chief," Charlie said. "EOC, this is Warren. I need to speak to General Mason, please."

There was a long pause over the phone and Mason came on the line. "Charlie! We thought... how did you... we're glad that you're alive, Colonel Warren," Mason finally regained his composure. "Your husband is on the way to the EOC. We thought there were no survivors. What's the situation where you are?"

"I remember hearing two explosions almost simultaneously," Charlie replied, rubbing her head. "My guess is that the center was hit with two RPG rounds. Probably Kolov's people."

"That's a good assessment, Colonel. We came to that conclusion ourselves a few moments ago," Mason agreed. "We'll send some transportation over to the site and bring you back to the EOC. After we're finished debriefing you, you and your husband can finally head home."

"Sir, that's not a good idea," Charlie said firmly. "We have a group of terrorists with a nuclear bomb loose in New York. I know where those people are headed, and I have a plan for dealing with them."

"Colonel Warren, with all due respect, your part of this mission is over. You've completed your objectives. We've secured the nuclear devices and neutralized the terrorist threat. NEST has airborne sensors deployed, and I have half a dozen state and federal agencies running after these guys. It's only a matter of time before they catch up with them."

"Do you have any people headed towards Compton?"

"No," Mason replied slowly. "Why?"

"Because that's where they're headed. I tweaked Kolov's pride when I mocked him about the people he sent to kidnap my sister. He has a giant-sized ego, and he has people in the Compton jail. I believe he's headed there right now with the bomb and what's left of his people to free them and destroy my family."

"That's an intriguing theory, Colonel. What do you want to do about it?" Mason asked. "I've got precious few resources to allocate to you at this time."

"Give me a detachment of SAS or Delta force troops and a helicopter, and I think we can handle it," Charlie said quickly.

"All right, Colonel; I think I can spare those troops. By the way, there's someone who wants to talk to you."

Mason handed the phone to someone. "Charlie!" David's voice came on the line. "I'm so glad you're alive! We all thought you were dead when we first heard about the center."

"I know, David. I'm glad to be alive," Charlie replied, trying to keep the grief out of her voice. "It's horrible around here right now. David, please convince the General that my idea about Compton is a good one. He'll explain it to you further. I love you, David, so very much. Please put General Mason back on the line."

"I love you too, Charlie," David said softly. "Here's the General again."

Mason came back on the line. "I'm back, Charlie."

"General, I need those troops and the helicopter as soon as possible. There isn't much time. I believe that Kolov is halfway to Compton right now. I plan to warn the police in Compton that they are headed that way. If we can get those troops there in time, we can avert a bloodbath."

"Okay, Charlie, I'll round up those assets and get them to you," Mason said, his tone warming up a bit. "Are you sure you're up to this? You've just been involved in a major disaster and now you're headed into a battle without any rest."

"I'm doing fine, General Mason," Charlie replied coldly. "People are dead, and the ones responsible need to be brought to justice. I'll rest when they're caught, or dead. Thank you again for listening to me.

"See you later, Colonel. Goodbye." She turned to Chief O'Hara. "Have the media people shown up yet?"

O'Hara nodded. "Yes they have. So far, we haven't told them anything."

"Good," Charlie replied. "I want you to keep it that way. Keep them back from the site. Make sure that the news helicopters stay away as well. I don't want the terrorists to know what kind of damage they've done. They will be monitoring the radio for news and information. I want them to think right now that there were no survivors from the explosion. It will keep their guard down."

"You're a sly one, lass, that you are," O'Hara said with a grin. "I can't believe you're English. Are you sure you're not just the least bit Irish?"

"I'm part Welsh, if that counts for anything," Charlie admitted. "I also come from a long line of spies, pirates and cutthroats."

A slow smile spread over Patrick Joseph O'Hara's face. "I pegged you for a mischief maker from the first moment I laid eyes on you, Colonel. We Irish have a nose for brawlers and roust-abouts, and you're a prime specimen if I ever knew one. Bit of the pirate, eh?"

"You might say that." Charlie replied, blushing violently.

A van marked "CSI" pulled up to a nearby fire truck. Joe Thomas got out, carrying his forensic kit. He glanced briefly around at the scene of devastation. "Looks like you beat me to this one, Charlie," he said in a conversational tone as he came up to them. His face became quiet and serious as he looked at her. "You were here when this one went off."

Charlie nodded mutely. Joe's face darkened with rage. "Are you okay?"

"I will be, Joe. As soon as I get the people who did this."

-0-

Mason hung up the phone and whistled. "Where did you find that woman, Stone?" he asked David, who was standing next to him. "She just got her command shot out from under her, and she's already gearing up for another major battle. When does she quit?"

"Never, as far as I can tell. She's tough, General. That's all I can say. One minute I'm ready to hug her to pieces and the next minute I'm ready to kill her for going off on some half-cocked escapade," David shrugged. "What can I do to help with things around here?"

"I'm getting on the horn to Rosson's people," Mason said. "We've already relieved the SEALs. ESU's taken over processing the prisoners and getting things straightened up. The EOC people are handling the decontamination of the tunnels, and we should have things up and running in this city in short order."

"Sounds like you're mission's almost accomplished, General," David observed.

"No, I'm actually finished with my part of it, that's all," Mason grinned. Ken Rawlings joined them. "How are things going on your end of the street, Ken?"

"My little canary has decided to cooperate, especially when I explained to him that I could charge him with at least half a dozen capital crimes unless he cooperated," Rawlings replied. "It's the same old story. Dubek got greedy, like a lot of traitors. Now that the money's gone, so is his loyalty. My people are about to lower the hammer on LuxVeritas."

"I'd like to be there when that happens, Agent Rawlings," David said.

"I'll see that you get a piece of the action, Stone," Rawlings said with a grin. "You've been a valuable part of this case, you and Charlie." He paused for a moment. "Has anyone heard anything about how Meyers is doing?"

"Got a report from the hospital this morning," Mason found a sheet of paper with some information he'd put down. "He's out of Intensive Care and has been moved into a private room. His partner's still with him."

A phone on Mason's desk chimed. "Hello? Yes, Colonel Rosson. We have a mission for your people. We need you to swing by here and pick up Stone. You're headed to Compton. What? She's alive, Colonel. Really? That doesn't surprise you? Okay, you'll pick her up on the way over. She'll brief you in the air on her plan. Yes, I'm sure it will be something completely off the wall. All right. See you soon. Out."

Mason turned to David. "Okay, your mission is to ride herd on that wife of yours, Stone. I don't envy you. Try to keep her in line if you can."

David looked at him dubiously. "I've been married to the girl for about six months, Nathan. So far, my track record stinks in that department."

"There's always hope," Mason grinned.

-0-

Charlie called the Compton Police Department as soon as she'd finished talking to General Mason. Joan answered the call. "Charlie! What kind of mischief are you mixed up in now, girl?"

"Joan, this is serious," Charlie replied. "We've got some more of those Russian goons headed your way. They're going to try to get their friends out of the jail."

"They can try, Charlie, but it's not going to happen," Joan said firmly. "Carl and I will take care of it. Don't worry."

"Just make sure you don't wind up getting hurt," Charlie's voice filled with concern.

"I can take care of myself, little girl, but thanks for the concern," Joan said warmly. "We'll take care of baby sister, too."

"Where is she now, by the way?"

"I sent her over to Trinity to help Angus with the rose bushes," Joan told her. "She's got a day off from skating. We haven't had any play practice since all that mess in New York City started. What's the story there?"

"Things are calming down, Joan," Charlie assured her. "I think once we get rid of these people, things will get back to normal."

"Honey, things haven't been normal since you blew into this burg back in September," Joan laughed.

"You know what I mean, Joan."

"Yeah, I do, honey. I do," Joan's voice softened a bit. "You don't sound too good right now, Charlie. You don't need to tell me, but I'm willing to bet that you've been through some pretty bad times, right?"

Charlie's voice broke a bit. "You're right, Joan. I... I can't think about that right now. I'm too busy. Just take care of yourself, and watch out for those pieces of scum headed your way."

"We will, Charlie. Take care."

"Goodbye." Charlie turned off her cell phone. The sound of an approaching helicopter filled her ears. It was a UH-60 Blackhawk.

The firefighters on the ground directed it to a point away from the explosion site. Charlie went to meet the aircraft as it landed. The cabin door slid open and David came out. He met Charlie halfway, and picked her up and hugged her fiercely.

"I'm so glad you're alive!" he shouted after he kissed her. "Charlie, Rawlings just got word that two vans shot their way through a National Guard roadblock about twenty minutes ago. They said the vans were headed east on the road towards Compton!"

"Come on, David!" she yelled back, freeing herself from his embrace and taking his hand. "Let's get on board! We still have work to do!"

They ran to the helicopter, which had not slowed its engines down since it landed. James Rosson and Donald MacKay were in the cabin, alone with six other soldiers from Delta.

"Good to see you again, Colonel!" Rosson shouted as Charlie got into the cabin. It was too noisy to carry on much of a conversation. Charlie simply nodded and squeezed his shoulder and Donald's. She went forward to the cockpit.

"I need to speak to you, Captain!" She shouted to the pilot.

The pilot in command, Ed Jeffers, nodded. Charlie produced a map and drew a route for him.

"We need to get to Compton as fast as possible, but avoid the main roads going into the town," Charlie pointed to the route she'd drawn on the map. "If we follow this route, we can use the terrain to mask the noise of our approach until the very last minute. We'll sweep around and take up a position northeast of the town. There's good masking terrain there and it will muffle the sound of our engines. We can come in low and fast. It will give us a tactical advantage."

Jeffers studied the map for a moment. "Looks good, Colonel. We can fly over the ocean most of the way. The road's away from the ocean, and we have some hills we can use to mask our approach."

Charlie nodded. "Okay. Let's go!"

The pilot nodded once more and looked over at the copilot. He briefly explained their flight plan. A minute later, the aircraft was airborne and headed south and east.

Charlie went back to the cabin and strapped herself in next to

David. She pulled out her map and briefed the team on her plan. "I've already talked to Joan about the people headed their way. She told me they'd be ready for them."

"You think those cops can handle a bunch of terrorists?" one of the Delta commandos asked.

"Brother, you don't know Joan Richards, and you don't know our cops," David said, shaking his head. "Those people are running into a buzz saw. I almost feel sorry for them."

"I don't," Charlie said stonily, looking out the window.

-0-

"We've got ten confirmed dead and six wounded when those vans shot their way through the roadblock," Rawlings informed Mason grimly. "NYPD wanted to go after them with everything they have, Nate. It took a lot for me to have the Chief to call them off."

Mason nodded slightly, his face set into a grim mask. "Believe me, Ken; there's nothing I'd like better than to turn those vans into flaming hunks of burnt metal. Unfortunately, Kolov has a twenty-kiloton device on board that van, and as long as he has that, we can't touch it. We've got to trust that Warren's plan is going to work."

"What about the situation at Compton?"

"That's our ace in the hole, Ken," Mason grinned. "I know those people. The Chief worked with me at Bragg. He and Stone ran my battalion Ops section. They're pros, so we're in good shape there."

"You think we're going to win this one, Nate?"

"I give us about a sixty percent chance of success," Mason replied soberly. "I wish we had better odds, but I'm just not sure at this point."

31

"Isn't this the road that those IRA people were captured on a few months back?" one of the Russians asked Ivan Kolov as the vans sped along the road towards Compton.

"Yes, this is the road where that woman captured all of those blundering fools," Kolov shot back. He had said very little since they had left New York City. "Are you sure that you saw no signs of life after our rockets hit that command center, Vasily?"

"Yes, Comrade Kolof," Vasily Luktin replied patiently. "The two rockets hit the targets center of mass. The explosion destroyed everything."

Kolov was still not convinced. He turned on the van's radio. "I want to make sure," he muttered, turning the dials. He finally tuned into a news-talk station. "… And in other news, police and fire officials confirm that an explosion on the New York docks this morning caused a huge fire and massive loss of life. We have no word as to what or who was involved in this disaster, but officials do confirm that the installation involved was part of the terrorist response team currently aiding New York in the recovery efforts. This is Brittany Craft, Cable News."

"See, Comrade Kolov? You have nothing to worry about," Lutkin said with satisfaction. "The Americans have no idea what happened."

Kolov relaxed a little. "Good. After we free our friends, we will kill the rest of Warren's family and then head out to the rendezvous point at Merit Cove." He glanced down at the large case containing the nuclear weapon. "Our clients will pay a fortune even for this one device, my friends."

The vans drove on, taking the eastern road towards Compton. Ten miles to the south and east of the road, the aircraft bearing Charlie and the team of commandos raced ahead, desperately trying to outrun the van. The curve of the earth, along with the low altitude of the aircraft, completely masked the sound of the engines.

"Your plan's a sound one, Charlie," Rosson said with approval after Charlie had briefed him. "My only concern is that we'll tip our hand once we land on the helipad at the hospital."

"There's no other choice, James," Charlie replied. "The helipad at the hospital is the only place this aircraft can land. We can't get any closer to the police station than that."

"We can split up and head in two directions after we land there," David pointed to the map. "I'm sure that by the time Joan and Carl get through with these people, all they'll be thinking about is a way out of that town."

"Carl's smart enough to not tip his hand ahead of time," Charlie agreed. "He'll have a normal number of patrols out, but nothing on the street to let the terrorists know he suspects anything."

"My chief is ex-SF, like me," David explained to the Delta Force commandos. "Our department may be small, but we've got pros running it. The lady who runs the detective department is an ex-Army drill sergeant from Fort Jackson. You may have run into her at Basic."

"I hope not," one of the commandos shuddered. "There was one female Drill Sergeant who was completely nuts. We all kept hoping she'd have a stroke or something. I've never been dogged so much in my life, and that includes Ranger, airborne, and Delta training. We called her 'Joan the Terrible.'"

"That would be her," Charlie said with a smile.

"Great," the commando groaned. " Just my luck. I run into Joan the Terrible on an op. I hope the Russians shoot me."

"Hey Jack, I ain't never seen you scared of nothin' before," one of his friends said in a joking tone. "What's so bad about some female cop who was your drill sergeant in Basic?"

"You'll find out when you meet her," the Jack Waskowski replied, beads of sweat breaking out on his face.

-0-

"Are you all nice and comfy, friend?" Joan asked the hapless Russian as she handcuffed him to the chair at the Desk Sergeant's location. The man now sat directly in front of the glass double doors that opened into the Compton Police Station.

"Try to remember that I have my rifle trained at the back of your head, and that I speak and understand Russian. If you attempt to warn your playmates, I'll blow your head off. Do you understand? Do you have any doubts in your wormy little mind that I wouldn't do it?" Joan asked, looking at the man with deadly seriousness. "Yip once, and your head turns into hamburger."

"I know you are serious," the man said in a terrified whisper.

Carl Davis came up and put his hand on Joan's shoulder. "Okay, Joan: that's enough playtime. We need to get in place now." He keyed his police radio. "All units: this is five-seven. Keep this frequency cleared for tactical traffic only."

"Five-seven, this is Echo-foxtrot," the pilot of the helicopter called out. "Our ETA is five mikes."

"Roger, Echo-foxtrot. We copy your ETA. Five-seven out," Carl looked over at Joan and the rest of the officers positioned around the station entrance. "Okay people: this is it. Stay sharp."

"Five-seven, this is Echo four-six. We have two vans approaching from the west," one of the patrol cars called in from a concealed location just outside of Compton.

"Roger four-six," Carl replied into his radio. "All units: hold your position until you hear my command. Five-seven out."

All of the officers in the station were dressed in body armor and carried machine guns. From the outside of the station, no one could see the trap that had been set. *I hope this goes off*, Carl thought to himself as he took his position.

-0-

"I need to run into the hospital for a minute when we set down," Charlie told James Rosson as they came up on their final approach to Compton. The pilot had been flying as low to the ground as possible for the last few miles into town. "We need to hold our position right now," she told the pilot.

"Roger," Jeffers responded, bringing his aircraft into a low hover behind a group of trees.

On the other side of town, the two vans approached the station. There was nothing out of the ordinary to tip off the terrorists as to what was about to happen.

"All right, here's what I want to do," Kolov directed his people. "I will go to that church and pick up the priest. I've been told that the child helps him in the morning. Meet me there after you have freed our comrades."

The van with Kolov made a right-hand turn on Main street and headed off to Trinity Church. The other van continued down to the police station. Rolling into the parking lot, the van stopped abruptly, and six men erupted from the back of the van.

"Let's go!" the leader called out to the other five men as they charged into the station.

They stopped short in front of the Desk Sergeant's desk where their terrified friend was waiting. "Vanya! What are you doing dressed in that uniform?" the man stammered as he looked at his handcuffed companion. Before the man could answer, the five terrorists were surrounded by police officers in tactical uniforms holding automatic weapons.

"Trick or treat, pond scum," Joan Richards sang out, pointing her weapon directly at the man's head.

The driver out front was watching his friends in the station. He saw the activity inside the station and knew that the jig was up. Gunning the engine, he peeled out of the parking lot.

Carl spotted him leaving. "All units: this is five-seven. We have a chicken trying to flee the coop. Bring him back."

"I've got him," a unit said as she pulled directly in front of the hapless van half a block later. The van screeched to a halt. "Freeze, moron!" the officer screamed as she got out of the car and leveled her pistol at the terrified driver. "Don't even breathe!"

-0-

"Okay, Captain: let's drop in on the party," Charlie directed the pilot. He nodded and lifted the aircraft out of the concealed position and headed for the hospital helipad.

A moment later the aircraft had landed at the helipad, and the commandos were outside the helicopter. Charlie jumped out of the helicopter and went into the Emergency Room entrance without telling anybody where she was going.

"We need to go to the police station and pick up our prisoners," Rosson said, ignoring her for a moment. "From what I gather, Carl and his people managed to do quite well without us. The station's only two blocks away, so let's head over there now."

"We still have one van left," David pointed out. "We don't know where that van is headed."

"Captain, I need you to take your aircraft up and see if you can find out where that might be," Rosson told the pilot. He looked around. "Where's Colonel Warren?"

"You mean the girl? She went into the hospital, I think," one of the commandos said.

David looked at Sergeant Major MacKay and Rosson. "All right, you guys go take care of the terrorists. I'll try to find out where Charlie went."

He walked into the busy emergency room and ran into Dr. Maggie White. "Did you see Charlie just come in, Maggie?" he asked.

"Yeah, she came in dressed in all that black stuff she sometimes wears," Dr. White replied. "She asked me if she could borrow my car. What's going on, Dave?"

"You gave her your keys?" David asked incredulously.

"Sure," Dr. White shrugged. "Why shouldn't I?"

"Oh no, that's just great," David groaned in despair. "Where's your car, Maggie?"

"On the other side of the hospital in the doctor's parking lot."

"She's way faster than I am and she's got a two minute head start," David sighed, trying to figure out what to do next. "I need to go out and tell Rosson what's going on." He ran out the ambulance entrance just in time to see the aircraft lift off. Rosson and the commandos were nowhere to be seen.

"I'm going to kill that girl when I get my hands on her," David growled. He keyed his mike. "Five seven, this is Delta eight-six. I need a unit and back up to come to the hospital to pick me up, over."

"Delta eight-six, this is five seven," Carl Davis' voice came over the small radio on David's shoulder. "Your people have just arrived our location. What's up?"

"My wife, that's what," David replied. "She bugged out using Maggie's car. I think she's headed to Trinity."

"Tactical, this is Echo-foxtrot," the helicopter pilot's voice broke in over their radio transmission. "I have a dark late model van parked next to a church. There is a man moving a girl and an older man into the church. He is armed, over."

"That's Trinity Church," Carl said, speaking to the pilot. "Echo-foxtrot: hold your position. All units, this is five-seven. We have a hostage situation at Trinity Church."

32

Angus was outside with Katya tending the rose bushes in his garden when the van pulled up. A tall man with dark hair and a short beard opened the door and came out of the van. He was carrying a machine gun.

"You two! Get into the church!" he commanded, brandishing the pistol. Coming up close to them, he grabbed Katya by the arm. "I know you! You're John Warren's brat! Get moving, now!"

"See here, young man..." Angus began, then stopped when Kolov shoved the pistol into Katya's side.

"One more word and I will kill this child where she stands," Kolov said, his eyes blazing with maniacal fury. He half dragged Katya into the church along with Angus.

"Shut the door," Kolov commanded. Angus did what he was told. "Come with me to the front of the church." They went to the front of the church, near the altar.

"Now then, we'll sit down and have a nice chat before I kill you both," Kolov gestured with his gun, directing Angus and Katya to sit down in the front pew. "I want you to know who is about to kill you."

-0-

"Floor it, Sam!" David ordered Sam Richards as the patrol car raced towards Trinity Church. He spoke into the police radio. "Five seven, this is eight-six. I am at Trinity. Officer is already inside. I am going in to back up."

335

He leaped out of the car without waiting for a reply as the car pulled to the curb a block away from the church. "Give me your rifle, Sam. Tell Carl to set up a command post here. Hopefully, this will be over in a minute or so."

"You've got it, Dave. I'll get Carl and Joan on the horn and give them a sitrep." Sam threw him the rifle. David caught it in midair and pulled the action back, cocking the weapon. He moved quickly up to the van.

A figure was slumped over the driver's seat. "Freeze!" David yelled as he pulled open the driver's side door. The very unconscious man nearly fell out of the van.

Sam Richards' car pulled up next to him. "Looks like Charlie got to him first." Sam said dryly.

"Yeah, that's my wife: the one-man army," David shook his head. "She must be in a better mood this morning. She didn't kill this one. I'm going around to the alley-side entrance, Sam. Set things up right here, okay?"

Richards nodded. "Okay. You've got five minutes before my wife arrives and breaks down the front door, Stone. That's all the time I can give you."

He went to the alley behind the church, David went in through the back door. He knew Charlie was already inside. Going around to the side, he cautiously opened the door into the sanctuary. He could hear voices inside. Slowly, stealthily, David crept into the side of the church next to the altar. Shouldering his rifle, he waited for the time to shoot.

-0-

Ivan Kolov was enjoying himself. Katya and Angus huddled in front of him on the pew, abject terror on their faces. *Charlie Warren has been blown to bits, and now at last I can destroy the last of John Warren's family,* he thought as he lovingly fingered his weapon.

A sadistic grin spread across his face. "I think I'll shoot you first, Katya. That way the old man can watch you bleed to death before I kill him." Kolov slowly straightened his arm and pointed his pistol at Katya's middle.

A single shot rang out, and Kolov screamed in pain. His weapon went spinning off into a corner of the church as Charlie's round shattered his wrist.

"The next bullet goes through your heart, Kolov," Charlie came up the aisle, holding her machine pistol out in front of her, ready to shoot.

Kolov stared in disbelief as Charlie came within ten feet of him. "You... you can't be alive. I saw the command center blow up!"

"You saw it blow up, but I was outside," Charlie's voice was filled with rage and hate. "You butchered all of those people, you spineless pig." She pointed her pistol at his knees. "Now get down on your knees before I shoot them out from under you."

"I will never kneel before you, Warren," Kolov snarled. Before Charlie could react, he leapt over to where Katya was sitting and wrapped his arm around her throat. Jerking her up in front of him, Kolov held the terrified girl as a shield. "Where are your brave words now?"

He tightened his grip on Katya's neck. "I'll crush her throat, Warren. I swear it. Drop your weapon, or the girl dies."

"No, Kolov, you will die," David came up the side aisle, rifle aimed at Kolov's head. "I've got your skull in my sights. Let her go, or you will die in five seconds. Five... four...three...two..."

Kolov looked into David's eyes. There was no doubt that David fully intended to pull the trigger. Kolov could see the tendons in David's hands squeeze slowly, inexorably on his weapon as he readied to fire. He loosened his grip on Katya at the very last second.

David gestured with his rifle. "Move away from my family, pig." Kolov shakily moved away from Katya and Angus. Suddenly his body was transfixed by half a dozen laser-targeting beams.

"Down on the floor, slime!" Joan Richards yelled as she raced up the aisle to the church to where Charlie and David were.

Katya rushed over to Charlie and buried herself in Charlie's arms, sobbing hysterically. Joan came up to Kolov and put handcuffs on him. She hauled him ungently to his feet.

Kolov looked over at Charlie, his eyes were black with hatred. "You will regret not killing me, Warren. I have followers who will hunt you down and kill you some day."

"I wanted to capture you alive, Kolov," Charlie looked up from her sister and replied in an icy voice. She came up to him and stared unblinking into his face. "If I had wanted you to die, you would not be standing here in front of me now. Be thankful that I was merciful, because I was prepared to kill you with my bare hands.

"Be grateful, Ivan Alexyevich, that the police arrived when they did. Otherwise, you would now be before God's throne facing judgment." She rendered the words in Russian.

Ivan looked into her eyes. They were cold, without life or compassion. For the first time in his life, Ivan Kolov felt fear. He knew that Charlie was fully capable of killing him on the spot, without mercy, without a second's hesitation. Kolov's heart started pounding slowly in his chest and a film of sweat broke out over his face.

Charlie nodded slowly, noting his involuntary reaction of fear. "Good. At least we understand one another. *Doswidenya*, Ivan Alexyevich."

"All right, pixie: let's get you out of here," Joan Richards not-too-gently pulled him down the aisle. Carl Davis came up to them and fixed Charlie and David with a withering stare.

"You two are starting to bother me," he said grimly. "David, I can excuse Charlie for not waiting around for backup, but you should know better. If you two ever pull something stupid like this again, I'll shoot you both."

His face softened. "Good work, by the way."

"What about the rest of these idiots?" David asked.

"They're being bundled up and taken back to New York." Carl replied as they walked down the church. "There are about a dozen Federal prosecutors waiting for them. They'll be spending the rest of their lives in jail and then some with all of the things they've done."

They walked out onto the church lawn where the rest of the SRT were waiting, along with the Delta commandos and Rosson. Joan was talking to one of the commandos who had been in Basic Training when Joan was a drill sergeant.

"Good to see you finally learned to use a weapon properly, Waskowski," Joan said admiringly. "I had my doubts about you."

"I owe everything to you, ma'am," the soldier said, a little nervously. "Seeing you still strikes fear into my heart."

"Yeah, well that's the way it should be, soldier," Joan said professionally. "My drill always told me you'd forget your boyfriends and girlfriends, but you'd never ever forget your drill instructor."

"I agree wholeheartedly, Ms. Richards," Sergeant Major MacKay said, coming up and joining the conversation. "I wanted to tell you I was very impressed with the way you handled that situation at the police station this afternoon."

"Tactics are tactics, Sergeant Major," Joan replied modestly. She looked over at Charlie, David and Katya. "I think it's time to send that family home."

"I agree with you," MacKay nodded. He went over to James Rosson. "Sir, I think that under the circumstances, it might be prudent to relieve Colonel Warren and Detective Stone of any further duties today and allow them to go home."

"I agree, Sergeant Major," Rosson said. "I've just finished talking to General Mason. "Now that the rest of the terrorists have been captured and the last of the weapons recovered, Colonel Warren is officially relieved of command."

He walked over to Charlie and saluted. "Colonel Warren, you are relieved of command immediately. You are hereby ordered to return to your home and resume your former life. We'll be in touch in the next few days, but for now, you and David and Katya need to spend some time together. Those orders come from General Mason, the Queen, and just about everyone else here."

"I stand relieved sir, with unutterable pleasure," Charlie replied returning the salute, holding David and Katya close to her. She released them and hugged James' neck and kissed him. "Thank you, James, for everything."

"You are most welcome, Lady Warren," James smiled. "It's been an honor to serve with you in battle. By the way, I had a most interesting proposition for you from the SEAL team commander. I told him you were married and declined for you."

"Really?" Charlie's eyebrows went up. "I'm flattered, James." She looked at David, who was staring at her disapprovingly. "It's a compliment, David; that's all."

"Uh huh," David replied skeptically. "I know all about SEALs, Charlie. It's definitely time for all of us to go home."

"We'll be seeing you tomorrow, Charlie," James said. "Nice job today. Glad all that training of yours came in handy."

"I had the best teachers," Charlie smiled. "All my best to Jane and the children."

"She has felt rather left out," James admitted.

"We'll be together soon," Charlie promised. James nodded and headed back over to the police van where Sergeant Major MacKay and the rest of the Delta commandos were waiting.

"Come on, people," Joan Richards said. "I've got orders from Carl to take you home. Don't even think of trying to disobey me, because I will cuff you and put you back in my patrol car if I need to."

"You heard the lady," David laughed. "Let's go home."

Angus McKendrick watched as Charlie, David and Katya got into the back of Joan's patrol car. "I'm so glad they're finally home," he told Carl as the car drove off. "Carl, could I trouble you to take me to hospital for a moment? My chest is… not feeling quite right."

Carl's jaw dropped. "Your chest is not feeling quite right?" he repeated. "Why didn't you say anything before now, Father McKendrick?"

"I didn't want to alarm anyone," Angus said mildly, "especially Katya. The child has been through enough today."

"You know I'm going to get into a world of trouble taking you there," Carl growled as he took Angus to his car. "Charlie will skin me alive for doing this."

"It's all right, lad; I'll make it right with her," Angus assured him as he climbed into the car.

33

Ron Meyers woke to find Brenda Reynold's head lying next to him. Brenda was deeply asleep, barely stirring as Ron tentatively put his arm around her shoulder. She sighed and nestled in closer to him. *This must be a dream,* Ron thought to himself happily, feeling Brenda's hair next to his cheek. *I've wanted to do this for so long.* A knife-like twinge of pain in his abdomen reminded him sharply that he was very much awake.

Brenda had fallen asleep next to him after Ron had been transferred out of the intensive care unit that morning. Ron had been taken off life support the night before and was fully awake for the better part of the night. Brenda filled him in on everything that had happened in the tunnels, including Charlie's rescue. It was obvious to Ron that Brenda now had a new respect for Charlie; all of Brenda's contempt for her had utterly vanished.

Ron decided to turn on the news. He reached for the remote, being careful not to disturb Brenda. A nurse came into the room bearing a dinner tray. Ron gestured to her to put it on the table. He mouthed "thank you," and smiled. The nurse looked at Brenda, smiled in return, and left the room.

"The crisis in New York came to an abrupt end this afternoon when American and British special forces captured the final group of terrorists with an atomic weapon in the small New York town of Compton," Brittany Craft's voice said with an element of triumph in her voice. "General Nathan Mason, the military commander of the operation, credited teamwork with the military and local police forces for the capture of Ivan Kolov, one of the world's most deadly terrorists."

Mason's face appeared on the screen. "I just want to say that it would have been impossible for us to capture these people without the cooperation of hundreds of dedicated military and law enforcement officials.

"The brilliant leadership by the officers in charge enabled us to capture not only the terrorists, but the nuclear weapons they had stolen with minimal loss of life."

"Way to go, Charlie," Ron murmured, shifting slightly in his bed. He tentatively reached out and started to stroke Brenda's hair. His movement woke Brenda up.

"What?" she said, sitting up with a jerk. She looked down at Ron and blushed. I'm so sorry, Meyers. I must have dozed off. What time is it?"

"News time, " Ron replied, pointing at the television. "They just had some stuff on about that op in New York City. The guy in charge didn't mention Charlie's name, but we all know who he was talking about."

"How about that," Brenda said. "Good for her. I knew she could do it," Brenda said with approval. She looked over at Ron's bandage-swathed abdomen. "Hey, I'm sorry I… fell asleep on you," Brenda touched his abdomen gently. "I probably crushed you to death, leaning on that incision."

"Don't worry about it, Lieutenant," Ron replied. He was quiet for a moment.

Brenda reached over and took his hand. "Ron, could you do something for me?"

"Sure, Lieutenant," Ron replied slowly, his heart beating loudly in his ears.

"Could you drop the 'Lieutenant' when we're alone? My name is 'Brenda,' and I'd really like it if you called my by my name," Brenda said softly. "In fact, I'll tell you a secret. I've always liked it when you called me by my first name."

Ron's face went scarlet. "Gee, I don't know, Lieutenant. People might… well they might think we're…"

"We're what?"

"Falling for each other," Ron said slowly. He looked away for a moment. "I've been hoping for this for two years now. I never thought anyone as classy as you would ever have anything to do with a mug like me."

A half-smile appeared on Brenda's face. "Really? I thought I'd run every guy off in my life. You were the only one who stuck around. Why did you do that?"

"I guess I liked you."

Brenda came close to him. "I'm glad you did, because, Mr. Meyers, I am very, very much in love with you, in case you haven't noticed." She kissed him for emphasis.

The phone rang several times before Ron reluctantly picked it up. "Hello? Charlie! Yes, Brenda's here. We just saw the news on TV. You're finally home? Good, you deserve it. Okay, we'll see you tomorrow. Hold on, I'll put her on."

Ron handed Brenda the phone. "Hey partner, how are you doing? I'm fine. Ron's kinda beat up, but he's getting better. Yeah, shooting bad guys is always fun. Really? Okay, tell Stone he still owes all of us dinner. He promised me. Uh huh, I know you will. Okay, we'll see you later. Bye."

Brenda hung up the phone. "We have a dinner date with Charlie and David after you get out of the hospital."

"Sounds great," Ron replied happily. Brenda leaned over and put her head on his shoulder carefully. "If I'd known I'd get this sort of attention, I would have gotten shot years ago."

"I'll shoot you again if you're not careful."

"Right."

-0-

"Things seem to have gone quite well, Sergeant Major," James Rosson said as he looked at the last of the terrorists being loaded onto a police van. They were back at the Compton Police Station finishing up the last details of their operation.

"Sir, General Mason wants to talk to you," one of the Delta commandos handed Rosson a portable phone.

"Thank you, Sergeant," Rosson said, taking the phone. "Colonel

Rosson here. Yes, General; we're about ready to fly on out back to your position. What? Yes, sir, Colonel Warren and her husband are now finally home. Detective Lieutenant Richards radioed back to us just a moment ago. All right, we'll be there shortly. Thank you, Sir."

He turned off the phone. "General Mason was just interested as to whether we'd finally gotten Charlie and David safely home. I told him that Joan Richards was taking them. He said that was good enough for him."

"We've got the lot of those terrorists safe in the van now, sir," Sergeant Major MacKay said, looking at his watch. "We're ready to return to New York City."

"Very good, Sergeant Major," Rosson nodded and then sighed. "The tidying up is always the longest of any operation. Now we have hours of debriefings and after-action meetings to look forward to."

"That's quite true, sir," MacKay nodded. "We probably have the rest of the day ahead us to take care of these fellows. Megan is already talking about resuming that play of hers, so you know where I'll be tonight."

Rosson looked around. "I'm glad things are finally settling down to normal around here once again."

"May I remind the Colonel that you said something like that a number of months ago," MacKay said darkly. "We then proceeded to have some rather irregular times."

"Thank you for reminding me, Sergeant Major: I stand corrected," Rosson observed wryly. "With Charlie Warren in the picture, normal does not exist."

34

The phone rang ten times the following morning before David finally answered it. Charlie was buried in a heap of covers next to him, so he had to reach over the mound where she was sleeping to reach the phone. "Hello?" he mumbled, rubbing his sleep-numbed face. "Oh, it's you, General Mason. I'm sorry, sir. We've both been unconscious ever since we got home. Hold on, I'll let you speak to the hand."

Charlie's hand had appeared from the pile of bedclothes while David was speaking. He handed the receiver to her and the receiver disappeared into the mound. Katya appeared at the door. "Where have you been?" David asked. "The phone's been ringing for ten minutes."

Katya shrugged elaborately. "No one ever calls me, David. It's always for you and Charlie."

"That's not true, Katya. Ever since you started your babysitting racket, you've gotten plenty of phone calls," David reminded her. "What time is it?"

"Past nine o'clock," Katya replied. "Megan's coming by in ten minutes to take me to skating practice and then we're going to meet with Jackie and have lunch."

She paused for a moment, looking down. Katya did this whenever she had something unpleasant to tell. "I... I need to tell you and Charlie something."

David looked over at the talking heap of bedclothes. "Wait until your sister comes up for air."

"All right, General Mason, we'll be there in about an hour or so." Charlie's head finally appeared as she concluded her conversation. "Thank you for calling. Goodbye," she hung up the phone. "Good morning, darling. What sort of news do you have?"

"Uncle Carl called last night after you and David went to bed," Katya said. "He told me that he had to take Grandfather to hospital after we came home. Grandfather told him not to tell you then, because you were so tired."

Charlie and David looked at each other. "Thank you, Katya," Charlie finally said, keeping her voice even. There was no reason to get upset with Katya. She was simply following instructions other adults had given her. "David and I will be going into New York today. What's happening in your world today?"

"I have skating practice today and then Megan, Jackie and I are going to meet and get the play going again," Katya replied with a smile. "Will you be home for rehearsal tonight?"

"We're going to try, darling. Things are still very busy in the city. You know we want to, more than anything." Charlie held out her arms and Katya came to her. "Darling, we've missed you so very much these past few weeks! I promise we'll make it up to you soon." She kissed Katya's hair and held her close for a minute. "Once all this nonsense is over, we're going to be together forever."

Charlie looked over at David. "I promise," she said, kissing Katya once more. "You need to run along and get ready for skating, darling. David and I will be along in a moment or so."

Katya left the room and closed the door. Charlie called the hospital and found out which room Angus was located. "Uncle Angus, are you doing all right?"

"You found out, child," Angus said, guilt tingeing his voice. "I was hoping you would get some needed rest before anyone told you I was in hospital."

"I understand and appreciate your concern for us," Charlie said, choosing her words carefully. "But you are part of our family as well. Please let us know what is happening to you."

"I know that, love. You and David have had an exhausting week, and I just felt yesterday that I didn't want to trouble you."

"Trouble us? Uncle Angus, you have never been trouble to

anyone. However, I have a thirteen year-old sister who adores you, and would be devastated should anything ever happen to you," Charlie said. She got out of bed and started to select clothes for the day. David had already gotten up and was busy in the shower.

"I understand that," Angus McKendrick said patiently. "I treasure you and Katya more than you'll ever know. Perhaps we can have supper sometime soon. Friday, perhaps?"

"I'll have to see what happens around here. There never seems to be a free moment. When are you going to be released from hospital?"

There was a pause on the line. "I'm not quite sure about that, Charlie. The cardiologist is supposed to see me sometime later today."

Charlie stopped. "What's going on, Angus?"

"I really don't know, Charlie. I'll have to get back to you on that. I'm rather tired at the moment, my dear," Angus' voice suddenly became old and weary. "Do call later when you get back into town. Goodbye."

"Goodbye," Charlie said in a small voice, staring at the receiver. David came out of the bathroom fully dressed, drying his hair.

"What's going on?" he asked. Charlie had sat down on the bed, apparently dazed by her conversation with Angus. "Charlie, is there something wrong with Angus?"

"I don't know, David," she replied slowly. "I really don't know right now."

-0-

Charlie and David could hear the raised voices halfway down the corridor after they got off of the elevator. A group of young men were gathered around the entrance to the EOC. They were all dressed in Navy dress uniforms. One of them was talking in an animated tone to another man who stood apart from the others, obviously not convinced.

"Look, Commander: I've got a kid brother in ESU, and he told me that a friend of his told him that this Warren chick killed two Russians in five seconds!" the young sailor said, flailing his hands out for emphasis. "I'm not lying! This chick, if you seen her,

Commander, she's not bigger than a fire hydrant, but she takes out these two Russian goons. Boom! Just like that! This guy my brother knows says they found the two bodies of theses guys Warren iced. One guy had a knife wound in the center of his chest, and the other dude had two nine mil slug holes center mass in his chest. These guys were like huge, Commander. Freakin' monsters. I swear on my priest uncle's grave: it's the truth."

"Look, McNally: you can swear on anything you like," Doug Simpson said firmly. "I just have a hard time believing that a girl that size could kill anyone."

McNally refused to back down. He looked down the hallway and saw Charlie and David approaching. "Commander, this Warren chick ain't no bigger than that little girl coming down this here hall right now. Maybe she's a little bigger, but not much. And my cousin Bernie says she's totally hot, Commander. A real fox, you know…"

"Right," Simpson said skeptically. "Warren's probably built like an Eastern Bloc female swimmer. Probably as ugly as one, too."

"The jury's still out on that one," Charlie said, coming up to the group. "I'm Charlie Warren," she said, holding out her hand to Simpson, who was now turning bright crimson with embarrassment. "You must be the famous Commander Simpson I've heard so much about. I believe you wanted to meet me, Commander. At least that's what Colonel Rosson told me." Charlie held out her hand for Simpson to shake. Simpson took it, shaking slightly.

"I… well, I… uh, yes, it's good to meet you, ma'am," Simpson finally stammered out. Charlie was obviously not what he had envisioned. "I wanted to say, ma'am, that I really admired… your plans for our operation, ma'am." He stared down at her. Charlie barely came to the top of his shoulder. "Forgive me, ma'am, but you seem so small for a girl, I mean woman, I mean female. I… I…"

"Relax, Commander," Charlie said with a smile. "It's all right. I understand. Is this where we're going to have the outbriefing?"

"Yes ma'am," Simpson stiffened as he held the door open for her and David. He followed in behind them, along with the other SEALs. Charlie could hear in the background the barely-suppressed snickers of the other men.

McNally was basking in the glory of the moment. "Did you see the look on the Commander's face?" he chortled to his team members.

"I ain't never seen him act like that." One of the team members said.

"I think he's digging on her." McNally smirked.

"Shut up, fool." One of his friends shoved him.

Simpson ignored the remarks and decided to put his game face on. "All right, sailors: find a seat and shut up. I'll deal with you clowns later."

"One of your fan club members?" David smirked as they sat down in the auditorium.

"Stop it, beast," Charlie punched his shoulder. "Behave yourself."

"I think he's experiencing what I did when I first met you, that's all. I call it the 'Charlie Warren Effect.'"

"Really? And what on earth is that, pray tell?"

"Complete and total surprise people have when they first meet you. You just don't come across like the lethal lady I've grown to know and love."

"It's my greatest asset," Charlie replied smugly. "Keeps everyone off balance."

"Is this seat taken?" Brenda Reynolds said as she sat down next to Charlie. She looked very happy and relaxed. "How are you doing, killer?"

"Just fine," Charlie reached over and hugged her. "How's Ron doing?"

"He's doing great," Brenda replied. "He threw me out of his room today. Said I was a distraction or something."

"I understand all about distractions," David said knowingly. Charlie nudged him in his ribs. "Brenda, there's something different about you. What's going on?"

"Nothing," Brenda replied dreamily. "If I told you, I'd have to kill you, that's all."

"Uh huh," David said skeptically, winking at Charlie. "I'm not that dumb, Lieutenant."

"Mind your own business, David," Charlie shoved him. She looked at her watch elaborately. "What time is this clambake supposed to start?"

"Two minutes from now," David said, looking up at the clock. "Mason runs a tight show. He'll start on time."

"Have you ever been to one of these things before?" Brenda asked.

"Yes, unfortunately," Charlie looked violently bored. "They drag on forever, and they're dull as dust."

"Not Mason's after-action sessions. They're more like Wild West saloon fights," David said. "He's got a few simple rules: no guns, and what's said in here, stays here. It's strictly a learning experience."

There was a stir in the room, and one of the SEALs bellowed, "Attention on deck!" as General Mason came into the room. Everyone stood until he arrived at the podium.

Mason looked around the room for a few seconds before beginning. "I hate briefings, and I hate after-action briefings even more. Anyone of you who's served with me before can testify to that. You all can sit around for the next five years and tell war stories on your own time, so we're going to make this short and sweet.

"Here are the ground rules: we're all adults here, so there will be no name-calling and no weapons drawn. You have personal problems with someone, settle it with them on your own time, not ours. One person at a time has the floor.

"Before we get started, I need to know a few things: did you have what it took to do your job? Did we do our job in allowing you to accomplish your mission? This is your meeting, your floor. Let me hear what you've got, people, because if you don't have any complaints, comments or suggestions, I'm going to adjourn this clambake and head back to Washington."

Deafening silence greeted his ears. "All right, I know you've got some gripes, so spill it. I also know that the SEALs are out there, and when they're quiet, I know there's trouble brewing."

His remark produced a chorus of howls and screams from the SEAL team. Mason held up his hand. "Okay guys, settle down. Just wanted to make sure you weren't out there sneaking around causing trouble."

"That's what we do sir!" one of them shouted back. His remark produced another upheaval from the SEALs. Mason waited for the noise to die down before proceeding.

"Anybody else?" Mason looked around the room. He produced a sheet of paper in his hand. "You guys are really starting to bother me. If I don't hear any more signs of life in here in the next few seconds, I'm going to have Colonel Warren come around and check you guys out for signs of life."

"She can check my pulse any time she wants to, sir!" someone called out. That produced another uproar that died down after two minutes.

Mason stood back for a minute. "Another remark like that and I'm going to suspend my 'no firearms' rule. Anything constructive on your minds, people?"

Charlie raised her hand. "Sir, I have a few observations I'd like to share."

"I was wondering when you were going to step up, Colonel," Mason nodded in approval. "In case you heroes weren't aware of it, this whole op was planned, coordinated, and executed by Colonel Charlene Warren. She was, and is, I might add, your commander." He turned to Charlie. "Okay, Colonel: what's your gripe?"

"Sir, twenty-six people were killed the other day because I failed to provide adequate security at our forward operations center," Charlie said quietly, turning around to face all the people in the audience. "Their lives were my responsibility, and I failed them. I am truly sorry for my lapse in judgment."

There was dead silence in the auditorium. Mason looked at her for a minute before responding. "There was security around the center, Colonel. You just failed to anticipate that the enemy would throw a sucker punch during his move to evacuate the city."

He looked up and addressed the rest of the audience. "People, this is what the really good commanders do: they assume responsibility and take the blame when part of the op fails. You're correct, Colonel, it was a major flaw, one that the enemy exploited. The operation was drawing down, the enemy was fleeing, disorganized, surrendering everywhere. The command element had left their operations center. We felt like we had them on the run. Let this be a lesson for all you heroes out there: never let your guard down, and never assume the enemy's finished fighting with you until you have his neck under your heel and his face is turning blue. It's a good comment, Colonel, and a good lesson to learn for the future."

A ripple of laughter went throughout the room. Charlie's opening comments had broken the ice, and soon Mason was fielding and refereeing all sorts of questions from other members of the operations team. The session was lively, sometimes heated but never acrimonious. It lasted about an hour. Even David enjoyed it, and contributed some insights into the operation.

Hank Blevins had the final say. "General, I want to personally thank you for putting that wild man Stone on my team," Blevins said, pointing to David. "If it weren't for that maniac, we'd still be holed up in that stupid tunnel pinned down by enemy fire.

"Stone's solution was simple, stupid, and just what we needed to do: throw all of our grenades and charge, shooting everything we had. I just wanted to point him out, because any time he wants to quit his day job and start working for a real police force..." he stopped for a minute as a wave of yells and hoots swept the auditorium, "he can come to work for us. Thanks, Dave.

"I also want to thank Colonel Warren, who turned the Russian's mines around so when they set them off, they killed themselves. That was a dirty, low-down sneaky thing to do, Colonel. And you look like such a nice, wholesome, clean–cut girl who'd never think up something nasty like that. Nice creative work." His remark produced another torrent of howls and cheers from the audience. Mason held up his hand after another minute or so of mayhem.

"I think that wraps things up nicely," Mason said, pleased with the results. He now had three sheets of notes written down. "I want to thank all of you for your contributions, and your hard work. New York is alive and recovering today instead of bleeding and dying because of your efforts. You are all patriots and heroes in my book. Even the SEALs."

This final remark unleashed another volley of yells from the SEAL team. Mason snapped to attention and saluted the audience. "Attention!" one of the Delta team commandos yelled as everyone rose to their feet. Mason left the podium, and the lights in the auditorium went up.

"That wasn't bad at all," Brenda said approvingly. "I thought it was kind of fun."

"Yeah, Mason runs a good debrief," David said, stretching. "Some of the after-action sessions run by other guys I've been at have been so boring you could hear crickets chirp."

He glanced down at Charlie, who was unusually quiet. "What's going on, Charlie?"

"I failed them, David. My stupidity let them all die," she murmured, tears streaming down her face.

"Charlie, that's not true," David sat down next to her. "You know that's not true. You heard the General. You did the best you could. Nobody's faulting you, okay?"

"Least of all me," Nathan Mason said, joining them. Charlie struggled to her feet. "I want to thank you again for all you've done, Charlie. Standing up there, taking the first punch: that takes guts. We've learned a lot today, and that's what this sort of thing is all about. It's not about patting each other on the back and cheering. It's about learning from our mistakes and trying to do better the next time."

"The General is quite correct," James Rosson came up, along with Sergeant Major MacKay. "We do these things to find out how we can do better."

Charlie looked at them. "Thank you all for your encouragement, but I'll always think about how I could have done things a different way."

"That's the burden of command, Colonel," Mason pointed out. "That's something no one can take away from you."

"Oh yes, I have two things for you, Charlie," Rosson produced a thick, official-looking envelope. "The first thing is from your big sister Jane. She wants you to come over to our home as soon as you can, and she wants you there when her softball team goes up for the league championship game."

"I think we can manage that," Charlie laughed.

"The second item is from Her Majesty. I was instructed this morning to deliver it to you personally." James handed her the envelope.

Charlie opened it up and read the message:

Lady Warren:

The first Elizabeth had Drake and his privateers. We have you. The world owes you a debt for your efforts. Thank you for all you have done.

E.R.

Charlie handed the note to James, who read it and handed it back to her. "I don't know what to say, James," she said slowly. "I've... I've never had anyone say that about me before."

"May I see the note?" Mason asked. Charlie handed it to him. He nodded his approval and looked around the room. "I'm going to snag that SEAL commander before he sneaks out of this room and show this to him. With your permission, of course, Charlie."

"Go ahead, General," Charlie said, acutely embarrassed. "I just hate having my back slapped all the time." She looked at David and Brenda. "Let's get out of here and go visit Ron, okay?"

"Hold on you three: you're not going anywhere until I get a crack at you." Ken Rawlings came up to them. "I've got a special assignment." He handed Brenda an envelope with some documents inside. "I want you to go over to LuxVeritas and arrest the CEO and his Head of Operations."

A cold light shone in Brenda's eyes. "It will be my pleasure, sir."

"May I see you in private for a moment before you leave, Charlie?" Nathan Mason asked.

Charlie glanced at David, "Sure." She followed him to a conference room just off of the main auditorium. Mason closed the doors behind them after they entered it.

"Charlie, I appreciated what you said out there this morning," Mason began, looking steadily into Charlie's eyes. "You have to understand something. This is not Iraq, and this was not a conventional combat zone. There was no way you could have secured the perimeter from a threat like those two RPGs. You didn't have the resources to do it. You didn't have air suppression. You couldn't have prevented them from firing those missiles. I wanted you to know that, because you did your very best to safeguard the lives of those people with the resources you had at your command. Do you understand me, Colonel Warren?"

Charlie nodded mutely, tears streaming down her face. "I woke up, Nathan," she whispered hoarsely, "I woke up, and I was outside. The trailers were blown to bits, and they were on fire. All I could think about was, 'I'm alive, and all those people are dead.'"

She looked up at Nathan Mason with a look of utter despair. "I saw them last night, General. I saw all their faces. I remember their voices. They will be with me as long as I live. I will never be free of them."

Nathan Mason shook his head. "Charlie Warren, you have nothing to be ashamed about. You did the right thing; remember that."

He fished around in one of his pockets and brought out a card. "This is the name of a therapist I want you to see." He handed it to her. "Don't blow me off, Charlie, not this time. You tried to do this on your own last November. It was a disaster to try it by yourself.

"What happened the other day was a thousand times worse. You're going to need professional help to deal with this one. This lady is the best. She's ex-military, and I've used her down at Bragg to de-brief my soldiers.

"I've scheduled you to see her next week. She's expecting you, Doctor. If you don't show, I'll have you arrested and brought to her in handcuffs. Are you clear on that, Colonel Warren?"

Charlie wiped her eyes and smiled. "Crystal, sir."

"Good," Mason nodded. "Now let's get out of here before people start rumors."

He opened the door. David was waiting for them.

"I'll see to it that she makes that appointment, sir," David said.

"I'm counting on that, Stone," Mason nodded. "She's too valuable to have her broken and hurting for the rest of her life."

"Did you tell him about this, sir?" Charlie asked.

"No, he didn't, but I guessed what you were talking about," David replied for General Mason. "I knew Nathan Mason long before you did, Charlie. I know what kind of commander he is, and I know what he told you. He's a pro, and you need to listen to him."

"You're right, David," Charlie nodded. "I intend to do just that."

35

Things at LuxVeritas were finally getting back to normal. Like all major corporations, operations had been virtually shut down since the nerve gas attack on Tuesday. Now that normal traffic was allowed back into the city, the building was now a humming hive of activity. The organization was completely oblivious to the disaster it had suffered on the previous day.

Charlie, David and Brenda were let through security with a minimum of fanfare and no warning to the upper echelons. As they entered the building, a swarm of FBI agents, ESU team members, accountants, and lawyers simultaneously descended on company operations at various points throughout the city. The operation was so sudden, so complete, that no one had the time to punch any "delete" keys on any keyboard terminals. LuxVeritas was overrun and conquered before the executives in charge of it had any warning.

Robert Decker was in the office of Haman Evans when Charlie, Brenda and David breezed into the assistant's office. "NYPD," Brenda said, showing her badge to the startled assistant. "I need to talk to Mr. Evans now."

"He's… he's in a meeting right now," the befuddled assistant said, looking down at her appointment book. "I'll let him know you're here."

"I'm sure he is. Don't bother: we'll announce ourselves," Charlie said breezily as they all entered the inner office. Evans and Decker were deep in discussions about the tunnel operation.

"I can't understand why we haven't heard anything from our

friends on the East River," Evans puzzled. Decker had no answer, and just simply shrugged his shoulders.

"That's because they're either dead or in jail," Brenda Reynolds answered as Charlie and she came through the office door. "Care to join them? We have plenty of openings in our luxury line of Super-Max Federal Prisons."

"What's the meaning of this?" Evans snarled.

"It's called an arrest, Mr. Evans," Brenda said coldly. "We do that sort of thing in the Police Department from time to time. You and your playmates are wanted for conspiracy to commit murder, terrorist acts against the United States, and a list of other charges three pages long. It's all in this packet of warrants. You and your lawyers can read it down at the Federal Building."

She turned the two men around and put handcuffs on their wrists. "Dr. Warren, Detective Stone and I were selected to haul your slimy bodies out of this building. I hope you don't mind."

"Call our lawyers!" Decker bawled to the assistant in her office as they were marched out into the corridor. The assistant did as she was told, only to find that the phone service had been temporarily disrupted. In fact, electrical service for the entire building had temporarily been shut off, along with all other communication systems. This allowed the FBI and other law enforcement agencies to swoop down on LuxVeritas and capture the operation before anyone could react.

"All units: this is Reynolds. We have the players," Brenda spoke into a small microphone attached to a police radio located on her belt. The power flickered back on as they came to the elevator.

"It's so nice to have power when you need it," Charlie observed cheerily as the elevator chimed and the doors slid opened.

"I thought you said this scheme was fool-proof," Evans ground out through his teeth to the heavily perspiring Decker.

"Sir, we really shouldn't say anything more until our lawyers are present," Decker choked out.

"Indeed you shouldn't," Charlie said in a friendly tone as the elevator continued downwards. "Your name, Mr. Evans, is an interesting one. Do you know that Haman was the name of a famous traitor in the Old Testament? Interestingly enough, his scheme to murder all the Jews in Persia was thwarted by Queen Esther. I'm sure your parents were unaware of the significance of that name when they christened you. They probably thought it sounded beautiful. I think the irony is beautiful, myself."

The elevator chimed as the doors slid open. "Time to meet your adoring public," Brenda said as they manhandled the two executives out into the lobby. It was filled with shouting reporters and a galaxy of exploding photographic flashes.

They moved swiftly to awaiting patrol cars, which whisked the two unfortunate executives off to the Federal building.

David was waiting for them in the lobby. "Did you girls have fun?" he asked.

"It was great," Brenda grinned. "Best time I've had since I broke Kolinsky's knee in a kickboxing match."

"I always feel better when I take out the trash." Charlie said with satisfaction.

Brenda's cell phone beeped. "Hello? This is she. What? When? All right, I'll be right there." Her face went ashen with shock.

"Brenda, what's wrong?" Charlie asked.

"I've got to get to the hospital. Can you drive me? My car's still over at the EOC," Brenda said, glancing around in panic, her eyes welling with tears.

"What's wrong, honey?" David's face was soft with concern.

"I… they had to take Ron back into surgery this morning," Brenda said tearfully. "There was some sort of emergency."

"Let's get going," Charlie said firmly, gathering her purse and finding her keys.

-0-

"We had to go in and repair some areas that started leaking," the surgeon told Brenda half an hour later. "I know this is a setback, but it's one of those things that we anticipated. These sorts of things happen with trauma patients. Considering the nature of his injuries, Sergeant Meyers is lucky to be alive. He'll be back in the Intensive Care unit on a ventilator until he's able to breathe on his own."

Brenda nodded stonily, tears coursing down her face. "Thank

you, doctor," she whispered hoarsely, turning to Charlie and David.

"How long do you think he'll be in the ICU this time?" Charlie asked.

"I don't know," the surgeon replied, her face frowning as she considered her answer. "It's difficult to say. We'll just have to see."

"I appreciate your candor, Doctor," Charlie said. The surgeon nodded and went back into the surgical suite.

Brenda sat down on a chair. "Ron was fine this morning," she said, trying to make sense of it all. "He was laughing and joking. He sent me away telling me that he was fine and I'd be able to see him later. One of the nurses told me that an hour later, he broke out into a cold sweat and said he didn't feel well. That's when they took him back into surgery.

"I don't understand what happened, Charlie," she said tearfully. "Why is all this happening to Ron? Is he being punished or something?"

Charlie put her hands around Brenda's. "No, Brenda; Ron is not being punished. These things happen. That's just the way things are in life. Ron is a good man, and he loves you."

Brenda nodded mutely. For a moment, she was silent, then she looked up at Charlie. "I'm trying to understand all of that, Charlie. You have to understand that it's difficult for me to accept," Brenda said quietly.

"We understand, Brenda," Charlie assured her. "Right now, let's focus on getting Ron better. We'll have time to talk about other things soon."

"Hey champ; we're here for you and Ron," David said warmly. "You let us know what you need, and we'll do it."

"I can't believe you're being so nice to me, Dave," Brenda said with wonder in her voice. "I treated you so badly in the past. How can you do that?"

"Because I want to, Brenda." David came up and hugged her shoulder, "because I love you."

Brenda started tearing up again. "Stop it, you big creep! I was just about over crying and now you've got me started again."

"Yeah, well, life is tough, sweetie," David said, laughing softly. Brenda's cell phone went off.

"Hello? Yes sir, he had a setback and is back in the ICU. Okay, I'll be over in a few minutes. Goodbye." Brenda closed her phone. "Can you guys give me a ride over to the EOC? I left my car over there. They need me down at the station to finish booking our little friends."

"Sure, Brenda," Charlie replied. "Ron's in good hands, and right now he won't know if you're there or not. Besides, there's work to be done, and you're the one who needs to do it."

"You're right," Brenda agreed. "It felt so good putting those scum away this morning."

"It sure did," David said. "Ron would have been proud of you."

-0-

Charlie and David drove Brenda over to the precinct and dropped her off. They then went to the Consulate. Lady Margaret and Rosson were waiting for them.

"I'm so glad to see you in one piece, child," Lady Margaret said, fighting back tears as David and Charlie came into her office. "James and I were discussing your latest adventures."

"I've had quite enough adventures, ma'am," Charlie said firmly. "Right now my greatest wish is to go back to Compton and live in peace. Where's Sergeant Major MacKay?"

"We gave him the day off," James replied. "After the debriefing, I sent him to Compton to be with Megan. He has a decision to think about."

"Does this have to do with becoming Jonathan Mathis-Smith's Regimental Sergeant Major?"

"It does indeed," Rosson nodded, "a very big decision for our intrepid man from Edinburgh. We discussed it before, and I just want him to make the decision that's best for him and Megan."

"What do you want him to do, James?" Charlie asked.

"You know how I feel about Donald," James said briskly. "He's a splendid man. He'd make an outstanding Regimental Sergeant Major, and there's no doubt the country needs people like him. From a purely selfish point of view, there's nothing I'd like better than to have him working with me here at the Consulate on a permanent basis.

"But I also know that Donald's always been about the Army and the SAS. Things may have changed in that department over the past few months. I'm just wondering if accepting that post is the right choice for him personally."

"We could always use him around here, James," Lady Margaret pointed out. "He really has a flair for intelligence work."

Lady Margaret's phone rang. "Hello?' she answered and listened for half a minute. "Why, yes, she happens to be here right now. I'll put her on." She covered the receiver with her hand. "There's a Joseph Schmidt asking for you Charlie. Do you want to take the call?"

"Yes, Lady Margaret, I do," Charlie took the receiver from her. "Hello? Yes, Mr. Schmidt, this is Charlie Warren. Oh, I see. Well, thank you for telling me. I'll be in touch with you soon. Yes, I'll come. Just let me know when. Thank you again. Goodbye."

She hung up the phone. "That was Joseph Schmidt. His father passed away last night. He wanted me to know, and to invite me to the funeral service."

"That was the U-boat commander, wasn't it, Charlie?" Lady Margaret asked.

"Yes, ma'am, it was," Charlie shook her head sadly. "I got a chance to meet him before he died. He allowed us to pinpoint the location of his U-boat so we could make our plan work. Mr. Schmidt said he died peacefully in his sleep. He wanted to thank me for giving his father the peace he wanted so desperately."

"You seem to be making the rounds of hospitals lately, Dr. Warren," Lady Margaret observed. "That's what a physician does, isn't it?"

"Yes ma'am, it is," Charlie acknowledged. "By the way, Angus was put back in hospital yesterday with chest pain."

"Is it serious?" Lady Margaret asked.

"Not according to him," Charlie said. "He had problems yesterday after Kolov came to the church. He told Carl Davis to take him to the hospital and not tell me anything about it."

"Give him our best when you see him next," James said. He looked at his watch. "It looks like we're finished with you for today. Why don't you head back to Compton and see how Angus is faring?"

Charlie and David rose from their seats. "That sounds like an excellent idea," Charlie agreed. "We'll let you know what we find out."

-0-

Megan O'Grady was busy in the high school auditorium checking light cues and sound when Donald MacKay showed up. It was highly unusual for Donald to be in Compton on a weekday morning, so when he appeared at the door of the auditorium, Megan feared the worst.

"Donald, what are you doing here? Is there something wrong with Charlie?" Megan asked, her face white with fear as Donald came up to her.

"No, Megan, there's nothing wrong with Charlie, or with anyone else for that matter," Donald came up to her and put his arms around her. "I've been given the day off by Colonel Rosson, that's all."

Megan looked at him sharply. Her voice changed instantly to one of high suspicion. "Donald, you've never taken a day off in your life, at least not since I've known you. What's going on?"

Donald blushed and looked at his feet, something he never did except around Megan and Charlie. "I received a call from Colonel Jonathan Mathis-Smith this morning. He's going to be promoted to Brigadier in a few weeks, and he wants me to be his Regimental Sergeant Major."

"Oh yes, you mentioned this might happen a while back," Megan nodded. "It sounds like a great opportunity for you, Donald."

MacKay looked at her for a moment. "It is, lass, but it isn't. I'm flattered that I was offered the position, but I'm not sure I want to take it."

He shook his head in confusion, trying to clear it. "I've had so many things on my mind I can't think straight."

Megan took his hand in hers. "Come on over here, Donald. Let's sit down for a minute. There's no one else in this auditorium, so we can talk in private." They went over to one of the rows of chairs and sat down. The set for the upcoming play was on the stage, three-fourths done. It was a beautiful reproduction of a Shakespearean theatre set.

"The set looks so beautiful, Megan," MacKay remarked, trying to change the subject. "I can't believe how fast it's come together."

"Modular constructions always do," Megan observed. "There's actually been very little original building. Katya and Jackie have simply combined existing pieces to come up with their set in a quick fashion. It gives them more time to rehearse the play."

Megan looked directly at Donald. "You came down here to find out what I want you to do, didn't you? You're afraid that if you accept the position, you'll have to leave me here in Compton. Isn't that it?"

MacKay was silent for a moment. He took her hands and held them. "Megan, this is your home. All of your friends are here. Charlie and David are here, and Angus and your brother Sean. I can't tear you away from them to go off and fulfill my own dreams and desires. That would be selfish." Donald said in a huge rush of words.

"Donald, what would make you happy?" Megan asked. "Because if taking this position would make you happy and content, then take it. I want you to be happy, above all else. I want to be with you, and if that means leaving Compton, so be it. You left your home in Scotland to come over here, and your family still loves you, right? Their love is strong enough to bridge the gap between there and here. My love for the people I care about is also strong enough. Wherever I go with you, I'll always be close to them."

"I'm glad to hear you put it that way, love. The real conflict is inside of me, Megan," Donald admitted ruefully. "The Army has been my whole life until now. When I met you, I suddenly realized that I wanted more from my life than simply what the Army had to offer. I wanted home and a family. I wanted someone I could love and care about.

"This job at the Consulate these past few months gave me the best of both worlds. I could serve over here in America, and be close to you. Now I have to make a choice, and that's what I've been grappling with."

"Well, you know now that you don't have to worry about what I think," Megan pointed out. "Because I'm going with you no matter where your choice takes you. That part of the problem is settled, Donald. Don't think you're going to get rid of me that easily." She kissed him for emphasis.

They sat in the darkness of the theatre for a while, holding hands. Megan finally broke the silence. "What do you want to do with your life, Donald MacKay? It sounds as though the Army is no longer enough. Maybe it's time to move on to a new part of your life. There's no shame and dishonor in that. It's simply a choice."

She paused for a moment. "You know, Sean's been wanting to expand his business. St. Matt's is finally taking off, and he can't be two places at once. He was talking to me the other day about it. You're a genius when it comes to fixing engines, and he adores working with you. I'm sure there would be more than enough for you to do around here in Compton if that's what you decided to do."

"I have enjoyed it," Donald admitted. "Your brother is a wonderful man. I can't wait for Dad to meet him. They'll get along splendidly." He thought for a moment. "Colonel Rosson was telling me the other day how much he appreciated having me around to help with all of the operations at the consulate. He said that before I came along, the whole thing was driving him daft."

"And then there's Charlie to deal with," Megan said with a smile. "Do you think David's going to be able to keep her in check if you're not around?"

"David's a fine man, Megan," MacKay replied. "He loves Charlie dearly, and he's an excellent husband for her, but she's slipped the leash twice in the past week, and I'm deeply worried about her getting in too deep."

"Looks like you're needed around here to keep things on an even keel with her," Megan observed. "You couldn't do that if you were the Regimental Sergeant Major, could you?"

"No, I very well couldn't," MacKay admitted. He paused for a moment. "You know, lass, I think I've made up my mind."

"It looks that way," Megan said in a neutral tone. "You made it up by yourself, Donald. No one else did it. You just listened to your heart for a moment."

"But you helped, lass. That's why I love you so much. You helped me listen, and sort things out," Donald kissed her again and held her for a moment. "Thank you for giving me the chance to talk to you about these things, Megan."

"It's why I'm here, Donald," Megan replied. "I'm not going anywhere, except with you, so get used to it."

"That I can live with," Donald said happily. His cell phone beeped. "Hello? Why yes, Charlie; we were just talking about you! Here with Megan. Oh, it was that obvious, was it? Well, would you like to get together for lunch? All right, we'll meet you over at Angelo's in a bit. Give my best to Angus. Bye."

He closed the phone. "David and Charlie just got back into town. They're going over to the hospital to visit Angus. We're supposed to meet them in an hour or so at Angelo's for lunch."

"Good," Megan rose from her chair and looked at her light plot. "I need you to help me focus and angle that one light on far stage left." She handed him a crescent wrench. "I'll get up on stage and let you know when it's in position."

"Right you are, lass," MacKay replied happily.

-0-

"I just finished talking to Donald," Charlie told David as they pulled up to the hospital. "He and Megan are going to meet us over at Angelo's for lunch."

"Sounds good," David nodded. "How's Donald doing?"

"I think he's made up his mind," Charlie said, a slight smile on her face.

David raised his eyebrows. "And?"

"We'll know more when we see them later on today," Charlie said breezily as she walked into the busy treatment bay of the ER. "Where's Maggie?" she asked Gwen Jones, one of the ER nurses.

"Over in Suture Two," the Gwen replied. "Hey, when are you going to do another couple of night shifts? We've missed having you down in the ER."

"I'll let you know in a week or so, Gwen. I've been rather busy with other things," Charlie answered.

Gwen's eyebrows shot up as she looked at Charlie. "So I've noticed. Congratulations, by the way."

Charlie blushed and looked down. "Thanks, Gwen. I'll see you later." She and David went over to the suture room. Maggie White was busy putting the finishing touches on suturing a farmer's leg laceration.

"Howdy, cowboys," Maggie called out to them, not breaking stride as she put the final suture in place. She looked up at her patient, a middle-aged farmer who'd come in after gashing himself on a piece of farm equipment. "Okay, Glen: come back in a week or so and I'll take those out, or you can have your family doc do it. Make sure you take those antibiotics, okay?"

Glen nodded, easing himself gingerly off the table. "Thanks again, Maggie."

"No problem," Maggie smiled as he went out the door. "Now then, what can I do you for? No more gunshots to treat, I hope? Man, that Russian dude was mad at you! The cops had to practically sit on him while I examined him yesterday."

"He'll live, unfortunately," Charlie replied, glancing at David. "If David hadn't been there to stay my hand, you would have had a stabbing victim to deal with."

"She's very strong when it comes to knives, you know," David added, handing Maggie her car keys. "I'm returning these to you, Maggie. Thanks, I think."

"Okay," Maggie sat down on a stool. "Now why are you really here?"

"How bad was Angus when he came in here yesterday?" Charlie asked quietly.

"I got his pain under control with nitro and morphine, Charlie," Maggie replied. "He's not responding to the oral nitrates like he used to, and you know what that means.

"Maggie, the man's eighty. He's not a good candidate for bypass surgery," Charlie said.

"Charlie, I'm an ER doc, not a cardiologist," Maggie said slowly. "But from where I stand, he's going to have to make some hard choices if he wants to stay alive for another few years. You know what that means."

"I'm afraid I do," Charlie acknowledged. "He'll have to give up Trinity Church."

"I know you're his only family," Maggie looked down at the table. "You're going to have to talk to him, Charlie, and it isn't going to be easy."

-0-

"We've got to stop meeting like this," Charlie said to Angus McKendrick as she and David came into the ICU room where he was located. "I see you're not giving these nice people too much trouble."

Angus' face adopted a look of extreme martyrdom. "I've been the perfect patient, haven't I, Stacey?"

"Of course you have, Father McKendrick," Stacey Michaels replied brightly, winking at him. "He's wonderful, Charlie." She glanced over at Charlie for a brief moment. "I'll be back with you all in a little while."

Charlie and David waited until Stacey had left the room. They came over to Angus and Charlie grasped his hand wordlessly. "We shouldn't be having this conversation right now, Charlie," he finally said, breaking the silence.

"Then when are we supposed to have it, Uncle?" Charlie asked quietly. "When I get the call that you've collapsed in front of the rectory? In the middle of the night from Maggie White telling me that you've gone into cardiac arrest? When do we get a chance to have this conversation?"

"They told me I need surgery, Charlie," Angus replied. "The drugs aren't doing anything for my pain anymore. I take my pills every day, and still I have the chest pain."

Charlie's grip on Angus' hand tightened, and her eyes filled with tears. "Angus, Angus: don't leave me in this world now. I'm going to have a baby. I want him to know you. I want to put him in your arms. Please stay around long enough so you can see our baby."

"Charlie and I have been talking about this for a while, Angus," David said. "We have plenty of room at our house. You can come and live with us. Katya would adore having you around. You could tend the rose bushes, and you could finally have some time to yourself."

"What about Trinity, Charlie?" Angus asked. "I've been there since 1946. That church is my home, and those people are counting on me. Will you lead them if I retire?"

Charlie's face went white. "Angus, this is not the time or place to discuss that. We're talking about you right now."

"No, Charlie," Angus shook his head, his voice getting stronger. "If we are talking about making tough choices, then this is part of that choice. You cannot separate the two. There are no seminarians or ministers the diocese can send to replace me if I retire. That means that Trinity would have to close, and the people would have to go to another church in another town. You and I both know that would be a disaster for Compton as well as dozens of families. Trinity needs a minister it can count on, one the people know and trust. I want you to take over Trinity, and the people want it as well.

"I talked to the vestry and Bishop Archer. They are all in agreement that having you take over the church is the best possible plan.

"The cardiologist said that if I undergo heart surgery, then I will have to make arrangements for someone else to take over services at the church. That means you, my dear," Angus said calmly. "I'm sorry, but that seems to be the only solution to the problem."

Charlie looked at him for a long moment. "Angus, will you have the surgery if I agree to take over at Trinity? Will you come home and live with us?"

Angus put his hand in hers. "Yes, Charlie. I will come home and live with you and David and Katya if you agree. You were called by God to pastor that church, I believe that with all my heart.

"I never thought in my wildest dreams that anything like this would ever happen, but I believe now that one of the reasons God sent you over to America was to help me with the church."

"Angus, I am not an ordained minister," Charlie said, shaking her head. "I am not qualified to celebrate Communion on my own. I have not been through seminary of any sort."

"The bishop and I have talked about that as well," Angus smiled quietly. "Arrangements can be made, and the details can be worked out. I'm sorry, Charlie, but all avenues of escape have been closed. You must yield to God in this matter."

"Checkmate is the correct term, isn't it, Angus?" David said.

"Not the exact phrase I would use, my boy, but close enough," Angus agreed. He looked directly into her eyes with a penetrating gaze. "Charlie, there is a deep hole in your heart, one that has always been there. You have wanted home and a family all of your life, and you have been denied that opportunity. Everyone in your life has been taken from you: your mother when you were five, your father when you were eighteen, and last year, your grandfather and your brother.

"Now God has sent you to America, and you have found a home here with David and your sister. You have a love for God and His people that is deep and real. I see the light of God in your heart, and it shines forth every time you ascend to the pulpit. The people love you and respond to the message of salvation when you are there. You were born to do this, Charlie. This is God's answer to that deep wound, Charlie, just as heart surgery is the answer to my heart trouble. We both need surgery, Charlie. God has provided a way. We can do this together."

Charlie held Angus' hand, feeling its warmth. She held it to her cheek, and tears ran down her face. David came close to her, and put his hand on her shoulder. She started to weep quietly as she pondered Angus' words.

"I will do this," She finally said, "I can do it, because I know what you have said is right, Angus. I don't know how I'll do the task, but with God's help, I know I can."

"Charlie, I know you can do this," Angus said. "You are already doing the lion's share of the work at Trinity anyway. You just haven't been aware of it, that's all."

"I don't feel like I do that much," Charlie replied.

"Well, you have been, whether you've been aware of it or not," Angus replied. He sighed and looked at the clock. "It's noon, or thereabouts. I imagine you'll be headed over to see Donald and Megan shortly."

"How do you know that?" Charlie asked.

"Because Sean told me," Angus winked at her. "He called a few minutes before you came. He's meeting you and Donald and Megan down at Angelo's. Give all of them my love, by the way."

"You have to get out of this hospital soon, Angus," Charlie

reminded him. "We have to conduct Richard Cartwright's service next week."

"That we do," Angus sighed. "We need to put the lad to rest. MacKay and I have already planned most of the service. It's going to be at Trinity, with full military honors. You are going to deliver the eulogy, by the way. Sean will assist at service, and Donald's going to be the NCO in charge as well as the pipemaster.

"You are probably going to have to conduct the service this Sunday as well. You have the keys to the rectory, so my library is at your disposal."

"Sounds like everything's been taken care of, Charlie," David observed. "Let's leave this man alone so he can get some peace."

Charlie reached over and stroked Angus' cheek. "I love you so very much, Uncle Angus. Thank you in so many ways for everything you've been to David and me."

"You are the child I always wanted, Charlie, but never had," Angus replied, hugging her. "I love you as much as if you were my very own."

Stacey Michaels came back into the room. "Angus, the cardiologist will be seeing you later on today."

"Good, I have some news for him," McKendrick looked at Charlie and David. "You can tell him that the treatment plan can proceed. Everything is now ready."

"God help us all," Charlie whispered.

36

Angus McKenrick's surgery was scheduled for the following Monday. Charlie spent the better part of the weekend drafting her sermon for Sunday. Since Angus was not going to be present on Sunday, Charlie opted to conduct the service of Morning Prayer. She spent a considerable amount of time talking to Steve Morton, the head of the vestry.

"I am not going to read Angus' resignation, Steve, and that's final," Charlie told him firmly on Saturday. "As far as I'm concerned, Angus is still the pastor, and I'm simply his assistant."

"I understand, Charlie," Steve nodded sympathetically. "No one is trying to pressure you into this. We all understand that this is an emergency situation. Unfortunately, the bishop was very candid about the fact that no new seminarians are available to step in and take over Trinity. That's just what we have to deal with right now."

"I will have to get a special dispensation from the bishop so I can dispense the Sacraments if need be," Charlie said. "I don't know what kind of shape Angus is going to be in following his surgery. At least I was able to convince him to come to live with us once he's out of hospital."

"That's the best part of this situation, Charlie," Steve smiled gently. "We know how much Angus loves you. If he has to retire, then coming to live with you is the best possible solution to that problem."

"I'm planning on visiting the bishop at the diocese on Tuesday and talk to him personally about all of this," Charlie said with determination. "I'm still not convinced that having me appointed as rector is the answer to Trinity's leadership problem."

Sunday morning finally came, and Charlie was extremely nervous. She barely ate any breakfast, and spent most of the morning going over her sermon, making final corrections and honing a few points.

David said nothing, allowing Charlie the space and time to work out her feelings and make the necessary arrangements to get ready for Sunday. "Is there anything else I can help you with, Charlie?" he asked as Katya and he waited for Charlie at the door of their home.

"You can tell everyone to please get the barrels of their guns out of my back," Charlie snapped, picking up her purse in a quick, angry movement. She stopped and realized what she'd said. "David, I'm sorry," she said tearfully, "I'm absolutely terrified about today. There are a million things racketing around in my head right now. I just want all of this to stop for a moment."

"I believe in you, Charlie," Katya said, coming up to her and putting her hand in Charlie's. "You are strong, and God is with you."

"Thank you, darling, but right now I don't feel very strong at all," Charlie put her arm around Katya's shoulders and stroked her hair for a few seconds. She composed herself. "All right, I'm better now. Let's go to the church and have service. You're serving at the altar today, aren't you, Katya?"

"Yes, Charlie," Katya replied. "It's my turn this Sunday."

"Good," Charlie said, her voice growing stronger. "At least I'll have you up there to catch me if I try to run away."

"I don't think you've run away from anything, Charlie," David said, opening the door to the outside.

"There's always a first for everything," Charlie replied steadily.

-0-

David parked their van in the alley behind the church. They had gotten half an hour before the service started, but the street outside the church was already lined with cars. "Lovely day for a hanging party," Charlie observed cynically as she climbed out of the front passenger side.

"Charlie, we're in this together," David hugged her. "Besides, compared to what we've been through these past few days, this is a cakewalk."

"Indeed," Charlie replied in a small voice. She looked up at the rear side of the church. "Why do I feel so small right now, David?"

"Because you're looking up, not ahead," David said quietly. He opened the rear door to the church. "Let's go inside."

David made his way to the sanctuary while Charlie and Katya got ready for the service. The sanctuary was packed with people this Sunday. Everyone in town had heard about Angus, and the situation at the church.

"Donald and I have been sent over here by Sean as reinforcements," Megan O'Grady said as David came over to greet them. They were sitting next to Carl Davis and his family.

"I understand," David swept his eyes over the rest of the congregation. "Excuse me for a minute," he said, getting up and crossing over to the far back of the church where a solitary figure sat on the farthest pew by herself.

"Charlie and Katya are in the service this morning, Brenda," David said, sitting down next to her. "I'd like it if you sat up front next to me."

Brenda Reynolds looked at him with blank astonishment on her face. "Ron's better, Dave," she began. "He got out of the ICU last night, and he told me to come here today and let you know."

She glanced around the sanctuary nervously. "I should be going now. Your service is about to start."

"Why are you leaving?" David asked quietly. "You're family, Brenda. Charlie would want you to stay. I want you to stay. What's the problem?"

"You don't remember how I acted here when we had Karen's funeral?" Brenda asked. "You don't remember how I slapped your face and called you a murderer and I wished that you were in that casket instead of Karen? How can you forget all of that and ask me to stay in this church?"

"Because I love you, Brenda, and I've forgiven you," David said. "This is going to be a hard day for Charlie. She needs your help right now. She needs you here. Will you help her?"

Brenda sat and said nothing for a moment. "Yes, Dave, I will stay." She got up with him and they went down to the place where Donald and Megan were sitting.

"Good morning, Ms. Reynolds," Donald said, standing up. "We're glad you're here today."

Brenda nodded politely, avoiding Megan's eyes. "I'm here because Dave asked me to be here right now. He said Charlie would want me here."

"I'm glad you're here today, Brenda," Megan reached across Donald and grasped her hand. "It's been too long."

"That's right," Sarah Davis said. "It's been too long, Brenda. Welcome home."

"Thank you," Brenda said slowly. She could detect no hostility in either of the women's voices. There was only friendliness and genuine warmth. *I don't understand how they can be this way*, she thought to herself. *I was horrible to them, and they're being so friendly*, Brenda thought to herself.

A door at the rear of the platform opened, and Katya came out, along with another girl. They lit the long candles flanking the altar and then sat down.

Brenda glanced down at the hymnal and the prayer book in front of her. "You're going to have to walk me through this, Dave," Brenda told him nervously. "I've not had too much experience with all of this."

"Don't panic, rookie," David said jokingly. "Everyone has a first day. I'm still wet behind the ears with all of this, too."

"That's why I'm here, Brenda," Carl Davis said jokingly. "I'm his backup." He winked at Brenda for emphasis.

-0-

Charlie came out of the vestibule entrance behind the altar and faced the congregation. She could see dozens of her friends in the congregation that morning. Some of them had come a long way to be there that morning.

The Rossons were there, along with their children. Lady Margaret was there with her family. Charlie saw Brenda standing next to David, trying to sing along in the hymn book. Brenda's eyes glanced up and caught Charlie's gaze. For a few seconds, they looked at each other. Charlie nodded and mouthed *thanks*. Brenda nodded back and returned to her singing.

The service of Morning Prayer continued, and at last it was time for Charlie to deliver her sermon. A deep hush fell on the sanctuary as she ascended to the pulpit.

"Dear brothers and sisters," she began, looking across the sea of faces turned in her direction. "As you have doubtless noticed, our pastor, Angus McKendrick, is not with us today. He is in hospital, scheduled to undergo bypass surgery tomorrow morning. I am sure I speak for all of us when I tell you that we pray for his continued health and speedy recovery.

"Father McKendrick and I talked the other day. He has been in consultation with the vestry of this church, as well as the presiding bishop of this diocese. Father McKendrick has told them, and has told me, that because of his health, he is no longer able to continue as pastor of this church."

A murmur rippled through the congregation. Charlie waited until the congregation quieted before continuing. "He informed me at that time that no new seminarians are available at this time to fill the pulpit, and that the priests in the diocese are unable to fulfill any new commitments that his resignation would leave in his absence.

"Father McKendrick has asked me to assume the role of leader of this congregation. I have reluctantly agreed to do so, only because without an ordained licensed member of the ministry to serve this church, the only alternative would be for the diocese to dissolve this parish, and have the members go to another church in another town. That is unacceptable, and that is why I have accepted the position."

Charlie looked down at the text of her sermon. "My text for this morning's message comes from the Gospel of John: '*Ye have not chosen me, but I have chosen you, and ordained you, that ye should go and bring forth fruit, and that your fruit should remain.*'

"The words of our Lord are plain," Charlie began slowly. "Although he spoke these words initially to his disciples in the upper room the night before he died, there is no doubt that he meant these words for all of his people, for all time. We are called upon to bear fruit in his name, fruit that honors him.

"It has been the tradition of the Church over the centuries to endow the clergy with special responsibilities and titles. But it is plain from a closer reading of the Gospels that the disciples of Jesus had no special rank or titles at the outset. All of them were of humble birth. They had no special rank or privilege. What they shared with each other was a willingness to follow Jesus."

Charlie looked up from her text, and her eyes swept across the congregation. Her voice gathered strength as she found the courage in her heart to deliver the message.

"This message has added meaning today, in this church, here and now. You are all ministers in the sight of God. You are all priests who labor in his name. Make no mistake about that. It is you who must bear the high and important calling of servant in Jesus' name. The fact that you have no title or rank in terms of clerical status does not excuse you from your duty to follow Jesus."

Her voice gathered warmth and conviction. "I love you all, and I thank you all for your prayers and support. I have known from the very time I came here to this community that this is a special church, a place of warmth and love. The heart of God rests in each of you, because you have made him welcome there.

"Each one of you bears the holy responsibility to be the people of God. It may be God's will for me to lead this church, to administer the sacraments and conduct the business of the parish, but it is your responsibility to bear witness to the power of Christ and to share the Gospel of life to a lost and dying world."

Charlie paused as a wave of love surged up inside of her. "We can do this together, you and I. That is how Father McKendrick has done it for so many years, and if it is God's will, so will I.

"Amen."

Charlie stepped back from the pulpit, and a deep silence filled the sanctuary. For a full moment, there was no sound in the space of the church. At last, the organist bestirred himself and began the final hymn. The congregation rose and sang, and remained standing for Charlie's final benediction. As the service concluded, most of the congregation came forward to congratulate Charlie on the message.

"Girl, you hit that one out of the park," Sarah Davis said, hugging Charlie. "We know you're going to do a terrific job."

"Thank you, Sarah; we'll see how terrific I am," Charlie said, looking up at the throng of people around her. David was some distance away from her, and it was several minutes before she spied him.

"Where have you been?" she asked when he finally got to her.

"Making arrangements with Angelo for a little celebration," he said with a huge grin on his face. "Way to go, kid. That was an awesome message."

"I'm not so sure about that," Charlie shook her head. "The words were easy. The actions are going to be the hard part."

37

The service ended promptly at twelve, but the last person didn't leave until after twelve-thirty. Charlie finally was able to change back into street clothes. "All right, David, let's head to lunch," she said, kissing her husband in the sanctuary. "Where's Katya?"

"She went with the Davis family," David replied, walking with her down the aisle. "Sarah managed to con Katya into babysitting for her while we eat. She's keeping the kids while we eat at Angelo's."

"Katya seems to have taken my place with the Davis children as their favorite aunt." Charlie observed, laughing. "I don't get attacked like I used to whenever I come through the front door. Instead, I get greeted with 'Where's Aunt Katya?'"

"That's all right," David said. "I'll still attack you whenever you like."

"Oh you will, will you?" Charlie kissed him once more as they went through the door. Someone was waiting for them outside, standing on the front steps of the church.

Brenda Reynolds stood hesitantly at the front of the church, as though pondering whether to stay or go. "Hello, Brenda. Would you like to go with us to lunch?" Charlie asked. "You know you're invited. We'd love to have you. Thank you so much for coming today." She went over and hugged her. Brenda returned her embrace hesitantly.

"Charlie, I... I have something I want to talk to you about," Brenda began reluctantly. She glanced at David. "It's something I'd like to discuss with you in private."

"David, please give my thanks to everyone at Angelo's," Charlie swiftly sized up the situation. "Tell them to start without me. I'll be along when I can, and if they can't stay, I'll definitely understand."

She turned to Brenda. "We can go over to the rectory and talk."

-0-

Most of the impromptu party had left by the time Charlie finally arrived an hour or so later. Donald MacKay was still there, along with the Rossons and Megan O'Grady. "Forgive me for being tardy," Charlie told David as she sat down, "that really couldn't wait."

She looked over at Megan. "Where's that deranged brother of yours?"

"He had some business to do at the diocese," Megan shrugged elaborately. "I don't know. Maybe one of the church members "tattle-tailed" to the Bishop about something. You can never tell with Sean. He's almost as hard to control as you."

"Thanks, Megan," Charlie stuck out her tongue at her. She sat down in a chair with a sigh.

"Where's Brenda? I thought you invited her to dinner?" David asked.

"She had to head back to New York," Charlie replied, picking up a menu. "Ron called and said he had something urgent to discuss."

"Urgent like what?"

Charlie glared at him over the menu. "Urgent like 'It's none of your business'. I didn't ask."

"That's because you already know," David said smugly. "He's going to propose to her, right?"

"My lips are sealed," Charlie said enigmatically. "We talked about all sorts of things. I will say that I think Brenda discovered someone today."

"And who might that be, lass?" Donald MacKay asked.

"God."

"Well, this is a great day to celebrate," David said, smiling. "We have a lot to be thankful for."

He handed her cell phone back. "By the way, I'm going to start charging you for taking all of your phone messages. This stupid little gadget has rung every five minutes since we got here."

David gave her a piece of paper. "You've got Angus' surgery on Monday, then on Tuesday you're meeting with Bishop Archer about begging out of the post at Trinity. That's a lost cause already, Charlie. You're going to lose on that one."

"Really?" Charlie raised her eyebrows. "How do you know that? Are you able to predict the future?"

"No, I just happen to know that everyone at Trinity wants you to take the post, sweetie, so get used to it." He rumpled the papers in an annoying, self-important way.

"Are you going to give me that, or am I going to have to take it from you forcibly and cause a scene?" Charlie asked in a light-hearted, yet menacing tone.

"I want all of these fine people to know what my bride is doing when she's not saving the world." David said with a smile, looking at the Rossons, who were sitting with profoundly amused expressions on their faces.

"You also have my softball tournament in July to pencil in," Jane added. "You're also going to be at our house on Friday next for a cookout. We haven't seen you in an age, you know."

"Except in an official capacity," James added with a wink.

"May I continue?" David broke in, resuming the reading of his list. "Tuesday afternoon, you have a memorial service to attend in New York at the EOC. Full dress uniform is required, and they expect you to deliver the eulogy."

"I expected that one, David," Charlie said quietly.

"All of this in addition to your normal duties as Medical Examiner and assistant to the director for the summer play," David folded up the list and handed it to her. "I'm sure there are more appointments coming down the pike, but I turned off the phone so I could visit with our friends."

"We're just glad to have you back here in Compton, safe and sound," Megan said, putting her hand on Charlie's. "You've been missed."

"I've missed you all as well," Charlie replied. "Now if you don't mind, I really have to eat something. I'm starved."

"You have to eat from time to time?" David asked in mock astonishment. "What a concept."

"Behave, David." Charlie concentrated on eating for a moment. David looked at her with an amused expression on his face. She looked up in exasperation. "All right, David: what's on your mind?"

"Nothing," David smirked. "I was just wondering if things are going to settle down once the baby comes."

"I don't think that question even merits a reply," Megan observed, winking at MacKay, who nodded in agreement.

"Thank you, Megan," Charlie said with a smile which turned into a glare at her husband. "Life will go on, dear sir, just as it has before."

"That's what I was afraid you were going to say," David sighed.

-0-

The setting sun glinted off of the spires of the great castle on the hill over Budapest, casting reflected golden rays on the two men quietly drinking coffee on a riverside café. The Danube was full of tourist boats busy running happy sightseers up and down the historic river.

It was a very public spot for a meeting. There was nothing about the two men that made them stand out from any of the other patrons of the café. Both of them spoke in fluent, idiomatic Russian, blending in with the dozens of other tourists around them.

Sir Leslie Gresham looked at the man across the table. He took a sip of his iced coffee before speaking. "Apparently our young colonel has done quite well for herself. You were correct in telling me she'd be an excellent intelligence officer."

"I knew that from the very beginning," the man replied quietly. There was silence between them for a moment or two. Both men tried to decide where the conversation would go next. It was an awkward lull for both of them.

"She is expecting a child in March," Gresham finally broke the silence.

A pleased light flickered in the other man's eyes. "Give her at least a year to enjoy her family. She deserves at least that consideration."

"I understand and sympathize with your concerns, but some things are out of my control. What about you, old friend? Is the time ripe for you to return to the West?"

The man sat back in the chair for a moment. "Kolov is now captured, but his organization in Russia is very much alive. My mission is not completed until it is totally destroyed."

Gresham nodded. "That was the Prime Minister's take on the matter. I wish for all our sakes that it was not so." He reached into his shirt pocket and handed the man a photograph. It was a picture of Mary Anne and Charlie at their graduation ceremony from medical school. "In so many ways, Charlie is a second daughter to me." Gresham said with genuine warmth and affection in his voice.

The man took the photograph and lovingly caressed it. A flood of emotions washed over his face as he looked at the two young women. "They look so young, Leslie, so happy. Is my Charlie happy now?"

Leslie reached across the table and clasped his friend's hand. "She is, and when you return, she will be even happier."

"I know that, Leslie," John Warren smiled as he returned the picture to his friend's hand. "With God's help I will be coming home soon."

Printed in the United States
78622LV00004B/62